IN THE DEPTHS O
marine biologist Cas
fungus covering a m

IN THE SLUMS OF CALCUTTA,
dedicated Dr. Jackie Dunbar encounters a killer
disease that she cannot identify or defeat.

IN THE MOUNTAINS OF IRAN,
Colonel Andrei Kurisovsky leads elite soldiers
disguised as Arabs into a high-tech arsenal, with
their ultra-modern weapons hidden and drugged
prostitutes as live bait in a deadly trap.

IN THE CAPITALS OF EAST AND WEST,
the leaders of the great powers begin to wake
to the danger that threatens them, and how
helpless they are to stop it.

**But someone, somehow, has to stop it—before
the missiles are launched, millions die, and
the dream of the future dissolves in a
nightmare of the past—**

PHOENIX STRIKE

PHOENIX STRIKE

by

Charles Ryan

AN ONYX BOOK

ONYX
Published by the Penguin Group
Penguin Books USA Inc., 375 Hudson Street,
New York, New York 10014, U.S.A.
Penguin Books Ltd, 27 Wrights Lane,
London W8 5TZ, England
Penguin Books Australia Ltd, Ringwood,
Victoria, Australia
Penguin Books Canada Ltd, 10 Alcorn Avenue,
Toronto, Ontario, Canada M4V 3B2
Penguin Books (N.Z.) Ltd, 182-190 Wairau Road,
Auckland 10, New Zealand

Penguin Books Ltd, Registered Offices:
Harmondsworth, Middlesex, England

First published by Onyx,
an imprint of Dutton Signet,
a division of Penguin Books USA Inc.

First Printing, November, 1993
10 9 8 7 6 5 4 3 2 1

To Bud

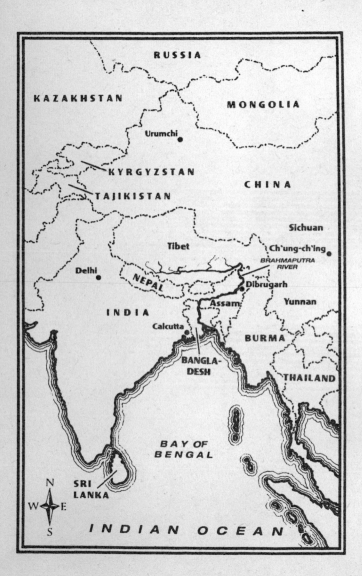

Prologue

Rabach Mountains, Iran
April 3, 1992

Colonel Andrei Kurisovsky always hummed softly to himself whenever the certainty of killing was near. It was a tuneless sound, deep in his throat. Wrapped in the robes of a Bedouin, he was seated on a scrawny-shanked camel with a red leather saddle and a scabbard containing an ancient Kashmiri long rifle. Behind him, on a boulder-strewn mountain trail, were nine other camels, seven of which carried Russian mercenaries all similarly dressed. Their light skins were darkened by amber pitch to simulate the deep, sun-burned color of nomads; each carried an assault weapon slung across his back.

Aboard the remaining animals were three women in hooded black *kajubas*. Their heads lolled back and forth with the rocking motion of the camels, and flecks of cottony saliva limned the corners of their garishly painted lips. They were prostitutes, kidnapped from the whore dens of Gwanda, Pakistan, two days before. Since then they'd been kept drugged by periodic shots of tar heroin.

Before the summit of the trail, Kurisovsky held up his hand and the little caravan halted. He dismounted and walked forward to a point where the trail started down the eastern side of the Rabach range. Stretched before him was a vast plain of open desert. A thin pall of sand dust hovered above it, tinted lavender in the last rays of evening.

Bracing his arms against a boulder, he swept the desert with binoculars. The landscape was empty save for a small cluster of lights at the base of the mountains. That, he knew, was the Iranian outpost of Qrar-e-Qund, which guarded the old trade road from Dharkeesh to Makran and the Gulf of Oman. He focused on it.

One of his men approached and stopped behind him. Without taking his eyes from the binoculars, Kurisovsky snapped, "Check your weapons and arm the charges, Sergeant. And be damned alert from here on."

"Yes, sir." The man hurried back to the camels. His woollen boots made no sound in the dust.

After a moment Kurisovsky also came back down the trail and remounted. He withdrew the Kashmiri rifle and laid it across his saddle. It had a polished brass butt plate and an open firing pan. At his signal, the caravan shuffled forward again.

The outpost sentry hut, no larger than an outhouse, was made of sandstone with a low roof supported by rusty pipes. Two Iranian guardsmen in shabby khaki uniforms were on duty. They looked barely older than fifteen. Each held a British Bren gun across his thin chest. When they spotted the line of camels approaching out of the darkness, they walked out to the edge of the light cast by the hut.

Kurisovsky stopped a few feet in front of them. He lifted the Kashmiri rifle over his head, his hand gripping the barrel. It was the ancient sign of non-hostility among desert tribes.

"What do you want?" the taller of the two guards shouted in a coarse Tehran dialect.

"Food and water," Kurisovsky answered in the same language. "Bandits have stolen our supplies."

"Go away. We have no food."

Kurisovsky turned his head slightly, nodding toward the prostitutes. "We will trade our women for food and water."

The guard leaned out and squinted at the females directly behind the colonel. After a moment he turned and walked back to the hut and spoke into a telephone nailed to the outside wall.

Two minutes later, a small, English-made Sandringham 6 Hotspur armored vehicle skidded to a stop beside the guard hut. An Iranian officer and a sergeant got out. The officer was very handsome, with a mustache and a yellow kerchief around his head.

Arrogantly he strode along the column, shining a flashlight into the faces of the riders. His holster belt squeaked as he walked. At the end of the line, he turned and came back to Kurisovsky. "Who are you?" he demanded loudly.

"Herdsmen from Besharum."

The officer's eyes narrowed. "You have a strange accent."

"We are At Ta'if tribe."

The Iranian snorted with disdain. He jerked his head toward the women. "They look like Indian whores." He continued studying Kurisovsky, then abruptly flicked his hand in a dismissive gesture. "Go back to the mountains. I don't waste food on jackals."

Kurisovsky stared coldly down at the officer. Then he whistled. Instantly one of the mercenaries fired a handgun from under his robe. It had a silencer, and the sound of it was like the spit of a striking snake. The bullet struck the Iranian in the face, snapping his head back as if violently jerked by an invisible wire.

As he crumpled to the ground, his sergeant gave a

small cry and clawed for his sidearm. Two more guns *thrupped* and their rounds went into his mouth and throat. The impacts spun him in a little pirouette.

Beside the hut, the two young guards froze. Kurisovsky pulled a 9mm automatic from his robe and shot them, twice each. The bullets knocked them back and down like wheat stalks in a wind.

One of the prostitutes started to cry, a tiny whimper like a little girl alone in a dark room.

In the shadows beyond the guard hut lights, the women were stripped naked. The night had turned cold and they huddled together between the camels, holding their arms over their breasts. Their bodies reeked of stale perfume and vaginal scent and fear. One of the Russians gave each another injection of heroin, shoving the needle into the thick vein behind the knee. They were lifted back onto the camels. In a moment they began to nod.

Kurisovsky, having donned the Iranian officer's uniform and head kerchief, climbed into the armored car and swung it around. Quickly the men jockeyed their mounts into line behind it. They started off toward the main compound of the post a quarter mile away, which was brightly lit by spotlights on thirty-foot poles.

As they neared, Kurisovsky kept scanning the buildings, taking in the lie of the place. They were made of the same sandstone as the guard hut, flat-roofed with tarred timbers protruding from the outer walls, grouped in a semicircle connected by walkways covered over with filthy canvas. He immediately noticed no machine-gun pits were visible.

Only one structure was made of wood and was located in the center of the arc of buildings. It had a narrow porch with chairs against the wall and looked like a mess hall. A dozen or so Iranian soldiers with slung rifles were hunkered down in front of the porch, playing a marble game in the sand.

They glanced up casually as the armored car came into the glare of the lights. Then one spotted the naked woman and pointed. The rest instantly sprang to their feet, calling excitedly to others inside the building. A moment later, more soldiers appeared.

Kurisovsky casually drove the armored car past the converging men, holding his head low. No one paid any attention to him. He continued a few yards beyond the mess hall, then turned around and parked beside a smaller building. It was dark inside.

By this time all the camels had stopped in the center of the compound. The Russians quickly dismounted and herded the animals into a tight clot surrounding the two carrying the drugged prostitutes. The camels tossed their heads, spooked by the sudden press of soldiers.

One prostitute sagged out of her saddle suddenly and fell to the ground. As the camels jerked away, she stretched out flat, her legs spread-eagled. Two soldiers rushed up to her and knelt down. They laughed and lasciviously ran their hands over her breasts and down into her crotch. All the other soldiers surrounded the animals, squatting to see under their bellies. Several more began bullying their way toward the woman, pushing the camels' rumps with the butts of their rifles.

Temporarily ignored, the Russians backed slowly away from the milling soldiers until they were strung out in front of the buildings. More excited soldiers continued coming past them and into the compound.

From his vehicle, Kurisovsky watched intently. When his men were all positioned, he took a small box from his shirt pocket. It was the size of a pack of cigarettes and had a tiny antenna and a red button on its face. He held it up. Instantly his men dropped to the ground, their heads down, ears covered.

He pressed the button.

A violent explosion shook the earth as charges of gelignite, hidden under the saddles of the camels, blew simultaneously. A concussion wave lashed across the compound, immediately followed by a back-suck of air as a ball of fire and dust hurled upward, laced with whirling, bloody pieces of animals and men.

The sound of the blast was quickly swallowed by the vastness of the desert. Only a distant echo remained, whomping through the canyons and gullies of the nearby foothills. Before it faded, the Russians were up and moving, disappearing into the buildings, their weapons drawn.

Kurisovsky lunged from the armored vehicle and headed for the mess hall, pulling out an Uzi. Two troopers joined him, each carrying Skorpion VZ-61 machine pistols. As they reached the door, an Iranian peered out for a split second, then ducked away.

One of the troopers pulled a grenade, jerked out the pin with his teeth, and flung it through the door. It exploded, hurling wood splinters and shattered crockery through the windows. Kurisovsky, going low, dashed in with the other two right behind him. Bracing themselves against a wall, they opened up, fanning their weapons back and forth.

At last they stopped. Cordite smoke fumed in the room, which was littered with shattered dishes and furniture. Two Iranian soldiers lay dead near a back door. There were several muffled bursts of gunfire from one of the other buildings. The three men turned and ran out, ejecting their empty clips.

It took three and a half minutes to clear the buildings of stray Iranian soldiers. Meanwhile, out in the courtyard, wounded men crawled around among their truncated companions. Some wept, others simply wandered about, dazed by the concussion. Their uniforms smoked. A single camel was still alive, lying in the explosion crater with its spine blown away. Now and then it bellowed with pain.

The Russians returned to the compound and began shooting the wounded. One after another, methodically, unemotionally. When that was finished, they shot the camel.

The missile storage area was underground, back from the camp a half mile where the first uplift of the mountains began. Two tunnels had been driven into a sheer rock face. On the flat ground in front were several storage shacks and a parked flatbed truck with a large compressor tank and high-pressure lines running into the first tunnel.

The Russians, having shed their cumbersome robes and wearing desert-camouflage jumpers, approached in good squad fashion, checking each outbuilding until they reached the main tunnels. The area was deserted.

The tunnels were ten feet square with their tops shaped into diamond arches to distribute the weight of the rock. Kurisovsky led them into the first. Directly inside was a platform with a large generator and exhaust pipes leading back out the entrance. Electrical boxes were bolted into the rock behind the platform. One of the men started the generator. Immediately overhead lights came on along with the whir of ventilation fans.

The room was large with timbers bracing the overhead. The beams had roof bolts driven through them, their plates black with resin seepage. Strings of bare bulbs were hooked between the timbers. As the men moved about, their boots stirred up a fine powdery dust that misted the lights.

Gear was everywhere: Stoper drills with long bit shafts, heavy Spad guns, shovels, stacks of timbering and canvased generators. At the back, three smaller drift tunnels branched off. The air smelled of electrical wiring and the faint, acrylic sent of dynamite.

Cautiously the men moved off into the drifts. Each drift tunnel contained side rooms. The first was a machine shop with tool chests banked against the walls and A-frame block-and-tackle dollys. In the second there were two small Russian STING SMS-120 mobile launcher vehicles, both covered with a thick layer of dust.

Leaving two men with the launchers, Kurisovsky and another trooper continued deeper into the drift corridor. Sixty yards from the main entrance it widened into a circular room the size of a basketball court. There they found several double metal racks holding two dozen Soviet BEARCAT SSR-214 low-range missiles.

They were twelve feet long, eighteen inches wide with a forward taper, short mid-frame wings, and cropped fins. They were painted white with a gray stripe around the solid-fuel packet compartments. Each had a TK-44 ignition-glide-ignition-glide turbofan engine. But the warheads were not attached, and the empty sockets with their four homing antennae looked like insect faces.

Kurisovsky prowled the missile bay while the other man began dismantling the rack covers. Wooden cases were stacked against the walls, some containing spare engines in Cosmoline and electronic gear and empty missile tanks.

At last he found what he was looking for, a seven-foot stainless steel door. Its frame fitted neatly into the rock. The door itself was crisscrossed with red stripes and a black death's head stenciled over the handle with warnings in Arabic.

He pried off the combination lock and swung the door open. The inside was lit with fluorescent tubes and had an antiseptic odor. The walls were packed with fiberglass and braced by wooden struts to absorb small seismic movements. In the center of the vault was a stainless steel matrix resting on a foundation of enclosed roller bearings. The entire assembly was anchored to the walls with spring cables.

The matrix was made up of twenty-four steel baskets, each containing a warhead. They were black, about the size of ten-inch naval barrage shells with rounded snouts. At the frontal curve of the snout was a single red circle. Stenciled on it were the German words: Achtung!! BIOLOGISCH GESCHUTZ//TT-12XX//PPB-3—GRAMRAUCHE MMS.

Kurisovsky lightly flicked his finger over the surface of one of the warheads. He smiled, pleased. His intelligence from Moscow had been right on the mark. In this room was enough killing power to decimate three million people. Each warhead contained concentrations, in inert suspension, of one of the deadliest organisms known to man: pneumococcal pneumonia bacteria, Strain Three.

The old Douglas C-47 came in low over the desert, running with only a single red light on the bottom of the fuselage. Kurisovsky's men had strung a line of burning fuel barrels to mark the touchdown point. Beyond was flat, hard-packed sand called *shash*.

It had taken over two hours to load eight missiles from the tunnels. With their warheads affixed, they placed two on each launcher and the rest aboard a weapons cart that the lead vehicle towed. Just to be safe, they took three spare warheads. By eleven o'clock they were headed southeast, straight out into the desert toward the ruins of Kuh-e-Zor. The night was very cold and turned their breath to frost.

The two C-47 pilots were Australians who sat out on the port wing smoking while the Russians shoved and bullied six of the missiles into the aircraft and lashed them down with cargo netting. The Aussies, like Kurisovsky and his men, were employed by Gulab Dau Singh, a Sikh border chief who controlled the Brahmaputra River plain in the Indian state of Assam.

The aircraft was old and painted jungle camouflage. During World War II, it had flown the Hump from China to Stilwell's troops in India. Now it hauled contraband: raw opium from the Assam foothills to processing camps on the Irrawaddy River in northern Burma, and weapons out of Afghanistan for Sikh rebels in the Punjab.

It was past three in the morning by the time the loaded aircraft finally took off. Rolling into a sharp bank as soon as it lifted from the hardpan, the wheels coming up trailing sand, the pilots turned north . This would take them along the Afghanistan–Pakistan border, which was free of radar nets. At Srinagar they'd turn southeast and follow the Himalayas to Assam.

Before it was out of sight, its shadow dwindling against the starlight, the Russians were again on the move. The two launch vehicles, free of the weapons cart but still carrying two missiles, ground noisily over the *shash* as they turned due south on a line that would take them straight to a stretch of deserted beach on the Gulf of Oman.

Her name was the *Java Queen,* a rusty shallow-hulled, broad-beamed sternwheeler. She carried tall black stacks that rose sixty feet over her water deck and was driven by twin steam engines in parallel. Built in

1909, she'd spent her first seventy-five years moving cargo and passengers in the upland rivers of New Guinea. She belonged to Singh and now hauled teak timbers down the Tazpur and Brahmaputra rivers to the mills at Chittagong on the Bay of Bengal.

The colonel and his men had to wait two days before the sternwheeler finally arrived at the beach rendezvous, her spoon bow breasting through the gulf swells just at sunset. Several Russians immediately waded out to lay a path of log floats as a guide through the series of sandbars that radiated out from the beach.

But the *Java Queen's* captain would have none of it. A thickly bearded old Swede named Gavborg, he drunkenly waved a bottle of rum at them. "Get the gott-dam hell out of de way!" he shouted. "I don't need no pig-fucking Bolshevik to tell me how to land my ship."

Backing two hundred yards off the beach, Gavborg wadded steam and rammed her over the sandbars until the bow was solidly wedged ashore. Up near the pilot house, several of Singh's militiamen, unfamiliar with seafaring, were pitched to the deck by the jolt. They glared furiously through the windshield at the captain but remained silent.

It was hellish loading the two launchers, working under lights. They swung the first one up with the boat's forward cargo derrick while Gavborg paced the pilot house deck and blew commands to his half-naked deckhands on a policeman's whistle. But to get the second vehicle aboard, they had to drive it out into waist-deep water so the after spar lines could reach it.

The task was finally completed and both launchers were securely lashed down and tarped. One was forward of the pilot house just above the boilers, the other aft, its chains snugged to the huge sponson brackets of the paddle wheel.

Kurisovsky sent three of his men to accompany the ship. Then he and the others picked up their gear and moved off down the beach in single file. They were to cross the Pakistan border at the Dasht River, head for Gwadar, and then filter back across India to Assam. Over their shoulders they watched as the captain took his vessel off the sand.

He had to grasshop her, using long poles cabled to a donkey-engine capstan. Slowly, laboriously the ship inched backward, her fireboxes glowing orange-red, the crack of blocks and the booming slam of her engines shattering the night.

At last she was free, beyond the bars, her great stern wheels gouging out a cascade of sand-thick water. With a final blast of his horn, Gavborg swung to starboard and pointed his ancient ship once more toward open sea.

1

Bay of Bengal
Coordinates: 15:03 N/84:85 E
June 5, 1992

The screams came from the ocean in a quick burst of sound. Then silence. Then there was another static-crackling blow, which fused into the constant chattering clicks and soft booms of deep marine creatures.

Aboard the submersible *Checker 3,* marine biologist Cas Bonner jerked upright in his pilot's seat. For the last few minutes he'd been idly swinging the antenna dish, taping the sounds of the ocean environment. "What the hell?" he murmured and pressed the headset tighter against his ear.

Another rush of human voices came, high-pitched screeches this time as clear as needles of glass. Again they faded. Bonner flicked up the volume knob as the hair lifted on the back of his neck. He shot a glance through the submersible's acrylic dome at the sheer wall of rock some thirty feet away. In the powerful glare of the strobes it appeared as gray as ancient granite, pockmarked with fractures and deep caves.

Beside him, Ed Burke, assistant head of mission for the Australian-mounted Tamcore Deep Probe survey, gave him a frowning look. "Problem?"

"I'm picking up screams."

"What?"

"Here, listen." Cas turned on the overhead loudspeaker. As the volume came up, the chilled air of the submersible was filled with the cacophony of sea life, sounding much like the crackling of a big wood fire. Then, slashing through it, a voice bellowed in agony. Immediately it diminished into a jumble of words and half sentences before it finally drifted away completely.

"What the bloody hell is that?" Burke cried.

"Somebody's in trouble."

Burke's eyes widened. "My God, not D-One?" The designation signified the submersible's service ship, the ASN *Digger*.

Bonner shook his head. "I don't think so. That sounded like Hindi. You catch any of it?"

"No." Both men leaned forward intently, listening for another burst.

The *Checker 3* was at a depth of two thousand feet, moving slowly along the western wall of the great Godavari Rift, an undersea gorge located on the bottom of the Bay of Bengal, two hundred miles northeast of Madras, India.

Impatiently Bonner hissed through his teeth. "I think it's a sub. And it's close." He swung around and gazed out the stern of the Submersible. The little vehicle's acrylic dome, made to withstand over ten thousand pounds of pressure per square inch, formed a nearly complete sphere, giving a panoramic view of the ocean. Except for the reflection of the strobes off the polished housings of the maneuvering motors, there was nothing astern but a solid wall of black.

He turned back, scowling. Bonner was a big man, six-three, with powerful shoulders that stretched his blue jumpsuit whenever he moved. From years in and around the ocean, his face and hands were tanned the color of mahogany, his close-cropped brown hair streaked with sun bleach.

"Can you get a signal fix?" Burke asked.

Cas was already swinging the antenna to do just that.

Immediately the sounds off the Rift wall faded. Then as the back of the antenna dish came around and faced away from it, they returned. He held that position and waited.

Several seconds passed. The voices returned, rushing up as if blown by a strong wind from a deep well. He quickly adjusted the antenna until the sound was loudest, then glanced down at the directional heading indicator on the radio panel: zero-nine-three degrees.

Using a small computer near his elbow, Cas punched in the directional heading and modulation level. In a second the readout showed a position fix of the sound source along an azimuth off the front of the submersible. It was coming from the bottom of the Godavari, nine thousand feet below them.

The screams diminished, then rushed back. Burke started to say something, but Cas cut him off with an upraised hand. The loudspeaker burst forth with static that riffled off, drawing the voices with it.

"I heard Russian," Bonner cried.

Again the voices came: first a jumble of screeches with Hindi words mixed it, and then, clearly, several Russian phrases. Cas spun his selector switch and keyed the telephone mike. "D-One, Checker 3, do you read? Over."

The service ship's radio operator came right back: "Checker 3, say again. Strong interference, over."

"Do you have us on track?"

"Affirmative, but encountering strong magnetic pulses below your sector. Are you in trouble?"

"Negative. But we're picking up converging telephone messages from source on bottom. Repeat, on bottom. Can you read also?"

D-One came back, but the message was garbled. Bonner keyed: "Say again."

"Negative on secondary message source. Explain."

Cas thought a moment before keying. "Run a full profile scan for location of possible downed submarine. Cover sectors . . ." He paused, searching for his sector map.

Burke had it. He read off the area designations along a half-mile path directly below: "Use 44-B, -C, and -D on lateral, 15-B and -C on azimuth."

Bonner relayed, adding, "Going off selector position for three minutes, over and out."

"Aye, Checker 3. Standing by."

He turned up the selector switch and brought back the voices. Burke was murmuring to himself. Cas touched his arm to quiet him. The voice splurges came four times, each one ending with the same Russian phrases.

"It's repeating itself," he said. "Must be on an automatic tape."

"Good Lord, Bonner, a submarine's hull couldn't retain integrity at that depth."

"Yes, a Soviet boomer boat could." He frowned. "But there's something odd about the signal." Head down, he closed his eyes in concentration. The next time the sounds came, he had it. "Those aren't phone impulses. There's no modulation warble."

"Then what the bloody hell is it?"

"I think it's pure sound traveling through the water."

"That's crazy. We're too far from the bottom for our gear to pick up natural sound."

"Well, it's doing it." He swung the selector back and raised the *Digger*. The radioman informed him the bottom scan was getting a distorted read: "We're picking up scattered layers of magnetic overlay. Thompson believes iron deposits are creating interference. Advise your intentions." Doug Thompson was chief of operations for the Tamcore.

Bonner keyed: "We're striking for bottom. Track us

down with ten-minute fix relays and continue profile scan.''

Burke grabbed his arm. ''What're you saying, man? Even if there is a sub down there, those poor dingoes aboard have already copped it.''

Bonner shook him off. ''We can't just leave them.''

''We understand you have intention to strike for bottom,'' D-One said. ''Thompson has cancelled request. Too dangerous. Over.''

''I bloody agree with him,'' Burke cried. ''We'll push our reserves.''

''We can handle it.''

''This is insane.''

Ignoring him, Cas keyed: ''D-One, I'm utilizing captain's perogative.'' As submersible operator, he was indeed captain of his little vessel. ''We're going down. Now, goddammit, track us.''

A few seconds later, Thompson came on. ''What the hell do you think you're doing, Bonner?''

''There's a sub on the bottom, and I intend to attempt location for a possible rescue effort.''

''I absolutely forbid it.''

Cas flicked the switch, cutting off the incoming signal. Burke gasped. Bonner turned to a side panel and began throwing more switches. Instantly the tiny stern thrusters that had been pushing them at a half mile an hour stopped. A moment later, the ballast tank pumps came on.

He waited a few seconds, then turned on the radio-telephone again. ''D-One, are you going to track us or do we go it alone?''

There was a long silence, then: ''What is your present environmental status?''

Cas gave the phone to Burke, who glared fiercely back at him. While the Aussie read off power and ballast readings to the service ship, Bonner turned off all

lights to conserve battery power. They were plunged
into near total blackness, the only illuminations coming from the green glows of the dials, their sonar
screen, and the tiny colored dots of switch lights.

They dropped.

Although they descended rapidly, it would take them
nearly an hour to reach the bottom. Periodically the
Digger updated their track status. Bottom scan, they
were told, was still registering distortion. Now and
then Cas would swing the selector to the voices. They
seemed to be increasing in volume.

Six thousand feet . . .

Eight thousand . . .

They passed through a squid swarm. The animals
squirmed and coiled against the acrylic dome, their
bodies strangely luminous. They made tiny squeaks
like mice that came in over the soft hum of the ballast
pump.

At ten thousand, three hundred feet, their side-scan
sonar began picking up the bottom. Bonner eased the
descent speed to fifty feet per minute and moved away
from the Rift wall as it angled toward the east. Burke
turned on the strobes. Through the beams whirled a
snowfall of bottom dust.

Over the past ten minutes, the *Digger's* phone signal
had become chaotic, surging and fading and riding
heavy modulation. Burke kept shaking his head anxiously. The inside temperature of the submersible was
now holding on 29° F. and frost formed in the air.
Condensation beaded the metal surfaces.

They reached the bottom of the Godavari Rift and
began the search.

The ship loomed suddenly into the strobes like a
gigantic pile of refuse and tree cuttings somehow carelessly deposited on the Rift floor. It was completely

covered with a thick layer of green, furry-looking moss that Cas immediately recognized as a fungial fume. In the lights, the layer seemed to breathe, and tendrils of it drifted in the current. Its thickness distorted the actual shape of the ship's hull, gave the spars and derrick posts streamers which resembled old men's beards.

They'd been very lucky to locate the wreck; rebound impulses from their small sonar unit had become distorted. At first glance Cas thought the thing was a rock formation and had started around it. Then he caught sight of metal fittings and, a moment later, the great twisted blades of a stern wheel. He cut power and hovered off the port side.

During the entire descent the overhead speaker had continued repeating its litany of screams and Russian–Hindi jabber. Now it was nearly continuous, sometimes murmured, then violently powerful.

Burke finally had enough. "God, man, turn that bleeding thing off. It makes my testicles shrivel."

Cas complied. The submersible fell silent as he eased on thruster power. They moved slowly around the ship. The strobes probed the lines of the hull: the pilot house, the deck layers and crumpled stacks. She had plunged stern first into the bottom and then broke in two, the upper deck completely smashing down onto the lower spaces.

One of her boilers lay partially driven into the sand. It had a great hole in its side, the ragged edges indicating an internal explosion. A few feet away, a vehicle of some kind lay against one of the main stacks, apparently having sheared it off. Protruding from the stern of the vehicle was the crushed after portion of a missile with collapsible fins. A second, similar vehicle rested thirty feet beyond it, nearly buried under the pilot house.

Bonner surmised what had happened. One of the

vehicles, lashed onto the top deck, must have broken loose and crashed down into the boilers. The resulting explosion had torn the ship's bottom out.

"Well, that's some bloody submarine, that is," Burke snorted. "That fucking pile of scrap's been settin' here for years."

Cas shook his head. "No, she hasn't been under for more than a few weeks. Look at her metal surfaces, very little rust or algae pock."

He completed one circuit, started on another. The wash of the submersible's rotors had by now stirred fungi off the scattered debris. It swirled up until the ship looked as if she lay in green fog. As bits of matter drifted past the acrylic dome, Cas leaned forward to get a closer look. *Serius Diastrolipium,* he decided, a common oceanic and riverine fungi. But he'd never seen such a concentrated fume of *Diastrolipium.* And judging from the way the mass moved and "breathed," he figured there was still a tremendous amount of reproduction going on within the core.

"Either way," Burke said, "there couldn't possibly be enough electrical power still aboard that thing to run a tape unit."

Cas settled back, his eyes thoughtful. "It's not a tape," he said finally. "The sounds are coming straight off the hull."

"Ach, how can that be?"

"Those are acoustic imprints of the crewmen's voices. Somehow they got imprinted into the metal as she plunged."

"That's bloody nonsense," Burke sneered.

Cas ignored the remark. "The imprints are probably on the boiler plate or the engines. They were the only things hot enough. Just the right amount of heat and pressure, coupled with the strong magnetic component in this area, and those metal surfaces became acoustic tapes. Now the current's reproducing the imprinted vibrations.'' He grunted at his own thought, caught by the bizarre prospect of these eerie, soulful voices screaming forever through the darkness of the Godavari.

The water had become so murky they could hardly see the ship. Bonner stopped his stern motors and engaged the bottom set. With a tiny tremble the submersible scooted sideways for a few seconds. As they cleared out of the fungial mist, he cut power completely. They drifted while Burke checked their power reserves.

"Are you satisfied now, Bonner?" he snapped. "We've only got six minutes more of bottom time."

Eight seconds later, the lights went out.

Bonner stiffened. His control panel was dark, all power gone. He felt an icy shiver down his back. Then he began throwing switches, hearing Burke curse in a panic. The lights came on for a moment, low-powered, yellowish, then went out again.

"The main batteries are gone," Cas said quietly. He felt over the control panel, found the reset button, banged it with his fist.

Nothing.

"Go to manual power."

"Oh, my God!"

"Go to manual power," Cas hissed. At last he heard the Aussie fumbling for the auxiliary, hand-pumped generator. The submersible rocked with the movement. He found a flashlight, flicked it on. It flared directly into Burke's stark face. The Aussie was sweating.

Cas swung the light to his control board, bent forward to read dials. Under their glass faces all the needles were jumping crazily. What the hell? Then it hit him. They must have drifted into a chaotic magnetic pocket. Instantly the circuit lines from the battery packs had lost magnetic linkage and locked open, shutting off all electrical power to the interior systems.

He scanned the environment panel above the control set. These instruments were static-operated and indicated such things as water temperature, salinity gradient, current speed, and composition analysis. With another shock his eyes fixed on the ambient aquatic gas readout. The automatic analysis registered far below normal levels for gases suspended within the surrounding water. All except the methane gradient. That was holding on a two thousand percent above-normal read.

Burke's pumping finally got the lights back on, but they were feeble, fading and rising with his arm movements. Bonner shut down the strobes and all unnecessary internal gear. He tried to start one of the stern motors. It spun gently but refused to come on fully.

"I told you we should have left well enough alone, you goddamned fool," Burke panted frantically, his chubby fifty-year-old body rocking back and forth over the pump generator. "Pull the plug and get us the hell out of here."

"Not yet," Cas countered. "I want samples of that fungi. The fume's shoving horrendous amounts of methane into the ocean. I want to know why."

Burke was so shaken by that statement he stopped pumping. The lights faded, then came on as he went back to it. His face was red with rage and mounting terror. "Fuck your bleedin' methane. I'm ordering you to get us up."

Instead Cas gently swung the *Checker 3* in a half circle and headed back toward where he figured the wreck was. They moved very slowly. Several seconds passed. He flicked on a single strobe. Immediately the interior lights sank as power was drained by the big exterior unit.

Directly ahead rose the tilted stack of the wreck. Cas veered slightly to the right, adding a bit of water ballast. The submersible went lower, skimmed just above the half-sunken boiler. He drew abreast of the deckhouse and hovered.

There was a series of tiny, sharp clicks as the battery switches closed. Instantly the lights came on full. Burke, gasping, sank back into his seat, eyes ablaze.

Retrieving the fungi sample was a delicate maneuver, with Cas manipulating the mechanical arm and sample basket. At the same time he had to power on and off to keep the current from pushing the little vessel into the deckhouse. They were so close, he could see scroll work on the forward bulkhead under the fungial layer. The curls and diamonds reminded him of Javanese temple carvings.

As the sample basket dragged across the bulkhead, it threw up a fresh cloud of matter that shimmered in the strobe like specks of beryl. Slowly he retracted the basket and waited for the tiny light on the manipulator board to indicate the sample had been pressure-sealed and locked aboard. When it flashed, he switched on the pumps to blow ballast. They whined softly and he felt the little vessel start to lift. For a fleeting moment his eyes held on the deckhouse for one last look. The green mist was thinning out, the current pulling it away. There, where the sample basket had scraped, he saw the ship's name:

Java Queen.

The three Burmese raiders stood in a line in the courtyard, their heads down. They were naked except for garlands of marigolds around their necks. Their

bodies were coated with a yellow oil that glistened in
the sunlight.

In front of them, Gulab Dau Singh sat astride a mag-
nificent black Arabian stallion. The animal snorted and
restlessly stamped its hooves on the cobblestones.
Singh, dressed in a flowing orange robe and massive
turban, was six-foot-six, with a massive chest. In his
right hand, its blade resting on his shoulder, he held
a British Guardsman's saber.

These Burmese had been taken during an incursion
across the Patkai Bum mountains, in the highland tea
belt south of Doom Dooma. Members of a rival opium
clan, they had struck at Singh's secret poppy fields at
Digboi. These three were the only ones left alive.

The courtyard was huge, half the size of a football
field. A wide gate opened in the east wall and, farther
in, balconies supported by marble pillars ringed the
compound. Below the balconies about a hundred of
Singh's militiamen in dirty *dhotis* and tall red and gold
turbans sat watching, an assault rifle resting on each
man's crossed legs.

At the western end of the courtyard, the great facade
of Lake House rose in the sun, a majestic structure of
pure white marble topped by peaked Deccani-temple
roofs fashioned from hammered brass and tile. Between the courtyard and house were gardens of scented
jacaranda and wild apple trees and pools crowded with
lotus blossoms. But the shrubbery was thick and un-
tended.

To the left, beyond a small grove of palms, the
ground sloped down to the lake shore and a small pavilion, its terrace extending out over the water. It, too,
was fashioned from marble and had intricately carved
stone screens.

Constructed on Namak Island, a small, pine-covered
ait in Lake Sonai, one of the numerous basin *etangs*

in the Brahmaputra watershed, Lake House had once belonged to a British administrator during the days of the Raj. Now it was Gulab Singh's headquarters.

The Sikh lightly touched the stallion's flanks with his boots, and the horse pranced in a wide circle around the Burmese men. They watched him, turning their bodies slowly. The eyes of two were glazed with fear, but the third glowered at Singh with a smoldering defiance.

Three times he circled before pausing once more. Then, with the tip of the saber, he pointed toward the open gate. "Run," he said in Burmese. "Reach gate, you free."

None of the men moved.

"Run!" Singh bellowed.

The man who had been glaring shot a glance toward the gate, then back. He had thick black hair and a wispy goatee. He studied Singh a moment, then again glanced at the gate. His body tensed . . .

Standing on a balcony above, Colonel Kurisovsky contemptuously watched the proceedings. It disgusted him: more barbaric bullshit, he thought. For a half hour Singh had tormented his captives with idiotic execution rituals: mustard oil placed on their palms, marigold garlands reaching their genitals, and cinnamon sprinkled over their buttocks. All of it had been accompanied by vengeful Dogra maledictions that were answered by the seated militiamen like a Greek chorus.

As a soldier, the colonel had been trained to kill an enemy with efficient dispatch, not torment him with senseless peasant rites. He lit a *bidi,* a native cigarette made of kendu leaf, and tossed the match over the railing. "Get on with it, you Indian baboon," he murmured scornfully. "Either kill the bastards or let them go."

Andrei Kurisovsky possessed a great deal of scorn for other, lesser men. Born in the bleak coal fields of Vologda, he'd learned early that only strength and courage in lethal proportions really counted in a world of chaos. But it must be ruthlessness with a purpose or else it became pointless. In his life, he'd discovered that few possessed such balanced qualities.

He had killed his first man at the age of fourteen—cleaved his skull in with a shovel during a fight in the mines. For that he had been committed to a work camp but soon escaped and joined the Red Army as an infantryman in the crack 178th Irkutsk Corps. With his fearlessness and unflinching obedience, he quickly rose in the ranks. At twenty-five he was a major, adjutant of a Spatnez unit. In 1979, he won his colonelcy and command of the dreaded October Force, an assassin group assigned to the KGB.

His OF men were all handpicked: ex-convicts, Spatnez commandos, and veterans of crack paratrooper units. Each was expert in infiltration tactics, demolition, and weaponry. For the next ten years he had led them on clandestine operations in Afghanistan, South Africa, and the Middle East.

Then his world began to change. First came the progressive doctrines of *perestroika* and *glasnost*, started by the now retired Premier Yuri Markisov. But his political heir, Viktor Seleznov, now president of the Commonwealth of Independent States and Russian prime minister, had continued these destructive policies. Eventually, everything fell apart. The USSR, once a land of warriors, dissolved into a morass of squabbling petty states, all shifting for power.

One of the main casualties was the Russian army. Uncertainty and a sense of formlessness haunted the upper echelons. Discipline fell apart in the ranks. Soldiers deserted, some even killing their officers. Bands of such freebooters prowled the countryside like wolves.

For the first time in his life, Kurisovsky lost direction and sank into despair. Quickly it turned to rage. Then slowly, clandestinely, he found other men who carried the same fury and frustration. Most were either active or retired army officers. Together they formed a secret brotherhood called Those of the Phoenix, and vowed to expend their lives in a rebirth of the old USSR from the ashes into which she had fallen.

Their leader was a deposed general named Valeri Zgursky, Kurisovsky's old commander in the 178th. After months of planning, they initiated a daring plan. The first step took Kurisovsky and sixteen of his OF men to India and Gulab Singh's marble palace on Lake Sonai.

Singh was the most powerful chieftain in northeastern Assam state. Originally from Jammu in the Kashmir, he was a direct descendant of the great Dogra warriors of the Rann of Kutch. In 1948 he had fought the Pakistanis, then led guerilla bands against Nehru's troops during the bloody riots for *swaraj* or Sikh independence.

The Chinese invasion across the Tibetan frontier in 1962, however, overwhelmed his scattered forces. Half his men were massacred. Taking the remnants, he fled south, then down the long eastern flanks of Nepal and Bhutan to the Brahmaputra River plain in northeastern India.

This vast area east of Bangladesh, had been in constant factional turmoil for years as native strongmen clashed with one another over territorial claims. Into this chaos Singh unleashed his war-seasoned guerillas with stunning ferocity. First he subjugated the aboriginal mountain tribes, then took on the lowland war chiefs. Within eight years he had gained complete superiority within the flood plain.

His timing was fortuitous. The Indian government, preoccupied with devastating famines and religious riots that swept across the whole of India throughout the late sixties and early seventies, left him alone while he expanded his power base. By the time the country recovered, Singh was so deeply entrenched it would have meant a bloody guerilla war to dislodge him.

The Delhi government chose an easier course. They granted him autonomous territorial status in Assam, thereby not only gaining the use of his militiamen to maintain peace there, but also the advantage of a buffer force against Chinese incursions across the old McMahon line, which marked the frontier between Tibet and India.

Now Singh lived in feudal splendor, accepting *baksheesh* from both peasants and rich landowners, skimming off percentages from every boatload of teak and tea or tanker of oil that went downriver. In addition, he developed a smuggler network for raw opium and arms shipments. . . .

Kurisovsky took another drag on his *bidi* and recalled his first encounter with the Sikh warlord. It had been touchy and dangerous. He'd come up the Brahmaputra alone, carrying the credentials of an arms dealer from Saudi Arabia. Singh's spies notified him of this rival, and Kurisovsky was kidnapped and taken to a basement room in Lake House. It had seeping walls and torches like a medieval dungeon.

After three days, Singh finally showed up. His black, blazing eyes studied the Russian for a long moment before he said, in English, "You not damn Arabian."

"No, I'm Russian."

Singh's lip curled. "I hate Russians."

"I've come to fight for you."

"Ah? Why?"

"I'm a soldier, trained to fight. My own country is dead and no longer needs me."

"I have plenny soldiers."

"But they don't have what I can give you. Long-range missiles and launchers that I can teach your men to use."

Singh frowned and paced back and forth, keeping his eyes on Kurisovsky. "Why I need these such missiles?"

"To kill BIM soldiers," the Russian answered. BIM stood for the Bangladesh Insurgency Movement. In addition to the Burmese opium raiders, Singh's main opponents were BIM guerillas who laid claim to the Meghalaya Mountains east of Bangladesh and the waters of the Brahamaputra as far as Tezpur. Recently these fanatical Moslem fighters had been attacking Singh's outposts and had actually bested the Sikhs in places like Shillong and Kampur.

Singh thought about that, then shook his head. "Impossible. Delhi government attack me if I am firing off these things."

"They wouldn't even know where they came from," Kurisovsky countered. "Only a few would be used at a time, low-level night launches into the river."

"River?" Singh guffawed. "We kill BIM bathing? Maybe like this many?" He held up a great paw of a hand.

"No, you'd kill thousands," the Russian said patiently. "These missiles would carry biological warheads." He looked steadily at the Sikh. "You understand?"

"Ah, biological."

"Once in the river, they'd infect half of Bangladesh, leave it wide open for your men to occupy long before Delhi could react."

Singh said nothing more. Scowling thoughtfully, he turned and left. But two hours later, Kurisovsky was released from his dungeon. He was given one of the field bungalows on the Lake House estate, and appointed to Singh's personal war council.

Immediately he sent word to his men, who had already assembled in Calcutta. Over the next week they came up the Brahmaputra, alone or in pairs, carrying their concealed weapons and forged permits as oil workers for the drilling platform on the eastern end of Namak Island. . . .

The Burmese ran.

With a bellow Singh rammed his boots into the stallion's flanks, and the horse exploded forward. The Burmese had scarcely covered twenty feet before the huge Sikh caught him. Bending in the saddle, he brought the saber down in a cross slash, severing the man's head. A low soughing sound lifted from the seated militiamen. The head, spewing blood, rolled onto the ground while behind it the headless corpse sprawled, arms and legs twitching in violent spasms.

Singh wheeled, the horse hooves crackling on the cobblestones. Bending again, he skewered the head with the tip of his saber and flung it toward his men. They dodged aside and struck at it with the butts of their rifles, sending it back out into the courtyard like a bloody basketball.

For a few seconds the remaining Burmese froze. Then one, crazed with terror, twisted and ran wildly toward the Sikhs. Two leaped to their feet, grabbed him, and threw him back into the courtyard. Instantly Singh was on him. He slashed twice with the saber, completely opening the man's spine.

Full of bloodlust now, the chieftain turned and headed for the last Burmese raider. The man stood there, unable to move. As the stallion reached him, it reared slightly, throwing its great chest forward. It smashed into the man and knocked him violently to the ground. Before he could recover, Singh rode over him, spun the stallion around and rode over him again. There was a loud crack of breaking bone. The man screamed in agony, rolled into a ball. Singh pulled the horse up and hacked at him. The man flailed, his open mouth screeching at the sky until the saber blade sliced across his throat, silencing him.

Slowly the militiamen rose and came down into the courtyard, walking high up on their toes in a kind of hot swagger. A conch horn blew from somewhere deeper under the pillars. The Sikh chieftain bolted on his horse this way, that. Blood was all over the ground, glistening brilliantly in the sun.

Kurisovsky did not move a muscle. Strung along either side of him at the railing were several of his own men. They chortled coldly at the carnage down in the courtyard. He took one final drag off his *bidi* and flicked it over the rail. It landed in a pool of blood, sizzling.

As if by some prescribed timing, the sudden crack of chains and machinery drifted over the silent courtyard. Kurisovsky glanced up. A half mile east of Lake House was a large oil-drilling platform at the very edge of the lake. Inland of it, intricate matrices of pipes led down to a tank nest and compound of workshops and barracks. The tanks were all painted bright yellow and emblazoned with SINGAPORE OIL logos.

A drilling crew had just started pulling pipe. As Kurisovsky watched, he was struck, as he had been in the past, by the stark contrast between the towering oil-stained monolith of the rig and the poetic marble beauty of Lake House. It was like India itself, he

thought, full of abrupt contradictions that created a
stifling mindlessness and ineptitude in its people. That
primal stupidity had already fouled his mission schedule and dangerously narrowed its time frame.

First off was the failure of the *Java Queen* to reach
Namak Island. No trace of it had been found, and
Kurisovsky was certain it and its drunken captain had
ended up on the bottom of the Indian Ocean somewhere. That meant another raid to obtain launchers,
more expended time and perhaps lost men.

Then came the accident aboard the barge used to
transport the missiles brought by the C-47 across the
lake. The loaders had carelessly braced the units to
the deck using only bales of hay. One missile broke
loose and went over the side. But before going into
the water, its warhead had violently struck the adjacent missile's tail section. Watching from the shore
through binoculars, Kurisovsky thought he saw a crack
in the warhead as it sank out of sight into fifty fathoms
of water. Later, the men on the barge said they had
heard escaping gas coming from it.

For their stupidity, Singh immediately shot two of
the loaders and fed their bodies to the crocodiles that
haunted the waters off the pavilion. But the damage
had been done. Without proper salvage gear, the missile could not be recovered.

That misstep haunted the Russian. Had the warhead's pressurized biological core been ruptured? he
wondered. Was its deadly virus even now moving
down the Brahmaputra River, infecting the people
along its banks? Such an epidemic could bring hordes
of government troops and medical teams up into Assam. If that occurred, somebody would eventually
stumble onto the presence of the other missiles stored
in Kurisovsky's bungalow.

He returned his gaze to the courtyard. Singh's men

had cut off the heads of the two Burmese and stuck them onto poles sunk into the ground near the gate. Singh stood beside his nervous stallion, rubbing its flanks and cooing softly. A militiaman went about with a box of sand, spreading it over the pools of blood.

Kurisovsky jetted a stream of spittle through his teeth and turned away.

2

"Oh, God!" Dr. Jackie Dunbar cried disgustedly. She had just stepped into a pile of human excrement on the sidewalk. Flies lifted, a foul bloom drifted up to assail her nostrils as she scraped the dark blob from the sole of her hospital-ward shoe. A thick throng of pedestrians, hurrying through the sweltering Calcutta night, flowed unconcernedly around her like water in a stream.

A few yards away at the entrance to a dark alley, a tall Bengali man in a dirty white suit anxiously called to her, "Please, daktar-missy, you must making great haste." She waved him on. He darted into the alley and, shouldering her way through the pedestrians, Jackie followed.

Thirty minutes before, the Bengali had burst into one of the emergency operating rooms of Victoria Hospital, pleading for help and wildly waving a fistful of rupees. He was immediately intercepted by one of the off-duty E.R. interns, a young Aussie named Becker.

"Hold it right there, mate," Becker growled. Roughly he shoved the Indian back into the corridor.

"Please, I am needing daktar," the Bengali cried. "Look, look, I have much money to pay."

The intern looked him up and down, scowling. "Why? What the hell's wrong wi' ya?"

"It is not I. My cousin, she dies."

"Then bring her in."

"No, no, I cannot bringing her here. She is bad breathing and her body is crazy."

At that moment Jackie had walked past. She was coming off a twelve-hour shift on the pediatric ward and had been heading for the rear parking lot to catch the hospital jitney for home. Curious, she paused beside the Admissions desk to listen.

"Look," Becker snapped impatiently, "we can't treat her unless you bring her in. Either do it or bugger off."

"Oh, please, you come." The Bengali shoved his money forward. "Here, you taking it."

The Admissions clerk, a massive woman with a bright red *puja* mark on her forehead, snorted contemptuously. "Bloody *goonda*."

Jackie glanced around. "*Goonda?* What's that?"

"He's criminal. Such men operate the black markets and prostitutions and drugs. Very dangerous and evil."

Becker started to turn away, but the Bengali, his eyes suddenly ablaze, grabbed his white jacket. "You come, I say."

The Aussie shoved him off. "Aye, keep the bleedin' hands off me, mate. Or I'll run your arse out of here."

Jackie stepped forward. "Hold it a minute, Becker." To the Bengali she said, "This cousin of your, you say she can't breathe?"

The Bengali whirled on her. "You are being daktar?"

"Yes."

"Indeed, indeed, she does like this." He gripped his throat, making choking sounds.

"How long has she been sick?"

"Two, three hour."

"Is she stiff in the muscles?" Jackie ran her hands over her own arms, across her chest. "You know, muscles?"

The Bengali's head swung back and forth in the Indian sign for yes. "Her body is hard as board and she makes crazy positions, very paining."

Jackie frowned. It was like the others, she thought. "Does she smell like kerosene?"

The Bengali stared, confused.

She turned to the nurse. "Translate for me."

The nurse complied. Instantly the man's face lit up. "Oh, yes, her breathing is smelling like *chula*." A *chula* was a small cooking stove that used charcoal or kerosene for fuel.

Things were falling into place. "Is she from Dibrugarh?"

"She is coming from there two days since now."

That cinches it, Jackie thought. All the other patients with identical symptoms had also come from Dibrugarh. Obviously, something was developing in that city near the headwaters of the Brahmaputra.

"All right," she snapped. "I'll come with you." She turned to Becker. "Loan me your kit, will you?"

The Aussie looked shocked. "Don't be a bloody fool, Dunbar. You can't go alone with this nong, he's a bleedin' criminal."

"I want to see this patient. She sounds like the others."

"What others?"

She had no time to explain. "Come on, move, get me your kit."

"It's against hospital regs."

"Screw the regs."

Becker shrugged. "It's your arse, luv."

Outside, the Bengali hailed a rickshaw for her. It was pulled by a man so thin he looked like a survivor from Auschwitz. Without another word, the Bengali took off at a trot with the rickshaw man following.

She glanced at her watch. It was seven-fifteen, another stifling June evening with the palm trees in the hospital grounds hanging limply in the torpid, sewer stench off the nearby Hooghly River. The two men raced down the long exit drive and entered the heavy traffic of buses and cars and oxen carts on Diamond Boulevard. Jackie settled back and hoped she wasn't making a mistake.

She had been in Calcutta for less than three months. A strikingly lovely women, thirty and model tall, she possessed quick, sparkling gray eyes that contained flecks of green in their depths. A graduate of the University of California medical school in Berkeley, she'd done her internship in Denver and afterward taken a position with the prestigious Holmes Clinic in nearby, exclusive Englewood. It paid two hundred thousand a year.

But one rainy afternoon a year later she threw it all away, along with a relationship with a lawyer that had, like the clients of the Holmes Clinic, become less than meaningful. Everybody was shocked. What the hell will you do? they demanded to know. In answer, she filed an application with the International Red Cross, requesting clinical work in a Third World country. They gave her Victoria Hospital.

India was a jolt, a world on a different level that bluntly abrogated most of the concepts she'd accepted all her life. She was overwhelmed by the massive amount of sickness, a mind-boggling diversity of suffering. All the bizarre diseases from the textbooks and some not came through the doors of the Victoria.

She struggled, forced herself to stand long shifts in a desperate attempt to condition her mind, her emotions, to the horrors she saw. At night, wasted with a fatigue that went into her bone marrow, she'd drag herself to her apartment on Chowringhee Avenue and brood in the twilight.

Then, three weeks before, a seven-year-old boy from upriver Dibrugarh had been brought into her ward. He was near dehydration from violent diarrhea and wracked by sporadic muscle spasms. His facial muscles were already afflicted by lockjaw; his spine was bent backward like a bow. His skin, breath, and stool carried the odor of kerosene fumes.

She diagnosed *Clostridium tetani,* or tetanus invasion, but blood work proved negative for that specific pathogen. Next, she considered hypobacterium tuberculosis. The tuberculin patch created no induration or erythema indicating non-bacillic presence. Desperate to do something, she chose to bombard the unknown vector with heavy doses of anti-tetanus vaccine, detoxification serums, muscle relaxants, and Demerol for pain.

None of it was effective. The boy went into respiratory paralysis within forty minutes, his body literally coiling itself tighter and tighter until his bones began to break.

A postmortem tissue examination reaffirmed the failure to pinpoint either *c tetani* or tuberculosis. However, high levels of lactic acid showed in the samples along with traces of methane in the feces. There was also an extremely faint residue of gram-positive bacteria in the cell wall tissue, but that was discarded as pathologically insufficient to cause death.

She badgered the lab technicians into doing further tests, more exotic blood chemistries. Since tetanus can occasionally exhibit similar symptoms to encephalitus and strychnine poisoning, she requested protein and toxicity readings. Again the results were negative. Eventually the ward's chief resident logged the death as due to ingestion of an unknown toxic substance, a very common event in India.

Two days later another case came in, this time a young woman. Soon after, twin boys and an old man were stricken. Same tetanus symptoms, same results with the standard anti-toxin drugs. All four patients died.

This time Jackie demanded full autopsies be performed. The hospital's chief pathologist refused. Pathology lab time was critical, he pointed out irritably, not to be wasted with expensive tests for something as ordinary as a poisoning. . . .

The Bengali, sprinting ahead through dense shadows, led her into the heart of the vast Calcutta slum known as Amand Nagar. It was a warren of makeshift shacks and tents squeezed between a railroad embankment and the Calcutta–Delhi highway. Eighty thousand people lived there, in a space no larger than three football fields.

The alley was barely six feet wide yet was filled with people sleeping everywhere on the ground, curled under sheets of *khadi* cloth and looking like corpses. There were no walls as such, only embankments of compacted hovels with candlelit rooms from which seeped the steady screech of Hindi music. A ditch ran down the center of the alley, filled with the dark sludge of human and animal excrement over which rats fought. In the humid, stifling air, the stench was horrible.

At last the Indian stopped before a shack built of cargo pallets and covered with a filthy canvas. He motioned her in. The single room was no larger than a closet, lit by three tall candles. Liquid feces glistened on the mud floor. In one corner a small image of Ganpati, the Hindu elephant god, sat with a garland of flowers and a fresh sandlewood-paste mark on its forehead.

The female patient, about fourteen years old, lay on a straw bed. Her filthy yellow sari was soaked with perspiration and runny feces, and her breath came in shuddering gasps through clenched teeth. Jackie quickly opened the medical kit and knelt to examine her. The girl's forehead was clammy but cool. She bent close and sniffed her breath, her skin. Kerosene.

Suddenly the girl's eyes shot open. Her pupils, Jackie saw, were constricted, the lids quivering spastically. "Easy, honey," she whispered and ran her hands over the girl's arms, chest, abdomen. The muscles under the dark skin were rigid. She straightened and took a syringe and a small vial containing 1,600 units of ampicillin from the kit.

The moment the needle sank into the girl's buttock, she trembled and instantly clenched up in a violent muscle spasm. Her arms locked against her chest, and she thrust her body into an arch, her feet thrashing in the mud. Her mouth drew back in a snarl, teeth bared, eyes rolling in terror and pain.

Jackie took out a second vial containing a powerful muscle relaxant. She drew up again and shouted to the Bengali, "Get an ambulance here. Right now."

He stood frozen.

"Move, goddamn you."

She plunged the needle in again. A single groan, trailing out like the scream of a woman in labor, came through the girl's teeth. A vertebra cracked. For one terrifying moment the girl, her neck veins popping out, fought for air and then her lung muscles went into full respiratory paralysis.

Cursing, Jackie began pounding on the girl's chest, pulled at her shoulders to force the lung muscles to function again. Sweat ran down into her eyes. She kept on wildly. It was useless. The girl was already dead.

A soft whinny of sorrow burbled out of the Bengali. After a moment he stepped close and knelt down. His fingers fluttered like bat's wings over the girl's face, the bulging eyes, the bruised breasts, whispering, whispering.

Jackie stood up. She felt suddenly utterly fatigued, wasted. Leaving her kit, she stepped around him and went back out into the alley. Its foulness assailed her in a renewed rush. She stood there motionless. Around her sounds meshed in the air: the banshee music, snores and snuffles, a humming like women praying. Something crossed over her ankle. She jerked back and squinted at the ground. A scolopendra, a venomous centipede a foot long, slithered off into the shadows.

Shuddering with repugnance, she felt a surge of nausea roil in her stomach. She wanted to run past all the filth, beyond the disease and the stenches. But she didn't. Slowly, forcing away the images of vileness, she re-entered the hovel. The Bengali was still kneeling silently beside his cousin. Jackie touched his shoulder. "Go and bring a morgue wagon," she said softly. She unpinned her hospital ID badge and held it out to him. "Show them this, they'll send one."

The man ignored her.

"Please do this," she insisted. "I want to take your cousin's body back to the hospital."

His head snapped up. "No, you will not taking my Aloka there."

"I want an autopsy done on her."

"You leaving now."

"You don't understand. This—this thing that killed Aloka might kill you. Maybe many more people. We have to learn what it is before it's too late. Please."

"You leaving now, daktar-missy."

"As a medical officer, I'm ordering you to do this."

The Bengali's eyes gleamed with ferocity in the candlelight. He reached into his coat pocket and shoved a wad of rupees at her. "Take money and go away. This moment you are leaving. Or you, too, are dying here."

Jackie felt his rage wash over her. She recoiled.

"Get out," he screamed.

Cautiously she retrieved the medical kit and backed out the door. Outside, she looked around, suddenly unsure of the direction from which they'd entered the slum. At last she made a choice and started off.

Within minutes she was hopelessly lost. The alleys converged with complex, formless patterns. She passed lepers with faces like gargoyles, naked Jain fakirs squatting in meditation. A little boy urinated on a canvas wall while a dog ate a live snake, its tail coiled over the dog's ear.

It was like plunging through a nightmare, among shadowy, grotesque creatures pinioned in a time warp. She clutched her bag and ran, faster and faster. More hovels loomed, voices whispered. And then the sound of trucks and traffic drifted toward her, the suddenly pleasant smell of diesel fumes. She burst out onto the busy boulevard. To the south she saw the river with boat lights drifting under the high crenellated towers of Howrah Bridge.

George Tadhunter, assistant to the British high commissioner for Singapore, sipped his cognac and watched a particularly lovely young woman dancing on the terrace. She was blond and deeply tanned. The eight-piece orchestra played a jazzy rendition of "Waltzing Matilda." Each time the dancer's partner whirled her, their feet interlocked so that their pelvises pressed against each other, giving the sensual impression of a whirling coitus. A bit distractedly, Tadhunter found that his penis had risen into a mild erection.

Beside him, a burly Australian executive of Singapore Oil named Podecker was growling about India and that "great bloody kafir Abu Singh." With an effort Tadhunter drew his attention from the dancer. "Yes," he said absently. "Yes, I can certainly understand your frustration."

"That's just the damned problem. Everybody understands but nobody has the bleeding arse to sack the bugger."

"Not much *can* be done. Singh does present a problem, but as long as Delhi continues to protect him—" He shrugged. "It's a matter of Indian priorities."

"Priorities, my dick," barked Podecker. He shoved his thumb and forefinger under Tadhunter's nose. "It's the rackets, mate. Cash, plain and simple. The whole Delhi gov'mint is on the take. And it's bleedin' us oilers starkers."

Around them milled Chinese businessmen, diplomats, a few general officers, lovely women in frilly cocktail dresses. Like fishermen working a stream, they waded about with glasses in hand, forming little clots of conversation that soon broke apart. This particular party was being given for the new Australian commissioner for Singapore in the home of the industrialist Tu Yehsheng. Five thousand square feet of high-tech chrome, steel, and white leather located on the slopes of the Fort Canning Rise, the most exclusive residential area in old colonial Singapore.

"Well, I'll tell you one thing." Podecker snapped. "Someday soon those jack-ups in Delhi'll be sorry they let that barstad run loose. Him and the BIM are fair tearin' up the countryside. And now, would ya believe, he's gone and got hisself fuckin' Russians to show him how to do it better.

Tadhunter's eyes snapped up. "What's that you say?"

Podecker chuckled. "Aye, that grabs your ear, does it?"

"Russians? What Russians?"

"Bloody mercenaries."

"How many?"

"I'm not sure. But the bullbucker on our rig at Sonai Lake says they've been with Singh for three, four months now. It's got his crews antsy as old ladies."

For a moment Tadhunter felt anger hotly touch his cheeks. Four months? And his people in-country had given no indication of any Russians in northeastern India? Well, he'd find out about that.

In addition to his duties with the British consulatory force in Singapore, George Tadhunter was also station head for the British Overseas Intelligence's network within the Malaysia/Burma/South India quadrant. Due to the dramatic changes throughout India and Southeast Asia over the preceding decade, Britain had found it more expedient to centralize her intelligence-gathering activities in the freer atmosphere of Singapore.

In reality, the MBSI field agents had very little to do these days. Unlike more active stations in the Middle East, the demise of the USSR had literally put them out of business. As a result, the organization had developed a definite sense of lassitude. Although he would never openly admit it, Tadhunter himself had found the old zing of intelligence gathering waning, filtered down to the humdrum of shuffling through monotonously similar agent reports.

The presence of Russian mercenaries in India, though, needed looking into, and quickly. He knew that it wasn't particularly unusual to find ex-Russian fighting men wandering aimlessly around the world, but most were gravitating to the Middle East, not India.

He abruptly excused himself from Podecker and went off to find his aide, Jack Booker. He located him in the kitchen, chattering with the Chinese cooks. Booker had once been a batman for a general of infantry and had never lost his keen interest in new dishes.

The two men passed through a back door and down a pathway to a pavilion with a tiny pool, the air above it thick with the scent of frangipani. Tadhunter informed Booker of what Podecker had told him. The aide, his perfectly bald head glistening in the lights from the terrace, grunted significantly. "Would seem Jeffry's been a bit lax, doesn't it, sir?" Norman Jeffry was the MI-5 on-site agent in West Bengal.

"Damned lax, I'd say. Now you get on the overseas and tell him I want some hard facts and assessments on these Russians."

"Yes, sir."

"I want to know how many there are. More important, what weapons they've managed to bring with them."

"Right, sir."

"In the morning send an aide-mémoire about it to London. I'll notify the Foreign Office myself. Now off with you."

Booker hurried back up the stairs. Tadhunter stood for a moment, gazing down into the pool. He sighed. Of all his territory, southern India was the most difficult to keep tabs on. The whole place was a maelstrom of confusion, dirty politics, absurd foreign policies. That buffoon Podecker had been right about that. It *was* a political dung heap festering in anachronisms, payoffs, and endless religious upheaval.

Not like the old days, he thought, the sixties and

early seventies when he'd been scientific officer stationed in New Delhi. The corruption had been just as pronounced then, but at least he'd had solid field men experienced in Indian ways. Fellows like Stewart and Weaver and even that crazy bastard Hak McCarran, who'd ended up going jungle-sahib from too much whiskey and too many Indian vaginas.

For a moment he allowed himself a bit of nostalgia, then returned to the house. Only to discover disappointedly that the lovely tanned dancer had left. Within minutes, he had recouped and was deep in conversation with the Eurasian wife of a French diplomat. He had already slept with her. As he talked he recalled how deliciously lustful she had been.

It had a core of darkness, an aura that Bonner sensed strongly. He eased away from the dissection table and took off his gauze mask and rubber gloves. Behind him, his mice chirped and whispered softly in their cages. He lit a cigarette, swung around, and withdrew a beer from his sample refrigerator.

Around him, the *Digger* rolled gently against her sea anchor. It was four A.M. and from his tiny lab room abaft the galley, he could hear the ship's cooks setting up breakfast for the crewmen who would be coming off watch. He'd been working on the fungi samples off the *Java Queen* since ten the night before. Running identification tests, nutrient cultures, and tissue studies from one of the mice that had died soon after exposure to the fungus.

The results were bizarre, creating a mounting mystery. His initial identification of it had been correct: a Thallophyta, non-chlorophyllic organism designated *Serius Diastrolipium*. It was as common as sand on the ocean floor and in some freshwater rivers. But these samples, he discovered, were a mutated form, containing grotesquely oversize mycelia, deep green coloration, and a contorted zoospores formation through compression of the uredinial and telial stages. The result was an explosive germination. Its growth rate was nearly five hundred times normal.

Granulated culture studies indicated wide-spectrum nutrient absorption, yet application of normal antifungial agents proved completely non-toxic to the organism. Yet it *was* susceptible to electric shock, he found. Its electrocution threshold created a splurge within the cellular mitochondria or energy function, creating a metabolic short circuit.

Moreover, even the presence of an electromagnetic source near the fungi caused it to react, like iron filaments to a magnet. Apparently it was this reaction force, instead of a magnetic pocket, that had in some way caused the sudden loss of power in the submersible's electrical system.

But it was the pathogenic reaction within the test mouse that proved most astounding. And ominous. After cutaneous injection of a fungial solution, the animal had almost immediately developed respiratory irregularity and muscle spasms. Tumor sites erupted on the abdomen and around the mouth. Within eighteen minutes the mouse went into fatal respiratory collapse with violent muscular contractions.

Dissection showed pathogenic invasion of all cell tissue accompanied by sepsis and profound toxemia. There was also metabolic decomposition of cellular protein into a methane-based enzyme exhibiting the distinctive odor of kerosene. More surprisingly, the biuret test for serum protein in brain tissue came up violet-blue, indicating minute traces of polysaccharide polymer, the component of a gram-positive but nonspecific bacteria.

It was this finding more than anything else that had

created the foreboding in Cas's mind. He was certain this unknown bacteria was the agent that had stirred the normally benign *Serius Diastrolipium* into its catastrophic mutation state. But what specifically *was* that agent? And how had it gotten way the hell down there in the Gadavari? He didn't like the answer he kept coming up with.

Thompson walked in, rubbing sleep out of his eyes. He poured himself a cup of coffee and studied Bonner. "Still at it, I see."

Cas nodded. He waited, expecting it to come. After returning to the surface the day before, he'd written up his report and presented it to Thompson. The man had remained stonily silent. Apparently he was still too furious to launch into the ass-chewing Cas knew he had coming for deliberately breaking operational dive rules against a direct order to the contrary.

"What'd you find?" Thompson asked.

Cas explained. The Aussie listened, quietly sipping his coffee. When Bonner finished, he frowned and squinted thoughtfully. "I should never have let you bring that specimen aboard," he said finally. "If that thing can kark a mouse that fast, it'll kill us all if it gets loose on this ship."

"Don't worry about contamination. I've got everything isolated and sealed." Cas took a pull from his beer. "But you're right, this thing is deadly, damned deadly. I've never seen mutative progression this rapid. And from what I observed on the bottom, it doesn't look like there are growth parameters to it."

Thompson scowled. "You mean it could infect the entire bottom of the Godavari?"

"I think it's possible."

Thompson grunted. "Well, thank God it's a long way down. We'll just be more careful in the future."

He pointed his cup at the dissection table. "But I what those samples dumped overboard. Right now."

Cas watched him a moment. "Have you notified the Indian government about the *Java Queen*?"

"No."

"You don't intend to, do you?"

"No."

Cas ran the edge of the icy bottle across his chin. "Then I'll have to."

Surprisingly, Thompson's mouth lifted into a rueful grin. But above it his brown eyes went flat. "Everybody told me you were a bleedin' crusader, Bonner. Always goin' off on your own and squarin' for a fight. I guess I should have bloody well listened to them."

It was true, Cas *was* a rebel, independent to a fault. At least where the sea was concerned. At forty-one, Bonner'd done just about everything in and around the oceans of the world, from running dolphin studies in Australia for the U.S. Navy to migration trackings of killer whales to running bottom surveys of the Great Philippine undersea gorge. And he carried a trigger-quick hatred for anyone, be it scientist or layman, who desecrated the marine environment.

All his life, the sea had given him something extraordinary. It was mistress, teacher, source of solace. In its balance and endless rhythm of life and death and rejuvenation, he glimpsed the infinite. For mankind, on the other hand, he had developed merely a sardonic cynicism for its endless greed and hypocricy.

Unfortunately, a too sharp crusader's blade sometimes nicks the wielder. His open disdain for oceanographic academia and the propensity to puncture sacred cows constantly got him into hot water. As a result, he was locked out of the normal channels of research.

When he did manage to garner assignments, mostly

through the intercession of old classmates from Scripps, he always added acid to the wounds. His mission results, usually gained through outrageously unorthodox methods, sparkled with brilliance. Even his enemies grudgingly admitted he was probably one of the finest natural marine scientists in the world.

"You can't let this thing lie, Thompson," he said.

"I can damned well let it lie. Right on the bottom where it belongs."

"You've forgotten about the missiles on that wreck."

"I don't give a shit about missiles," Thompson shot back, "If there were any. You're not certain about that."

"Yes, I am."

"Burke isn't." From somewhere in the ship came the sound of machinery starting up. Thompson paused, seemed to listen a moment. His smile was gone. "He wants you off the project."

"That figures."

"God dammit, man, you broke dive rules. Defied my direct order. That could have gotten both of you killed along with the loss of the *Checker 3*."

"I couldn't just leave men dying on the bottom."

"There weren't any men and you couldn't have helped, anyway."

"That didn't matter."

"Maybe so. But what does matter is this project. And that's why no word of that ship or that fungus will be forwarded to the Indian government. I'll not compromise my mission by getting entangled in internal Indian affairs."

Bonner sat forward. "Dammit, Thompson, don't you realize what we're looking at here? The *Java Queen* was hauling missiles and mobile launchers. I know a goddamned missile when I see it, for chrissake. That means someone in India, somebody the government doesn't know about, is arming himself with heavy ordnance.''

"It could have been a normal military shipment for the Indian Army.''

"Aboard a wreck like that stern-wheeler? Not likely. That was a clandestine shipment. For God's sake, man, at least check it out.''

"It's none of our business,'' Thompson countered stubbornly.

Cas whirled around, picked up his notebook. He jammed a finger at an entry. "See this? Polysaccharide polymer residue. You know what that means? There was bacterial metabolic decomposition in the fungi. I'm certain it was that bacteria that triggered the mutative explosion. Now, where do you think it came from?''

Thompson took a sip of coffee before answering. "Some unknown bottom species.''

"I checked all our water samples. There's no viable bacteria at that depth.'' He shook his head. "No, it was the missiles. More specifically, the warheads that probably got breached during the plunge. They were biological.''

Thompson blinked slowly, twice. "That's speculation.''

"Are you willing to take the risk that I could be right?''

Out in the corridor two crewmen went past, laughing, the jingle of their belt keys like Christmas bells. Thompson finished his coffee in one gulp and looked at Cas from under his heavy eyebrows. "I'll say it once more, Bonner, we're standing clear.''

"You're a fool.''

"And *you're* bloody fired. Our supply plane will be here at oh-six-hundred. Have your gear ready.''

3

Hak McCarran lay on his belly at the edge of a small bluff and listened to the crocs attacking the buffalo carcass down on the southern bank of the Brahmaputra River. In the darkness the sounds formed an eerie, hellish cacophany of thrashing water, clicking teeth, and half-retching gags as the animals swallowed chunks of flesh.

From his position he could just make out the line of beach forty yards away and the darker shape of the rapidly diminishing mass of the buffalo. He had killed it the day before and staked it to posts driven into the sand to draw in the man-eater that had killed two native women from the Assam village of Hojai.

This particular animal was huge, at least eighteen feet long. Hak had been hunting it for nearly two months as the croc wandered the river islands northeast of the town of Bishnath, occasionally taking human prey. Twice he had had a chance at it, but each time it escaped into fringe swamp. Now, with the latest kill, Hak knew the animal would remain within the general area for a while. Crocodiles are cautious and patient beasts. One this old and experienced usually studied the habits of shore game, including women who came to identical spots on the river to get water.

But would it come to the bait?

He turned and whispered to his hunting companion,

Dabu, a Tamil from Silghar. Dabu handed over a bottle of whiskey. McCarran took a swig and nestled the bottle into the sugary sand, smelling of river reeds. With his chin resting on the breach of his .404 Mannlicher, he studied the beach.

Light began to flush the sky. The river, in the low season, was still night black, but way out the scattered islands were fusing into view as if rising out of the water.

On the beach dozens of crocodiles were savaging the buffalo carcass, their tails slamming back and forth as they tore flesh. They made lines of white foam.

Dabu lightly touched McCarran's shoulder. "Dead animals," he said and pointed toward a spot a hundred yards upriver. The shadows were still deep there, but Hak could make out a second cluster of crocs feeding on the carcasses of three of their dead companions that had apparently crawled high up on the beach and into the scrub grass. Their white underbellies looked luminous in the dawn light.

McCarran was surprised at the unusual sight. Unless killed by hunters, dead crocs were rarely seen that high on the land. Always the carcasses were immediately taken by other crocs back into the river so that decomposition could set in enough to allow their blunt teeth to tear them apart.

There was an old belief among Indian hands that maintained that a croc, when shot in the water, would always come to land instinctively so as not to drown. But Hak knew no other hunters had been working this part of the river. No, something else had driven these animals that high on the shore.

His eyes slid back to the buffalo carcass just as Dabu hissed a warning. And there it was, the man-eater, an enormous croc walking up the slope of the beach, its height at the level of a man's waist. The smaller saurians moved aside as the killer took hold of the buffalo's chest and ripped out a huge chunk. The forward quarter of its body tilted up as if the animal were going to toss the meat, the tail snapping around to hold balance. In three gulps it swallowed the chunk.

Hak eased the butt of the Mannlicher up to the recess of his shoulder. He scanned the tip of the express sight along the edge of the water until it fixed on one of the buffalo's horns. To the left, he could see the croc turning, headed back toward the safety of the river.

He put the sight directly on the back of the croc's head as it lumbered closer to the water. Holding his breath, his finger began an even, steady pull on the trigger. The animal turned slightly, its jaw entering the water. Hak realigned, aiming for the curve of skull bone where the fist-sized brain cavity lay.

The .404 went off with the wallop of a cannon as its 400-grain high-velocity bullet was fired. Hak was momentarily deafened as he ejected, rammed in another round, and fired again.

Down on the beach, the croc rolled over and over, and its tail whipped froth into the water as the other animals skittered wildly back into the river. Twice more Hak shot, the rounds exploding into the animal's body with powerful impacts. At last it lay still, shivering with nervous impulses still emitted by its dead brain.

As they gingerly approached the carcass, it lay at the water's edge like a beached log. Quickly Dabu hitched a cable around its jaws, ran it back to loop over the tail in case the animal still had life in it.

Up on the bluffs, people from the village materialized out of nowhere. They looked down as Dabu sliced open the croc's belly and stomach wall, making two long slits. Both men jerked back, gagging, as the stomach contents fell out in a slimy mass. Enmeshed in it were the putrified leg and arm of a woman, along with four copper arm rings that gleamed in the new sunlight, polished by the croc's stomach acid.

In little groups the villagers came down the bluff and approached the dead animal. They stared at it for a little while and then spat on the carcass, lightly kicking its genital appendage with their bare feet. Without a word, they then went back up the bluff and disappeared.

Upriver, Hak and Dabu examined the remains of the other dead crocs. There were only shapeless remnants of two, but the third was only partially eaten. The air smelled of blood and raw flesh—and something else.

Dabu held his nose. "Stink different," he said. "Like got-dam *chula* smoke."

Hak knelt and sniffed the torn-open belly of the croc. It was true, the odor bore the distinctive smell of burning kerosene. He peered at the bloody flesh. It was speckled with globs of bright green that were encased in the tissue.

He dug a bit of it out with the tip of his hunting knife and held it up to the sunlight. The blob instantly contracted, as if repulsed by the heat. He studied it closely. It smelled strongly of kerosene. Gently he returned it to the belly tissue, rammed his knife into the sand a few times until it was clean, then stood up.

"Get gasoline," he snapped to Dabu. "We've got to burn these carcasses. And tell the villagers to stay away from any others they find on the shore."

Dabu trotted off.

He stared down at the green globs again. They were moving, spreading and contracting within the tissue like crystals of green liquid. He felt his hackles rise. He'd never see organisms like this in anything he'd ever killed. Was this what had killed them?

* * *

At nine in the morning, Jackie had been on the ward for four hours. The day wasn't even really started and she was already tired, testy. She'd spent a brutally humid night with only restless moments of sleep. As usual, the electricity had gone off several times during the evening, shutting down her air conditioner and television set in the middle of a vapid movie with its heavily made-up, round-faced Bombay actors mouthing their overripe dialogue.

At last she'd retreated to her patio, sat out there naked in the sultry darkness, coated with mosquito repellent. Below, traffic steamed along Chowangee Boulevard and the air was a torpid mixture of scents: jasmine, industrial fumes, and feces. Now and then she heard the faint, chilling roars of the white tigers in the Zoological Gardens near the Maidan.

After two warm Bangu-Station beers, she finally managed to doze off. But then came flying starkly up out of it with the horrible vision of dark men climbing over the balcony to get at her. By four in the morning, she gave it up, showered, and went to the hospital.

Now headed for a tea break, she caught sight of Dr. Bartlet-Simms, the hospital's administrator on the third-floor terrace. At her call, he paused and swung around, his starched white smock gleaming in the slanting sunlight.

He lifted an eyebrow impatiently. "Not now, Doctor. I'm in a hurry."

"This'll just take a minute."

He sighed and started off again. Jackie fell into step beside him.

"I'm encountering some difficulty with Pathology," she said.

"So I've been informed. Dunbar, isn't it?"

"Yes."

"Doctor, there are certain rules here at Victoria that are implemented out of necessity. One of those rules pertains to control of unnecessary pathology tests."

"I understand, but—"

Bartlet-Simms held up a long finger. "As you now know, we're an extremely overworked institution. As a result, diagnostic and laboratory priorities must be maintained."

"Yes, I know that. But I've encountered a new and extremely virulent pathogen. Five patients in less than two weeks, all with the same peculiar, acute symptoms." She ticked them off with her fingers. "Tissue and fluid odor of kerosene, rapid degeneration of lung tissue, violent muscular contractions with total non-absorption of normal anti-toxin agents. There's something going on here, Doctor. All I ask is that we run a few stage-five autopsies to see if we can isolate this damned thing."

"Impossible."

"Then can I at least have some reevaluations of the tests already done? And a check through recent admissions records to see if any other similar cases might have gotten by?"

Bartlet-Simms stopped, turned to face her with folded arms. "Dunbar, I strongly suggest you leave these administrative decisions to me."

"God dammit, Simms, I lost a young girl last night from this thing. She went into pulmonary collapse in a matter of minutes. Even milial TB isn't that violent."

The administrator studied her coldly, his head bent back as if she had just made a rude sound. "You've been here for three months, is that correct?"

"Give or take a few thousand hours," she snapped. She could feel her temper rising uncontrollably. It made her scalp prickle.

"I recommend you spend a longer period here before you attempt to formulate judgments." His lip lifted in a sneer. "After all, India isn't Colorado."

Her temper blew. "Colorado, my ass," she cried. "Look, I'm a good enough doctor to recognize the signs of what could become a potential epidemic."

Bartlet-Simms's eyes widened at her impertinence. "This conversation is terminated," he barked, wheeled, and strode away.

Jackie watched him go, glaring. "Pompous jerk-off," she murmured disgustedly.

The superintendent in the Port Authority's office was a tiny sparrow of a man who continuously adjusted things on his desk. Bonner had waited nearly three hours to see him, seated in a dilapidated lobby with yellow chairs and pictures of Hindu gods on the walls.

Earlier that morning he'd come into Calcutta harbor aboard the *Digger*'s supply plane, a Russian-built Be-12 Mail seaplane, gull-winged and slow as a wounded bird. He'd slept all the way in.

His departure from the ship had been muted. Thompson handed over his wages, then silently shook hands. Earlier he had locked the ship's lab to prevent Cas from taking samples of the fungi. With only his sea bag, Bonner rode the jack boat across to the aircraft bobbing on the ocean.

"Yes, I am most interested in this," the superintendent said. The desk name plate read *Suran Chatterjee*. "Very most interested."

"Then you have a *Java Queen* registered?"

"Oh, yes, yes. We keep wery precise records of our shipping here."

"And she's been reported overdue, right?"

"That is the most interesting portion. She is decidedly safe."

"What?"

"Oh, yes, her home port of Dibrugarh signifies she is on the riwer carrying her wonderful loads of teak."

"When did you last check on her?"

Chatterjee looked surprised. "I am checking this wery morning."

Oh, yeah, Cas thought. Apparently Thompson had already notified the Port Authority about him, probably told them he was a newly fired malcontent and not to be trusted.

"If there was no problem," he asked, "why did you check at all?"

"It is my duty," Chatterjee squeaked and hurriedly readjusted three pencils on his desk until their erasers were precisely aligned.

"But why that particular ship? And why this morning?"

"I am most cautious to see that all my shippings deliwer their cargos on a precise dot."

Cas grunted and stood up. "By the way, did Thompson mention missiles?"

For the tinest moment Chatterjee's eyes quivered. Then he looked blank. "Missiles? Nothing of missiles were talked of."

Bonner gave him a sly grin. "Right," he said.

Once more outside, he walked along the waterfront to the big Brahma dock nearby. Several oceangoing freighters were off-loading iron ore, and across the Hooghly River he could see the Botanical Gardens, a lush swatch of jungle that cascaded down the embankment to the river.

All along the river's edge were stone steps called *ghats* where hundreds of people gathered to bathe in the sluggish brown water. Above them were several cremation fires burning, stacks of sandalwood with the dead bodies lying on top. Untouchables continually fed the flames with fresh wood while naked *sadhus*, holy men smeared with burned cow dung, droned mantras and flung the residual ashes onto the river. The bloated carcass of an oxen drifted by in midstream, twisting slowly amid the wakes of high-sterned *dhows* laying bream nets in the channel.

Bonner watched all this with narrowed eyes. He didn't particularly like India. The place was too congested, an endless swarm of people like ants in a dung heap. He'd been in-country twice before, the first time as a second mate aboard a schooner owned by a Saudi Arabian shiek.

Back then Cas had just been fired from his first civilian job, the directorship of biological research for Hawaiian Marine on Oahu. Fresh out of the navy after four years with Seal Team One in Vietnam, he'd married the daughter of an ex-senator and publisher of the *Honolulu Sentinel,* Adrian Silham. With that kind of influence behind him, he'd easily won his appointment.

Unfortunately, Carolyn Silham turned out to be a very unstable, self-centered young woman. All speed and no substance. She took to heavy cocaine use and slipped into endless affairs. Cas tried to pull her out of it, but she cursed his efforts. One day he found her screwing a Kuhio beach boy on the kitchen floor. That was the last straw. He tossed the beach boy through a window, packed his gear, and departed. Two days later, he signed on the schooner.

As it turned out, the shiek ran them aground off Bombay, and Cas and four of the crew ended up in a vicious bar brawl with French sailors. They had to spend two weeks in a military cantonment before finally returning to sea.

The second time he'd worked for the Indian government as a marine consultant on fishery grounds in the

Andaman Islands. Their supply base was Calcutta. During that time he'd quickly learned how infuriating it could be dealing with the stifling inefficiency and corruption of the Indian bureaucracy.

So as he strolled along the riverbank, he considered his position. It seemed untenable and for a moment he wondered if it was really worth the effort.

There were times when Bonner actually grew irritated at his own passions. His temper led him into conflagrations that other, more rational men avoided. Thompson had called him a crusader. Maybe he should have said Don Quixote, Bonner thought.

He was tempted to forgo the whole thing. Perhaps his conclusions about the fungi were way off base. Had those grotesque green shapes ten thousand feet underwater really been missiles?

But the questioning was only momentary. And he knew it. When something got under his skin, it chafed at him until he finally worked it out. No, he hadn't been wrong about the missiles in the Godavari. He lit a cigarette, sat on a wall, and mulled over his alternatives.

Any hope of going further up in the Indian government, he knew, would prove useless. With Thompson cutting his trail, actively discrediting anything he said, he'd merely get brushed aside as he had been with Chatterjee. Well, he thought, perhaps the *Seriaus Diastrolipium* side of it would clear a way. If he could find solid evidence of other incidents of fungial mutation caused by bacterial contamination, he might at least open a few doors, create a few doubts.

During the Andaman project he had done a lot of research in Calcutta's Medical College Hospital. It possessed a large library of oceanic data. Deciding to start there, he headed up Kidder Pore Road to the underground railway station at Diamond Harbor. From there he took the crammed express across the city to the Bhowanipore district and the Gothic-arched college.

Until late afternoon he pored over research papers and international journals in a dusty, stone-cooled basement with two intense, turbaned medical students. At dusk the librarian shooed them out. Cas wandered upstairs to a small doctors' lounge where he remembered taking cups of thickly sugared Darjeeling tea and milk sweets called *gulab jamuns* during the Andaman days.

Several doctors and nurses were on break. They eyed his shorts and dirty T-shirt but said nothing. He sat by a leaded window that looked out on the skyline of Calcutta, skyscrapers among the colonnades and ramparts of the Raj, everything shimmering in the afternoon heat. He went over his notes.

He'd found very little information about *Seriaus D:* one item dated 1981 on human bile formation due to accidental ingestion of the fungi; another on riverine colonies in the upper Ganges during the drought of '78. But nothing on mutational capacity or formation of intra-cellular matrices triggered by bacterial contamination.

A young woman quietly slid into the chair opposite him, and he glanced up. She was beautiful, tall with dark reddish-brown hair and gray eyes. She wore a doctor's smock with an ID tag that said DUNBAR.

"Only medical staff's permitted in here," she said evenly.

"That so?"

"That's so."

"Let me write that down," he said and thought, Who the hell is this?

"You're Casimir Bonner, aren't you?" she said.

"Should I know you?"

"No. But I remember you from Scripps."

"Oh? I don't remember you."

"You once beat up my father."

Dunbar? For a moment it didn't register. Then it came back. It had been a long time ago. A professor named Michael Dunbar had taught him marine geology at Scripps when he took his doctorate there. Everybody called Dunbar "Red Mike," a burly, belligerent man who seemed to harbor a particular dislike for Bonner and rode him constantly. It eventually ended in a fistfight out on a beach where Cas mauled him. Although the fight was grounds for Bonner's dismissal, Dunbar had inexplicably failed to mention it to the school authorities.

A slow grin crept onto his face. "So, you're Big Mike's daughter. Now I understand the eyes."

She slowly took in his clothes, the three-day stubble on his chin, and snorted. "Got shit-canned again, didn't you?"

Cas sipped his tea, watching her over the rim.

"Daddy always said your temper and big mouth'd ruin your career." She chuckled. "He thought that was too bad. Particularly since he considered you the finest marine biologist he'd ever come across."

He looked askance at her.

"It's true," she said. "Daddy was always rough on people he liked, that was his style. Apparently you were too dense to understand that." Suddenly her eyes became still. "He was killed two years ago on a dive off New Hebrides."

He put his cup down gently. "I'm sorry."

"No, you're not." She stood up. For a moment she continued to stare at him. Abruptly she turned and headed for the door. Then as she reached it, she paused and came back. She picked up a napkin, scribbled something on it, and tossed it in front of him. "In case you need to mooch a free meal, biologist. My place. Eight. Don't be late.''

And then she was gone.

That same afternoon, BIM guerillas mounted simultaneous attacks on three of Abu Singh's militia units. Coordinated by a young Muslim ex-student from Dakha named Sadanand Luckoo, the strikes were for the most part successful.

The first attack, personally led by Luckoo, was on a jungle camp on the Kapili River thirty miles east of the Assam capital of Gauhati. Twenty-two Sikhs with several women had paused there for the night, setting up their tents under an ancient banyan tree.

Just after sunset, the jungle grew still, the calls of stone curlews and nightjars stopped abruptly. The Sikhs' horses, tethered along the riverbank, jerked and snorted restlessly. Thinking a leopard was near, Singh's men reached for weapons.

The hush continued for a few seconds, then came the shrill *kok kok kok* of an alarmed wild peacock. This was instantly followed by the staccato crackle of bamboo drums and an horrendous explosion of gunfire from the surrounding undergrowth.

When it stopped, everyone under the banyan tree was dead. Two wounded horses thrashed at the water's edge. Luckoo and his men stripped the bodies and hung them upside down on the aerial roots of the tree, gathered all the weapons, and melted back into the jungle.

The second attack targeted a bus outside the tea town of Jorhat. A barricade of *saja* logs had been put across the dirt road. Aboard the bus were eight Sikhs. A firefight started as Luckoo's men, dressed in camouflage fatigues and red bandannas, rushed from the jungle. Women shrieked and frightened roof riders plummeted to the ground in the darkness as the BIM men opened up. Bullets slammed into the side of the bus, and then its gas tank exploded, hurling bodies and chunks of metal and billowing black smoke. Afterward, the guerillas killed the wounded and tossed their bodies onto the fire along with the logs.

The last of the attacks did not turn out so well. It was launched against eighteen horse-mounted Sikhs on the Assam border with Nagaland state. The area was open grassland with scattered boulder castles where the guerillas had waited in ambush. But their leader panicked and ordered the attack prematurely, before the horsemen were fully camped.

Singh's men, used to fighting in the open, immediately remounted and charged up into the rocks. The exchanged fire was short but vicious. At last the guerillas retreated to a second line of boulders. From there they sniped at the milling horseman, who also soon pulled back.

The Sikhs lost eight men and four horses, the guerillas fourteen men. As the two sides regrouped and pulled farther and farther apart, jackals slinked down from higher ground and fed on the carcasses under a night sky blazing with stars.

In another place there were also stars, but here the night was not still. Off the southeastern coast of Africa, the Great Somali jet stream whipped the sea as it blew up from the deep southern waters, pulling moisture up into itself on its sweep northward. Soon it would cross the equator and gradually be turned eastward by the Coriolis effect of the earth's rotation.

One branch was destined to drive across the Arabian Sea, sucked onward by the low-pressure areas over India, until it made landfall along the Malabar coast. A second branch would turn farther southeast and en-

ter the air vortex above the Bay of Bengal. Twisted
north again by centrifugal force, it would sweep across
northeastern India, converge with a separate storm
movement coming up from the Indonesian quadrant,
and then slam into the barrier of the Himalayas. Each
branch, bearing horrendous amounts of rain, would
deluge the land in what is known as the summer monsoon.

Already meteorologists with their satellites and sea
stations were tracking its beginnings. Yet despite all
the high-tech gear and knowledge, precise dates for
the monsoon's arrival over the Indian subcontinent
could only be pinpointed within a forty-eight-hour time
frame. Still, forecasts were predicting that the southern branch would reach Assam state in nine days.

4

Jackie's apartment was on the second floor of a three-story building, an old colonial residence that had been turned into apartments. The front yard was hard-packed ground, and what had once been a garden was now a weedy, circular stone walk.

Cas arrived at one minute before eight. In the entry hall he checked the mail slots for her name and then rode an ancient cage elevator to the second floor. She awaited him, casually leaning against the sill in a loose-fitting gauze dress, sea-foam green and scoop-necked. She was barefoot and her hair, pulled starkly back into a single braid, gave her face a fresh, young-girl glow.

"I heard the elevator," she said. "Nobody uses that death trap, so I figured it must be you." She took his proffered wine bottle, smiled thanks, and went in. Cas slipped off his shoes and left them just inside the door.

The apartment was small, two rooms and an alcove for cooking. The walls were half paneled in a pink-reddish wood, and a screen door led to a terrace with bougainvillea entwined around a Victorian metalwork railing. The furniture in the main room was a half settee, a lounge chair and table, all in white rattan. He glanced into the other, which had a large, square bed suspended from chains in the ceiling beams. An air conditioner rumbled from somewhere overhead. The place looked like the set of a 1930 Humphrey Bogart movie about Cuba.

Jackie brought him a Bangu-Station and returned to the alcove. "We're having *murgi kari* and *kesar chaval*," she called. "That's chicken curry and saffron rice. But be warned, I'm a lousy cook."

Bonner stretched his legs out and took a pull on the beer. It was lukewarm. He watched her, noting the splendid lifts and curves of her body under the dress. Absently she brushed a curl of hair off her forehead, and the movement caused the material to cling to the line of her back, along the indentation of spine where it plunged into the rise of her buttocks.

It had been some time since Cas had made love to a woman. A man who lives most of his life at sea learns to bank his lust for long stretches of time. But here in this momentary coziness, with the scent of curry and saffron in the air and a beautiful female doing charmingly domestic things, he experienced the old arousal.

He said, "You always eat this fancy?"

She adjusted the burner. "No, usually I take something at the hospital. Everything's spiced enough to burn out the insides of a horse, but it's filling."

"How'd you know I'd show up?"

She gave him a glance over her shoulder. "Because I figured you're probably flat broke."

"Not really."

"Then why did you come?"

"Curiosity. And the chance to hear an American voice again."

"Amen to that."

Allowing things to simmer, she brought her beer over and flopped onto the settee. After a long pull she studied him. "What happened this time?"

"My mission head and I had a disagreement over priorities."

She chortled. "Daddy used to keep track of your escapades in the ocean journals. That time you took on the Japanese fishing fleet really gave him a laugh. 'Jesus Christ,' he said, 'Bonner's at it again.' "

Cas drank his beer without comment. The episode she referred to had actually caused an international incident. It happened off Tahiti, where he was part of a Woods Hole research team tracking migrating whales. Japanese trawlers were also fishing the same area with long drag nets. Eventually a pod of female whales and their calves got entangled. In the ensuing panic most of the calves and several adult females drowned.

Bonner was so infuriated, he'd gone out in a Zodiac boat and cut all the net floats, sending thousands of feet of netting to the bottom. The Japanese took a few shots at him, and the captain of Cas's research vessel rammed one of the trawlers in retaliation. It was tense for a while. Finally, Washington and Tokyo got involved and things were smoothed over. But, as usual, he was sacked.

She watched him. "You're a real Geronimo, aren't you?"

"I try." He was aware that a subtle tension had formed between them. A challenge of some kind that held a vague tinge of sexuality to it. He found it not unpleasant.

They ate on the terrace on stainless steel trays with a *punka* wick to hold off the mosquitoes. A night race was going on at the horse track near the south end of the great thousand-acre park called the Maidan. The track was alive with light like a huge bowl filled with radium, and they could hear the occasional thunder of the horses and the cheers of the crowd like an undertone from the sea.

Jackie's meal was indeed terrible: too much curry with the chicken underdone. But they both kept doggedly at it for a few minutes, sweating in the heat and sweetening the food with the Chittagong wine. Finally she gave it up and laid her tray on the floor.

She cupped her chin in her palm and gave him a coquettish smile. "Is it good?"

He hurried a piece of raw chicken down his throat. "Oh, great."

"You lie. It's ghastly. Sorry about that."

She carried the leftovers back inside and returned with two fresh beers. They fell into silence, listening to the cheers and the traffic down on Chowringhee. Cas lit a cigarette.

Jackie watched him a moment, then leaned over. "Let me have a drag." He handed the cigarette over. She inhaled twice and let the smoke drift out into the scorching air. "Makes me dizzy. I quit two years ago."

He took it back. "Don't start again."

"I've been thinking about it." Her eyes narrowed and she gazed off thoughtfully. "Only three months in this place, and my nerves are already shot."

"India does that to you."

"Those imbeciles at Victoria don't help it any," she said bitterly.

"Mm? Problems?"

She went at it slowly, scattered bits and pieces of medical talk coming out with the frustration. There were a lot of "those damned fools" and "that bastard Simms." Cas was content to listen, trying to grasp the core of the issue. Then something she said hit him full bore.

He leaned forward. "Hold it. What did you say about kerosene odor in these patients of yours?"

She nodded. "All five of them have exhibited the same smell of burning kerosene. In their skin and tissues, even in the feces." She looked at him, puzzled. "Why does that strike you?"

He thoughtfully tapped his thumbnail against his teeth, then sat back. "Go over this disease thing again, Jackie. But easy with the medical terms, I'm not a physician."

She did, covering it all, right from the beginning. She interpreted the pathology results, explained her diagnosis and futile treatments. Now and then Cas grunted, particularly at her mention of Dibrugarh. She finished with her recent visit to the medical college in the unsuccessful hope of talking somebody into running backup tests.

Bonner sat frowning.

"What is it?" Jackie asked.

He inhaled, let it out slowly. "Well, I could be way off base with this, but I think you've been treating for the wrong pathogen. It's not bacterial. It's a fungus, a mutated form of *Serius Diastrolipium*."

Jackie stiffened. "How do you know that?"

Now it was his turn to explain. Jackie grew more and more excited as he talked. She got up and paced around the small terrace, occasionally stopping him with a question. But she was focused on the medical aspect of it and apparently hadn't yet made the link between the mutation and the missiles.

He went back over it, emphasizing that aspect. She nodded and nodded and then suddenly put her hand to her mouth. "Oh, my God! You mean there's warhead bacteria loose in the river?"

"Apparently, yes. Somewhere around Dibrugarh."

"Sweet Mother!" She was shocked motionless for

a moment, then she hurried through the doorway. Cas could hear her talking on the phone. After a couple of minutes, she returned, her face stark. She sat down gingerly and stared at him.

"That was the hospital. I talked with the on-duty assistant administrator. He thought I was crazy." She hissed. "Damned idiot."

"What'd you tell him?"

"That there might be a bacterial agent from missiles in the river that is creating a deadly fungus. He laughed. The bastard laughed! My God, what are we going to do about this?"

"I've been thinking. I'm heading for Dibrugarh."

But she wasn't listening. She kept getting up to pace anxiously about before dropping back into her chair. Finally, without a word, she once more rushed into the sitting room. When she came out she had on a pair of pumps.

"I'm going to the hospital," she informed him. "Maybe I can get that stupid A.A. to listen to me."

He stood up.

"No, you stay here," she snapped. "You've already been discredited over this thing. If they check on you, we'll blow it. Now, dammit, don't leave till I get back." She hurried through the apartment and slammed the front door.

He watched her disappear up Chowringhee in a purple taxi. But his mind kept homing on a single thought: *It's loose in the Brahmaputra!* That meant that somehow other warheads like those in the Godavari had gotten into the river. But how? Had they been deliberately fired into it? No, he reasoned, if that had occurred, thousands of sick people would be pouring down the river, not just five. Then perhaps it had been seepage from stored units. If so, how extensive was the contamination?

Then he cautioned himself. India was a country overflowing with disease and Jackie was a newcomer. Maybe she was building disasters out of what was actually normal sickness. Still, the correlations between his findings and hers overlapped too much to be mere chance. No, there *was* a link, he was sure of it.

For the next hour, he wandered restlessly around the apartment. Around ten the electricity went off and he retreated to the terrace. The horse races were still going on. He got himself another beer and thought about what he would do once he got to Dibrugarh.

He'd never had any experience in provincial India, but it was reasonable to assume that the official bullshit dominated by local chiefs would be even worse than in the large cities. For another thing, all of northeastern India beyond Bangladesh was restricted. How would he even get there? Well, he thought, where there's a will there's a way. The challenge enticed him.

He sighed and shifted in the chair, feeling his lack of adequate sleep sift through his body. He closed his eyes and let the memories and converging images play with his mind. Slowly Jackie's face emerged, watching him with a feisty-eyed, twinkling smile. He was aware he chuckled as he dropped into sleep.

Kurisovsky passed the oil rag one final time over his bayonet and then slid it back into its scabbard. He and his troopers were in the field bungalow, cleaning weapons. The men lounged around a long teak table, their guttural Russian conversation muted and languid from the tiny sticks of *majum,* Indian hemp, they smoked.

The bungalow was set on a small, grassy hill two hundred yards from Lake House, surrounded by a grove of blue gum and cedar trees. Unlike the ornate Moghul splendor of the main house, it had the lines of a Simla hunting lodge: open-beamed with a

screened porch across the front and a thatched roof
made of bo-tree branches. The eaves were carved into
delicate gingerbread trim.

Inside were small *zenanas,* or sleeping areas, off the
main room and a kitchen with an earthen oven built
into the rear wall. The main room was walled in teak
and sandalwood, on which hunting trophies of *mar-
khor* upland goat and panthers hung. Except for the
teak table, the sitting furniture was made of polished
horn and unstripped wild oak branches.

A flurry of footsteps on the porch was followed by
a soft knock at the door. One of the troopers answered
it. A small, compact Sikh peeked inside and asked for
the "Col-oh-nel." Kurisovsky rose and walked over.

The Sikh snapped to attention with a British grenadier's double boot stomp, arm snapping into a palm-
forward salute. "Sor! General Singh says you are
coming immediately. He is most angry."

Kurisovsky strapped on his Beretta, and he and the
Sikh runner walked down the slope toward Lake
House. He could heard shift whistles and the steady
drone of machinery from the oil platform. Yet over it
was the intermittent but powerful roar of crocodiles.

The runner led him to the lakeside pavilion. Singh
was standing at the edge of the terrace that went out
over the water. One of his men worked a long pole
from which the rotting, half-eaten body of a pi-dog
was suspended a few feet above the surface. Below it,
in a foamy, churning maelstrom, were ten or fifteen
small crocodiles. As the man bobbed the carcass en-
ticingly, now and then a croc would lunge up to grab
meat.

Kurisovsky approached the Indian from behind.
Singh often played with the crocs for sport. But now
the Russian could sense outrage in him. The man's
huge body almost trembled with it, and his great wavy

beard shook with blue highlights. He remained silent, eyes glaring down at the crocs.

Kurisovsky waited patiently. Far to the right, he noted a dozen off-duty oil workers sitting on the wall near the drilling derrick, watching the crocs. Their hardhats glistened brightly in the lights from the rig.

"The filthy ones have struck me," Singh suddenly cried. He turned blazing eyes on the colonel. "Three times. Many men dead."

"Where?"

Singh told him while another croc surged into the air.

"Then strike back," Kurisovsky said. "Right now, before Delhi decides to send troops to quell the fighting."

Singh scoffed. "They no send goddam troops. I order them to stay away. This is my battle."

"Then mount a foray immediately. Punish them."

Singh snorted with contempt. "Foray! You talk like *bibi* memsahib. I will crush them, feed their filthy hearts to jackals." He swept his thick arm in a gesture of dismissal. "Prepare your men."

He turned and snapped something in Kashmiri. Instantly one of his men sprang forward with his assault rifle. Holding it at arm's length. Singh opened up on the crocs. The rounds blew out so rapidly that the pavilion was filled with a single explosion of sound. Down the beach, the oil workers got nervously to their feet as the bullets slammed into the contorted bodies, throwing up geysers and chunks of crocodile meat. The wounded animals rolled and thrashed and the water turned bloody, looking gray in the blue light.

Kurisovsky returned to the pavilion. Sergeant Varentov met him on the porch. "We just received a signal from Mr. Andropov, Colonel." This was the code name for *Phoenix*. "Intelligence has located a launcher for us, a Sparrow VLS. It's at a Thailand border base called Kau Moo Rah."

"A Sparrow!" Kurisovsky swore. "That means we'll have to modify the damned thing to take the 214s."

"Andropov said that was the only one they could find that was vulnerable to squad assault, sir. The airfield has only a small contingent of border militia."

"All right, get the men ready. Hold Perotsky, Zhdanov, Ilney, and Shelepkin for the mountain strike. The rest of us will be going on a foray with the Indian baboon."

"Yes, sir." The sergeant hurried back into the house.

Ten minutes later, nine fully armed troopers waited before the bungalow. Inside, Kurisovsky gathered the four remaining men around the teak table. He reviewed their attack procedure quickly, then looked into each man's face. "Remember, do not allow yourselves to be taken. And if you're wounded, prepare to die. Your comrades will kill and burn you."

Each man nodded silently.

As the four began packing their cold-weather gear, Kurisovsky went into the kitchen. He pulled open the door of the earthen oven, which still was impregnated with the odor of potato *pakoras*. Inside was a large Rastorov XB-118 shortwave radio with a Morse code key attached. He switched on the power and began ranging through frequencies, occasionally tapping out his call letters. Splurges of talk, tiny snippets of code, popped from the speaker, everything clothed in static.

At last he heard a weak splay of Morse code: "Andropov, zero-one-Alpha-Alpha . . . holding for transmission."

Kurisovsky's message was short and concise: "Approve coordinate designation Kau Moo Rah, hold . . .

Phase two operation also in motion, hold . . . Strike designated monsoon plus two, out.''

He had just notified Mr. Andropov that the Phoenix strike would be launched two hours after the onset of the monsoon over Assam state.

''Bonner, wake up.''

Cas drifted through amber dreams, something rising from mist, the drift of it tinkling oddly until it crystallized and became Jackie's voice. He opened his eyes. She was bent over him.

He cleared phlegm from his throat. His T-shirt was soaked with perspiration. ''What time is it?''

''After midnight. Come on inside, the air conditioning's on again and I've fixed the settee for you.''

He followed her in, rubbing the sleep out of his face. ''How'd you do at the hospital?''

''It was useless. Everybody thought I was an idiot.'' She picked up a half-finished glass of wine and took a sip. ''I did at least get that boob A.A. to order depth checks for fungial pathogen presence if any more suspicious cases come in.'' She twirled the glass. ''I want to go upriver with you.''

He shook his head. ''I don't think so.''

''Why not?''

''I'll be shooting in the dark on this thing, Jackie. All I've got is Dibrugarh. This isn't the U.S., you know. You don't just go to the local library and find out where missiles are stored.''

''Lord, if I hear one more person tell me this isn't the States, I'll scream.''

Chuckling, he dropped onto the settee and stretched. ''Besides, this could get dangerous.''

''No more for me than you.''

He tiredly waved her away. ''Look, I don't want you with me, so that's that.''

She put down the wineglass and stared stonily at him. "If you think I'll sit here and watch more people die, you're crazy. There's a disease out there, Bonner. And if there's the slightest chance I can find out what it is and why it is, I'm going to look. With or without you."

He studied her eyes. The irises were dark, the grayness suddenly opaque, deep. He grinned. "I just caught sight of your father in your face."

"Thanks for the compliment. So, what's it going to be?" She became suddenly almost coquettish. She lowered herself to the edge of the settee and ran a fingernail down the curve of his pectoral muscle. "There's one little thing you don't know."

"Oh? What's that?"

"Access to the upper Brahmaputra is restricted. Only people with official permits can travel in that zone. How do you figure on getting one?"

"I'll manage."

"No way, you're on the government's suspicious list already." She tilted her head. "But as a doctor I've got automatic entry anywhere in India. So, you see, you need me."

"So you can get a permit. How does that help me?"

"I could designate you as my medical assistant."

As close as she was, Cas was vividly aware of her touch, the scent of her hair and skin.

"Come on, Bonner," she said softly, cajolingly. "Don't be a turd about this. We can do it together."

He lifted his hand and lightly rubbed the back of his forefinger against her cheek. "You have any idea what you could be letting yourself in for?"

"I'm willing to risk it."

He shrugged. "Okay, don't say I didn't warn you."

"I won't."

Neither of them moved. He saw her eyes shift, a

faint frown coming to them as they searched his own. Her full mouth went a little slack, lips parted. The look that often comes into a woman's expression when she's caught off guard by a sudden, unexpected emotion.

He bent to kiss her.

Her eyes changed again, lit by a mischievous twinkle. She planted two fingers against the bridge of his nose and playfully pushed him back. "In your dreams, Geronimo," she said.

Then she whirled to her feet and pranced off to her bedroom, calling over her shoulder, "Reveille's at four-thirty. See ya."

By this time of night Supreme General Qin Kanghou was usually saturated with alcohol. Nevertheless, he rarely seemed drunk, although his daily consumption totaled two quarts of the fiery Chinese wine called *unkape*. Impatient and restless, he stood in a campaign shirt at the open suite window of his hotel and looked out on the sleeping city of Urumchi in the Xinjiang Uygur Autonomous Region of China's remote western frontier.

Far to his left he could see the dark shadows of the Tian Shan Mountains against the moonlit horizon. In the lower loess highlands were the flickering camp fires of Zunghar nomads who were moving their sheep and goat herds to summer pasture. From just outside the window came the rumble caused by long lines of trucks and tanks entering a staging area south of the city. Their headlights formed serpentine lines like festival dragons in the desert. These were units of Qin's Green Banner Army: missile, paratrooper, and armored divisions pulled from their regular garrisons in Tibet and Manchuria to reinforce the western frontier with patrols, launching bases, and new airfields.

The general had been given command of the vast Northwest Bureau three months earlier, reassigned from his regular staff position with the Ministry for Military Affairs on personal orders from the Supreme Chief of Staff of the People's Liberation Army, Marshal Peng Shushi. Military strategists had predicted the possibility of a problem along the borders with the former Soviet republics of Kazakhstan, Kyrgyzstan and Tajikistan. The disintergration of the old USSR had given other nations the opportunity to move their spheres of influence into these areas.

Iran was the most aggressive. Chinese intelligence indicated Tehran had already allotted tremendous funds for the spread of Islamic fundamentalism into six post-Soviet republics, including those on the Chinese border. Mosques were being restored, agents sent into the area to stir revolt, and arms shipments continually poured across the linking frontiers under the auspices of the so-called "Caspian Alliance."

From the toilet-room, he heard someone start to hum. The tune was soft and lilting and made him smile. He touched his flaccid penis, squeezed it, felt it respond. "Hurry, *siumaau*," he called. "I grow restless again."

Qin was a robust Chinese, imposing even in near nakedness. He had been a soldier forty of his fifty-four years, and had become one of the most powerful military men in China. He even had his Beijing residence within the politically elite Zhong-nanhai compound outside the Forbidden City.

He had been pleased at Peng's decision to send him out to bolster the western frontier. He, along with other powerful generals, despised their premier's hesitance in moving immediately into the old Russian republics. Qin felt now was the time, while the Russian nation was in chaos. Once and for all they should abrogate that cursed St. Petersburg treaty of 1881 that had given ancient Chinese lands to imperial Russia.

Still, the movement of the Green Banners was a step forward. Very soon his orbit garrisons in Burgin, Kaski, and Taxkorgan would be so entrenched, no Islamic *gau* would dare intrude. They would be powerful enough to invade once Premier Sichen and his timid factions were ousted.

He heard the soft rustle of bare feet on the rug. He turned. A young man of twenty had come from the toilet room. He was slender as a girl, with flowing, dark hair. He smiled at the general, his face painted pure white like a geisha's. Delicately, seductively he stretched himself onto the rumpled bed.

Qin felt his heart grip with lust. Absently he flung his bottle of *unkape* out the window, and lunged across the room.

5

Prakash Ghate, the guide Bonner hired, was a short, fat Bengalese who sweated constantly. He had feminine eyes, talked in rapid bursts, and wore dark glasses stuck up on his head. Cas got him for fifty rupees a day from the Indian Tourist Bureau on Shakespeare Sarani. While there, he had also cashed his *Deepcore* check, exchanging half of it for Indian money.

Meanwhile, Jackie headed off for Victoria Memorial to inform Bartlet-Simms she was taking a week off. She expected him to be outraged. Still, she was entitled to the time. Afterward, she would go to the General Post Office, where the Commission for Travel was located, and get their travel permits. She was to meet them at Howrah station at noon.

Cas and Prakash, whose nickname was Sugar, arrived at the station a little before twelve. It was situated on the banks of the river, a big redstone building with towers and old cannon emplacements. Inside, it had a vaulted black ceiling with clerestory windows that threw beams of sunlight down through a perpetual fog of smoke and dust.

People were everywhere, the air thick with the sweltering, sour stench of compacted human bodies, garbage, and train exhaust. Throughout the building, squatters had taken up residence, and their open cooking fires added to the smog. Beggars lurked in dark corners and vendors worked the crowd, selling everything from pencils to prostitutes. Thin, filthy children squealed and chased each other among mounds of cow dung.

Cas chose a pillar and stretched out against his sea bag while Sugar went off to find something to drink. A little girl of about seven, pretty but with dull, penetrating eyes, immediately approached him. She wore a man's *dhoti,* the ends trailing in the dirt. Very deliberately she asked, "You are giving me money, sahib?"

He smiled at her. "What's your name, sweetheart?"

"You are giving me money?" she repeated.

He tried to remember the Hindi word for name. "Your name, honey. What's your *sarif?*"

"Me Maya. You are giving me money?"

"Okay." He handed over two rupees. The little girl ran off, but within a minute she was back with three other children. These had sores on their lips and smelled of urine. Dutifully he handed over more money. Quickly he was surrounded by an excited, chattering circle of children.

Sugar sprinted back up the platform, cursing loudly. When the children spotted him, they scattered. One threw an empty tin can at him.

"*Acha!*" Sugar yelled. "Little bloody beggars." He turned to Bonner. "Sahib Bonner, you are please not giving these chilrens monies. They are making nuisances."

"Hell, they're just hungry." He looked after them and shook his head sadly. "Tragic."

"Oh, no, no, not being tragic," Sugar cried. "They are making nuisances."

The Bengalese had purchased two bottles of cold mango juice and some curry puffs called *samosas* wrapped in newspaper. Bonner took a drink. The juice was heavily sweetened and tasted faintly rotten. He lit a cigarette and studied a large cinema poster affixed to a nearby pillar that showed a heavily painted starlet, her breasts as round as cantaloupes, fighting off a leering *dacoit* highwayman.

As his eyes shifted, they locked into the steady stare of an Indian man leaning against the third pillar down. He was thin, dressed in a purple *longi* with twin yellow puja lines horizontal on his forehead. For a moment they studied each other; then the Indian glanced away and nonchalantly scratched his crotch.

Cas frowned, sensing something familiar about the man. Hadn't he seen him earlier that morning? He finally shrugged it off and finished his mango juice. When he looked again, the man was gone.

Sugar chattered away, telling Bonner about his life and travels. He'd been to America and Australia, he said, and once even visited a cousin who was a croupier in a Las Vegas casino. "Oh, I am liking Newada a most great deal. So many monies and I am werry pleased to be fucking pretty showgirls."

"Right," Bonner said with mock seriousness. "Showgirls are always the best kind."

"Yes, yes, I am agreeing. They perform many delicate good feelings."

Jackie finally arrived around three in the afternoon, hauling two suitcases. "I've never seen such bureaucratic idiocy," she snapped petulantly. "Four damned hours I waited at that stupid travel office."

Bonner grinned up at her. "Well, be ready to wait four more. We haven't gotten the tickets yet."

It was a complicated process. First they had to stand in line to obtain a ticket to purchase the tickets. Then another line for the actual tickets. They purchased a two-up, first-class A.C. compartment for themselves and a third-class for Sugar. Next they had to wait while the passenger lists were made up and posted.

They finally boarded about six-thirty amid a furious scramble of passengers, some climbing straight through the windows of the third-class cars. Their compartment was the size of a kitchenette containing two sleeping shelves and an ancient air conditioner, a varnished box covered with soot and filled with chunks of ice.

At last the train began to move, out the east track past soiled blocks of foundries and jute mills and grimy apartment buildings. These gradually thinned out and became shanytowns of cardboard shacks with tin roofs and cooking fires and men squatting beside the tracks, shitting stolidly as the train lights flashed past them. Finally they entered the West Bengal countryside, where the kerosene lights of scattered hamlets shone in the night.

Bonner and Jackie went to the dinning car. It had a shabby elegance, chipped silverware and torn leather seats. There were tiny cockroaches in the buffet. They ordered *pakora*, meat and vegetable patties cooked in a batter with *tikkiya* potato cakes.

Jackie poked at her food, searching for unpleasant things. "A dollar to a doughnut I get dysentery," she said sourly. "God, what an unhygienic country this is. It's no wonder everybody's sick."

His eye twinkled. "Get used to it. It gets worse."

She gave him a smoldering scowl. "You're really enjoying this, aren't you?"

"Let's just say I like to watch memsahib on safari."

"You know, Bonner, I sense a big streak of asshole in you."

"When traveling with Romans."

She gave him the bird.

Cas smiled gleefully, betraying the youthful exuberance he always felt when starting out on a new adventure. Despite the frenetic press of humanity around him, he could feel a storm on the horizon, could sense its distant electricity in the air. The future might be dangerous, but it offered excitement, an anticipatory high.

He continued to scrutinize Dunbar as she probed her *pakora* and wondered idly what she was really made of. He'd already seen hardness in her. But was it steel or sandstone? He let his gaze wander along the fine, straight line of her nose, the high forehead, the deep-set eyes he suspected could flash with ecstasy as easily as fire. He was struck again at how lovely she was. A bit sweaty and jagged, but she nonetheless projected the aura of a—what? Into his head popped the image of a clean-cut Malibu surfer girl.

She caught him staring. "What're you looking at?"

"You ever surf?"

"Sure, at Balboa and Malibu."

He laughed.

"What's so funny about that?"

"Nothing."

"You're an idiot."

They returned to their compartment. Soot was pouring through the window, and the cooler box reeked like wet fish sacks. The floor rumbled and shook. They got into a squabble over who would get the top bunk, Cas arguing just to irritate her. Finally she ordered him out and climbed into her berth to read a copy of the *Chandigarh Tribune* someone had left on the floor.

He bought two beers and stood out on the coupling platform. A cadaverous-looking Tamil was squatted beside the door. Out of the wind, he methodically extracted tobacco from a cigarette and then tamped in grains of opium. When he lit up he inhaled deeply and closed his eyes.

Jackie was asleep when Cas returned to the compartment. He stretched out on the lower bunk and soon dozed off. Sometime in the night he was awakened by the revolving thuds of the train's wheels going over bridge ties. He looked out and saw a river below them. The water level was low and the banks gave up the stench of mudflats. There were fishing boats out with kerosene lanterns on their prows. He checked their map and found the river was the Ganges at Faraha.

Abu Singh's retribution against the BIM was swift and barbaric. Within an hour after his order to Kurisovsky, thirty-five heavily armed Sikhs and the Russians boarded two *dagoons,* the flat, motorized rafts used to haul the missiles, and crossed the lake to the small airstrip carved out for the C-47. It awaited their arrival, engines idling and running lights on.

Before leaving, Singh held a war council. Kurisovsky remained silent during the discussions, content to let the chieftain's lieutenants suggest methods for the punitive expedition. There were six, all big men, thickly bearded. They sat in a circle in the pavilion looking like Moghuls from the steppes of Aristan. Each in turn rose to speak, first going through a vitriolic tongue-lashing of the BIM dogs before giving an opinion.

It was decided to focus the strike against the guerillas who had ambushed the Sikh patrol at Dimapur. This particular band had taken casualties and, unlike the others, was in open country. Singh was certain they would head into the Nagaland mountains rather than run the risk of crossing the Lumding plateau to the sactuary of the Hojai forest. The meeting completed, he stuck a heron's feather in his turban, the ancient sign of blood feud, and led them to the *dagoons.*

The flight to Dimapur took two hours, the C-47 going low over the jungle with its lights out. The Sikhs sat in the darkened fuselage and babbled all the way across, slapping their weapons and proclaiming complicated oaths in Kashmiri, whipping themselves into a frenzy. In contrast, Kurisovsky and his men remained silent and watchful, occasionally lighting a stick of *majum* and passing it around.

They landed on a strip of paved road three miles from town where Singh's men had strung out burning piles of cow dung. The pilots brought the aircraft down hard, ramming brakes, and the plane fishtailed, shaking, as it lost speed. The Sikhs half squatted, murmuring nervously.

The leader of the patrol that had been ambushed met them with an old Chevrolet flatbed four-wheel-drive truck and fifteen horses he'd commandeered from a nearby tea plantation. Singh and his lieutenants, including Kurisovsky, took the first horses with the survivors of the ambush using the remainder. The rest of the men climbed up onto the flatbed.

As the C-47 roared back into the sky, the horses started out with the Chevrolet grinding behind. The land stretched away in the moonlight, rolling hills of elephant grass and blue-shadowed rock formation. Up ahead in the foothills they could see the dim, flickering lights of tiny hamlets.

Twice they had to stop to put water in the truck's radiator, which steamed and hissed in the chilly air. When dawn came, the Barail Range formed an indigo line against the southern horizon, slowly lightening until its peaks and cliffs were draped in scarlet. High overhead a jet's contrails drew a red, feathery ribbon in the sky.

Soon after sunup they reached the site of the ambush. The elephant grass was still crushed and scarred by the Sikhs' wild charge, a wide swath where the bones and partially eaten remains of horses and humans still lay. Kurisovsky dismounted and walked through the carnage, trying to recreate the battle in his mind and pick out the direction in which the guerillas had fled. Singh and his men would not enter the killing zone. Instead they merely circled it silently three times, their eyes blazing. The horses snorted nervously at the gamy stench that hung in the air and shook their heads, making their harnesses jingle softly.

From here the land began to rise steadily. The truck went slower and slower, and finally the men had to get off and walk beside it. An hour later they passed through a village surrounded by tiny fields of withered corn. The houses were low and flat with stone roofs. Women squatted on the hard-packed earth making cow dung patties, and scrawny old men in filthy *dhotis* came and stood silently as the contingent passed through.

Two miles beyond the village, a speck appeared on a ridge. It came at them swiftly, stirring up a line of dust. A Sikh rider pulled up, his horse lathered and blowing hard. He talked to Singh a moment, who then turned and signaled for Kurisovsky to approach.

He pointed at a series of sharp ridges in the southeast. "Up there Jakarat. Hill station with Buddhist monastery. My man say wounded BIM men are there."

The Russian nodded.

Singh looked off, frowning. "Monastery is holy place. If BIM inside, *you* must get them. I cannot kill in holy place."

Kurisovsky shrugged—he was a godless communist, after all—wheeled his horse and returned to the line.

It took them seven hours to reach the series of ridges. The land grew ever steeper, and the elephant

grass thinned out into open escarpments with scattered
stands of Sikkim pine, their branches thin and dry.
They were forced to abandon the truck, and the men
trudged behind the horses, pouring sweat under their
gear.

Sometime after noon they reached a winding mountain road. Soon it became so narrow the horses slipped
and balked, their chests steaming in the air, which had
turned cool from the elevation. Far below was a small
lake that sparkled in the sunlight like a bowl of chocolate pudding.

At last they rounded a treacherous hairpin turn and
spotted Jakarat a quarter mile away. The village clung
to the sides of a ridge, its houses made of wood and
set into the rock face. On the main ridge rose the Buddhist monastery like a fortress. Its walls were brilliant
white stone, and it had a gilded brass roof and square
turrets of dark wood that hung precariously to the
sides. There was a small courtyard in front of the
building and a road lined with houses. The place
seemed deserted.

Singh held a council, his men crowding around him.
Even after the long climb they were seething to get at the
guerillas. They kept glaring up the slope toward the
monastery, muttering maledictions. Behind them,
the Russian troopers squatted in the road and checked
their weapons.

The attack was like a cavalry charge, Singh standing
in his stirrups, bellowing. Behind him came the other
horsemen and then the dismounted men, sprinting
through the whirling dust, their assault rifles held
straight up in the air, everybody making an eerie ul-
ulation. Up the slope they went, the horse hooves
pounding like thunder.

The Russians came more slowly, in dual file, jog-
ging with their weapons held at high port. Singh had

ordered Kurisovsky to keep his men out of the fight unless BIM guerillas were in the monastery. He wanted this to be a Sikh bloodletting, if possible.

The horses flew past the houses toward the monastery courtyard. The houses had goat skins hanging over the doors and windows, and the rush of the horses made them riffle in the wind. There was still no sign of habitation.

At last Singh drew rein before the courtyard. It had a wooden gate and a circular flagstone walkway. A large black stupa, the image of the Buddha, stood in the center of the courtyard. The facade of the monastery was covered with pastel frescos of flowers, and there were prayer wheels with tiny bells under a small overhang. In the middle was a great gold-colored door with delicately carved peacock windows on each side.

Singh pranced his horse back and forth before the gate, bellowing challenges for the guerillas to come out and fight. The other horsemen jostled and wheeled behind him. Then the dismounted men came up and began methodically bursting into the houses, ripping away the goatskin coverings. A woman screamed.

As the scream faded there was a single rifle shot. It came from the monastery, sounding clean and clear in the high air. A Sikh horseman tumbled off his mount, striking the ground on his back. Instantly a heavy fusillade erupted from two monastery windows. Bullets flew around the wheeling horseman. Two more men went down along with a horse that rolled over, thrashing, its belly covered with blood.

There was instant confusion in the road, Singh raging at the guerillas, his men trying to control their screaming, rearing mounts. The men began firing into the air but would not aim at the monastery. Another long burst of automatic gunfire roved through the milling horsemen, and a rider hunched over, gripping his animal's mane to keep from falling off.

Kurisovsky and his men reached a point fifty yards away. He dropped lightly from his mount as his men opened up on the monastery, their fire focusing on the two upper windows. The rounds stitched holes in the white stone.

After a moment he and three troopers, under the covering fire, skirted the wheeling horsemen and sprinted across the courtyard to the prayer wheel over-hang. Moving in pairs, they crept around the corner of the building. A flight of stone steps led up to a third floor. Gunfire burst through the floor of one of the wooden turrets. The bullets *whanged* off the flag-stones. All four men returned the burst, blowing the wooden floor apart, before they raced up the stairs.

A wooden door opened onto a narrow corridor with thick columns on one side and open cells on the other. Gunsmoke drifted in the still air, mingling with the thick smell of incense. A saffron-robed monk with a shaved head darted across the end of the corridor. Then an Indian carrying an assault rifle. Kurisovsky's burst caught him before he crossed, blew him off his feet.

They hurried down the corridor, checking each cell. All were completely bare except for straw matting and prayer candles in brass jars. The corridor curved to the right and turned into a *cherisi,* a large prayer chamber with more frescoes and thick matting and a dais where small worship drums and little copper prayer wheels were laid out. To the left a doorway led to a balcony that overlooked a gorge a thousand feet straight down. Across the room were several smaller corridors branching off.

Again they formed pairs and began exploring the corridors. At the end of one Kurisovsky found a dead guerilla beside a window, his forehead blown away. The blood had pooled and was already coagulating.

Kurisovsky heard a whimper and swung around. Two BIM guerillas in bloody loincloths squatted in a tiny side room, heads down, their weapons on the floor. They were weeping softly. They tried to kiss his boots as he came up. He slid their weapons back out the door.

Another burst of gunfire echoed through the building, followed by the sound of a man retching. Kurisovsky motioned for his trooper to investigate. The retching went on for several seconds, and then he heard the muffled coup de grace shot to the head and the retching stopped. He lifted his Kalashnikov and laid the muzzle almost gently on the top of the head of the closer guerilla. His finger tightened.

At a soft rustle behind him, he whirled. Standing in the doorway was a girl of about thirteen with the high cheekbones of a Tibetan. Dressed in a white gown that went to her bare feet, she had deep black eyes that stared directly into his with a strange tranquility. He was aware of the two Indians behind him prostrating themselves on the floor, heard them murmur, *"Kumari-ayah."*

Kurisovsky had read of the legends of the Kumari-ayah, the handmaidens of the living Hindu goddess, Uma. They lived in isolation in hidden temples or dual-religious monasteries like this one. There they would remain out of sight of all men save the monks until their first menstrual period, at which time they would be replaced because their bleeding had proven them human. These virgins were revered figures, even to Muslims like these guerillas.

Drawn by her calm, even stare, he stepped closer. She was small and delicate. He looked down into her eyes and for a moment thought he sensed an energy there, a motion that was not a motion, like the shift of light on the bottom of a deep pool.

Without a word, she lifted her hand and placed her index finger between his eyes. The touch was whisper-light, yet he felt it so precisely that he could even distinguish the ridges in her skin. A momentary warmth seemed to flow to him.

Strangely stilled, he stepped back, bent to retrieve the guerillas' weapons, and left the room, glancing over his shoulder at the girl. Her eyes followed him all the way down the corridor.

He and his troopers searched the rest of the monastery. There were no other guerillas. When Kurisovsky returned to the road, Singh had dismounted and was planted defiantly beside the stupa. Some of his men had also come stealthily into the courtyard, where they discovered a tiny red statue of the Hindu monkey god, Hanuman, in an alcove in the monastery wall. They stood in front of it, putting their palms together and bobbing their heads in *namastes*.

"All dead but two," Kurisovsky said. "Those are disarmed and wounded."

Singh smiled grimly. "Bring all out."

Kurisovsky whistled. In a moment his troopers began throwing bodies out the upper-floor windows. They landed on the steps in contorted postures, their skulls striking with the dull plops of heavy melons. There were four. Singh's men retrieved the corpses and dragged them toward the gate, leaving blood and excrement smeared on the flagstones.

At last the Russians brought out the two wounded guerillas, prodding them with the muzzles of their Kalashnikovs. The men were nearly paralyzed with fear and would not look up. They were rushed by the Sikhs, who grabbed handfuls of hair and hurled the men across the courtyard, spitting and kicking at them.

The corpses were laid out in a line before the gate. Singh walked along the line and methodically beheaded each. His sword blade, quickly bloodied, rang metallically as it cut through spinal bone. The other Sikhs stood, shifting their weight excitedly, their eyes hot. One of the guerillas fainted.

Next the houses along the main road were set afire, the men running from hovel to hovel with cloth torches. The structures blazed up quickly, roaring, and billows of smoke fumed into the air, casting oily shadows on the road. Panicked villagers in dirty pantaloons and sheep vests scurried out and fled toward the monastery, dragging their children and tethered animals. From the monastery windows, the frightened faces of shaven-headed monks peered helplessly down.

The two guerillas were dragged to the edge of the village and laid on the ground. Ropes were tied to each of their limbs, then lashed to eight horses. The men groaned and screamed as the lines went taut. A slow, rising sound lifted from the Sikhs, their tongues fluttering against the roofs of their mouths. It rose to a crescendo. Whips slashed down on the horses' flanks. A single scream, twin voices coiling around each other, exploded from the guerillas' mouths as their bodies were pulled apart. The sound was shockingly loud, a thick ripping like the violent sundering of wet canvas. Blood erupted, spewing onto the clothing of the closer Sikhs. The horses plunged away, dragging the body parts in the dust.

Throughout the entire procedure Kurisovsky and his men had stood aside. When the drawing and quartering was over, they turned and walked off down the road, some of them spitting in disgust.

Kurisovsky walked with them, leading his horse. He thought about the odd incident with the girl in the monastery and touched his forehead. Where her finger had been seemed cold, as if an icy coin were being pressed against his flesh.

That night they camped a mile from the ambush. The men made mats of elephant grass and laid out a rope ring around the camp to keep cobras from coming among them in the night. Jackals prowled beyond the firelight, and the smell of them drifted on the breeze.

Around midnight a rider came in from Dimapur. He consulted with Singh. A moment later one of the lieutenants awakened Kurisovsky. The leader was studying the moon thoughtfully as the Russian came up.

"News from my spies in Calcoota," Singh said. "American man is making questions of *Java Queen*."

Kurisovsky stiffened. "What? When?"

"It is now two days. He also making mention of missiles. What you think?"

The Russian was silent for a moment. "Where is this American now?"

"Spy say he is taking train to Guahati with woman doktar. What you think?"

"Kill them," Kurisovsky said.

6

Secretary of Defense Richard "Jack" Moffett III had just completed a distasteful chore, hosting an office party for one of his retiring secretaries. She'd been with him most of his political life, from young congressman all the way to the Cabinet. Moffett was a rather cold, stiff man, and the emotional atmosphere of the party had been uncomfortable for him.

On his way home, in the parking area under the central concourse, he was hailed by Captain Tony Peck, a senior officer on the staff of the Chief of Naval Operations.

"Excuse me, sir," Peck called, trotting up carrying a flight officer's overnight bag. "Have you a moment?"

"Of course."

"There's something I've been meaning to bring to your attention."

Moffett glanced at the bag. "Leaving town?"

"Yes, for a couple of days. My son's getting married in Boston. I've got a nine o'clock flight out of Washington National."

"Come on, I'll give you a lift."

The secretary always handled his own car, eschewing drivers. Although it seemed out of character, he owned a black 1979 Corvette that he personally kept in mint condition. The two men climbed in, and a moment later, Moffett eased into the traffic on Jefferson Davis Highway.

Peck got right to the point. "I've been going over some of the mock-ups from JAD covering military unit movements inside China," he said. JAD was the Joint Analysis Directorate, a strategy think tank connected to the Pentagon's National Command Center. "They're coming up with conclusions that conflict with CIA scenarios."

"Concerning what movements in particular?"

"Those in western China, along the border with the old Soviet republics. Satellite documentation is clear on the repositionings, and intelligence reports pinpoint elements of the Green Banner Army."

"Yes, I'm familiar with the data." Moffett flipped the wheel and expertly passed a Greyhound bus. "If I remember correctly, the CIA boys figure it's to protect against the burgeoning influence from Iran in that area." He snorted mirthlessly. "Can't say I blame the Chinese. I wouldn't want an open frontier with those loonies in Tehran either."

"That would seem a logical conclusion. But I recently talked with Scott Clark. He had some interesting comments." Clark was co-chairman of JAD. "First off, he pointed out that the Green Banner Army is essentially a combat and assault force. Paratroopers and mobile cavalry units, not garrison troops."

"Weren't they in garrison in Tibet?"

"Yes, but only their missile teams for the most part. The bulk of their M.C. units have been stationed along the Manchurian border ever since things got hot and heavy with the Soviets back a few years."

Moffett grunted.

"Second," Peck went on, "intelligence indicates that command of the Green Banner was given to General Qin. That old boy's an extremely aggressive field general, not a garrison officer.''

Moffett was silent for a moment as he swung off the highway and down the curving entry road toward the airport. Washington National was ablaze with lights. As the Corvette leveled out, Moffett said, ''You're saying JAD thinks the Chinese are mounting for an invasion of the old republics?''

''At least two mock-ups pointed in that direction.'' Mock-ups were run in a basement room of JAD's headquarters. On a regular basis experts from various fields gathered there for war games in which certain scenarios would be thrown at them. Computers countered their reactions and the results were than analyzed and formulated into policy recommendations.

''Why hasn't any of this come across my desk?'' the secretary snapped.

''Clark felt there wasn't sufficient data to submit a blue paper.''

''How far did they take the mock-ups?''

''From an invasion across the border and into at least a sixty-hour reaction frame.''

''And?''

''Occupation of the old republics would be rapid, with very little resistance. And world reaction would most likely be mild, limited to notes to Beijing. Depending, of course, on how much they took in Kazakhstan. They still have a fair share of nuclear missiles.''

''What about reaction inside the CIS?''

''That's the big mystery, sir. Clark says analysis gets into a shadow area here. Nobody is certain whether the Independent States would or could react in unison over an invasion.''

Moffett's thoughts were moving ahead. ''And if they

did unite, would that initiate the return of right-wing Russian central control?''

"Exactly."

Moffett scratched his nose. "Interesting." They had reached the main terminal ramp, and the secretary eased to a stop behind several taxis lined near the entrance. Peck opened the door but paused, waiting.

"You keep on this, Tony. And stay in contact with me. I'll talk to Clark myself in the morning."

"Very good, sir." They shook hands.

The secretary thoughtfully watched Peck disappear into the terminal and was struck, as he often was, by the odd way important data really got transferred in Washington. The place was so bogged down with protocol that if it wasn't for these momentary, informal contacts between thoughtful men, nothing of substance would ever get done.

On the ride home, he taped some of his thoughts and instructions to himself. Particularly he intended to study up on intelligence reports concerning China's political factionalism and Sichen's control. At the moment, he knew, the Chinese premier was in a head-to-head fight with conservatives in Beijing over economic policy. But where would Sichen stand in JAD's computer-created scenario of invasion?

"That's goddamned interesting," he said aloud as he passed over the Potomac. Down on the shoreline he could see the tiny, twinkling lights of fires where homeless people were camping.

Dawn found the train on the outskirts of Raiganj, two hundred miles from Calcutta. Bonner awakened to the noise of people passing along the aisle. He got up and looked out the window. The countryside was flat and dry, gray in the early light. To the north the foothills of Sikkim and Bhutan rose sharply, completely covered in cedar forests. Silhouetted against the eastern horizon, its snows made pink by a sun not yet risen, towered the peaks of the Himalayas.

Jackie was still asleep, tightly curled in the fetal position. He went off to the communal toilet in the carriage. It was a small closet with a large copper water tank over the single toilet and a cracked tin basin with a pump. The copper tank was tarnished green, and the room had a thick, foul stench.

A few minutes later, Ghate found him in the dining room getting tea. The Indian was already sweating and bounced from foot to foot, making his chubby shoulders bob. "You are sleeping well, sahib?" he cackled, then leaned close. "Not eating the breaking-of-fast here. Soon we are arriving Jalpaiguri. Number one hotel there."

The Bengalese went off to his third-class car, and Cas returned to the berth carrying two plastic cups of tea. Jackie was up, combing the sides of her hair and tightening her braid.

"How you doin?" he asked.

She gave him a smile. "Not bad. I slept better than I thought I would." She drank her tea with relish. It was thickly sugared and lightly spiced with cinnamon. "Where are we?"

"Just passed through Raiganj. Sugar says we'll be in Jalpaiguri in about an hour. We've got a three-hour wait there before we change trains."

She glanced out the window and gave a little cry. "Oh, look! Are those the Himalayas?"

"Yes."

"They're beautiful." She looked and looked, her eyes wide and girlish. "Darjeeling's up there, isn't it? When I was a little girl I used to have cut-out dolls of English officers in the Raj. You know? And their ladies, all in taffeta and satin. I used to pretend they lived in magical places like Darjeeling and Bangalore and Katmandu. Kipling places with—'' She turned, saw him smiling at her. She flushed slightly with embarrassment. ''You're laughing at me.''

''Not at all.''

She finished her tea and sighed. ''Well, the reality sure tears hell out of the magic.''

''Doesn't it always?''

She studied him from under her brows. ''You ever do anything romantic in your life, Bonner? I mean just for the romance?''

''All the time.''

''I find that hard to believe. I see you more as mister macho. I'll bet you even wore a leather jacket when you were in high school. Right? Tooled around on a big ole Harley? Or stood on street corners spitting and scratching your crotch?''

''That hurts,'' he said, but he was laughing.

''I'll bet.'' She took to scratching her arm furiously. ''God, I feel like I've got every icky bug in India on me. This thing have a shower?''

''No. Maybe you can wash in Jalpaiguri. Sugar's taking us to a hotel.''

They refilled their plastic cups and sat out on the coupling platform watching red hawks swoop in the sky and men moving along with oxen carrying wooden plows pulled up over their massive haunches. The heat came as soon as the sun was securely above the horizon, and it poured up off the train's wheels, blowing little lines of dust through the seams in the wooden platform.

Soon they reached the outskirts of Jalpaiguri. More shanties and people and dusty animals, with rats as huge as mongeese scurrying off the tracks and leaping into the dry grass.

The station was a great rusted building with metal

grille work and peeling paint. When the train pulled to a stop, there was a furious exchange of people, passengers shoving and pushing to get off while hordes of dirty children scooted between their legs carrying buckets. They ran along the aisles and darted into the toilets to draw water from the basins and copper tanks.

Once more they stood in line to get their tickets punched for the change of trains, then Sugar guided them down into the town. It had the appearance of an American frontier town, with a wide central dirt road packed with traffic: cars and scooters and bicyclists carrying loads of hay, oxen carts and wandering cows with shrunken sides showing ribs, and two elephants with log harnesses.

The wooden buildings were three stories high, all with ornately carved balconies where clothes hung drying. On the bottom floor were hundreds of tiny stalls selling foodstuffs, jewelry, incense, *durries* (carpets), and flowers. Kites and paper lanterns dangled from the overhead under which squatted snake charmers with cobras in baskets, sword swallowers, puppeteers, lei makers, and storytellers.

The hotel was called the Lancer. It had once been white, but the paint was faded and the shutter brackets were rusty. A wide veranda ran across the front, where people were eating under jacaranda trees at Victorian metal tables with banana leaves and small earthen bowls. The waiters wore sarongs, and short white jackets with big yellow turbans.

Jackie got a room with a bath. Cas and Sugar found a table on the veranda and drank *arak* until she came down, scrubbed and glowing. Then they had breakfast, fresh mangos and bananas, and thick, moist rice cakes called *idlis* and *sambar* purees of vegetables with chutney and fresh strawberry jam. It was delicious, and Cas and Jackie imitated Sugar, eating with the fingers of their right hand and washing everything down with icy earthen mugs of rice beer.

The second train was an ancient, greasy H.M. Woolsford narrow-gauge with a high puffer stack and open fire box. There were no sleeping berths. All six of the carriages had splitting wooden sides painted ochre. There were wooden seats, broken windows, and the floors were littered with chicken bones and sticky banana leaves. The three of them managed to get seats in the last car, and they finally pulled out of the station at nine-thirty with people hanging from the sides and tops and huddled over the bare couplings.

It would take them the remainder of the day to reach their terminus at Guahati on the Brahmaputra River, two hundred miles away. From there they would continue by riverboat to Dibrughar. This would afford Jackie the opportunity to search out the strange fungial malady among river villages.

It was impossible to talk on the train over the steady slam and hammering of the locomotive. Jackie sat sweating and morosely staring out the window. After a while Cas, bored, climbed up the side of the carriage and squatted on the roof beside an old man with a long, yellowing beard who offered him bits of fish and rotten onions.

At noon they reached Dhuburi on the Brahmaputra and paralleled it for thirty miles. The water was very low and muddy, and buffalos were submerged up to their nostrils in the shallows. Soon they left the river and entered an area of scrub jungle, then crossed a tributary named the Champamati, the train slowing almost to a walk as it crossed a dilapidated wooden scaffold bridge. One last leg to Gauhati remained, which Sugar said they'd reach at dusk.

Cas was dozing, his head resting on the old man's gunny sack, when he felt someone poke him in the forehead. He opened his eyes to Sugar's face, creased with strain from holding onto the side of the carriage.

"Sahib Bonner, come quick. There is bad trouble."

Cas sat up. "What's the matter?"

"Hurry, hurry." Sugar disappeared over the edge of the roof.

Cas scrambled back down and through the window. Jackie was sitting there looking confused. Ghate kept bobbing his head anxiously, trying to see up the line of carriages.

Cas grabbed his arm. "What the hell's wrong?"

"Sikhs, sahib," Sugar hissed, his eyes frightened. "Four are getting aboard at bridge. They have weapons and are searching for you and the lady."

Oh, shit, Bonner thought. It's starting. "How do you know they're after us?"

"They go from car to car asking for American man and lady doktar from Calcoota."

"My God," Jackie gasped.

"What can we do?" Sugar cried. "They are coming to shoot us all." Other passengers were beginning to take notice, turning to look.

Cas twisted and glanced at the back of the carriage. It had a wooden door that led to a small rear platform. He shoved Sugar toward it, turned, and pulled Jackie to her feet. "Come on. Hurry."

"What about my things?"

"Leave them."

"But I've got medical supplies."

"Take those but leave the rest. Come on, dammit, move!"

They jostled their way to the platform, which was filled with people. Jungle rose on both sides of the tracks. Bonner leaned over the railing and studied the speed of the ground moving past.

"What are you going to do?" Jackie shouted over the clack of the wheels.

"Get the hell off this train."

"What?"

Sugar held up his pudgy hands. "Oh, no, sahib Bonner. We will fall under the wheels and die."

The train was entering a curve, slowing slightly. Cas estimated its speed at about twenty miles an hour. As the other passengers watched curiously, he unlatched the railing gate. Then he turned and pulled Sugar up to it.

"Jump away from the tracks," he yelled into his ear.

The Indian groaned, bracing his legs against the railing. "I cannot, sahib."

"Go!" He put his shoulder against Sugar's fleshy back and shoved him off. He went with a little squeal. Cas turned and pulled Jackie to him. "When you hit, roll. Let the bag take some of the shock."

"Oh, shit," she said shakily, staring at the rail ties flashing past.

"Just do it, Jackie," he yelled. She hesitated a moment, and then she was off, her braid flapping straight out. He watched her land in a flurry of dust, and roll. Then he braced his feet and jumped himself.

The landing was a jolt as he rolled off into a clump of dry grass. Instantly he popped up, headed for Jackie and Sugar, yelling, "Get down in the grass. Hurry." He dived in after them.

Down the track, the train was moving around a slight curve. He peered out between grass blades. On the top of the last carriage, he saw two large Sikhs walking on the footboard, holding small machine pistols with the muzzles to the sky. They paused for a moment, then turned and went forward again.

He waited until the train was completely out of sight

and then stood and walked back to the others. Jackie was sitting in the grass cursing softly, studying her elbow. The fall had torn her blouse under the right arm. It had also broken Sugar's dark glasses. He was sadly studying the empty frames.

Cas squatted beside her. "You okay?"

"Yeah, I'm fine, fine."

He turned to the Indian. "What other towns are between here and the Brahmaputra?"

"Look, look," Sugar cried disconsolately. "My beautiful glasses."

"To hell with the glasses. What towns?"

"No towns, only villages."

"How far?"

"Four, five kilometer."

He looked up at the sky, gauging the time. He figured it was after three. He reached over and hefted Jackie's medical bag, then pulled her to her feet. "Let's go. I don't want to be in this damned jungle after dark."

They crossed the tracks and headed due south. The land was covered in scrub jungle of *saja* and *kulu* trees and short, flat lowland oak. Interspersed between the stands were open stretches of knee-high grass. Now and then dust devils danced through the trees. The heat was fierce and throbbing. It made their eyes hurt, their noses feel stuffy.

They moved in single file, Bonner leading. Although he wanted speed, he went cautiously, his eyes searching ahead for the telltale gleam of a snake's scales in the shady areas. This was viper and cobra country, he knew, where a careless step could be fatal. Overhead, tailless vultures drifted in the heat currents and crows called raucously from the trees.

Directly behind Cas, Jackie plodded grimly. But

Sugar Ghate kept mumbling to himself, occasionally bursting out with fearful predictions of Sikh savagery.

They crossed a series of hills with termite mounds and then descended into an area of scattered dry potholes where floodwater had formed tiny pans. Their sides were white with alakai crystals and pocked with bee-eater holes and rat burrows. As they passed, a seven-foot cobra emerged from a burrow. It lifted, flaring, as it caught their foot vibrations. Its warning hiss was like the sound of a broken air hose.

Sugar yelped, *"Naja, naja."*

Everybody froze. The snake swayed a moment, its hood white and slashed with brown striping. Then it dropped and glided into a second burrow. Jackie released her breath and touched Cas's shoulder. He felt her shudder.

As evening approached, the jungle began to change character, turning green from the deep groundwater off the distant river. The oaks and *kulus* gave way to stands of eucalyptus and peepul trees and the occasional neat clump of bamboo. Cas spotted a game trail and followed the tamped grass as it curved slightly to the left. Soon they reached a narrow dirt road and started following it. Darkness was coming on rapidly, the sky bleeding first orange and then crimson.

They could smell the village before they saw it: the musky drift of ox-dung fires and penned animals. They heard an oxen low, and then village lights appeared through the trees.

A quarter mile before the village was a small temple with a wooden gateway. A tiny brown monkey was tethered to a pin in the top. It screamed at them as they entered, baring its teeth. Beyond the gate was a small courtyard around which were low, crumbling stone buildings strewn with vines and faded paintings of jungle gods. In the center was a ten-foot *gopuram,* a tower, its stone bas-reliefs worn to indistinguishable shapes.

The rear of the temple courtyard was formed into a rock alcove with a single three-foot shaft of black stone set behind a still black pool filled with algae. At the foot of the shaft were garlands of marigolds and coconut offerings.

They passed a rear gate and continued on to the village. The huts were all made of wattle and mud, some with corrugated tin roofs. They surrounded a central plaza containing a well and a bare tree stump, apparently some sort of meeting site. A slightly larger hut outside the plaza had dirty glass windows and smoke issued from its mud chimney. Several bicycles were leaning against the wall, and four half-naked Indian men squatted in front of the building, smoking shag tobacco in rolled strips of newspaper.

Sugar spoke to them, then turned to Cas. "We can call for taxi from Gauhati here, sahib Bonner. They have radio." He looked at both Cas and Jackie, grinning. "And young girls if you are wanting."

"Oh, lovely," Jackie said.

When they went inside, they found a single room with a chandelier made from the top of an oil drum that held a dozen thick candles. A bench stood against one wall and the dirt floor was scattered with old newspapers. Three young Indian women lounged on the bench. They were barefoot and wore dirty saris and nose jewels. One was trying to breast-feed a tiny dark baby wrapped in a towel. The child squirmed, refusing the tit.

A man in a *longi* and ragged turban came through a side door. He was tall and thin and had an ugly scar on his forehead. He paused, staring at Jackie, who had walked over and was tickling the baby's head and smiling down at it. At last he shifted his gaze to Bonner.

"Fifty rupee for one fucking," he said, nodding toward the three girls. "Lady can have for forty."

"I understand you got a radio," Bonner said.

The man scowled at him. "You no want young girl?"

"Just the radio. We need a taxi from Guahati."

"Fifty rupees for the radio."

Cas snorted disgustedly at the price but took some bills from his belt. He counted fifty rupees and handed them over. The man stuffed them into his turban.

Sugar leaned closer. "I will go with him, sahib," he whispered. "To see he is not cheating you." The fat little Indian seemed nervous, and his eyes darted away when Cas looked at him.

"Do that," Bonner said.

Sugar and the proprietor went into the room. Jackie was still with the girl and her baby, examining the child more closely now. The other two prostitutes chattered, and one reached out and touched Jackie's braid.

Bonner eased across the room and stood beside the door through which the others had gone. The proprietor and Sugar were talking rapidly in low voices. He caught the words *Sikh* and *rupees* several times. His eyes narrowed icily. You little prick, he thought.

"Bonner, bring my bag," Jackie called.

He did so. She was peering into the eyes of the girl with the baby. "I am doktar," she said slowly. "You understand? Your baby is sick. Understand?" She held up the child's chin. The lips had a dark scaly deposit. "See? Sick." She bent and snapped open the bag.

Cas looked at the baby. It squirmed and its breathing was shallow. "What's the matter with it?"

"She's got a bronchial infection. Probably *Laryngotraceo-bronchitis*. If that gets a hold, it'll kill her.'' She was drawing up a hypo. "This child needs to be in a hospital."

The mother saw the needle and shied away. Jackie kept talking to her soothingly, but the girl refused to let her touch the baby again.

Bonner tapped her on the shoulder. "Do what you have to do but make it fast," he said softly. "We're getting out of here."

She frowned at him. "I can't leave now. I've got to watch this baby for at least three hours."

He shook his head. "No. Sugar turned us."

For a moment that didn't register. Then she cursed and turned back to the woman.

The proprietor returned.

"Where's my man?" Cas asked him.

He tossed his head. "He go making shit. He be back." He looked at the needle in Jackie's hand. "What she do?"

"She's a doctor. The baby's sick."

Surprisingly, the man looked concerned. He walked over and stood frowning anxiously at the child. Jackie said, "Tell the girl this is medicine. If she won't let me give it to the child, it'll die soon."

The man shouted something at the girl. She still hesitated. He shouted again and she finally let Jackie inject the needle. The baby squealed as it went into her buttocks. Jackie wrapped the syringe in a cloth and handed it to the proprietor.

"Throw that away," she ordered. "But don't touch the needle. And tell the mother to clear the baby's mouth of mucus. You understand mucus?" She made a coughing sound and a vomiting gesture with her hand. "Every fifteen minutes. Understand?"

The Indian nodded and spoke to the girl.

Cas picked up the medical bag. "Let's go," he said. Jackie looked at him. "Are you sure?"

"I'm sure."

She shook her head, gave the baby a final glance, then followed him to the front door.

The proprietor shouted, "You are not staying for the taxi?"

"We'll wait outside. It's too hot in here."

They went into the plaza. The squatting Indians were still there, and the proprietor watched them from the door. They walked over and sat on the rim of the well.

"Damn that Sugar," Jackie snarled. "Why'd he do this?"

"To cover his own ass. He probably told that joker back there he'd get the money off our bodies after the Sikhs were through."

"So what do we do now?" Jackie asked.

"Wait till he goes back inside and then head for the temple. I don't think they'd look for us there. Later tonight, we can hook two of those bicycles and head for Gauhati."

She put her head down and was silent for a moment. Then: "Who the hell are these Sikhs, anyway?"

"Obviously they're connected with the missiles. Come on, he's gone." She rose and started back in the direction of the temple, but Cas grabbed her arm. "No, we'll continue up the road and then come back through the jungle."

It was hellish coming back in the darkness. The jungle whispered and rustled with furtive movements. Owls called among the shrill chirping of nightjars. Tiny tree frogs, their bodies reflecting the faint moonlight through the trees, glowed on the trunks, looking like little luminous coins.

They finally reached the temple and went through the back gate. On the other side of the courtyard, the tethered monkey raised a ruckus but then abruptly settled down. They crossed to the alcove where the holy shaft was and slid behind it. The wall of the alcove was covered with fine moss, and they could smell the wilted marigolds and soured coconut milk and lemon oil offerings. Moonlight shone in the courtyard, making the stones white.

Jackie hugged herself. "Do you think they'll find us?"

"No."

"I'm scared."

He didn't say anything, but he put his arm around her shoulder. She nestled against him.

"You ever get scared, Bonner?"

"All the time."

"You don't show it."

"It's a waste of energy."

"God, I wish I could be that unemotional. First I get panicky and then I get mad."

"Mad's good, holds off the fear."

She was silent, listening to the night. Finally she said, "What happens when we get on the river? Do we turn back or go ahead?"

"I'm going to Dibrugarh."

She turned and eyed him quizzically. "Why are you doing this? I mean, what the hell does India mean to you? So another disease, a military coup with missiles scourges the scene, a few thousand people die. So what? It'll be absorbed just like all the rest has been absorbed for centuries."

"You really believe that?"

"I wish I did. But I don't."

"What do *you* want to do?"

She sighed heavily. "God forgive me. Stay with you, I guess."

Once more Bonner said nothing, but he liked her answer. The quality of Jackie Dunbar's rock was beginning to show, and it wasn't looking like sandstone.

She said, "Are we safe from snakes in here?"

"You're never safe from snakes."

"God, are you always so damned practical? Don't you ever stroke?"

He stiffened.

She felt it and hissed, "What?"

"Something's coming."

The sound of a vehicle was very faint, a distant hum that was almost a part of the jungle sound. Then it seemed to break free, surging, close. In a moment it roared past the temple toward the village.

Jackie groaned softly.

Cas pulled away from her and crept out into the courtyard. He paused a moment, then scurried to the rear gate. He could see a Land Rover parked in front of the whorehouse. Two men were sitting in it and he made out the shapes of gun racks beside the windshield brackets. As he watched, the driver got out, crossed the headlights, and went into the building. He was tall and lean, wearing an Aussie bush hat and khaki drill shorts.

A few minutes later, he came out again, climbed into the vehicle, and wheeled it around. It tore off down the road on the farther end of the village. Cas returned to the alcove.

"Was it the Sikhs?" Jackie asked in a harsh whisper.

"I couldn't tell. But they went south."

"We won't be able to use the road now."

"No, it'll be all right. We'd hear them before they come in sight."

They sat, not talking. The night seemed to drift past like a dark mist. Alerted by a rustle beside the alcove, they saw a long, dark snake slither across the courtyard toward the gate, pausing occasionally to test the air.

The vehicle returned, this time coming with a gunning of its engine. Bonner felt his adrenaline start its cold pumping, experienced its tingling in his fingers, his temples. He got to his feet.

"Where are you going?" Jackie asked desperately.

"Stay here. Don't move, no matter what happens."

"Cas, goddammit."

He slipped out of the alcove. The vehicle was passing back through the village. He frantically searched the moonlit courtyard, spotted a stone. He sprinted over to it, dashing lightly on the balls of his feet, and scooped it up.

The Land Rover skidded to a stop in front of the temple, and the tethered monkey started screaming. The engine dropped into a slow idle, and there was the sound of boots on the ground.

Holding the rock with both hands, Bonner eased up against the front gate. His skin shivered each time he put a foot down, toes first, easing weight, then moved the other. Above him the monkey scurried frantically back and forth on the gate, its chain snapping against the wood.

Two men appeared before the gate, silhouetted against the Rover's headlights. One carried a shotgun, the other a short machete. They stepped through the gate, less than five feet away.

His blood was drumming in his ears. Tensing his leg muscles, he waited. They passed him. With an explosive lunge he leaped forward, rock held high, aiming for the man with the shotgun.

The two men jumped away instantly and whirled about. A bright light snapped up into his face, for a fleeting second blinding him. Then he saw the muzzle of the shotgun extended beyond the light source. In the awkward, arms-raised position, his momentum took him a few feet, the light moving with him and the weapon lowering until it was pointed directly at his stomach.

He froze, his whole body gripping down, blood going to ice, as he waited for the blast to tear him apart.

7

U.S. Navy Commander Jack Rockliffe, captain of the nuclear-propelled attack submarine SSN-771, the USS *Yuma*, started his fifteenth lap of the missile compartment. He was working off Tactical Division's pizza, which he'd consumed for supper. Each division of the sub took turns making pizza for the entire crew. Unfortunately, T.D.'s specialty was notoriously over-spiced, with a crust that sat on the stomach like lead.

The long compartment gleamed under its overhead fluorescents: matrices of serpentine piping, circuit boxes, control panels, and switching consoles. Yet everything was dominated by the line of twelve, brown-painted vertical-launch tubes strung out down the center of the space. All but one contained Tomahawk SSM missiles. Tube number nine, however, had been altered slightly to take a different missile, one designated an XGB-3AS.

At the moment the *Yuma* was midway between the northeastern coast of Australia and the island of Bali. Twenty-one days earlier, she had left her home port of Bangor, Washington, for her normal patrol area, which included the deep South Pacific and the Strait of Molucca. On this patrol an additional assignment had been given to her. She was to achieve station at coordinates 83:15 E/08:30 S in the eastern Indian Ocean by June 8.

At that time she would test-launch the new missile. The target was a shallow upthrust of ocean bottom a thousand miles to the southwest called the Mascarene Plateau. Already standing off the target area was the National Oceanic and Atmospheric Administration research ship *Explorer,* which would track the missile's flight and run post-explosion tests of the area.

The overhead crackled: "Would the captain come to the C.C.?"

Rockliffe instantly broke off his lap. An athletic man of thirty-one, he wiped the sweat off his face and hurried forward through the reactor compartment and machinery space to the companionway that led up to the Control Room/Attack Center located below the sub's sail.

His executive officer, Lieutenant Bill Duquette, was on the conn. He turned as Rockliffe entered. "We have contact on bearing zero-four-nine at range of twenty thousand yards, sir. It is classified as warship with active sonar source."

"Very well. I relieve you of the conn."

"I stand relieved, sir," Duquette answered. He turned slightly and called, "Quartermaster, the captain has the conn."

The quartermaster repeated.

Rockliffe paced slowly. "On the deck, man battle stations. Chief of the deck sound general alarm."

The commands were instantly relayed and acknowledged as a Klaxon clanged throughout the ship.

"Depth?"

"We have zero-eight-zero feet, sir," the dive officer answered.

"Up scope," Rockliffe ordered. "Use one hundred-foot masthead height, high power." The command was relayed and the gleaming, polished trunk of the scope slid silently out of its well. Draping his arms around the handles, he swung the scope, then held. "Mark the bearing zero-four-nine. Designate contact on the horizon as Tack-One."

"Contact Tack-One is so designated."

"Final bearing on number two scope is zero-four-nine."

"Final bearing is zero-four-nine, aye."

"Down scope." As silently as before, the trunk slid out of sight. "Officer of the deck, rig ship for ultra quiet." As the command traveled throughout the submarine, unnecessary machinery was instantly shut down and off-watch crewmen hustled to their bunks and climbed in.

In the Sonar Room, banks of computers ingested the incoming sounds from the entire marine environment. These were filtered into discreet bands and then displayed as vertical lines on the sonar men's screens and compared to the ship's library of sounds for identification.

A few minutes later, the C.C. speaker barked, "Conn, Sonar, we have contact Tack-One classified as Australian warship based on active range sounding." The Aussie, probably a destroyer, was lashing the area with active sonar pings. Undoubtedly she had already picked up the *Yuma*.

"Very well," the captain said. "Quartermaster, place our position within local Australian operating zone."

"Bearing three-five-eight and fifteen miles on the log, sir."

"All right, bearing correlates to Australian operating zone. Quartermaster, work out course for egress from zone on plot."

"Aye, sir."

Reports from the Sonar Room updated the changing position of the Australian ship. A moment later, the quartermaster called, "Captain, recommend course three-five-zero to avoid all contact."

"Very well. Helm, right to steady course three-five-zero. Ahead two-thirds."

The course and speed commands were repeated.

"Helm, on the dive make it two-zero-zero feet."

"Two-zero-zero feet, aye."

"Secure fire-control tracking party," Rockliffe said. "Chief of the watch, rig ship for control quiet."

Sliding deeper into the sea, the *Yuma* headed almost due north. Fifteen minutes later, she exited the Australian patrol zone, set up a new course to the west, and disappeared into the blue-black gloom of the Indian Ocean.

"Hold it, lad," the man with the shotgun said quietly. "Go easy and put down that ruddy rock."

Cas, still caught in the mind-stultifying moment of expectation, didn't move. A second light came on. Both beams shone on his face.

"The rock," the shotgun man repeated.

Bonner dropped it.

"That's it, lad. Now, where's your lady friend?"

"I'm alone."

"Very gallant." He said something in Hindi to the other man, who hurried across the courtyard, flashing his light on the crumbled buildings.

"What's your name, lad?" the man said. His words had a slight Scottish lilt.

"Cas Bonner."

"Why're the bloody Sikhs scouring the countryside for you?"

Cas felt the energy pulses of his body decelerating. He kept glancing at the other man, who had passed the *gopuram* and was nearing Jackie's alcove. In an attempt to distract him, he snapped, "Who the hell are you?"

"Name's Hak McCarran."

"What do you want?"

"I've been told you're in a bit of a stew."

"So?"

"Thought I'd jot over and save your bloody arses."

"You're not with the Sikhs?"

McCarran snorted. "Hardly."

The other man found Jackie and brought her back across the courtyard. "Well, here we are," McCarran said and shone the light on Jackie's face. Her eyes were wide and frightened.

"No need for concern, missy," McCarran went on. "Nobody's going to hurt you." He returned the light to Bonner. "Now, I'd say we'd best vacate this area before the bloody kafirs arrive."

"Where're we going?" Bonner asked.

"To the river."

Cas hesitated. "Why are you helping us?"

"We can discuss that later. Miss?" McCarran stepped aside to allow her to pass.

He drove very fast down the dirt road, the headlights throwing quivering illumination into the towering trees, making them look like the sides of a tunnel. He and the Indian sat in front, with Cas and Jackie scrunched on the tiny backseat.

After a while, McCarran yelled over his shoulder. "This is my mate, Dabu." The Indian turned and grinned at them.

"What's your name, missy?"

"Jackie Dunbar."

"You really a doctor?"

"Yes."

They flew on. The vehicle, Bonner noticed, was loaded with hunting gear and packs and rolls of fishy-smelling, leathery material he assumed were crocodile skins.

McCarran took a bottle of whiskey from the glove compartment, lifted it a moment, then handed it back. Cas took a swig. It was scotch and smelled like nail polish. Jackie refused it when he offered, so he took another slug and handed it back.

Jackie leaned close. "Can we trust these people?" she whispered loudly.

"We don't have much of a choice, do we?"

Thirty minutes later, they saw lights up ahead and soon reached a little procession of men walking along the edge of the road. They carried torches and had nets slung over their shoulders. McCarran skidded to a stop beside them. For a moment he and they talked in Bengalese, the men all jabbering at once and pointing to the east. At last Hak shifted into gear and they zoomed off again.

"Bloody Sikhs were coming at you from two directions," he called back. "I'm wondering how they found out you were in that village so soon. These people don't usually talk to Sikhs."

"Our guide sold us out to that pimp back there," Cas yelled.

"Aye, that sounds about right."

"How did you know?"

"Word travels fast hereabouts if you know where to listen. I heard about you people within an hour after you left that train. Common sense said you'd head for the river."

Another half hour passed. Slowly the jungle began to thin out, replaced by stretches of dry rice paddies. Far off to the south they caught sight of the Brahmaputra River under the moon, with the scattered lights of tiny fishing communities along each bank.

McCarran lived on a houseboat tied to a huge peepul

tree. Along the bank on either side were makeshift shacks of logs and tin strips and cardboard. Numerous boats were anchored off the banks with floating log walkways to them: *cammacs* with high spoon-shaped bows, *dongas*, and sailing boats like Javanese *praus*, their triangular sails reefed. Some of the larger boats had high straw-and-thatch after houses, glowing cozily from kerosene lanterns. Most had people fishing off the sterns with long, thin poles that had sealed bottles of oil and burning wicks to attract the fish.

As McCarran pulled to a stop beside the peepul tree, Jackie glanced up and was startled to see a man squatting on one of the thicker branches. With hair draped over his shoulders, he was completely naked, an immense penis dangling between his legs.

"My God!" she cried. "Look at that."

McCarran was unbuckling the rifles from the windshield brackets. He chuckled. "He's a fakir. I call him Percy. Been up that bloody tree for ten years now. Gets his kit hoisted up to him each morning and he lowers his slops each night. Healthiest bastard on the river."

Dabu trotted off to his own shack, and Hak led them across a gangplank made of two-by-fours to the houseboat's screened veranda. The sound of a generator whined softly from somewhere. The water directly below looked oil-shiny. A dead rat, caught in a back pool, bobbed against the aluminum hull, and flying black beetles banged against the screen.

Inside, the houseboat was spotlessly clean, lit by overhead fluorescent lights. Beyond the veranda was a single large room hung with colorful Malabar rugs. There were three windows on each side of the boat with *parda* curtains made of bamboo strips coiled on top. The floor also had a rug and the furniture consisted of one large, well-worn leather chair, a wicker table, and a bookcase filled predominantly with history books. Bonner took particular notice of the three battle honor insignias on the bookcase, British Special Air Service shields emblazoned with the regimental motto, *Qiu ose gagne*.

In the right-hand corner beside a doorway was a small stand with an image of Ganesh. It had a long trunk and its painted eyes were bright below a fresh mark of sandalwood paste. On the other side of the door was a heavy Hallicraft XB-134 transceiver, its antenna wire running through the nearby window. Above the radio were three rifles in stud mounts: twin Cogswell & Harrison .375 H & H Magnums and a .458 Brno, all the stocks worn with usage. A smaller cabinet held boxes of cartridges.

All of it instantly described McCarran to Bonner. He'd met such men before, expatriates who had found their own kind of significance in strange lands. Bearing highly personal and usually peculiar ideas of what was important, they possessed a certain standoffishness that was, in its own way, a manliness rarely found among other men. Cas had always liked the McCarrans of the world; within himself existed the same qualities and disaffections.

Hak placed his shotgun and a .404 Mannlicher onto the two empty racks, then leaned through the doorway and called softly in Hindi. A moment later, a middle-aged Indian woman in a blue sari came out. She was quite beautiful and graceful. He introduced her as his wife, Malli, with the emphasis on the *i*.

Malli smiled, showing straight white teeth. "You are most welcome here," she said, performing *namaste*.

Both Cas and Jackie returned the greeting.

She slipped back into the other room as Hak took

off his bush hat and tossed it onto the radio. Above the line of the brim, his forehead was stark white, balding slightly, with salt-and-pepper hair cropped close. In the light, he appeared to be in his sixties, his features long and narrow, nose sharply pointed. But it was his eyes that drew attention. Little wrinkles radiated from their corners, and their color was the light blue of a crystal-clear pool in open sunlight.

They sat out on the veranda atop delicately embroidered pillows. Malli brought out iced mugs of rice beer. Hak lit an Indian cheroot, took a long pull of beer, and eyed Bonner. "Well now, lad, let's have the story."

Bonner told it, starting right at the beginning when the voices had come out of the ocean. McCarran listened intently, his eyes narrowed with interest. He grunted and mumbled, "Extraordinary," when Cas mentioned the missiles and again at the description of the fungi. Meanwhile, Malli kept their beer mugs filled.

When Cas finished, Hak sat for a long time, staring out through the screen at the river. Finally he said, "Tell me, could this fungus of yours affect animals as well as humans?"

"Very probable," Jackie answered. "I assume its vector trail is through the intestinal system. Maybe the lungs, too. But either way, animal metabolic processes are similar enough to humans that it would be just as toxic."

Hak nodded. "I think I've seen the bloody thing. In dead crocs up near Hojai. Their belly flesh had this slimy green substance. Bloody thing looked alive. And there was the strong smell of kerosene fumes in the flesh."

Jackie gave Bonner a quick glance. "Then it *is*

here.'' She turned back to Hak. ''Where exactly is this Hojai?''

''About a hundred miles upriver.''

''Have you seen any other signs of it? I mean, people with TB- or tetanus-like symptoms?''

''That's hard to say. This country's full of disease. Malaria, blackwater fever, cholera, typhoid, rabies, hepatitis. You name it, missy, it's here.''

''What about the missiles?'' Bonner asked. ''Obviously the Sikhs are the ones moving them. But who exactly are they?''

Hak's eyes hardened. ''Abu Singh's people, that bloody *pagal maila*. Singh's a Kashmiri who's made himself the bleeding *prabhu* here in Assam. Whole damned country kites to him, including those idiots in Delhi. Now I hear he's even got Russian cadres with him at Lake House. Probably showing the son of a bitch how to kill more efficiently.''

''Russians? Then those were Russian missiles.''

''Very likely. It'd be just like that madman to launch biological missiles into Bangladesh.'' He shook his head sadly. ''Lord save us all.''

''How much weight do you carry with the authorities, McCarran?'' Bonner asked. ''They didn't believe me when I told them. Maybe they will you.''

Hak smiled coldly. ''Not much chance there. Delhi thinks I'm a bit cracked, a bloody gadfly. I've been buggering the bastards for years to protect their game animals up here. Especially the tigers and rhinos. They go through the motions, but it's all a bloody farce. Poachers keep killing horrendous numbers of animals, and Delhi gets the *baksheesh*.''

He took a deep drag on his cheroot before continuing. ''Besides, Singh has his lapdogs inside the Indian Intelligence Bureau who'd protect him. They don't want another bloody Amritsar. And, believe me, trying to cut through the layers of corruption in Delhi or even Calcutta would try the patience of a bloody saint.''

"How about the English embassy?''

McCarran shook his head. "They'd need precise physical evidence before they'd chance making charges. Something like this could damage Indo-British relations if they approached it half-cocked.'' He snorted contemptuously. "Ever since Independence, those bleeding Foreign Office blokes are running scared, afraid to pee in the wrong place.''

Outside, the beetles continued to thrash against the screen, trying to get to the light. There was the sudden screech of a peacock. It sounded like a woman in distress.

Bonner studied McCarran a moment. "Why'd you get involved with us?'' he asked. "This could be risky for you.''

Hak snorted. "I hate the bloody Sikhs. Frankly, I rather relish taking a bleeding prize from 'em. They're an arrogant, volatile lot who'd slit your bloody throat as look at you. And this Singh's the worst of the crop. He's mucked up this whole area. Some of the stories I've heard of his savagery would curl your hair.''

"I noticed croc skins in your Rover. You a hunter?''

"Only for man-eaters.'' His eyes twinkled icily. "And a *maila* poacher now and again just for spice.'' For a moment he slipped into his own thoughts, then: "And one of these days I'll cop off the head poacher of 'em all, that thieving, cheeky bastard Pal Jungali.''

Malli interrupted with dinner. They ate with bowls in their laps: strips of beef and vegetables on skewers and banana patties in a thick curry sauce. Halfway through, Hak glanced at his watch, excused himself, and went into the main room. Soon they heard the radio and the stentorian voice of a British announcer from the BBC Overseas Service giving the latest racing news from England's Doncaster, Epsom, and Kepton Park tracks.

When Hak returned, he had a fresh cheroot and mug of beer. "How good are you with weapons, Bonner?" he asked.

"Good enough."

"Ex-soldier?"

"SEAL."

"Bravo, lad." For the first time he flashed a warm smile. "I've been thinking that maybe you and I could do a bit of scouting upriver."

"Good idea," Jackie said cheerily. The powerful beer had given her eyes a sparkle, her mouth a sleepy little grin.

"I want a closer look at those missiles. And we might even be able to slip out with some physical evidence for the B.C. At least enough so they won't laugh us out the door."

"When do we leave?" she chirped.

McCarran smiled indulgently at her. "Not advisable for you to come along, missy. You stay with Malli till we get back."

"Bull puckie," Jackie snapped. "You forget I came up here to do a job. I intend to do it."

Cas grinned at her. "You're tipsy."

"Oh, shut up." To Hak: "Well?"

"Determined, isn't she?" he said.

"More like stubborn." Cas leaned over and tapped Jackie's knee. "Look, honey, there's a good chance we're gonna get shot at."

"*You* look, honey. I can handle a weapon just as well as you. Now, I'm going upriver, alone if I have to."

Chuckling, Hak stood up, stretched lazily, and

smiled down at her. ''Then you'd best get some sleep, missy. We'll be leaving before daylight.'' He nodded to the outer walkway. ''The loo's around the side. Watch for snakes in the bowl. Sometimes they come out the mooring line.''

8

Sergeant Yuri Perotsky peered through his night scope at the small Chinese frontier outpost a half mile away. It consisted of a thirty-foot round blockhouse made of stones and two rock storerooms connected with blizzard lines. A single light shone in the tower; everything else looked gray-green through the scope.

The outpost was situated beside the narrow road that ran through the Nyamyang Chu Pass, a rocky valley on the southern slope of the remote Himalayan Chang Tang plateau in southeastern Tibet. Bracketing the outpost were steep, twisting hills, and beyond the pass the land leveled into great salt pans before climbing precipitously into the snows of the higher peaks. Campfires of *drokba* nomads twinkled on the pans, and five miles to the east, its single light clear in the thin air, was a second Chinese outpost.

Perotsky glanced at his watch: it was 11:57. He tapped the trooper, Ilney, who lay beside him. "No one outside," he said, his breath frosting in the air. "Move out. Check for trip wires."

Instantly Ilney and a third trooper named Shlepkin rose to their feet and went off down the road, hunched over, their padded boots silent. Each was armed with a Kalashnikov AKS-74 with spare clips of notched ammo, making them like dum-dum rounds on impact. Hooked to their H-harnesses were MK-3A-2 concussion grenades. Like the others, their gear was wrapped in ordnance tape to prevent rattling.

The sergeant watched them through his scope. When they were halfway to the blockhouse, he and the fourth man, Zhdanov, shouldered their weapons, picked up the canvas-wrapped body of the dead Indian they'd brought, and followed. Perotsky carried an American Stoner 63-A light 5.56mm machine gun, Zhdanov a Polish PMK-DGN assault rifle fitted with a grenade launcher.

The sergeant was a *stariki*, an old hand, at insurgency tactics. A veteran of Afghanistan and border strikes in Manchuria, he had once been a lieutenant in a *spetsnaz* naval brigade. But he'd killed a fellow officer over a prostitute and spent two years in a penal battalion before returning to the *spetsnaz*. The others had been in airborne brigades.

With a jeep stolen from a teak logging outfit, it had taken them nearly twenty-four hours to reach the pass. First they had traveled through the heavy jungles of the Assam river plain, then into the foothills, terraced in rice and tea, and finally the high forests of pine and spruce and wild apple groves. Little red-roofed villages nestled in steep ravines where waterfalls misted the valleys, and the bridges were made of cantilevered logs.

At last the trees gave way to bare rocky slopes and the road narrowed with its kilometer markers on *mani* prayer walls made of rocks thin as tortillas. Occasionally they passed pilgrims, all in maroon robes and twirling their brass prayer wheels with each step. One, a tall Tamil, they killed with a bullet through the forehead. Then they dressed him in the stolen uniform of a 9th Bengal Grenadier, wrapped the body in canvas, and strapped it to the hood of the jeep like a deer.

They had reached the bridge at Tsangdhar at dusk.

Two miles beyond was the Thang La Ridge, which formed the Indo-Chinese frontier, the old McMahon line demarcated during the time of the Raj. In 1962 Indian soldiers had battled crack Chinese troops in these ten-thousand-foot mountains over Chinese territorial claims. The Indians had been pushed back nearly thirty miles, but U.N. pressure had forced Beijing to order a return to the old line.

A hundred yards from the blockhouse, Perotsky and Zhdanov went to ground. The sergeant unshouldered his Stoner and braced it atop a rock. Both men were breathing hard in the thin air. He waited a moment, then looked through his night scope. He could see Ilney and Shlepkin flat on the ground, each at a forty-five-degree angle to the building. He checked his watch: 12:13.

The explosion of the Stoner was like a cannon. Perotsky threw a series of bursts, two or three rounds each, watched the bullets blowing into the sides of the blockhouse, every fifth one a tracer that made a tight white line before impact. Beside him, Zhdanov opened up, too, the combined reports echoing among the rocks.

A moment later, Zhdanov sent a grenade into the blockhouse. It blew a three-foot hole through the wall near the ground. He flung another. This one tore off the left corner of the building. Instantly both men stopped firing and lunged to their feet, sprinting down the slope. Ahead, the other two had already reached the breach, both hurling grenades through the hole.

A machine pistol cut loose from the blockhouse roof. Perotsky heard the bullets *whanging* into the ground ahead of him. His chest was burning with oxygen need. Ignoring the pain, he swung the muzzle of the Stoner up and sprayed the roof. The machine pistol stopped just as the two grenades went off, hurling debris back through the hole.

Before the echoes ceased, Ilney and Shlepkin dived through the breach, shouting back and forth to each other, firing their weapons in sharp, intense bursts. These were answered with screams and the higher-pitched rap of Chinese rifles in a full firefight.

When Perotsky and his partner reached the hole, he hollered to identify himself and went through. The inside of the blockhouse was torn apart, part of the loft floor down. It was cloudy with smoke and rock dust and stank of explosives. Bodies were strewn around a hearthfire that still glowed red in the center. From overhead a beam of moonlight descended through the shattered floor, forming a delicate shaft through the smoke.

Backs against the wall, the Russians blew everything they had. The rounds hurled rock chips, cut through beams, made the bodies of the already dead Chinese jump. They were dressed in sheepskin jackets and red skullcaps and had laceless tennis shoes worn over thick yellow leggings.

All firing stopped. In the sudden vacuum of silence the men called to one another, then began moving stealthily among the dead. A Chinese soldier, half his face blown away, moaned. Ilney shot him. Zhdanov found a broken wooden barrel of *chang*, barley beer, and scooped up a palmful to drink.

Perotsky threw a quick burst through the remnants of the upper floor, then started up the stone steps that curved along the outer wall. As his head cleared the floor, a shadow lunged up in front of him. His finger tightened on the Stoner's trigger. He felt a horrendous pain plunge into his chest just below his heart. His eyes misted for a second as he felt his weapon go off. The shadow disintegrated and then he was toppling backward, seeing the handle of a shovel protruding from his body. The pain was so powerful, he didn't feel himself hit the floor, nor did he hear the others blowing the ceiling apart.

The troopers carried him out to the road and laid him behind a rock. He stared up at the moon. Oddly, his vision was so clear that he could actually see the dark shadows of its mountains. Zhdanov knelt beside him while the others returned to the blockhouse to find fuel oil.

Struggling with the words, Perotsky said, "Put—body inside—breach." Each syllable sucked pain into his throat.

"Yes," Zhdanov said. After a moment he drew a Beretta 9mm from his harness. He held it against his knee, staring at the sergeant.

"Do it," Perotsky gasped.

Zhdanov obeyed. He placed the muzzle on the bony ridge between Perotsky's eyebrows. "Farewell, comrade," he said and fired.

Afterward he stripped the body of munitions, placed Perotsky's blue *spetsnaz* beret on his chest, doused the corpse with fuel oil, and ignited it. Then he and the others retrieved the Indian corpse and put it inside the grenade hole of the blockhouse. The fire of Petrosky's corpse sent dark smoke up against the moon, and the thin air carried the stench of burning flesh.

The three men went back up the road, going in single file, saying nothing. On the border side of the Indian hill station they waited among rocks. Farther down, Indian soldiers were quick-stepping toward the border, their weapons across their chests, ammo canisters clinking.

Forty-two minutes later, Chinese reinforcements began shelling the hill station with mortars. The Indian *jawans* formed a skirmish line and fired back, and then their own mortars began lobbing shells into the pass.

In the confusion, the three Russians made their way back to the jeep and started the long return trip to Assam.

At 3:31 A.M., Delhi time, Indian Secretary for State Affairs Amit Chedi received the Chinese ambassador in his office deep within the North Secretariat building. In a room down the hall were members of his staff whom he'd called in after receiving a telephone message from his intelligence watch officer about the firefight in the North East Frontier Area. Now they were frantically analyzing updated reports from the Tsanghar outpost.

The Chinese ambassador, Tian Xiangan, was a thin, dapper little man who had once been a professor of Asian studies at the University of Kentucky. Although his manner was calm, his dark eyes were hard.

While Chedi sat behind his great mahogany desk inlaid with patterns of tiny lotus blossoms in gold, Tian read a letter of protest from Beijing. Its wording was formal but explicit, clearly threatening. The government of China, it stated, deplored the unprovoked attack of its frontier station and the killing of at least fifteen Chinese soldiers It demanded an explanation and an apology from Delhi. Further, it warned that any more acts of terrorism against Chinese frontier troops would be considered provocations of the most serious nature, ones that could result in a major confrontation between the two nations.

The reading completed, Tian stared fixedly at Chedi. "Now, Mr. Secretary, how does your government intend to answer mine?"

Chedi leaned forward and put his elbows on the desk, his fingertips together. For a moment he studied the ornate ceiling, a tiny, cold smile playing across his full lips. Finally he said, "I must say, Ambassador, I am taken aback by the threatening tone of your note."

"It was intended to be so. Fifteen Chinese soldiers were killed. My government does not consider that a minor incident."

"We seem to have a conflict of facts here, Ambassador Tian. From reports I have received, it was your troops who opened fire."

"A lie."

Chedi stiffened and the vague smile snapped off. "You say I am lying?"

"I meant your facts are incorrect."

"Then we must ascertain which facts *are* correct before an answer can be given."

"And when will that be?"

"When it is," Chedi answered sharply. He stood, a signal that the meeting was over.

Slowly the Chinese rose also. "I must have some time frame."

"I will speak with the prime minister immediately. Afterward I'll contact you with a statement as to our posture."

Tian bowed and withdrew.

Ten minutes later, Chedi, still seething, drove the half mile to Rashtrapati Bhavan, the Presidental Palace, to confer with Prime Minister Jurigan Anduri.

Meanwhile, far to the west, Green Banner General Qin was also moving. Wakened by a direct call from Beijing, he had regretfully left his sleeping lover and rushed to his headquarters on the outskirts of Urumchi. There he received constant updates on the incident in Indian's NEFA, as well as intelligence and strategy communiqués from hurried meetings of the

State Council and the PLA General Staff in Beijing. Everybody there was outraged, even P.M. Sichen.

Within the first hour, Qin had issued a barrage of orders. All Green Banner missile and infantry units along the entire Indo-Nepal-Bhutan-Chinese frontier were put on red alert. Transiting divisions were speeded up, with some being returned to the Tibetan region in order to reinforce depleted units. His staff, working in close conjunction with PLA headquarters, began formulating defensive/offensive and air-support contingencies.

The general was then driven to his base heliport. Beijing wanted a personal assessment of the situation along NEFA. As he rode, staring out at the barren, moonlit landscape and sipping his bottle of *unkape,* he considered the myriad aspects of the situation.

Why had India done such a thing? he wondered. Was it, as some in Beijing thought, a prelude to a territorial challenge? If so, it was tactically a foolish move. Who precedes an invasion with a warning skirmish? Was it a diversion, then? Could other forces even now be massing in the north, in the marcher lands of the Kashmir frontier?

He paused, sensing something else. Gradually it began to emerge. What if this challenge, he reasoned, was actually being mounted from the north, from the old Russian republics? This pathetic little incident, rather than having anything to do with India, could in actuality be the beginning gambit of a Caspian Alliance move. This seemingly unconnected incident could be used to test China's reaction and strength in an actual border crossing.

Possible, he thought. Perhaps even probable.

He snapped forward and picked up the car phone. In two minutes, his mind racing as he spoke, he gave the complete directive for a readjustment of mobilization plans. Units would not all be returned to NEFA; instead some would continue concentrations along the frontiers of Kazakhstan, Kyrgyzstan, and Tajikistan. Further, six complete divisions were to be airlifted from Gansu, Quinghai, and Manchuria to increase offensive strength there within forty-eight hours.

He sat back, pleased. For a moment he idly wondered at the reaction in Beijing to his bold adjustment. He immediately scorned it. Even those progressive imbeciles in the capital, Sichen chief among them, would have to admit that the possibilities of his concept were too dark to ignore.

Once that was absorbed, he knew, the rest would follow: the acceptance that China's borders were, and would continue to be, open to challenge in a rapidly shifting and chaotic world. Thus, to protect herself, she must strike first, reclaim those buffer lands that had long ago been stolen from her by arrogant Russian czars.

Secretary of Defense Moffett was attending a cocktail party in the Mayflower Hotel in downtown Washington when he was called to a private phone. It was his Deputy Secretary of Intelligence, Thomas Walsh.

"The Ranch just called, sir," Walsh said. "Foreman wishes to see you as soon as possible." The "Ranch" was the White House, the "Foreman," the President.

"All right. Stay close." He hung up.

Moffett immediately made his excuses to the hostess, a beautiful lady senator from Arkansas, and left. From the phone in his Corvette, he called Walsh back. The phone was a scrambler unit with a short time lag. "What's up?" he asked as soon as Walsh came on the line.

"There's been an Indian attack on a Chinese outpost

on the northeastern Indo-Chinese border. Some place called Tsanghar.''

India? Moffett thought, shocked. What is this? "How extensive?''

"We've got very little so far, but there were at least fifteen Chinese soldiers killed and one Indian grenadier. No unit ID on him yet.''

"Fifteen to one,'' Moffett mused aloud. "Is it still going on?''

"No, sir. The Indians have pulled back. There was a mortar exchange, but it seems to have quieted down now.''

"How did we know about it?''

"British Intelligence intercepted field communiqués between Tsanghar and Delhi. They passed it to our watch station in London.''

"What's Beijing doing?''

"Nothing concrete yet, but our sources in-country say there's a lot of activity within PLA headquarters. And rumor has it Beijing's already whipped out a strong note of protest to Delhi.''

"Any response?''

"We don't have anything so far.''

"Keep in touch.''

"Yes, sir.''

The President was already in conference in the Cabinet Room. Present were Assistant for National Security Affairs William Novak, and Deputy Director of the CIA David Bade, acting on behalf of the director, Leo Shantz, who was in California. Everyone was in casual dress: the President wore a silk, metallic blue bathrobe, Novak a sweatsuit, and Bade one of his old Marine Squadron VI sweaters.

Moffett was brought up to speed by the President. Apparently there had been an extremely strong note sent to Delhi. So far the Indian government had not formed a response.

Finished, the President sat back and surveyed the three men. "So, gentlemen, what's going on?"

"It could merely have been a spontaneous thing," Bade said. "Antsy soldiers eyeing each other across a line for too long tend to get trigger-happy."

"No," Moffett countered, "this was planned. Too many Chinese were killed for it to have been a casual exchange of bullets."

"Then what?"

"I think it was a test of Chinese strength in the area," Moffett answered. "As you know, the Chinese have been doing a lot of repositioning all along their western frontier. Many of the units sent north were pulled from those very sectors."

"Come on, Jack," Novak cracked. "You don't really think Delhi is working up to an open challenge to China, do you? Admittedly, the area's always been a bone of contention between them, but what would India gain by putting on the gloves now over a pissant bit of land?"

"Wait a minute," Bade countered. "There could be something to that. Maybe it wasn't Delhi per se. Maybe certain elements within the government set this up."

"Why?" the President asked, swiveling his chair around to look directly at Bade.

"The purpose could be to embarrass Anduri," Bade explained. "After all, he's a progressive. His policies have been shredding the conservative power base of the Congress Party ever since he got in. Our reports consistently show a growing panic in the C.P., as well as among the military, to wrest control from him."

Moffett glanced at the President. He himself hadn't thought of that angle, but it did make sense. He jumped on it. "That could be it, sir. Remember, the last time China and India went head to head over territorial claims in '62, it brought Nehru down."

The President grunted twice, scratched his chin. Then he glanced at Novak. "What do you think?"

The NSA man shrugged his massive shoulders. "Hate to admit it, but it's a viable angle."

"So where does this—" The tiny chime of one of the telephones in a bank beside the President's chair sounded. He picked it up, listened a moment, said, "Thank you," and hung up. He looked at the others. "Well, the Indian shoe just fell. Delhi's apologized and agreed to pay reparations."

Everybody relaxed.

The President sighed and leaned back in his chair, crossed his arms. "Well, if this *was* a setup, the conservatives'll have their issue. Undoubtedly, the Congress press will label Anduri's acquiescence a capitulation and chop him good. But thank God the bastard had enough guts to make the right decision." He leaned forward again. "The only trouble is, will they try it again?"

"Could be, sir," Bade offered. "But there's one thing that might limit that possibility. The monsoon season's about to start all through that area. Once it does, it'd be militarily disastrous for anybody to start anything over there."

"How far off is it?"

"I'm not certain. Perhaps a week, a bit more."

"Well, there's still time for it to be touchy. Everybody keep a tight eye on this thing. I'll tell Bains to pull it up on the agenda for U.N. discussion." He rose. "Thank you all for coming."

The others instantly came to their feet, said their good nights, and headed for the door. Moffett hesitated, turned back. "Sir, could I see you a moment?"

The President waved him back to his seat. "What's the problem?"

Moffett recounted his recent conversation with Captain Peck over the heavy concentrations of Chinese troops along the borders of the old Soviet republics and about the mock-up results JAD had come up with. He had personally discussed it with Scott Clark that morning. After he completed the summary, he added, "I didn't want to mention it in front of Novak, sir. After all, JAD's in his bailiwick."

The President frowned. "I don't like the sound of this, Jack." He thought a moment. "You think this Indian thing could have any link?"

"I doubt it, sir."

"My God, if China starts crossing into old Soviet lands, we could end up with one confoundedly confused situation on our hands." He thrust himself to his feet, walked about, his silk bathrobe rustling softly. "It could mean a return to a unified Russia and a major war all in one swoop."

"Well, it's merely theoretical as yet, sir," Moffett said. "As Clark pointed out, even if China did try such a move, the CIS could be too fragmented to respond. They might just let the Chinese have the damned land."

The President gave him a sour look. "Except that theories have a lousy habit of turning out to be true." He paused opposite Moffett, placed his palms on the table. "I want you to investigate this, Jack. All aspects." He considered a moment. "But just to keep egos out of it, go through your own intelligence network. Make your JAD requests for specific mock-ups low-key. But instruct Clark this is red-light stuff, and we want him to run every mock-up twist he can think of."

"Yes, sir," Moffett said and rose. The President walked him to the door.

Dawn brought with it a sudden dust storm across the vast Gangetic Plain, driving black clouds of dust and dry wind across central India. Created by a rapidly developing low-pressure area from the constant lift-off of heat over the parched interior of the subcontinent, it roared across the Haryana and Rajasthan plateaus with gusts reaching fifty knots. By mid-morning, the cities of the Plain, including Delhi, were covered in a whirling darkness. Called a *rohini,* such windstorms are the heralds of the monsoon.

Far to the west, the southern African coastline was being pounded by the wind-driven surf of the Somali Current as it churned up from the equator. Vast blocks of ocean air, displaced by the thrust of the main storms, were already curling eastward, turning the Arabian and Indian oceans choppy. Gale warnings were being posted in the Maldive Islands, while fisherman on the Malabar and Sri Lankan coasts feverishly worked the vast schools of tuna, *chala,* and shark that were being drawn into shallow water by the colder flows coming down from the north.

Meanwhile, a second force, also driving off the equator, was headed for the Bay of Bengal, Sumatra, and the Malaysian peninsula. All along the Bengal and Indian Ocean coasts, storm birds drifted in on the high, hot winds. Meteorologists, watching the rapidly forming isobar vortices on their charts, realized that the crossing of the monsoon fronts over land would occur earlier than expected. Perhaps by as much as thirty hours.

9

McCarran's boat was a twenty-footer called a *seram*. Its name meant silk and was derived from the silken sails an ancient river god had used as he searched for the headwaters of the Ganges. The hull was formed of overlapped teak strakes like a Viking warship. In profile, it looked as if it were traveling backward, the prow low and blunt with a gradual rise to a high, narrow stern.

Hak had shifted the huge tiller to the starboard side and replaced the centerline with a long, vaned propeller shaft linked to an old Morris Oxford four-cylinder car engine mounted inboard. A wooden cabin covered with thatch sat amidships. It was cluttered with freshwater tanks, hunting packs, and McCarran's rifles. At a steady cruise the boat could make fifteen knots.

Hak had roused Cas and Jackie while it was still dark. The river was blanketed in mist. Malli made them a breakfast of sweet cakes and thick coffee, and Hak suggested they change out of their tennis shoes. ''Ruddy unfit for jungle,'' he said. He loaned Bonner a pair of his own, and Malli gave Jackie *cappals*, soft boots made from goat skin. Then she went off to perform her *savera puja*, the morning prayer, with special flowers to Indra, patron of travelers, to protect them on their way.

It was cool on the river as McCarran guided the

seram into midstream. Fishing boats were already out, their kerosene lanterns drifting past like floating jinns. But gradually light began to filter through the mist until the sky glowed lavender.

Soon the mist dissipated completely before a slight breeze. The river was very low, its bank high and dust dry. People were wading in the muddy current casting flowers and bits of food into the river. Young boys washed oxen along the mudflats, the animals standing on their own reflections in water shining like gold.

Quickly the breeze turned hot, and the sun rose into a dry haziness that made it look like a red plate above the horizon. Jackie, who had been silently riding forward with Dabu, retreated to the cabin. Bonner went aft and hunkered down beside McCarran.

"How far do we have to go?" he shouted over the open rumble of the engine."

"About four hundred kilometers. It'll take us a couple of days."

"How do we approach this thing?"

"I figure we can reconnoiter Lake Sonai first, maybe spot something if we're lucky. Might be a little touchy, though. Singh's headquarters are on an island, and there's a bleeding oil derrick there, too. Lots of patrol boats in the area."

They fell silent for a few minutes. High over the river, ring-tailed eagles drifted on the heat updrafts. Hak took a shot of whiskey, passed the bottle to Bonner.

Handing it back, Cas asked, "How long you been in India?"

"About thirty years, off and on."

Bonner shook his head. "I don't think I could cut it out here that long. Too many people."

"Aye, that there is. And a damned sight more that'd

make a Madonna weep. But it's got its own kind of magic, too. Gets in your ruddy blood.''

"I noticed your Air Service shields. Second World War?"

"Aye." For a while Hak was silent, then he began to talk. Slowly, matter-of-factly, he told Cas about his past. Born in Aberdeen, Scotland, he'd gone into the military at sixteen, served time in a commando unit at eighteen. Later, he became a veteran of Special Forces campaigns in Malaya and Borneo. "When the Red Star insurgents were cocking off plantations one a week," he chuckled. "Made the Foreign Office bloody perturbed."

Later, recruited into British Intelligence, he spent time in Sumatra, the Solomons, and finally India. Eventually he had grown tired of it. "All that cloak-and-dagger thrust and parry. Rather a silly way to live a man's life." He brought out the bottle again and watched as Cas took a hit. "You mind if I settle a curious, Bonner?"

"What's that?"

"What made you take that ruddy submersible of yours down to the bottom despite captain's orders?"

"Curiosity, mainly."

"That sort of curiosity can get you booted from ranks."

Cas nodded. "Yeah, it's done that often enough."

Hak smiled, his pale blue eyes twinkling. "That's what I thought."

They talked and drank, swapping stories of each other's pasts while the old *seram* plowed steadily through the green-brown water. The land beyond the banks changed gradually. In places the jungle came right down to the river, and they saw elephants working back in the forests hauling logs. There were riverside villages Hak called *agraharams* where women, their saris hiked up to form breeches, beat clothes on rocks and young toughs threw stones out at the boat.

Here and there they noticed little processions of villagers coming down to the river, carrying red and yellow banners and makeshift tridents, the symbols of the god Siva. Chanting in unison, the people would dip them into the river, swing them in three circles, and then cast them far out into the water. Hak explained that they were calling the monsoon.

After a while, Bonner, feeling a bit giddy from the whiskey, went forward to the cabin. Jackie was dozing. He tapped her arm. "How's it going?"

She sat up, sweat shining on her face. "I've seen better."

"Seasick?"

"A bit." She glanced back at McCarran. "You two've been having quite a talk session. Get everything worked out, did you?"

He grinned at her. "Heat make you bitchy?"

"Among other things." She frowned at him. "You're half drunk."

"Not quite." He shook his head, feeling a headache coming on. "But if I keep downing that rotgut of Hak's, I will be."

She groaned boredly and held her face to the scorching breeze that swept over the bow. Dabu was sitting cross-legged up there eating a fish wrapped in a greasy newspaper.

"How long before we get to Dibrugarh?" she asked.

"I'm not sure. McCarran said we're almost to Bishnath. Up beyond it is where he found the dead crocs."

"Tell him I want to put into some of the villages up there, to check for symptoms."

Cas nodded and went aft again.

The land changed once more, this time into long stretches of *killi* grass dotted with six-foot anthills.

Now and again they could see distant villages shimmering in the heat haze, surrounded by the pale green of sugarcane fields. Little bamboo towers stood in the fields with strings of tin cans dangling that chased off the wild boars that came at night to feed on the cane.

North of Bisnath, they came upon a funeral procession moving along the edge of the river, fifty or sixty people all very excited and milling. In the center four men carried a bier made of bamboo. On it lay a body wrapped in red linen, the sign that it was a woman. A large yellow garland was draped over the corpse.

It was past noon and the sun made the air heavy with a fierce heat. Beyond the riverbank, the land was marshy, forming open stretches of muddy water and mudflats, where purple herons and ibis fed. Hak said it was ideal croc country.

He pointed upriver to a collection of hilly islands. "Those are the Majulis," he said. "It was in those *jheels* out there that I found the crocs with your bloody fungus."

Jackie instantly requested they land so she could get a glimpse of the body. Hak shook his head. "You don't interfere with these people when they're in *ronadhona,* missy. Mourning creates a strange frenzy in an Indian. Besides, you wouldn't be allowed to examine the body."

"Are they going to cremate it?" she asked.

He nodded. "Back at that woodpile." A half mile downstream they had passed a large mound of teak being prepared by two thin Indians in *dhotis.* Hak identified them as members of the Dom caste who performed cremations for a fee.

"Will they at least permit us to watch?"

Hak gave her a narrow look. "You ever see a cremation ritual? It can be a bit disturbing."

"You forget I'm a doctor."

He shrugged and edged the prow of the boat into the muddy bank. Leaving Dabu aboard, the three of them walked off to join the procession, keeping to the rear. It seemed a strange affair, both sorrowful and festive at the same time. People carrying flowers babbled, wept, held up their arms, laughed. Now and then one of them would dart in and touch a man in the lead with a shaved head. He, in turn, would press his palm against their arm or shoulder, and the touched villager would then retreat, grinning wildly.

"That one's the eldest son of the dead woman," Hak explained. "Apparently he's recently returned from a pilgrimage, probably to Kashi. By touching him these people share in his *darshan*, the blessing from the god's shrine."

"Why the shaved head?" Bonner asked.

"It's a sign of mourning. Until his hair grows back, he's entitled to particular respect."

They reached the funeral pyre. The men carrying the bier released it to the two Doms. The cremators went about their business methodically, very business-like, placing the corpse onto the pyre. Then the mourners all shouted at once and began circling it, each dropping or tossing flowers onto the red linen.

At last the eldest son approached. He was holding a heavy wooden club. He stood perfectly still at the head of the corpse while the Doms doused the wood and bier with fuel oil. They lit a handful of grass and handed it to him. He bent and tossed it on the pyre. There was a soft whoosh as the oil caught fire. Smoke lifted off into the still air, first black, then a greasy white as the dried teak began to burn.

The son closed his eyes a moment, then lifted his club and brought it down with great force on the corpse's head. It struck with the sharp crack of a baseball striking a bat. Both Cas and Jackie jumped. A moment later a dark stain formed on the red linen.

"God!" Jackie cried, inhaling sharply. "Why'd he do that?"

"It was his duty," McCarran answered evenly. "The skull has to be opened to release the soul."

The fire was roaring now, smoke going up to hang in a flat cloud. And then the stench of burning flesh came, the linen curling, exposing the body. The shafts of the bamboo bier split in the heat, and the suction of the fire made strips of it whistle like trapped birds.

Jackie turned away and walked back toward the boat. Cas and Hak followed, walking among some of the villagers. McCarran started a conversation in Hindi with one of the men. His eyes were yellow and moist, and he continually blinked. He proudly showed Hak his arm where the woman's son had touched him.

After a few moments McCarran whistled for Jackie to come back. When she did, he looked at her a long moment before speaking. His sky blue eyes were hard. "You got anything in that bloody medical kit of yours to counter this fungus?"

"Anti-serum." She got excited. "Why?"

"This woman was the fourth person to die here. In the last two weeks. And all had the same symptoms, horrible body cramps and finally asphyxiation."

"Oh, God, it's here!"

The cushions were of silk, high and billowy soft, the color of scarlet and amber. Sunk into them, two young Indian girls writhed, hands and mouths fluttering over each other's bodies. Sweat glistened on their dark skin, and they moaned and twittered in a sexual heat enhanced by *thandai,* milk laced with cannabis.

Across the high, red-and-yellow-striped tent, Abu Singh watched them with hot, wild eyes. He too was naked. With him were two other girls, one with Oriental features. She was bent forward between his legs, pressing her breasts together against his immense penis. The other suckled his nipple.

Singh's lips drew back, relaxed, drew back again in response to the sensations surging through his body. At last, groaning, he drew himself to his knees. Twisting the girl who had been on his chest, he laid her on the pillows. In one violent plunge he entered her. She made a choking sound of pain and ecstasy, her legs snapping around his huge buttocks. Pounding, he arched, bit her neck, drawing blood. The other girl began licking his heaving back.

Orgasm trembled thickly through his loins, rising to a crescendo. He bellowed as he came. Still he plunged on. The Oriental, whimpering, coiled herself around him like a snake, wedging her body between his and the other girl's. Singh withdrew from the first, adjusted his knees, and slowly entered her exposed rectum.

The ground began to shake. Across the entrance flap, tiny silver bells hung on tassles tinkled softly. From outside came a rising thunder, the sharp cracking of tree trunks. A long, drawn-out cry was followed by a chorus of automatic fire.

Puzzled, Singh paused, still embedded in the girl. A slash of bullets tore through the side of the tent with the vicious sibilance of shrapnel. The Oriental girl lunged forward, disengaging. She started to stand but was instantly knocked down by a fresh train of bullets that tore into her face.

Horses screamed wildly, interspersed with the frenzied shouts of men and continuing gun bursts. The thunder increased until it seemed to envelop the tent, everything shaking. A Petromax lamp fell into the pil-

lows, instantly burst into flame. Through the chaos
sounded the furious trumpeting of elephants.

In one sweeping lunge Singh was on his feet. Still
in full erection, he scooped up a sword and made for
the entrance, tore the flap aside. Fifty feet away, an
elephant was charging straight at him, its trunk coiled
on its chest.

Out in the Sikh encampment, other elephants ram-
paged, trampling tents, tossing men into the air. Beyond, partially hidden by the jungle, BIM guerillas
fired into the melee.

With a roar the huge Indian reached back and ripped
away the string of bells. Whirling them in a circle, he
ran straight for the elephant. As he and the animal
closed, he hurled the bells into the elephant's face.
Instantly the behemoth veered slightly and lumbered
past him, smashing into the tent. As it passed, Singh
slashed the hamstring of its rear leg, swinging the
sword with both hands. The elephant fell to its side,
the great rump crumbling, folding down into the fallen
tent. A girl's shriek rose, was quickly cut off.

By now the elephants' charge had carried them
through the camp and into the jungle opposite.
Wounded and confused, they continued on, tearing
through the trees, their screams echoing back. The
firefight was now full-blown as the Sikhs got themselves organized and opened up. Through the maelstrom Singh strode, bellowing, his pendulous penis
quiescent.

Gradually the firing from the jungle slackened and
finally stopped as the guerillas, leaving their wounded,
melted back into the brush. The Sikhs followed, frenzied with bloodlust. They combed the area and found
three wounded guerillas. These were instantly decap-
itated and their *churkis,* pony tails, tied to the barrels
of the executioners' weapons.

They also found a wounded elephant down in grass near a small river. It had been lung shot and blood pumped from its trunk. It was wild-eyed with fear. It tried to rise when the Sikhs approached. They hammered away at it with hundreds of rounds that tore chunks of skin from its body, mud and blood spitting out into the water. Then they left it, still alive, as crocodiles began cutting wakes far up the river.

Back in the shambles of the encampment, Abu Singh, still naked, prowled like a tiger, eyes blazing. Dead horses and Sikhs lay all around. The elephant he had hamstrung continued to trumpet, still lying in the smashed tent, which was now burning strongly. Singh ordered someone to kill it lest it draw the others back. One of his men ran over and poked the muzzle of a heavy-bored rifle into the animal's ear and fired rounds until it went still.

By count, fourteen Sikhs had been killed, half as many wounded. Two of the harem girls were also dead, as were eight horses, and the rest had disappeared into the jungle.

Singh finally took himself off to sit beneath a peepul tree while the others cleaned up the mess. As he sat, the bloodstained sword across his knees, twilight crept through the jungle. His mind whirled with insane fury and thoughts of revenge. He knew who would pay, BIM sympathizers from the nearby logging operations at Moranhat, ten miles south of Dibrugarh. He knew that that was where the guerillas had gotten the elephants.

His first impulse was to mass his men and make a night attack on the logging camps, kill everything in sight. But then the savagery of his thoughts focused on another method. Yes, he'd destroy more than just a few loggers and their animals. He'd administer a profound warning to anyone who would dare challenge him in the future.

He summoned one of his lieutenants. The man came humbly, afraid to meet his leader's eyes. "Radio Lake House," Singh hissed. "Instruct Pramud that he is to take one of the metal boxes that hold the sickness the Russians brought and empty it into the river."

"Where is he to do this, Feared One?"

"At the docks of Dibrugarh."

Through the binoculars, the woman's face was homely, Slavic-wide, and puffy. Yet for the past two minutes General Zgursky's attention had been riveted on her. He was reading her expression. Like the telltale tremble of a single thread in a wind, heralding a coming storm, he was using her face to gauge the mood of the fifty thousand people around her. Hers was sullen and angry.

It was late afternoon in Moscow, and it had drizzled all day. Despite that, people had gathered in Red Square: factory workers, shoppers exiting from the nearby GUM mall and its empty shelves, aimless soldiers, clerks, street girls. Everybody drifted in spontaneously to stand silently like dark mourners outside the grim red walls of the Kremlin.

As the size of the crowd increased, the Moscow police, growing anxious, sent in more and more horse-mounted officers to patrol the perimeters. Dressed in blue parkas, their animals' harnesses gleaming dully, they prowled the radiating boulevards and avenues. No attempt was made to disperse the crowd, yet the officers were clearly edgy.

With them came the opportunists, pickpockets, and political activists, mostly from the pro-Communist Tridovaya Moskva and Nashi unions. Soon red Soviet flags and portraits of Josef Stalin appeared. Murmurs riffled through the crowd, punctuated by shouts calling for the downfall of the traitor Viktor Seleznov and his capitalistic policies that had plunged the country into near chaos. A small band materialized and played the Soviet anthem over and over.

As Zgursky watched, the woman in his binoculars suddenly lifted her arm, fist clenched, and shouted something. "Yes," he growled. "Now! Order Taranenko to strike at once. The mob is ready."

Two hours earlier, when informed of the gathering in Red Square, he and his Phoenix associates had immediately leaped at the chance offered. He sent several men into the crowd. All were armed with camcorders that carried concealed 9mm Berettas with silencers. Then he and his aides, both young ex-paratroopers, took up a station in a shabby hotel on Kujbyseva Avenue to monitor the proceedings in the square.

At his command, one of the paratroopers took out a small hand radio and spoke into it. "Where are you, T.?"

The answer came back as clear as a telephone call: "East side of stand."

"Activate."

"*Da.*"

Zgursky swung his glasses from the woman and across the crowd to the far end of the huge reviewing stand near the east wall. A small clot of mounted police were gathered there. Eyes narrowed, he picked out the tallest. He was broad-shouldered and sat very straight in the saddle.

Suddenly the policeman jerked slightly, as if a stick had been jammed into his back. Turning slightly, he slipped out of the saddle and fell to the ground. The unexpected movement made his horse skitter to the side. Instantly several officers rushed over and knelt to examine him.

"Good, good," Zgursky shouted happily. "Again. Now!"

He shifted his glasses to a second mounted policeman. The man's head snapped to the left, and a burst of blood spewed from one cheek. The kneeling officers all leaped up, and a woman screamed. Then things began happening rapidly down in the square.

More mounted policemen converged onto the two fallen officers. Frantically people began running, trying to get out of the way. One of the approaching officers was knocked completely out of his saddle and went somersaulting over the horse's flanks.

For a few moments total confusion reigned near the reviewing stand. Then one incoming policeman, enraged, swung his horse to the left and bored directly into the crowd. He slashed left and right with his whip, knocking people aside. One woman went down under the horse's hooves and tumbled, leaving a swath of blood on the wet cobblestones.

Like a charging lion, a second officer drove into the mass of people. He bellowed, holding his machine pistol up in the air. There was a shot. The officer twisted, grabbing his arm as the weapon clattered across the ground. A young man in the crowd ran forward and picked it up, swung around, and threw a burst at the horse and rider. The animal reared, screaming wildly, and crashed down.

Four distinct bursts of automatic fire erupted from the policemen, and the man with the machine pistol was lifted into the air. Beyond him, people dropped to the ground, trying to crawl out of the line of fire. Farther out, people began running hysterically, heading for the sanctuary of the GUM and the grassy knolls of Oktober Boulevard.

The police, driving spurs into their animals' flanks, tore after them, focusing their fury on anyone with a banner or a sign. Isolated shots sounded, little muffled pops. Another policeman was knocked off his horse. Reserve police units thundered in from the radiating avenues, and right behind them armored vehicles and ambulances. Their sirens warbled and echoed between the buildings.

The general lowered the glasses. He was short, robustly built with thick, coarse gray hair and jagged teeth. "Come, we've seen enough," he snapped.

The three men left the room and descended a stairwell to a dark lobby with brown wainscotting and tattered furniture. The concierge and his wife were standing in the doorway, excitedly trying to see out into the street. The men edged swiftly past them, ducked into a parked Zil, and sped off.

The general gazed thoughtfully out the window, smiling and nodding his head as reports from Taranenko came through the radio. Fire hoses were being used, and the police had fired more bursts. There were many dead and wounded. At this last statement Zgursky uttered, "Wonderful!" and shook his two fists in the air.

Forty minutes later, in a house overlooking the Moscow River, he met with his two highest-ranking co-conspirators. One was General Alexi Ostalsky, chief of staff for Marshal Ivan Sudenkov, commanding general of the Commonwealth armed forces. Ostalsky had recently been voted to head the Dashka, a group of five thousand active officers who had met in Moscow to form a union to represent the military in political discussions with the CIS. The other was Sergei Granov, who had once been first chief director of foreign intelligence for the KGB.

Ostalsky opened the conversation with the latest update of casualties in Red Square. Twenty-three dead, he said, at least two hundred wounded. More important, the populace was seething over what appeared to be a brutal and unprovoked attack by the Moscow police.

"Seleznov is tearing his hair out," the general said with grim pleasure. "Reports are already coming in from St. Petersburg, Chelyabinsk, and Rostov of spontaneous reactions occurring there, too. Even in the capitals of Georgia, the Ukraine, and Turkmenistan there are demonstrations mounting."

Granov sipped his vodka, his narrow, ferret-like face frowning. "Perhaps this is not as good a situation as we might think, comrades. It could bring things to a head too quickly. We're not ready to move yet."

Zgursky waved that off. "No, it will not explode yet. Seleznov will maintain control, but this will leave a sour residue. Now some of those who have been hesitant will come to us."

"I agree," Ostalsky said. "As far as the Dashka is concerned, my officers will be outraged over this. There were soldiers injured today. But, I fear, they will still hesitate."

Zgursky sat forward. "Now is the time to probe, Alexi. Take this opportunity to find out precisely who we can count on when the time comes."

The general nodded.

Zgursky turned to Granov. "What have you managed to pick up about the Chinese?"

"My reports are still fragmented, but something definite is happening." Although KGB listening posts around the world had been literally dismantled when the USSR fell, there was still a cadre of intelligence personnel in most countries, including China. Granov, with his personal contacts, was able to assemble cogent intelligence data. "Lots of Beijing military meetings and rumors of heavy troop movements out of several provinces. All headed west."

Zgursky gleefully slapped his palm on his knee. "Good old Qin, holding true to form." Zgursky personally knew the Chinese general. As a young officer, he had been assigned as a military liaison to the PLA. Although he had contempt for Qin's homosexuality, which had been known for years, he greatly respected the man's abilities as a field tactician and his highly aggressive nature. "Yes, it all begins to fall into place."

Then, remembering something, he went to a desk and took out a radio transcription. It was from Kurisovsky, relaying his preparations for his attack on the Thailand base along with the latest meteorological update of the Indian moonsoon.

Granov was the first to read it. After doing so, he glanced up. "It is ironic comrade, how neatly the schedule is fitting. Even nature seems with us."

"What is it?" Ostalsky asked.

"The monsoon is predicted to strike India within five days, a full thirty hours sooner than expected."

Zgursky held up his glass of vodka. "Comrades, to the Phoenix and the Indian monsoon."

10

All through the long, brain-numbing heat of afternoon, Jackie Dunbar administered to another stricken Indian woman they had found in the village. She saturated her with anti-toxin, kneaded her muscles when the terrifying spasms hit, and cleaned away the bloody sputum and watery diarrhea that fouled the floor of her hut. Now and then the woman would thrash uncontrollably, hissing wild-eyed at her like an animal tortured beyond sanity.

Meanwhile, Cas, Hak, and Dabu prowled along the riverbank to find the precise source of the fungus; they probed through the mudflats with sticks and examined the hut foundation stilts where they entered the moist ground. Squinting against the stench, they went through mounds of human and animal feces. Some of the women and children curiously followed them around, squatting on their haunches and jabbering.

Cas periodically returned to check on Jackie. The Indian woman had worsened. He watched as Dunbar cut into her neck to insert a rubber tube to assist her breathing. He was impressed at how calmly and expertly Jackie went about the procedure, blood dripping off her gloves while she probed with her finger to separate the distended muscles and fibers around the windpipe. When she inserted the tube, it looked grotesque, like a thick yellow leech protruding from the woman's body. He took off his T-shirt and wiped the sweat off Jackie's face.

Afterward, they stepped out onto the catwalk for some fresh air. It came across the grassland, freighted with heat. "Well?" Cas asked.

"The anti-toxin isn't strong enough." She gazed distractedly across the sluggish river.

"Look, take a break. Go back to the boat. I'll watch her."

"No. Where's McCarran?"

"Still searching."

She turned away, but he took her arm. "There's no sense killing yourself, Jackie. This heat's going to hit you, you're not used to it."

Angrily she jerked her arm free. "Just leave me alone." She bent to enter the shack, then paused and turned around, smiling ruefully. "Hey, I'm sorry. It's just that I have to sit and watch this poor creature die. I feel so goddamned helpless." She disappeared into the shack.

Dabu found the first sign of fungi, on a discarded banana leaf with bits of fish meat and hardened kernels of rice stuck to it. McCarran brought it to Bonner. "Is this your fungus?"

Cas squinted at the bits of food. In the flesh were minute dots, the color of pearly sapphires. He nodded. "Yeah, that's it."

"Bloody hell," Hak hissed. "It was under one of the shacks upstream. That means somebody besides that woman's ingested this godawful stuff."

He gathered the villagers together down on the mud-flats and showed them the fungus. There were mostly women and children and a few old men. The younger men had already returned to their fishing following the funeral procession. In Hindi, he explained that the green substance was very poisonous. *Dehant hara,* he called it, green death. He told them to search all over for it and burn anything that had been touched by it. Even their animals.

Each villager approached, peered down at the banana leaf, then stepped back, face closed down with that absurd blankness Indians get when they think they're being deceived. Any thought of killing their animals over some tiny green dots was absurd. Although they knew and trusted McCarran, this simply couldn't be accepted. Shaking their heads and murmuring, they walked away.

Hak watched them leave, shaking his head. "I didn't think they'd buy it."

"What's the matter? Don't they believe you?"

"Why should they? That fish came from the river. Their gods put it there for them to catch, and gods don't do anything to hurt people."

Just before sundown, an old man came trudging slowly across the grassland. Over his shoulders he carried a boy of about eight. The boy was very ill and the old man's back was covered with watery diarrhea that had soaked into his *dhoti*.

As he neared the far end of the river village, several of the returned fishermen stopped him. Brandishing machetes, they made him lay the boy down on the hard-packed ground. The child's body was thin, contorted.

Hak went out to talk with the old man. After a moment he came back and told Jackie she'd best go have a look. "I think the kid's got the thing, too."

"Bring him in."

Hak shook his head. "Can't, he's from a lower caste than these people."

"So?"

"They won't allow him in. He'd contaminate them."

"Well, shit," Jackie snapped and then followed Hak

back out to the boy. Cas went along. Her examination told her it was the fungus infection. The boy was racked by violent muscular contractions every few minutes, and from his sunken eyes and extremely low blood pressure, she knew he was also suffering acute dehydration.

As night came on, Jackie shuttled back and forth from the shack to the little spot in the grass with Bonner hauling lanterns and water pails. McCarran and Dabu continued their search for more fungus, their lanterns bobbing about down on the mudflats. Out in the grass, jackals prowled.

Around nine-thirty the woman slipped into a coma and died within ten minutes. Hak immediately informed the village men, and one of them untied his boat and went to fetch the Doms. Jackie returned to the boy.

After a while Hak came out. "I think it's time we move on," he said quietly. "We'll take the boy along and leave him in Dibrugarh."

"I agree," Bonner said.

"All right," Jackie said. "But what about the old man?"

"He comes, too."

Dabu came running up. Hak swung around at the sound of his footsteps. They talked rapidly in Hindi for a moment, and then McCarran glanced at Bonner.

"Seems we've got some company, lad," he said. "Horsemen. Out in the grass."

Scott Clark took a thankful bite of his jelly roll and washed it down with a gulp of steaming coffee. It was the first food he'd had since seven that morning. Now it was mid-afternoon in Washington.

He, along with four other men, was in the JAD War-Game Room, known as R-32, located in the basement of the Pentagon. They had just completed a simulated reaction scenario centered on the recent Indo/Chinese situation, and had started the post-game discussion called the "hot wash-up."

As always, Scott was struck by the almost locker-room aspect of this particular part of the simulation protocol. The men were still slightly hyped from the action-reaction aspects of the game, like ball players after a challenging contest. Present were General Jake Hind from the Army War College in Carlisle, Pennsylvania; NCO Staff Captain Ross Gould; Senator Lee Osburg of Arizona; and a think-tanker from the Harvard-based RIM Corporation, Roderick Tamaguchi.

The senator moved about, slapping everybody on the shoulder with a meaty hand. "Helluva coordinated effort, gentlemen," he boomed. "We make a damned fine team, don't we?"

"I still think our fleet reaction in the Med and Indian oceans should have been quicker and stronger," General Hind said. "Hell, that third scenario damned near got the Chinese all the way to Delhi before U.N. intervention started having any effect at all."

"That's the point, Jake," Osburg countered. "U.N. reaction was too slow. The President should have forced an emergency session within two hours after the invasion."

Captain Gould shook his head. "Wouldn't have done any good. Whatever resolution came out of it would have taken days, weeks to implement. The Chinese moved too fast."

Scott listened intently to the talk. This kind of relaxed conversation often held more insight than the game itself. He knew that the players, regardless of their credentials, usually had the tendency to downplay facts and trends, reacting instead to hunches based on their feelings when interpreting signals. It was called playing the "gambler's board."

Yet he had to admit that in this particular situation, he was haunted by his own gut feelings. At forty-two, Scott was normally a man of controlled passions, despite the casual impression given by his longish brown hair, beard, and persistent "uniform" of checkered work shirt and Levis. It was just that something about this Indo/Chinese thing bugged him. It sat out there like Gatsby's green light. As he had pointed out to the Secretary of Defense, his gut said it could involve the Russians.

This particular game was the ninth in a scheduled series of twelve. Obeying the President's instructions to keep the whole thing low-key, he had run small games, not utilizing the SINBAC network of linked commanders around the world, or the mainframe computers at the National Defense University at Fort McNair, D.C. When all twelve were completed, he intended to write up a blue paper for Secretary Moffett. Then, based on the reaction that brought, he'd probably ask for more powerful simulations.

He turned to Tamaguchi, who had been silent. "What do you think, Rod?"

"I agree with the general and captain that a show of force immediately after the invasion of either side would prevent escalation," Tamaguchi answered. He was small and nattily dressed in a brown silk suit. "But I sense something else here."

Scott leaned forward slightly. "What's that?"

"Russian involvement."

"In the invasion or its aftermath?" Scott shot back.

"In the aftermath. I don't believe this incursion had anything to do with Indian politics or Alliance intrigue. I think it was a Chinese ploy, similar to Hitler's demonstrations in Czechoslovakia. Except that the main target isn't India at all but rather the old Russian republics and the rising influence of the Alliance.''

Osburn scoffed. "That's a helluva scenario, Yamaguchi. Chinese killing Chinese? Hell, our game results already discounted any Russkie reaction. Ivan isn't powerful enough anymore to even piss on a high stump.''

The Japanese said evenly, "I don't mean Russian border reactions.''

"Then what the hell do you mean?''

"Internal ones.''

Oh, yeah, Scott thought. He probed further. "What reactions, precisely?''

"A return to centralized Communist power in Moscow.''

"That's always a possibility," General Hind put in. "But I see it as remote. The Chinese would certainly be aware of that risk. They wouldn't take on India, the Alliance, *and* a reformed USSR all at once.''

"Perhaps they perceive the results as worth the risk. They need western buffers.''

"What about an Alliance probe of the Chinese will to fight?" Captain Gould countered. "Our intelligence out of Iran is, frankly, shabby as hell. For all we know, those crazy bastards are armed and gunning.''

Scott eased back. The conversation was slipping out of the glow of his green light again, the players returning to the gambler's board. He let it run for another ten minutes, then called a halt. Thanking everybody for attending, he ushered the four men out.

As he walked around the green baize-covered game table gathering the players' pads and his own notes, he munched thoughtfully on another jelly roll. Something was missing in the scenario, he thought, a direct link that would put all the pieces neatly into place.

Just before leaving, he paused long enough to write a short memo to Secretary Moffett. In it he asked that a diplomatic request be sent through channels to the Indian Intelligence office for data on recent insurgency and terrorist activity in the entire NEFA sector, with particular attention to Assam state. As an afterthought, he included a second request for similar data from the British Intelligence field station at Singapore.

Kurisovsky's attack didn't go smoothly at all.

The tiny Thai base of Kau Moo Rah was as remote as a Mayan ruin in Belize. It was situated in a valley at the base of a nine-thousand-foot mountain just east of the Burma–Thailand border. Surrounding it were thick teak and silver oak forests, and a mile to the southeast, under jagged cliffs, ran the chocolate brown Kuthawaddy River.

At precisely 8:03 P.M. Thailand time, Kurisovsky sent four of his nine-man force parachuting into the jungle near the river. Quick, static-line leaps at four hundred feet, the heavily armed troopers disappearing out the side of the C-47 in the faint lingering twilight.

Immediately after, the Aussie pilots swung the aircraft south, ran for ten minutes to allow the downed troopers to get into position around the base, then made a one-eighty and headed back toward Kau Moo Rah.

Both pilots were bitching openly. They'd never been into this particular airfield, which had been bulldozed out of the jungle. Coming in at night with cliffs on the right and foothills on the left was going to be a ''bleedin' Buckley's chance,'' they said.

Playing the starboard engine throttle to give the impression of distress, they started swinging the radio and calling ''Mayday,'' the international sign of distress. Nothing came back from the Kau Moo Rah transmitter. They kept on, the dark hills rising through the windows and the ground coming on quickly. The faint outline of the runway remained out there between the trees in the faint light.

Kurisovsky, seated just aft of the cabin bulkhead, noted a small collection of camp fires he hadn't seen before along the sides of the river cliffs. Then they touched down, the C-47's wheels hitting hard and clattering across the metal matting of the runway.

By the time they got stopped and turned around, headlights were coming their way. A few moments later two jeeps filled with Thai soldiers pulled up beside the aircraft's port wing. In the blinking lights the Russians could see .50-caliber machine guns mounted on each vehicle and the Thai soldiers carrying M-16 rifles.

One of the soldiers began jabbering and shoving the muzzle of his rifle up at the pilot. The Aussie killed his engines, the cylinder explosions dropping suddenly and the huge blades swinging with momentum. The Thai started shouting again.

"Speak English, you bleedin' swiggie," the pilot yelled back. "You makee English talk-talk?" Behind him in the fuselage, Kurisovsky's men took positions beside the cargo door.

"Who you?" the soldier shouted back. "What you fuck want?"

"One o' my bleedin' engines is gone, mate. Din't you hear it?"

"No can stay here. You get out." Several soldiers climbed out of the jeeps and stood under the wing, slamming the butts of their rifles against the metal.

"I can't, you bloody choong," the Aussie yelled. He shot an anxious glance back at Kurisovsky.

"I say you get out," the soldier shouted. "Got-damn Yank. We—"

He never finished his sentence. Kurisovsky's men flung open the cargo door and opened up on the soldiers. Thai bodies went flying in all directions. There was one returning burst, which blew the port tire of the C-47.

Instantly a machine gun from the main part of the base opened up, arcing tracer rounds over the top of the aircraft. Two Russians leaped down and ran over to the jeeps. Swiveling the mounted .50s, they banged away at the opposing gun and it soon fell silent.

Using the vehicles, Kurisovsky and his men headed for the main compound, laying down a steady barrage into the huts as they went. There were a few, sporadic returning shots but nothing concerted. As they neared the first group of huts, sounds of more firing came, from far off to the left where the river cliffs lay and the troopers had jumped. Kurisovsky stood up in the jeep's passenger seat, glaring in that direction.

They roared into the compound. All of the huts were made of bamboo with peaked roofs and fenced pigpens. A Thai dashed across an open space, his shadow against light. They cut him down. A small burst of automatic fire flared from one of the huts to the right. They answered it with a concentrated barrage. The bamboo walls blew apart and the firing stopped.

The Russians dismounted and darted through the compound, holding to good fire-and-movement technique. A grenade blew a hut to pieces, the bamboo splinters zipping through the air. Another went. They were through to the outside perimeter. There were storage barns there, also of bamboo, and two 155mm gun pits, the howitzers canted high. Between them, its wheels and lower carriage sunk in cement, was an American BM-27 MLRS rocket launcher.

Sporadic fire continued from the river cliffs, but gradually it diminished. Kurisovsky hurried his men back through the compound once more. Except for fifteen dead Thais, it was empty. The main force had apparently retreated into the jungle after the initial attack.

They prowled through the huts. The whole cantonment was in a state of deterioration: grass and weeds sprouting between emplacement sandbags, outside weapons uncanvased and showing rust, inside weapons lying in pools of rainwater. They found the reason in the storage sheds. These were filled with contraband, stacks of boxes filled with antibiotic and surgical instruments, bales of high-grade marijuana and kilos of raw heroin. There were also bags of rough gems, rubies, and sapphires, and between the huts a series of wash boxes, high-pressure hoses, and vibrator jig belts used to filter ore.

The officers' hooches, in contrast, were opulent, with silver and porcelain dishes and cases of champagne and silk bunks covered with female garments smelling of powdered cinnamon bark called *thanaka* and vaginal fluids. Obviously, the entire base force had been more occupied with smuggling than keeping border guard.

The firing from the river started up again, this time closer. Kurisovsky ordered two men to take a jeep and find out what was going on. They roared off across the runway. At the other end, the Aussies had gotten repair lights out and were standing around staring at the blown tire.

Then the sniping started, scattered shots from the jungle accompanied by Thai obscenities. The bullets snapped through the hut roofs, and everybody, including the two Aussies, hit the ground. Pumping his arm, Kurisovsky sent his men out after the snipers. They melted off into the trees.

Suddenly a fresh, furious chatter of Kalashnikovs

blared from the south end of the runway, their muzzle flashes visible in the underbrush. Then the jeep drove in, the men aboard firing back into the jungle. Yells and screams came from the trees, and a moment later the shadows of running men broke free of the undergrowth and raced after the vehicle.

The jeep screeched to a stop near the cantonment headquarters building, and everybody bailed out, falling flat on their stomachs. On came the charging men, the lights from the buildings flashing on lifted machetes and a few revolvers. The Russians in the camp and those back in the woods opened up, laying a vicious field of fire across the runway. Bullets came back, singing and zipping through the air.

The momentum of the charge carried the foremost men to the very edge of the lights. They were Tangkhul tribesmen, bellowing and half naked, their heads shaved like Iroquois. In the steady, methodic Russian fire, the front ranks crumbled. Those behind came up against the fallen, hesitated, then turned and ran wildly back to the protection of the jungle.

One of the troopers crawled over to Kurisovsky. His head was bleeding. "There's a miners' camp down on the river, sir," he said dispassionately. "Didn't see them until they came out of holes in the cliffs like damn vermin and overran us."

"How many men gone?"

"Two."

Kurisovsky cursed and stood up. One sniper was still popping away from behind the camp. The colonel ignored him. He whistled, twirling his arm. Within a minute, troopers converged on him. Snapping curt orders, he set up a perimeter of fire around the cement-encased launcher and sent three troopers to the plane with one of the jeeps. It was loaded with sandbags from the gun emplacements to protect the C-47's engines.

The next four hours were hellish. While three men worked at dismantling the launcher, the others watched for gun flashes from the jungle and then blew rounds at them. Once another charge materialized but was quickly driven back. In frustration, the Thais skulked around in the underbrush, even throwing stones and sharpened bamboo spears.

Laboriously the work continued, the teams changing places periodically. Even Kurisovsky took his turn unbolting rusty components and manhandling them to the jeep, where they were hauled back to the plane and loaded aboard.

He was grim with rage. The information about the launcher from Moscow had been incorrect. It wasn't a Sparrow VLS. That meant they'd have to revamp the essential components of the MLRS even more at Lake House so it would take the Iraqi missiles. New firing sleeves and rails would have to be built, and heavy reinforcement and baffling plates mounted around the after housings to prevent explosive pressure and shock waves from blowing the whole apparatus apart during launch.

The pilots added another glitch. The aircraft tire couldn't be repaired, they said. The only plausible solution was to winch up the strut and place a skid under it. But that presented a problem. With the added weight of the launcher and the slower takeoff run due to the drag of the skid, they might never get off at all. Kurisovsky ordered them to make the skid.

With the midnight moon forming blue-white shadows through the encroaching trees, the dismantling of the MLRS's usable components was finally completed. Next, they turned to constructing the sawbuck scaffold on the runway in order to winch up the aircraft. The

Aussies had ingeniously fashioned a skid from a beveled teak log and encased it in strips of bamboo. This was frame-bolted to the strut.

But the pilot was adamant about off-loading some of the launcher parts. "I'm tellin' you, mate," he growled to the colonel, "we try takin' off wi' all that bloody metal, we'll fair wallop them trees for sure."

"Nothing comes off," Kurisovsky snapped.

"Then I ain't bloody flyin' her."

Kurisovsky stepped close, his voice as icy as an arctic breeze. "Yes, you will, comrade."

The Aussie couldn't face him down. He went back to the strut, cursing.

At last it was finished. The sandbags were removed from the engine cowlings, and the pilots hit the starters. The roar of the engines was like thunder. In the camp, they could see men moving back into the compound.

As a final gesture, Kurisovsky wired the throttles of both jeeps, pinned four delay-fused grenades to each seat, and sent them jouncing back toward the compound. One flipped over just as it reached the headquarters building, but the other blew into the porch and through the bamboo wall. When the grenades went, the explosions threw huge orange-white flashes up against the jungle trees.

Going slowly, the pilots brought the C-47 around, using full brake on the good wheel. By the time it was pointing back down the runway, the compound was in full conflagration. The fire made the distant trees look solid.

With the engines screaming, the Aussies built up power while still on brake. The aircraft surged and bounced, and runway debris slammed back into the after surfaces. The pilot was having a hard time holding against the surge of the aircraft with only one wheel braking.

But finally they got moving, the plane going heavily, sluggishly, the drag of the skid coming up through the floor, the burning compound of Kau Moo Rah closing and then it was right off the starboard wing. Thais were running around, their darting silhouettes looking like Aborigines around the mouth of a lava conduit. Two bullets crashed through the windshield and slammed into the bulkhead with a ringing sound. Both Aussies started cursing.

Ahead, the trees came up fast. Slivers of firelight danced in the higher branches while beyond, down the slope, the moonlight formed a vast blue-white tunnel between the river cliffs and the foothills.

Closer and closer came the line of trees, and still the C-47 remained aground. The scrape of the skid became loud enough to hear over the engines, and the fuselage shook violently.

Five hundred feet . . . four hundred . . .

Kurisovsky, face expressionless, watched the trees growing in height.

Three hundred . . .

At last there was a slight feel of lightness. And then the aircraft lifted off the Marsden mats, the pitch of the engine rebound changing slightly. Treetops loomed as if seen from the cab of a racing locomotive. A second later, they slashed across the windshield and front of the aircraft. The entire plane was jarred as the propellers tore through branches, hurling chunks of wood that slammed and banged all the way back along the fuselage.

But she was free, straining for altitude, the moonlit tunnel flattening out behind as the moon jerked and bounced through the side window.

Kurisovsky chuckled and tapped the pilot's shoulder with his knuckle. "Good," he said.

The Aussie whirled around, face contorted with rage. "Fuck you, you bleedin' Bolshevik barstad."

Still chuckling, the colonel turned and went aft to check on the launcher tie-downs.

11

The flare went off with a hollow, popping sizzle. Instantly the grassland, the shacks, even some of the river, were engulfed in a brilliant orange-white glare. Two hundred yards off, formed into a line, were nine horsemen.

"Sikhs," Hak said. He quietly issued Dabu an order, keeping his eyes on the horsemen. The Indian ran off, headed back toward the boat. "All right, Bonner," McCarran continued. "Let's make this slow and easy."

Cas hooked a hand under Jackie's arm to lift her. She pulled back. "What about the child? We can't just leave him."

"He'll be all right," Hak said. "They won't hurt him."

"No, I'm staying right here."

"Like hell you are," Bonner growled. He pulled her to her feet and shoved her toward the river. She shoved him back, and for a moment they jostled together. The old Indian rose and stood looking confusedly from one to the other.

"Damn you, Bonner," she cried, exasperated. "Either we take him or I stay."

"Come on, people," Hak crooned casually. "No bloody time for a lovers' quarrel."

Cas hissed an oath through his teeth, then turned

and scooped up the child. They started toward the fishing shacks, everybody walking normally, not looking back. Overhead, the flare drifted in the sky, trailing a faintly visible line of smoke.

There was a shout, then the pounding of hooves. A man bellowed a drawn-out cry as the horsemen charged.

Everyone broke into a run. Bonner, lifting the boy's body until it was just under his chin, could hear the child groaning, could smell the feces and kerosene scent of his breath. The thunder of the horses neared, the earth trembled.

The three reached the hard-packed ground above the shacks and crossed between overturned boats and goat pens. The animals, frightened, plunged against the wooden barriers, their eyes glistening in the flare's light. An automatic pistol opened up. It made tiny pops with even spaces between each explosion. Bullets whispered overhead. Jackie gave a little squeal and covered her head with her arms.

They went over the crest and down the bank, their legs sinking knee-deep into the foul-smelling mud. Ten feet away was the nearest shack. The entire village seemed suddenly deserted. Jackie stumbled and went down face first into the mud, still clutching her medical kit. Before she could extricate herself, McCarran bodily lifted her and hurried her under the shack's stilt platform.

Bonner struggled behind them, trying to keep his balance in the mushy ground. It sucked at his legs, distorted his gait. Cursing, he kept at it. In the air the thundering hooves seemed so close they formed an envelope of pounding sound.

Through it came two more bursts of gunfire. The wall of the shack splintered apart as the rounds ripped through and into the river, sending up tiny geysers.

Bonner could see Hak and Jackie crouching. Another burst followed. He heard a bullet strike flesh, felt the boy's body jolt upward and become stiff.

Nearby he heard the sharp, frantic whinny of a horse. A split second later, their merged shadows silhouetted against the fading light of the flare, a horse and rider burst into view above the crest of the bank. The rider was trying desperately to turn his mount, but it was too late. The animal threw its head back, hind legs driving against the ground as, in slow motion, the two hurtled out beyond the crest, sailed for a moment in a frenzied tableau, and then crashed headlong into the shack.

The flare went out.

Bonner lunged to the side and fell down, the boy slipping from his arms. He twisted up in time to see the riderless horse plunge through the shack and go into the river upside down. Following a soft whoosh, the mud and water beneath the pilings burst into flame from a shattered lantern. In its light, he saw McCarran clutching Jackie protectively, both lying on the upside of the bank. The horse thrashed in the water, screaming.

Another figure rose in front of the flames, popping up so swiftly it seemed to materialize out of the mud. The rider, his baggy white clothes black with mud, saw Bonner and swung his arm up, a machine pistol in his hand.

Before he could pull the trigger, Cas lunged at him, driving his shoulder in with all the force he could manage off the slippery, sucking bank. They went down together, almost gently into the mud. Hands clawing, Bonner climbed up the Sikh's chest, felt his face, felt the man's teeth clamp for a moment on the fleshy part of his palm.

Cas threw his body to the left, curling his arm over

the other's. Bracing, he arched back, the Indian's outstretched arm twisted under his armpit. With a loud snap Cas broke his elbow. The Sikh screamed and crumpled. Bonner flipped him over and, gritting his teeth, pressed the man's face down into the mud. Seconds whipped past. The Sikh struggled violently and then went limp.

Another shadow loomed. Cas, blood screaming in his head, whirled to meet it. It was Hak, feeling around in the mud. He came up with the machine pistol.

Up on the crest of the bank, the other horsemen were dashing back and forth, firing bursts down into the bank and river. The plunging shadows were blurred and moon-dappled, faintly tinged by the rapidly fading lantern-oil fire. Not a sound or hint of movement came from the other shacks.

"Take cover under another house," Hak shouted to Bonner. "I'll throw a burst and follow you."

Silently, Cas obeyed. He found Jackie still stretched on the bank. She was panting hard and murmuring with panic, little meaningless phrases. When he touched her, she jerked around and opened her mouth to scream. He clapped his hand over it.

"Don't!" he hissed into her face. "It's me."

"Oh, Cas."

"Come this way."

"Where's the boy?"

"Back there. He was hit." He heard her make a tiny cry in her throat. On their bellies, they scooted toward the bank, Cas hauling her and himself along by pulling at roots and shack stilts.

Hak waited a moment, then sprayed a burst across the crest. Horses shied instantly, men bellowed, and then a blast of concentrated fire came back, throwing up clods of mud and wooden splinters. With a low, throaty explosion, a second flare whirled up into the air, trailing sparks. A few seconds later, the area was again brilliantly lit.

By now Cas and Jackie were deep within the thicket of stilts. The flare cast sharp beams of dancing light through the breaks in the catwalks. Bonner cursed steadily, clenching and unclenching his hands in frustration and adrenaline surge. A moment later, Mc-Carran crawled up beside them. Out in the river, the fallen horse had reached the shore and was trying to climb the slippery bank.

"Damn!" Hak cursed. "This bloody piece is empty." He tossed the Sikh's machine pistol aside and stretched forward to look up the bank. For the moment, they seemed safe. The horsemen were on the far side of the collection of shacks, and their occasional bursts whipped the bank fifty feet away. But before long, they all knew, the Sikhs would come down to the river.

"Where the hell is Dabu?" Bonner asked in a harsh whisper. "We've gotta have weapons." He squinted up at the sharp, hot orb of the flare through the slits in the catwalk. "I'm gonna make a run for the boat."

McCarran nodded, his face stiff and slashed by the matrix of light beams. "Aye, Dabu should have been back by now. But you'd best wait till that bloody flare's down before you show yourself, lad."

"Right."

"Cas?" Jackie croaked.

But he was gone.

By the time he reached the far end of the shacks, the second flare had landed in the river with a sizzling burst. But he could still see light out there. The first flare had set the grass on fire, and a large patch was burning, sending up sparks that rode the updraft. He caught sight of the old Indian still standing out in the open, numbly gazing at the flames.

He climbed over a tin boat, went across a small plank walkway, and then reached solid ground again. Something slithered across his calf. He jerked away from it, pulled himself up, and stuck his head above the crest. Several of the horsemen had dismounted and were heading along the catwalks, searching the shacks and peering down into the water, their weapons at the ready.

Fifty yards away, he caught sight of Dabu running along the bank. He had Hak's rifles and two bandoliers over his shoulders. Bonner started to rise. Just then a horseman loomed out of the grass. Cas dropped and pressed himself as flat as he could. For a second the horseman came straight toward him, moving slowly, his horse picking its forelegs up high. Then the Sikh caught sight of Dabu. With a shout he wheeled his mount and drove spurs into it.

"Shit!" Bonner gasped.

Dabu saw the horseman coming. For a second he stopped, then turned and started running back toward Hak's boat. Cas moved, too, frantically half crawling, half running just below the crest. The horseman was in full gallop now, his body lifted in the stirrups, rapidly closing the distance to Dabu.

The little Indian twisted his head to throw a terrified glance back. He dropped first one rifle, then the other, sprinting as hard as he could. Bonner saw the Sikh extend his arm and pull off a burst. It caught Dabu in the back, hurled him facedown into the water. So close was the horseman that he went flying past before he could turn his mount. He fired again into Dabu's body.

Bonner reached the first rifle. He jacked the bolt back slightly, caught the soft brassy glint of a chambered round, relocked it, and threw the butt to his shoulder. Just over the sight dot, he saw the face of the Sikh turn toward him, faintly flame-etched, and then the man's arm came up.

The recoil of the Cogswell and Harrison .375 was like a bull's hook. Instantly the Sikh was lifted out of the saddle and disappeared over the other side of the horse. The animal veered and ran off into the grass.

Bonner retrieved the second rifle and scurried to Dabu. The little Indian jerked slightly as Cas felt for a pulse in his throat. There was none. Quickly he stripped off the bandoliers. One had been ripped open by the bullets and was sticky with blood. He fumbled a cartridge out, rapped open the bolt of his rifle, inserted it, and slammed it home. Then, keeping to the shadows formed by the crest, he started back toward the shacks.

He heard a horseman thunder past, then another. They didn't see him. He paused and looked back toward where Dabu lay. The first rider dismounted and slid down the bank to examine the body. Bonner moved on.

He found a Sikh standing directly above where Hak and Jackie were hiding. Bonner froze in the deep shadow cast by the bank. The man remained for a moment, then ducked into a shack. Cas quickly scurried to the catwalks and disappeared underneath. It was faintly lit under the pilings, and he caught a tiny glint. It was Jackie's wristwatch. He crawled over.

Tightly Hak said, "The bastards got Dabu, didn't they?"

"Yes."

There was a moment of utter silence. Then Hak said evenly, "Give me a rifle."

Cas handed over the Brno .458 and one of the bandoliers. The rounds were in leather loops, thick as cigars. Moving with slow deliberation, Hak withdrew a bullet and quietly chambered it. Then he took out three more rounds and placed them between the fingers of his left hand. He rose, bent forward slightly beneath the catwalk. They could hear the Sikhs shouting inside the shacks.

"What're you going to do?" Bonner said. He stood up, too.

"I've had enough of bloody hiding," Hak answered. His voice was low, tensed into tempered steel. "It's time for a face-down. Come if you want, stay if you want."

Cas felt his insides chill. A frontal attack against the Sikhs was foolish, he knew. Rifles against automatic weapons. But their choice was simple. Either they stood up and fought or they'd die like rats in a mudhole. Yet there was something beyond that stark fact. He studied Hak's dark face, the features unclear in the shadows, and he felt something move between them, form a bond. It touched him way down inside where the adrenaline still crackled. He gently slipped three cartridges from his own bandolier and finger-locked them.

Jackie whispered harshly, "You can't show yourselves, you fools."

Cas knelt beside her. "When it starts, run. Don't look back or stop. Go for the boat and get the hell out of here."

She grabbed his arm. "You'll die out there."

"Do like I tell you."

He pulled free, and he and McCarran walked out from under the pilings. The brush fire had spread away from the fishing village. Above it billowed a cloud of smoke that made the moon look dirty. They stood in the mud, ten feet apart.

A Sikh emerged from one of the shacks. Hak blew him away, the big-bored Brno exploding like a cannon that numbed Bonner's ears. The other Sikhs started yelling, and automatic fire snapped overhead like ripping cloth. Cas fired at the closest burst, his shoulder jerking back with the recoil. He heard a man scream and at the same instant he caught sight of Jackie, holding her medical kit against her chest. She emerged from under the shacks and skittered along the bank.

Beside him, McCarran was methodically chambering another round, and he did likewise. As his hearing returned, he picked up the sound of horses and swung around. The two riders down near Dabu's body were coming in. He lifted the rifle and fired. The horse in front went down, heaving its rider over the crest of the bank.

The Brno went off again, another horrendous wham! This time the return fire came directly at them. Bullets smacked into the mud, throwing up pockets of water. Cas, heart pounding, heard the bullets zing beside him.

Suddenly a burst of gunfire opened up from a completely different direction, out beyond the upside of the shacks. Cas caught sight of a horseman wheeling into sight, then heading wildly off toward the fire. More rifle shots followed.

For a moment he was confused. He glanced at Hak, who had paused in reloading and was looking up toward the new gunfire. A Sikh ran from a shack. Cas threw up his rifle, but the man disappeared, then reappeared, chasing his mount, which was also fleeing toward the flames.

A lull of silence was so profound that the ringing in Bonner's ears filled the whole night. He moved closer to McCarran. "What the hell's happening?"

"Apparently we've just found some friends," Hak said, his voice emotionless.

Men began to materialize on the bank near the shacks, their silhouettes sharp against the brush flames. Some came down onto the catwalks while others remained up on the bank. A flashlight flicked on, pinioning first Bonner and then McCarran. A man laughed.

"What da hell you doin' down dere, HakMcCarran?" the man called down with the lilting, calypso rhythm of a Caribbean native.

Hak laid the rifle across his shoulder. "Hello, Jungali," he said evenly.

"What dese crazy Sikh mountain monkeys want wid you?"

"Apparently they were trying to kill me."

Jungali laughed again, a throaty, happy sound. "No, no, you goddom Englishman. Only me will kill you, I tell you dat."

Pal Jungali, as Hak later explained, was the *prabhu,* or chief, of a poacher gang that roamed all over northeastern India but focused most of their hunting in the national parks. He and McCarran had known each other for over fifteen years and harbored between them a strange, enemy-friend kinship. Both of them knew that someday one would kill the other.

Born in Trinidad of a Carib prostitute and an East Indian smuggler, Jungali had been a thief all his life. As a boy, he had poached crocodiles and box-bill turtles in the Windward Islands, later turning to piracy. He eventually wound up hauling dragger boats full of illegal guns from Guyana across the Boca del Dragon strait to the nationalist insurgents who were challenging the British in Port-of-Spain.

At twenty-nine, he was imprisoned on Tobago. He would have died there except for a judge's *praja,* the repayment for a favor done. Jungali had once saved the man from a tiger shark. In return, the judge freed him with the admonition that he "get the bloody hell out of Trinidad and stay out."

He migrated to India, where for ten years he worked the slums of Bombay and Calcutta as a petty thief and procurer until he moved to the jungles and swamps of Assam. There he became a master poacher, smuggling the skins of leopards, tigers, long-snouted gavials, and blackbucks. Occasionally he also took rare *barasingha* deer skins, elephant ivory, and the horns of the Indian rhino to the tourist shops of Rangoon and Chittagong. Although he was sixty-two years old, he still retained the gutter-French and Carib speech of his youth.

Squatting on the bank, a short, husky man with a round, light-skinned, merry face that held a grin full of crazy teeth, he watched McCarran, Cas, and Jackie come up the bank.

"*La barbe*, HakMcCarran," he called loudly, "You fight da shit outta dese mountain monkeys." He focused his dancing eyes on Jackie. "You be da lady doctor I bin hearin' about?"

She nodded.

"Good, good. You be comin' wid us. My son he be sick."

Hak paused for a moment before Jungali, then turned and silently strode along the bank toward where Dabu lay. Cas followed as Jackie disappeared around the corner of the shack cluster to hunt for the boy's body.

The poachers watched in silence, ragged men in filthy, discarded clothing. Most carried old bolt-action rifles, Swedish Mausers and Lee-Enfields, with narrow-bladed bolo knives called *ags* lashed to their waists. Two had braced bows made of horn and wrapped in electrical tape slung over their shoulders with quivers of long arrows.

McCarran reached Dabu and knelt. He placed his finger on the corpse's carotid artery, then sank back on his haunches. He murmured something soft, almost delicate in Indian. Rising at last, he lifted the little Indian's body and carried it along the water's edge to his boat. He laid it on the prow, climbed in, and deposited it in the cabin.

Jungali came down and knocked on the hull. "Come on, Englishman, we got to go now."

"Not till I finish."

"Ain't no time for dat. My son be needin' dis lady doctor."

Ignoring him, Hak moved to the stern and unhooked the fuel line of the Morris-Oxford and let raw gasoline stream out onto the floorboards. Back at the village, people were coming out onto the catwalks and looking furtively downriver. Beyond, the grass fire had moved to the edge of the river, its sparks drifting out over the water like tiny, flaming kites.

"I not be waitin' for you, mon," Jungali said.

"Then get out."

The Carib shrugged, jerked his head for Jackie to proceed ahead of him and his men. "Go to, lady," he said, "and be pretty goddom quick about it."

Jackie threw a terrified look at Bonner. He lifted the muzzle of his rifle, setting the butt against his hip. "Hold it," he shouted.

Jungali stopped and glanced over his shoulder, flashed his crazy grin. "Who da hell are you, mon? An' don' be playin' games wid dat weapon, else I be takin' it from you."

"Easy, Bonner," Hak said quietly. "His men'll drop you where you stand. You go ahead now. When I've finished with poor Dabu, I'll be along."

They went beside the river for a quarter mile, three men walking in front, then Jackie and Cas, followed by Jungali and the others. The poachers stank with the dark effluvium of dried blood and the callow salt tang of skins. As they passed the fishing shacks, they caught sight of the old man shuffling down to the water to retrieve his grandson's body. After a while he came back up, struggling with the weight of it, and walked back across the now scorched grass, the stiff mannequin of the corpse propped against his stooped shoulders.

Three old, beat-up Land Rovers were parked on a grassy bluff above the river. Two were loaded with rolled animal skins, several gaur heads with their great curved horns, plus the single stump of a rhino horn, resembling a massive gray-black fang. The third Rover held cans of spare gasoline and ammunition.

Cas and Jackie were put into the third vehicle with Jungali at the wheel. Now and then he would burst out talking, various comments, as if he were discussing something with himself.

As the trio of Rovers headed out, with the grass slapping against the fenders, they saw McCarran set his boat afire. All the villagers were out of their homes now, walking around the hard-packed earth, taking stock of the damage. Then the *seram* exploded as the fire reached the main fuel tank. A blinding eruption of white silhouetted Hak's figure.

Jackie leaned forward to yell at the poacher leader over the wind. "What is your son's sickness?"

"I don' know," Jungali hollered back. "He jus' be goddom sick like the others. First one of my mon gettin' the sickness, den another. Der bodies all coilin' and dey screamin' wid pain. Both of dem mons die." He flashed his crooked-tooth smile. "But now you here, be keepin' my son alive."

"I'll try."

"No, lady, you don' be tryin', you be doin'."

She sat back, casting a furtive glance at Bonner, who squatted on a gasoline can, the Cogswell and Harrison across his knees. They raced on, the stars jumping around above them in the moon-washed sky.

They passed into thin scrub forest and finally reached a road thick with dust, which whirled up and made the headlights of the following Rovers look dim and orange. Now and then they saw animals crossing the road, small groups of sambar or musk deer. Momentarily mesmerized by the lights, they would stare, eyes glowing, and then whirl and rush away. Once, over the whine of the engine, they caught a clear, reverberating scream that Jungali identified as a leopard.

The poachers' camp was situated just beyond the boundary of the Rantamkumar National Park. It was demarcated by a buffer stand of eucalyptus. Beyond the line of trees the land was covered with thick *tarai* grass and spindly scrub-oak where herds of blackbuck browsed in the moonlight. But Cas noticed tiny lanterns out there, too, from graziers who snuck into the park at night to illegally gather fodder for their animals and cut the scrub-oak for firewood.

Once the preserve of a maharaja, the Rantamkumar was now Jungali's private hunting domain. Using payoffs throughout the levels of government designated to oversee the park, he was able to take anything he wanted. But the combined attack of poacher and farmer would soon decimate the entire reserve. Already the denuded ground had created deadly floods in 1989.

The camp was comprised of a dozen or so makeshift lean-tos constructed of eucalyptus branches overlaid with layers of grass. In the center of the compound was a large fire pit still glowing with embers. Metal grates formed a matrix over the coals.

Back near the buffer trees were three ancient flatbed trucks with tanks for gasoline and fresh water steel-banded to their beds. Several women, thin-legged and wrapped in blue-and-pink-striped blankets, were standing near the fire pit as the Rovers skidded to a halt.

Instantly Jungali slid off the seat and motioned for Jackie and Bonner to follow. He led them to the largest lean-to, featuring softened leopard skins hanging across the front. Inside were thatch-stuffed canvas bags for beds, leather water bottles, and *ags* sheathed in brass scabbards hanging on the boughs. A single, ancient flintlock rifle was propped against the lean-to's strut. The hut reeked of kerosene fumes and excrement.

On the straw bed, a man of about twenty-five lay completely naked. He was beautifully built, with smooth, muscular shoulders and thick legs. His skin in the flickering lantern light was the color paper makes just before it curls into flame. He was drenched in sweat and coiled tightly into the fetal position.

"Dis is my son Raghubir," Jungali said. "You be doin' dat medical magic now, you lady doctor."

Jackie knelt beside the man, and he opened his eyes. She examined him, already knowing he, too, was infected with the fungus. Undoubtedly he was going to die.

She opened her kit and gave him two shots, one an anti-toxin, the other a painkiller. Raghubir's skin felt so hot that it heated the air above it, like a candle flame. She turned to Jungali, who squatted near the flintlock, his eyes darting back and forth between her face and his son's.

"He's very, very ill," she said softly.

"I already know dat."

She hesitated, then said, "He's dying."

"No, no," Jungali snapped irritably. "Don' be sayin' dat."

"It's true, Mr. Jungali. This disease is caused by a

strange new fungus. I don't have medicine strong enough to fight it.''

The poacher kept bobbing his head, his eyes twinkling their peculiar merriment. "You be doin' fine, don' worry.''

Frustrated, Jackie glanced at Cas, then back at the Carib. "I'll do the best I can, but be prepared for the worst.''

Jungali sucked spittle loudly through his crooked teeth, baring them for a moment. He spat, stared evenly at her, the merriment gone, his eyes dark with the reflection of the lantern flame in their depths. "You be takin' dat demon outta Raghubir pretty goddom quick, lady doctor.'' He lifted a stubby finger and pointed it at her left eye. "Or me gonna put a goddom bullet in yo' eyeball, I tell you dat.''

It took Pramud several hours to reach the outskirts of Dibrugarh with the warhead. He came straight downriver in a 1930s speedboat, a relic from the time of the British administrator, which was berthed at the oil dock on Namak. He passed through the island shallows of Dangori and Talap and then entered the long reach of river, a mile wide, above the city.

Pramud was a cousin of Abu Singh and was excited over being given such an important assignment. As a result, he had come alone, unwilling to share the glory the completion of the task would bring him. Crouched over the wheel, he watched the foredeck spotlight spread its flared beam thirty yards ahead of the boat.

Long before he reached Dibrugarh, he saw the glow of its oil fires burning off pressure in the drilling yards. Then the lights of the town merged out of the darkness. The water traffic increased, forcing him to slow. Dugouts with reed fish baskets balanced across their gunwales and high-sterned sailing *dhows* carrying tiny red after lights slipped past him. Then he was on the edge of the main wharf area. To the right were drilling derricks and oil storage tanks, festooned with lights. Out in the roadstead river tankers were anchored, their huge steel hulls washed in moonlight.

Pramud eased closer to the left bank. There the city came down to the river: precipices of dirty white walls below gilded mosque domes. Moored boats were so thick on the banks they formed a solid mass. Here and there, resembling English buses, were triple-decked *sonas,* the filthy dormitories where oil workers lived.

He cut the motor and drifted. The river, sluggish and foul-smelling, gently began to push him back out toward one of the anchored freighters. Quickly he lifted the helm seat and took out the warhead. It was surprisingly heavy, at least a hundred and thirty pounds. But Pramud was a powerful man and, firmly gripping the heat-expanding cannular grooves in the stern of the canister, he placed it on the after seat.

Next, using a cold chisel and hammer, he attempted to punch a hole through the side. The metal rang with each slam of the hammer, but the chisel didn't penetrate. He kept at it for several minutes, even trying to puncture the red circle on the nose. Still no results.

He stopped, panting. A hundred yards away loomed a freighter. He could see someone standing on the bridge wing, the tiny, rapid glow of the man's cigarette like a blinking firefly. Frustrated, he went back to work, this time pounding the canister directly with his hammer until his arm grew tired. It didn't even dent the black metal.

An idea struck him. He could *shoot* holes in the bloody thing. Happily he lifted the warhead and placed it on the narrow wooden spacing of the transom. Withdrawing a Luger 9mm from beneath his robe, he knelt in the stern well until the canister was silhouetted against the lights of a distant causeway. He put the gun muzzle into the center of the red circle on the nose of the warhead and pulled the trigger.

The gun boomed in the night. Instantly following was a second, pressure explosion: softer, lighter, filled with hissing modulations. Propelled by the outburst, the canister rolled along the seat and went over the side into the water.

Pramud was struck in the face with a blast of tiny pellets, so small they felt like grains of wheat. They smelled rotten like the stench from suppurating wounds. He recoiled, vaguely hearing the canister still swooshing and bubbling fiercely for a few seconds before it sank.

A spotlight from the nearby freighter snapped on. It swept about for a moment and finally held steady on the speedboat. A man yelled something, but Pramud paid no heed. The pellets had caught in his throat. Like a man who had inhaled sawdust, he coughed and gagged.

Finally, recovering slightly, he stopped for a moment. His eyes were filled with tears. Through them he looked down at the water. The spotlight made it shiny, polished, and little things caught in the current drifted into the beam and then out again. He studied the spot where the warhead had gone down. There was no trace. He began coughing again.

In less than an hour, he was dead.

12

Bonner sat cross-legged outside the lean-to and watched Jungali's son dying. Like the woman and young boy, the passage was grotesque. Raghubir agonized through muscle spasms that would have brought screams from a lesser man. Watery feces exploded from his rectum, driven by powerful abdominal contractions. It was an unwholesome scene, void of any dignity.

For the past two hours Jackie had tried to hold off the steady decline. She dosed him again and again with the anti-toxin, washed his body of its kerosene sweat, cleansed his soiled straw mattress. But it was a losing battle.

Around them, the night went on in its ageless unconcern. Beyond the eucalyptus the blackbuck continued to feed. Jackals prowled and barked. Now and again a tethered lizard hissed at its captivity.

Jungali wandered around the camp talking to himself. Periodically he'd pause beside his son's lean-to to take in Jackie's ministrations. Meanwhile, the rest of the poachers were quietly fed by the women, furtive creatures with the blankets pulled up to hide their faces in the presence of a white man. Afterward, the men stood around awkwardly, murmuring at Raghubir's decline. But gradually they moved off to their own lean-tos and left two young boys to guard the fire.

During this activity Bonner had remained at his post near Raghubir's tent, the hunting rifle across his knees and his eyes slitted. He had been absorbing the entire layout of the camp. He knew the young poacher would die, but he didn't know precisely what Jungali would do when it happened. Had his threat been real? He had to assume it was. That meant he had to formulate a plan of escape.

At last he moved to the lean-to and pulled the canvas cover aside. "Any improvement?" he asked softly.

Jackie shook her head. Her hair was matted with river mud, and perspiration had left little chocolate lines down her cheeks.

"When do you figure he'll die?"

"By dawn. The anti-toxin's being overwhelmed. I think it's working, but the fungus in him keeps producing more and more poison." She turned and gazed almost wonderingly at him. "When he dies, is that man really going to kill me?"

"I don't know." He shot a quick glance across the camp. Jungali had momentarily stopped beside the guard boys and was smoking a long-stemmed pipe. Cas moved closer. "But we're not waiting around to find out. When I get the chance, I'm gonna work my way around to the Rovers. I'll disable two and steal the other. When I come back across that compound, be ready to move and move fast."

Jackie lowered her head and placed her forefingers on the bridge of her nose. When she looked up again, her face was drawn. "I can't just run off and leave this man to die."

"Bullshit, Jackie. There isn't any more you can do."

"I know." After a moment she nodded. "I'll be ready."

Raghubir made a grunting sound and jerked up suddenly. His eyes shot open, neck thickly distended as another racking muscle spasm struck. Jackie touched him, cooed softly. At the fire, Jungali turned and looked over. Raghubir's teeth gnashed but gradually the spasm subsided.

Jackie sank back, frowning thoughtfully. "Dammit, I keep thinking I've missed something here," she said.

"What?"

"Something, I don't know." She brushed a lock of wet hair from Raghubir's forehead. "Tell me again what you found in that ship's lab."

"Forget it. There's nothing that'll help now."

"Just do it, all of it. Please."

He did, going quickly over his tests on the organism and the results of his experiments on the mouse. Far in the distance, a jackal chorus started. When he reached the organism's susceptibility to electrical energy, she put her hand on his arm.

"There it is," she said.

He looked at her, puzzled.

"Don't you see? Electrical energy destroys the fungus."

"So? What good does that information do us here?"

"We can do it."

He leaned back to study her. "What are you saying? Shock him?"

"Precisely."

"That's nuts."

Her eyes were flashing with excitement. "No, we can do it, I tell you. It's the fungus continually producing new toxin that's killing him. If we can destroy the main organism, the serum'll have a chance to stabilize him."

Bonner thought about that. It made sense. But to do it here was impossible. "We don't have the equipment," he said.

"There must be some source of electricity we can

use.'' She looked frantically around the still compound. ''Those Rovers, we could use their batteries. Couldn't we hook him up to a battery? We'd just need a single jolt.''

Cas shook his head. ''No, those units have self-contained circuits, they don't go to ground. Besides, there's not enough amperage in them to overcome his body's resistance.''

''Dammit, Bonner, there must be some way we can rig it.''

''Okay, suppose we could generate enough juice, wouldn't that kill him? In his state, any electrical charge could stop his heart.''

She nodded, but the look in her eyes didn't waver. ''Yes, it might initiate respiratory collapse, even ventricular fibrillation. But at least I could fight against that with artificial respiration and heart massage.''

He still looked skeptical.

''It's worth an attempt, for God's sake. Isn't it? This man's going to die if we don't do something.'' She rose to her feet. ''I'm going to talk to Jungali.''

Cas grabbed her, forced her back. ''You've forgotten something, Jackie. Even if we could convince him into letting us electrocute his son, what if it failed and you couldn't bring him out of fibrillation? He'd die within minutes and so would we. There'd be no chance to escape then.''

''This could be the key to destroying this—this monstrous thing.'' Again her eyes searched his face. ''For that, I'm willing to take the risk.''

He stared at her.

''I can do it,'' she said. ''I know I can.''

Gradually a sardonic glint crept into Bonner's eyes. ''Well, I hope your medical instincts are as good as your guts.'' He rose. ''Let's give it a shot.''

The Carib looked at Cas as if he had just told him

the moon was falling when he said they would have to wire up his son and send a jolt of electricity through his body. The poacher reared back, scowling. "You goddom crazy, mon. You tink I let you send *bang*"—he slapped his palms together—"electricities in my Raghubir body? No, dass all, mon."

"Then your son'll be dead by sunup."

Jungali shook his head. "No, the lady doctor, she fix him up fine, mon."

"Her medicine isn't strong enough. We have to kill the . . . animal inside first. You understand animal inside?"

Jungali's eyes widened. "What dis animal you tellin' about? It be like Vodun *dupee*?"

Bonner had spent time in the Caribbean and knew that the term *dupee* meant a demon that could inhabit a human body. He leaped at his opening. "Yes, the *dupee* is what is killing your son. We have to drive it out, destroy it."

Jungali's lips pursed, making oohs and ahhs. He flung away from Bonner, squatted across the fire and quickly made the sign of the cross. The two guard boys, noting him, looked frightened.

"I don' like whot you be tellin' me, mon," the Carib growled.

"Then let us try." Cas pressed.

"Dis lady doctor not *mambo*. The spirits ain't gon listen to her when she tellin' dem to leave."

"The electricity is the demon killer."

"Ah, my heart got no name," Jungali sighed. He made the sign of the cross again, twice.

Cas looked up at the sky and pointed at the moon behind its gauzy veil, playing the scene out. "The moon is flying, Jungali. Soon it's too late."

The old man gazed into the fire's embers for a long time. They ebbed and glowed with orange and blue, the soft crackle like hushed spirit whispers. At last he nodded, sharp dips of his head. "Den do it now, mon."

It proved to be a complicated affair trying to draw enough of a charge from the Rover batteries. Cas first used one, then two linked in series, and finally three, utilizing the leads off a pair of jumper cables that were inserted into tiny slices Jackie had cut on Raghubir's left chest and another in his groin. Each time they touched the wires to him, there was no perceptible muscle reaction to indicate an electrical charge had passed into his body.

The activity had roused the rest of the poachers, and they were squatting curiously in a half circle around Raghubir's lean-to, whispering with puzzlement. Jungali took up a position at the edge of his son's mattress, his rifle butted into the dirt and his eyes narrow slits.

Jackie had fashioned a mask to place over Raghubir's mouth when and if artificial respiration became necessary. Any direct mouth contact would have transferred fungus-laden saliva to her own system. She had cut it from a piece of dried leopard skin, tough as a strip of thin metal.

The failed attempts left Cas frustrated and very uneasy. He hadn't liked pulling the third Rover's battery, since that left them completely without any means of escape. But by then the challenge of the thing had stirred his interest. He paced around and tried to figure a new approach.

He had a glimmer. If he replaced one of the batteries in a Rover, he thought, then ran double wires from the vehicle's generator to Raghubir, he'd get his charge. It would be very strong, maybe too strong. It could send the man into immediate cardiac arrest. But there was a solid plus: he'd have the only usable vehicle in the camp with its engine running.

As he returned to the vehicles, Jungali stepped in front of him. "You magic ain't be workin', mon," he said menacingly. "I tink dat maybe you be givin' me shit."

"We need a stronger electrical spirit," Cas explained. "I'm going to run one of the Rovers and line off its generator."

Jungali looked him up and down, considering. He nodded. "You betta be right dis time, mon. Or you and dat goddom doctor be hearin' da cries of Hell, I tell you dat for sure." He turned and strode back to his position beside the mattress.

With the Rover parked beside the lean-to, its engine idling, Cas brought the leads in and knelt beside Raghubir. The young man's eyes rolled, looking at the wires. He cried out and jerked his head aside. Jackie whispered to him. After a moment he calmed a little, panting.

She put her hand out. "Give me the second wire."

"Wipe him off first," Cas said. "Otherwise the charge could travel through his sweat."

She did it, swabbing the young Indian's chest, his arms, down the long, convulsed line of his legs. She tossed the cloth aside and put her stethoscope plugs into her ears. For a tiny moment she paused, her eyes meeting Cas's. They were wide open but calm. She nodded to him.

When the jolt hit Raghubir, he grunted and his back lifted slightly off the filthy mattress. His eyelids fluttered. Around the lean-to, the poachers buzzed and Jungali leaned far forward to see. For a second Raghubir settled. Quickly Jackie dropped the wire and placed the stethoscope bell on his chest.

A moment later, his mouth emitted a deep, wrenching gasp. "Shit!" Jackie yelled and threw herself over him, straddling his thrashing hips. "He's going into respiratory collapse. The mask, put the mask over his mouth and force air in."

Jungali leapt to his feet, swinging his rifle up. "You killin' him," he bellowed. The other poachers also rose and pressed in close, their faces ominous.

Bonner waved his arm and shouted, "Stay back." He scooped up the mask and fitted it over Raghubir's open mouth. The man tried to wrench it away. Cas fought against his uncanny strength.

Above him, jerking up and down as Raghubir thrashed, Jackie placed her palms over his sternum, braced, and shouted to Bonner, "Breathe into him, goddammit. Hurry!"

Bonner finally got one of Raghubir's arms under his knee. With his free hand, he gripped the other arm and held it off. Quickly he bent, cupped the top of the mask with his mouth, and blew in. Once. Again. A third time.

Stiff-armed, Jackie began pressing down on Raghubir's chest. She kept at it for a few seconds, then shouted, "Again." Once more Bonner breathed into Raghubir's mouth. He felt someone trying to pull him off, but he managed to brush him aside. When he lifted from the mask, he bellowed, "The demon's coming out." Instantly Jungali lunged backward, frantically waving for the others to do likewise.

Raghubir went abruptly limp, his mouth and eyes wide open, the pupils dilated. Instantly Jackie put the stethoscope to his chest. "Fibrillation!" she cried. She reared back and began pounding on his chest with clenched, wrapped fists. She continued for a few seconds, then bent to listen to his heart. Once more she pounded, listened. Resumed pounding.

The last time she listened, her eyes shot up to Cas.

Sweat poured over her cheeks. "We're getting it," she murmured. "His rhythm's stabilizing."

Gradually, agonizingly, Raghubir's normal heart cycle came back. His pupils constricted. His fingernails lost their bluish tinge. But still he lay motionless, in a coma.

Cas eased over to Jackie. "Is he still alive?"

"Yes. Now we wait."

"How long?"

"There's no way of telling." She dug into her kit, came out with another hypo.

"All right, I'll play for time. But if he goes, say nothing. Just get up and walk out to the Rover we were using."

She nodded.

He rose and walked over to Jungali. "The *dupee* is gone," he said.

"He look like he bein' dead."

"He's only sleeping."

"Ah, I see, I see." Jungali went over and took up his vigil beside the mattress.

Cas turned off the Rover and disconnected the leads from the generator. He retrieved his rifle and sat beside the lean-to to wait.

McCarran arrived with the sun, walking across the grassy plain with his large-bore rifle across his neck, his safari shirt and shorts caked with blood and mud and sweat. He came across the camp and squatted beside Bonner.

"The bloke still alive?" he asked.

"He was in a coma, but he's come out of it." He explained what they'd done.

While McCarran listened, he surveyed the camp. Jungali had momentarily gone off into the eucalyptus with some of the men to shit, and the women were preparing breakfast. Visible in the full light were piles of skins beside the lean-tos. Leopard, crocodile, a single tiger pelt, all stiff and pathetic. There were also stacks of horns and antlers. Hak shook his head. "Bloody butchers," he murmured.

When Cas finished, he said, "What are his chances?"

"I don't know."

Hak rose and crawled into the lean-to. Jackie was sitting cross-legged, eyes closed as if she were practicing yoga. He leaned over and looked down into Raghubir's face.

"Hello, you bleedin' *kafir*," he said.

"Hello, bloody Englishman," Raghubir answered.

Hak touched Jackie's shoulder. She opened her eyes slowly, as if from some pleasant dream. For a moment she stared at him, then said, "McCarran." She brushed her hands across her eyes. Beside her knee, Raghubir sat up suddenly and smiled at her.

"Jesus!" Jackie said.

They squatted in the grass: Cas, Hak, and Jungali, talking quietly. In the full morning light the air was saturated with heat. The vast grasslands shimmered with it as they rolled away toward the distant jungle.

"Oh, yes, I know dem Russkies, sure enough," Jungali said in answer to Hak's question. "Dey bein' over at Lake Sonai wid dat goddom Sikh bastard Singh."

Hak winked at Bonner. "I thought you liked Singh, Pal," he said straight-faced.

The Carib grew somber and he spat viciously on the ground. "Dat sombitch crazy, mon. Ain't no decent. He kill two of my men, bloody slice dose boys like dey was pigs." His eyes hardened. "But me one hard nigger, too. You know? I cotch two of his bloody boys and cut dere goddom pricks off." He laughed. "Now wen dey go to dere goddom paradise, ain't gonna do no fuckin', dat's for truth."

"What are the Russians doing at Lake House?" Hak asked.

"Marchin' dem Sikhs around like penny soljers."

"What about weapons?"

"Oh, dey got lots of weapons."

"Missiles?"

"Sure."

Hak shot Cas a glance. "You certain?"

"I seen da goddom tings, I tell you. Twice as long as you standin' up, mon, wid dem shiny black noses." He nodded to emphasize his words. "Dem missiles I seen when the Sikhs took 'um 'cross da lake."

"They ever fire any?"

Jungali shook his head. "No, I ain't seen dat."

Hak sighed and settled on his haunches. "Well, lad, there's our proof. I fancy maybe it's time we brought someone else in on this affair. Before that crazy Sikh puts the whole thing in the bloody bin."

"Right."

To Jungali: "You got a radio in this slaughter pen of yours?"

"No, no radio. But I know where we can be findin' one." He pointed off toward the distant jungle. "Dat bugger Shaunnessy's loggin' camp."

"Then let's be off."

JoJo Shaunnessy was a drunken York Peninsula half-Irishman with a face full of red veins and eyes inflamed with a perpetual, fiery rage. He was head foreman for an Australian lumber company and was known as a cruel jobber who beat his men, mostly farmers recruited from the dry Assam flatland villages.

He lived right at the edge of thick jungle in a white

bungalow with neat green shutters. It was always kept clean and painted by his mistress, a thin, homely Sudanese woman.

He was standing on his porch in spotless khaki work clothes when Hak, Cas, and Jungali pulled up in the Rover. Behind them came a second vehicle filled with the Carib's men. Shaunnessy watched sullenly as they dismounted. From deeper in the jungle came the trumpeting of elephants and the shouts of mahouts bringing them up to the cutting zone.

"Well, well," the Aussie remarked snidely, looking at McCarran and Jungali. "You two nongs a team now, are you?"

"Morning to you, JoJo," Hak said easily. He walked up onto the porch and sat on the railing. "I hear you have a radio. That correct?"

"What's it to you?" Shaunnessy watched Bonner come up the steps without comment, but when Jungali started up, too, he put his hand out. "No bloody niggers up here, mate."

The Carib gave him a big grin. "You got dat all wrong, mon. Dis nigger goes where he want."

Shaunnessy glared as the poacher continued up the steps. He wore an old ring-butted Walther strapped around his waist, but he didn't try for it. Jungali sat on one of the cushioned rattan chairs.

Hak waited a moment, then said, "I want to use it."

"Bugger off wi' ya," barked Shaunnessy, still eyeing the Carib.

"It's important."

"Who cares?" He shook his head. "My wireless is for official business only."

Patiently McCarran studied him. "Where is it?"

"Flyin' over the Celebes, mate."

Hak nodded at Cas. "Go find it."

As Bonner started past the Aussie, he cried, "Hold on, now. What's this crap, McCarran?"

"I intend to use your radio, JoJo," Hak answered in the same quiet, even tone. "You can make it easy or you can make it hard."

JoJo's eyes squinted. "An' how hard would that be?"

"A bullet in the head if that's what you want."

"Would you, now?"

"I would."

Shaunnessy stared vengefully for a decent enough moment, then hissed. "One of these days, I'll come bustin' into *your* digs, ya bloody English barstard."

"Always welcome."

He jerked his head. "It's in the back room." He looked at Jungali. "But that one stays out here."

Again the Carib gave him a grin. "I don' be wantin' to go into your house, mon. It be stinkin' of white."

The set was a new, multi-band Winston Metro 300 with a padded brass mike. The room, stacked with cases of Australian whiskey, was cool from a window air conditioner. Hak immediately seated himself in front of the radio, clicked it on, and began swinging through channels. Shaunnessy dug a bottle from one of the cases, cracked it, and leaned against the door.

McCarran flipped through a lot of radio traffic, music, what sounded like military calls, and some weak amateur stuff from far out. Finally he leaned back. "Dammit, consulate's changed its bloody frequencies." He turned and glanced at Shaunnessy. "Give me a drink of that."

Shaunnessy handed the bottle over, and Hak took a long pull. He held it out for Bonner, who also took a swig and then returned it to JoJo.

Shaunnessy said, "Which bloody consulate you talking about?"

"British, Calcutta."

"Never do it, mate," he scoffed. "You'd first have to get into the bleedin' Indian Military net. Priority is issued through those nongs now."

"I'm talking covert line."

The Aussie paused, eyeing Hak closely. "Covert line? How the bloody hell would you know about a covert line?"

McCarran ignored him, returned to the set. He began fanning frequencies on either side of the guarded radio positions he had known when he was with British Intelligence. At each stop he would call, utter an old code phrase, listen, then swing on.

Ten minutes later, he got a response: "Sickle Round, this is Babbitt-One. Receiving you on guarded frequency of one-zero-fiver. Who the bloody hell are you? Over."

"There we are," Hak said with a smile. He had just gotten into the British consulate's radio-screening room. Although the code phrase Sickle Round was outdated, it was, as he had hoped, still within the system's log bank and had automatically shunted him into the S.R. Undoubtedly Babbitt-One was attempting to track his signal.

He keyed: "Must speak with your O.S. intelligence officer. Extremely important."

"Sickle Round, you are transmitting on closed-guarded frequency. Identify yourself immediately or cease transmission."

"Identify as Friend."

There was a tiny tick sequence of static, then: "Friend has non-file designation. If valid, go to MarcryDix security gear."

Hak's thumb came down hard on the mike key. "I'm transmitting on a Winston Metro with no blasted security gear."

"Then get the hell off the line."

"Listen, you blithering idiot, I have a force-status report, urgent. Now quit mucking about and get your bleeding I.O. on the horn."

Shaunnessy stepped forward and reached out to grab the mike. "Hold it, you son of a bitch," he growled. "Those nongs'll be trackin' the signal right back to me. I want no stoush with them B.C. dingos."

Cas put his palm on JoJo's chest and eased him aside. "Go back to the door and shut up."

Shaunnessy glared at him. "Who the bloody hell are you, anyway?"

"Never mind. Just settle down."

Into the mike Hak said, "Come on, lad, get on with it."

There was another pause and then the consulate came back: "What is designate of this force-status?"

"Russian."

"Site?"

"Assam."

Another long silence followed. Hak drummed his fingers on the table. At last he punched the key. "All right, you've had long enough. I know you've verified my signal source by now, so get it on the plate."

"Sickle Round, go ahead with message."

"Russian paramilitary contingent at Lake House on Lake Sonai. Heavy weaponry, including bio-missiles. Repeat, bio-missiles. Believed to have released substance into Brahmaputra that is creating deadly mutated form of riverine fungi infecting upper river. Alert medical departments to utilize electrical shock in countering fungial infection."

He paused.

"What the bloody hell is this gibberish, Sickle Round?"

"Dammit," Hak said softly. He pictured the operators in Calcutta looking disbelievingly at one another. Probably stolid low-echelon types with mold on their testicles who would dump the whole thing into the discard bin. Still, in light of what he'd just said, he couldn't really blame them.

For a moment he considered. He'd have to tag some weight to the message that would carry it up through the layers. He knew what he *could* use, his old code name. But he had hoped to avoid that, since it could conceivably taint anything he had to say. Unfortunately, he no longer had a choice.

He keyed: "Transmit to Delhi embassy immediately. Designate source Tiger Stripe."

In the next lull he knew the S.R. operator was running through his agent logs. At last Babbitt-One came back, matter-of-factly: "I have transcription, Tiger Stripe. Over and out."

McCarran swung around on the radio seat, plucked a bottle from one of the cases, twisted the top, and took a drink.

Shaunnessy's eyes flared with rage. "If you've gone and got me in the slops with B.C., you flamin' limey barstard, I swear I'll come gunnin'."

Hak took another drink and tossed the bottle to Cas. "Fair enough, JoJo," he said, smiling.

13

At precisely 4:36 A.M., Calcutta time, the Dutch cruise ship *Vorchack* ran into a tumultuous sea south of the Maldive Islands, four hundred miles south-southwest of the tip of India. Wind gusts, caused by the incoming monsoon's Bay of Bengal front as it began its northward swirl before crossing Sri Lanka, reached thirty-six knots. Wave crests ran fifteen feet and were frothed with bottom debris.

The *Vorchack*'s captain dutifully ordered full deployment of the stabilizer wings, cut to weathering speed, and pointed his ship toward the Maldivian port of Male to wait for a break in the weather. Soon most of the three hundred passengers were experiencing varying stages of seasickness. Some of the hardier ones, however, gathered on the upper decks to watch a sunless dawn rise out of the wind-whipped sea.

Twenty-two hundred miles due south, the NOAA survey ship *Explorer* gently rode at sea anchor in a very different ocean. Far beyond the curl of the Bengal vortice, she was onstation under a brilliant sunrise, awaiting the arrival of the XGB-3AS from its underwater firing position beyond the equator.

Sleek and white, the *Explorer* would have been mistaken for a luxury cruiser if sighted on the horizon. Up close, the plethora of antennae and tracking dishes gave her away, as did her decks, which were loaded with scientific gear and a slender finger crane on the stern, used to deploy the bright yellow submersible chained to her after deck. In addition to her NOAA crew, she carried twenty-two scientists representing a wide spectrum of disciplines that included marine paleontology, oceanic geology, and meteorology.

Designated under a secret, joint-assignment program combining NOAA, the Pentagon, and the Department of Energy, her mission was to thoroughly explore the post-explosive environment of the Mascarene Plateau. The plateau was a microplate barely two miles across and lying under only a hundred and fifty feet of water in one of the remotest areas of the earth, two thousand miles due west of the western coast of Australia. It had been formed by an ancient pressure upthrust at the convergence of the Mid-Indian, Ninety East, and Amsterdam deep-sea ridges.

Once the missile reached the Mascarene, homed to it by the slightly higher temperature gradient of the water over the plateau, the scientists would begin immediate grid tracking of the entire area to take magnetic, gravitational, and seismic recordings of the surface of the undersea environment. These would give a geological profile of the plateau, which would then be used to determine formational components and archaeological status. A secondary aim was the location of oil anticlines. DOE was actively exploring the feasibility of open-ocean drilling in international waters.

The project, however, was mainly financed by the Pentagon and as a result, its primary research goal was centered on the performance of the XGB-3AS.

Created at the Pollack Research Facility in Amarillo, Texas, the missile represented a completely new approach to tactical target assimilation. Utilizing a thallium-based nuclear reaction with a nearly zero radiation throw-out, its impact would create an intense heat field that, under combat conditions, could completely destroy all life forms within the target area without the accompanying fallout of normal nuclear ordnance.

This was to be the first operational field test of the XGB.

Overall mission director for the project was David Bass, an MIT graduate in ballistics and high-speed aerodynamics and head of the Training and Control Systems Division of the Ford Point, South Carolina, Missile Depot. Extremely tall and lean, he was a Californian with a penchant for trying out novel ideas. He'd been in on the development of the missile project from the beginning, particularly during the designing of its homing system.

He just finished breakfast in the officers' mess with a second quart of orange juice when Charley Mirisch, protocol assistant for the operation, poked his head through the door. "They just got a status report from the *Yuma,* Dave."

"All right!" Bass cried happily. "It's about time."

Mirisch shuffled in. He was short, pudgy, and blond. "Not all right."

"What's the matter?"

"The sub's developed a minor glitch in its launch system."

"Oh, no! How bad?"

Mirisch shrugged. "They claim it should be on-line in six, maybe seven hours."

"Why don't they use the redundancy system?"

"The captain says no. Since this isn't an attack launch, he wants everything shipshape before going green."

Bass sighed disgustedly. "Well, there goes our observation schedule."

"I know. So Towne wants to know if you want to

scrap until tomorrow.'' Albert Towne was the captain of the *Explorer*.

Bass thought a moment. Once the missile came in, assuming the sub's projected time for operation was correct, they'd have about six hours of light left. He'd need at least that much time to run even the initial phases of the post-explosive scan. But that would also mean the DOE boys would have to hold off their tracking procedures until morning. The precision of their thermal and gravitational readings would undoubtedly suffer.

''Where's Garretson?'' he asked. Doug Garretson, a meteorologist, was head of the Department of Energy contingent.

''Up with the captain. He wants a scrap.''

''No, no scrap. I'm sick of sitting out here on the ocean with my finger up my ass. Tell him—'' He uncoiled his six-foot-six frame from the chair. ''No, I'll tell him.''

They went up through the ship to the bridge. The captain and Garretson were huddled near the ship's data encryption panel on the starboard side. The *Yuma* transmitted its messages to the ship in microwave from a towed communications buoy using a pseudo-random analogue ciphering system. This in turn was decoded by the *Explorer*'s AN/PRC-68 receiver, the message printing out on a teleprinter sheet. Both men glanced over as they came in.

Towne said, ''Well, what's the decision?''

''How definite is the *Yuma* on-line forecast?''

''A leeway of an hour, either way.''

''Then we'll go.''

''Dammit!'' Garretson cried. ''That'll fuck up most of our readings.''

''Not necessarily,'' Bass answered. ''We'll combine sweeps.''

The captain sighed. "That'll mean a fair amount of reassigning of gear priorities."

"We've got six hours to work it out."

"Shit," Garretson mumbled and stomped off.

Bass watched him depart, smiling wryly. He and the DOE boss did not particularly like each other. "Bit testy this morning, isn't he?"

Towne grunted. "Son of a bitch is always testy."

Landing the C-47 proved to be a problem. Straining with the weight of her cargo and the down wheel and strut, the old aircraft finally made it back over the peaks of the Kuman Range and crossed the Brahmaputra flood plain at treetop level.

Once they reached Lake Sonai, both pilots flatly refused to put her down on the strip nearby until daylight. None of Kurisovsky's threats could change their minds. So they spent an hour and a half circling over the lake while below them the lights of the drilling platform seemed to float like a suspended circus on the lake mist.

Finally, the copilot shouted back for everybody to strap themselves to bulkheads, and they began the final downwind approach to the jungle-encircled strip. Below, the trees drew closer as the C-47, lumbering like a wounded eagle, dropped lower and lower.

The first touch was gentle, almost feathery as the pilot, holding full flaps, floated his ship in. There was a slight rising sensation and then the lift dissipated and the aircraft came down hard, the skid and single wheel slamming. The ship lurched in that direction, then straightened, but its weight was settling too fast.

Desperately the pilot rammed power for a brief instant to lighten up. The engines sent momentary tremors through the fuselage before dying away as the plane settled and the loud rumbling scrape of the skid came up through the flooring.

Four seconds later the skid tore away.

The plane tilted sharply, twisting violently to the left. A tremendous crash erupted through the floor plates. Back tensed against the forward bulkhead, Kurisovsky glanced through the window and saw the port wing dig into the ground, hurling grass and dirt like smoke. Half the wing snapped off, its control cables trailing as the ship rolled even farther to that side. He heard things blowing, sounding like electrical transformers shorting out.

Silent and wide-eyed, everybody clung frantically to straps and cargo nets. Aft, the netting and cables tiedowns over the launcher parts were so strained they squealed metallically. Finally an entire section broke apart and sent some of the smaller parts crashing against the bulkhead.

It seemed an eternity of sound and blurred motion before the plane finally began to slow. By this time it was completely side skidding, like a flipped dragster hurtling off momentum. The port tail section tore off, forming a gaping hole through which rocks and sand blew back up the fuselage, pinging like shotgun pellets.

The retaining cables of the launcher carriage snapped and came whipping forward. One sliced across the chest of a trooper and nearly cut him in half. Blood sprayed across the floor as the carriage's full ton weight blew through the side of the aircraft. A great wash of sunlight and ground heat flooded back through the massive hole as the carriage continued on across the ground, turning cartwheels and hurling dust.

The C-47 at last came to a halt on its side, with the starboard wing shot up into the air, the engine hanging from the mounts like a molar torn half out of its socket.

Dust and smoke fumed through the fuselage, and everywhere metal groaned and ticked.

There was a concerted rush for the hole formed by the carriage's departure, now half buried in the dirt. Fearing an explosion, the troopers leapt through and ran off. Kurisovsky paused long enough to check the carotid of the wounded man. He was dead. The pilots came aft, crab-walking on the bulkhead. They were livid, mouths grimacing with rage. Wordlessly they passed Kurisovsky and ducked through the hole.

Everyone assembled two hundred yards away, stood around muttering and looking back at the wreckage. The aircraft had left a deep scar the length of the field. From the rim of the jungle, natives began emerging. Some paused to squat beside the gouge in the earth, shaking their heads. Others wandered around picking up shapeless pieces of metal strewn all along the scar line. A few clustered around the still heated hulk of the port engine, which had been torn off soon after the skid failed, probing it delicately like children around a dead bullock.

The chief Aussie pilot pointed a finger at Kurisovsky. "Oh, you bleedin' Russkie son of a bitch," he bellowed. "You'll pay for this. Wait till Singh finds out what you've done to me bloody ship."

"Will there be a fire?" the colonel asked quietly.

"Oh, I hope she burns like a bleedin' bonfire," the pilot screamed, running about throwing up his arms. He seemed near to tears with frustration. "I hope there ain't nothin' but a pile of ashes left. Singh'll shit in his boots. Then, by God, he'll blow your fuckin' heads off."

Kurisovsky turned slowly to look at the pilot. "I asked you a question."

"Fuck you!"

The other pilot was trying to calm him down.

"Come on, mate," he said, pushing on the other man's chest. "Ease it off now before you get us both karked." He glanced over his shoulder at the colonel. "No, she won't burn. She'd have gone up by now if she was."

Kurisovsky snapped his head and the troopers instantly trotted back toward the wreckage to begin recovery of the launcher parts. He walked over to the two pilots. "Get out of my sight," he said with frigid menace.

The excited pilot had somewhat regained control of himself. The rage in his eyes was replaced with a look of trepidation. "Hey, Colonel," he said nervously. "I'm sorry. I shouldn't 'ave—"

"Now!"

"You got it, mate," the second pilot said quickly. Both men hurried off toward the jungle, not looking back.

For the rest of the morning, the troopers, shirtless and drenched in sweat and aided by a few Indians pressed into service, hauled launcher parts. Back across the field they went and down through the marsh to the wooden dock. Kurisovsky continually hurried them along, periodically lashing out with obscenities like a safari hunter urging his bearers across a Kenyan grassland.

The three troopers from the raid on the Tibetan outpost had spotted the crash and came across the lake in one of the *dagoons*. Zhdanov immediately gave his report about the raid and Sergeant Perotsky's death. Kurisovsky showed no emotion.

"Where's Singh?" he snapped.

"Still in the jungle, sir. He was attacked two days ago, apparently it was bad. His men say he'll be in the area by tonight."

"All right, strip down and start hauling. Ilney, take a man and go get the other barge."

"Yes, sir," Ilney said and trotted back along the dock.

Zhdanov hesitated. "There's something else, sir."

Kurisovsky grunted.

"The Sikhs took one of the spare warheads."

The colonel didn't say anything for a moment. He just stared, his eyes flinty. "What do you mean they took it? To where?"

"Downriver, sir. One of the women told us Singh ordered it. It was to be dumped into the river north of Dibrugarh."

Kurisovsky's nostrils flared, blood flushing his cheeks. For a fleeting moment it seemed as if he would strike Zhdanov. Yet the trooper remained motionless, eyes straight ahead. At last the colonel walked off down the dock and stood watching the *dagoon* head back across the lake.

It was well after noon by the time they got the first load to the island. They off-loaded onto the small beach beside the pavilion and carted the launcher parts up through the gardens to the central court.

Down the shoreline, the drilling rig was going full blast as the crews tried to get in as much depth as possible before the onslaught of the monsoon. One of the drillers, curious, climbed up to the derrick crown and glassed the activity at the pavilion. Kurisovsky pointed a machine pistol at him, and the man immediately climbed back down.

When all the parts were in the court, the colonel called a short break. He sent one of the *dagoons* back across the lake with the natives, and then he and his men trudged wearily back up to the bungalow.

It was cool and silent. The men stripped off their gear while two went off to the kitchen to prepare food.

Kurisovsky walked out to the porch and sat on the railing. A pheasant cooed pleasantly from under the porch as he swung his gaze downriver. On the western horizon the cloud cover formed a brown band like smog. Through the heat he could feel the damp weight of the air, almost smell the rain that would soon be sweeping in. A day and a half, he estimated, maybe two.

His inner clock ticked feverishly against his temples. Would there be enough time? Or would Singh's damnable blunder bring Indian troops swarming up the river before he could get the launcher activated? He hissed through his teeth, swung around, and bellowed, "Out! Out! Everybody back to the courtyard."

Instantly men rushed through the door, pulling on boots and munching on cold *peroshkis*. Raggedly they walked back down the hill.

Rolling drowsily with the lunges of the Rover's rear seat, Bonner squinted at the sky. Forward, McCarran drove while Jackie was scrunched uncomfortably in the passenger seat, trying to sleep. Up high, vultures rode the updrafts, their black silhouettes stark against the thin cloud cover. He watched the floating bodies, their wings perfectly motionless arcing in wide trochoidal circles. Thunderstorm circles, they were called, harbingers of an approaching storm.

He leaned forward and tapped Hak on the shoulder. McCarran steered past a large pothole in the dirt road before turning around. "We've got a storm coming," Cas yelled over the whine of the engine.

Hak nodded. "You ever been in a monsoon, Bonner?"

"Once. It's a bitch."

"Indeed. Those roads upriver will be soup before we get to Sonai."

"Maybe that's good. We could use the cover."

"Maybe."

Bonner settled back, his arms crossed. He felt bone weary, yet there was a sparkle of expectation down inside. For a moment he thought about the strange interlocking of events that had brought him to this place. At first glance, they might have seemed unconnected, merely random circumstances.

Yet he knew they were more likely parts of a pattern. A kind of destiny. He was always being nudged and eventually hurtled into such situations. He wondered if he would have preferred it any other way and knew he wouldn't.

Earlier, Jungali had offered to help them against Singh. "Dat goddom crazy bastard?" the Carib croaked. "He gotta get his back broke, mon. Me, I be likin' to scotch off his big balls, I tell you dat." He smiled at Jackie. "Besides, dis lady is owed one big favor. Ole Jungali, he don' fo'get such tings."

It was decided that Hak, Cas, and Jackie would take one of the Rovers and head straight for Dibrugarh to inform the authorities about the missiles and the fungus in the river. They would then head for Sonai to meet Jungali and his men at a native Garo shore village.

They reached the Jamalpur–Dibrugarh trunk road sometime after noon. Dibrugarh was still a hundred miles away, Hak told them as he swung north and entered the stream of trucks, motorbikes, cars, and packed black minibuses called Tempos. Around them rose sparse stands of yellow-barked acacia, thicker groves of oak and wild lemon, and small meadows where turbaned men worked oxen in tiny rice paddies.

At three o'clock they reached Moranhat, where the jungle became dense and the heat very oppressive as they crossed the Jaipur River, a tributary of the Brahmaputra. The river was low but crystal clear. They saw crocs resting on the bottom while others sunned themselves on the sandbars. Farther on, logging gangs were working the jungle. Their elephants were covered with chalky mud, and some of the men worked at the river's edge completely naked.

At last they broke out of the jungle and could see, across a long stretch of marshland where pink flamingoes stalked the tidal shallows, the Brahmaputra. Bonner gazed placidly at it. It seemed so utterly peaceful way off there, yet he felt a peculiar sense of foreboding.

Jackie felt something akin to it, too. She turned and looked back at him. Her face was faintly dusty, yet the glow of an earlier bath lingered, gave her features a clean, precise vibrancy. She just looked at him, her eyes still for a moment, wondering.

He winked at her.

Reggie Hollis had been standing Screen Room watch in the basement when the peculiar call came in. Hollis, in-country for only six months, was a low-level assistant to the British Consulate General, Calcutta. The consulate offices were located in an ancient building of red brick and Edwardian columns that had once housed the Bengal Military Club.

At first the call angered him. He didn't need any extra work. But there *was* the term *Sickle Round,* which, on checking, he'd found to be that of a defunct code call still on the logs.

He had tried to pry more information from the caller. All that got him was some utter garbage about Russians and bio-missiles and fungi in Assam. So he accepted the message, checked the logs for a ''Tiger Stripe,'' and discovered that it was the code name of an inactive MI-5 agent.

"Probably from some old India hand gone bloody cock-up," he groaned out loud. "Ought to flush the tripe down the bleeding drain." But he couldn't do that, he knew. It was already time-logged and someone would surely ask questions.

He prowled around for a moment, thinking. If he sent up a report to the C.G., he would undoubtedly have him up for one of his tiresome lectures, this one on proper message reception. The vice-consul, a fairly decent chap, was out of office.

Finally he lowered himself into his seat and ran off a teleprint of the entire transmission. He coded it EM-BASSY: LOW-PRIORITY, stuffed it into a plastic tube, and shot it up the pneumatic pipe to Operations. There it would be placed into the daily dispatch, which would go out on the regular two o'clock Vayudoot Air flight for New Delhi.

That would both bury it and get him off the hook.

14

George Tadhunter had been at his office in the Commissioner's Building since four in the morning. Earlier, Thai troops in Bangkok had opened fire on pro-democratic demonstrators who were demanding the resignation of the country's prime minister, Supijat Kachinda. Several people had been killed, dozens wounded. Throughout the long morning Curzon House, MI-5's London headquarters, barraged him for updates on the situation.

To comply, he'd insisted on half-hour reports from his agent in Bangkok. So far, he was told, the government had declared a state of emergency in the capital and four surrounding provinces but were stopping short of martial law. Still, indications showed that certain Thai generals were putting heavy pressure on the P.M. and a military coup was possible.

To cover all bases, Tadhunter had also logged reports from agents in Burma, Laos, and Malaysia to see if any pattern might develop. Among the mass of papers coming in was an unusual bulletin that caught his eye. He didn't quite know what to make of it and red-penciled the item for immediate investigation once the Bangkok situation cooled down.

It was from the Rangoon agent, who had heard a rumor from a Thai newsman about an attack on a Thailand border base by white mercenaries. *White mercenaries?* The phrase had struck him instantly. No further information about it was available, and apparently the Thai military, with other priorities to deal with, were keeping it close to the vest. The item soon slipped to the back of his mind in the flood of data from Bangkok.

He was on his tenth cup of coffee when Jack Booker entered the office. "Excuse the interruption, sir," he said. "But we just received a signal from Jeffry on those Russians in Assam."

Tadhunter leaned tiredly back in his chair and rubbed his temples. The caffeine overdose had given him a blistering headache. "Bloody hell, that's all I need now. Well, let's have it."

Booker handed over the transcription. It contained a bit more than an earlier report, upping the number of Russians to between twelve and eighteen. Norman Jeffry had been unable to extricate any precise information on units the men had come from or any weaponry other than normal automatic field gear. Their purpose seemed to be the training of Abu Singh's militia.

He did, however, have a partial identification of the leader. He was a colonel called either Kurisovsky or Kurensky. The agent closed with a request for clarification on whether or not he should attempt an actual penetration of Namak Island.

Tadhunter tossed the signal onto his desk and studied Booker for a moment. "Tell Jeffry to steer clear of penetration for now," he said finally. "I don't want these people getting suspicious and altering their routine. Just keep him digging."

"Yes, sir." Booker departed.

He rubbed his temples once more. Russians again, he thought wearily. It suddenly occurred to him how ironic it was to have *them* in the mix. Like old times. But a deadly situation nonetheless. Finding a contingent of Russian mercenaries anywhere was like detecting a viper in your bed.

He was on his way to the Transcription Center down the hall to contact Curzon House when he recalled the rumor out of Burma. White mercenaries. He paused in the corridor. Could it be possible they were the same? No, impossible. Such a connection made no tactical or strategic sense. He continued on.

It took his radioman a few minutes to raise London's signal, which was linked by the TelSet-4 Mediterranean satellite. When Curzon House was on-line, Tadhunter adjusted the headset from the LMI Speech Scrambler, which was cable-interfaced with the main VHF transceiver, waited for the operator to exit the room, and then punched his key.

"John, George again. How is signal?" John Williamson was Director of MI-5's E-Branch, responsible for all overseas intelligence.

"Clear, go ahead," Williamson said.

For the next few minutes, he gave the latest update on the Bangkok situation, along with the rumor out of Rangoon. "And one other item. I got a bit of an update from A-3 on those Russians in Assam. Nothing really enlightening except the possible name of the leader."

"Good. Now, that disturbs me. Bloody Russians mucking about in India. What have you got?"

"Two possibles, Kurisovsky or Kurensky." He repeated both names.

"All right, I'll tap our P.F. files and see what we have. I think I'll also give Army and the Foreign Office a run, see if anything turns up on this bloke in their diplomatic dispatches. Shouldn't take but a few ticks. You'll hold?"

"Of course."

It took twenty minutes. When Williamson came

back, he said, "The name's Colonel Andrei Kurisovsky. He's an ex-Spetsnaz commandant. Reputed to have had connections with the October Force."

"My God, an assassination team?"

"Quite possible. But the number of men in this doesn't ring true. Too bloody many. Still, I don't like this, George. Kurisovsky's a high-powered covert operative. Something's up."

"Yes, I agree, of course. Do you advise we attempt a cover penetration immediately?"

There was a long pause, then: "Not quite yet. But I do think you ought to get some people in to help A-3. When we have more solid intelligence, we'll put a man in."

The first time General Valeri Zgursky killed a man, the experience had given his blood an astounding rush. It also melted the fear of death that had come when the Germans attacked his village in 1942. He was thirteen then, an ignorant farm boy. The war swept violently over him. He was given a partisan gun and told to kill Nazis.

That first kill came in a forest glen near Stalingrad. His partisan camp had been probed out by forward patrols of the German 6th Army. A firefight ensued and Valeri, hands trembling on his weapon, saw a German soldier appear through the rain. He fired. The bullet tore the man's throat to pieces. Everything seemed to proceed in slow motion: the crack and recoil of the rifle, the suddenly appearing wound, the gush of blood, and the slow descent of the German into a pool of mushy ice. It was then his body had given song. He'd never known fear since.

He was experiencing something of that same lift in the blood as he sat in his house overlooking the river, receiving ongoing reports from his Phoenix people.

Everything looked promising. Earlier, General Ostalksy had reported that the incident in Red Square had indeed stirred discontent within the officer corp of Dasha. Even normally tight-lipped officers were openly voicing outrage.

In addition, Granov was sending in reports from his own cadre, who were circulating through the hostels and dining clubs where many of the delegates to an upcoming meeting of the Congress of Deputies were staying. They were scheduled to open a three-day session in a day and a half.

Here, too, Granov was finding deep dissatisfaction with Seleznov and his policies. Already, certain middle-of-the-roaders had for the first time showed interest in the idea of a change. Some were even planning to challenge Seleznov vehemently when he gave the opening address at ten o'clock the morning of the convention.

In addition, a recent report from the agents he'd sent to monitor the Chinese moves along the Sino-Kazakhstan border said that Qin's incoming forces were already taking positions in division strength along the frontier east of the oasis of Ining and in the desert plain south of a lake called Ozero Balkhash.

The general left his desk and stood before the window. Below him the early afternoon sun sparkled on the river. As he watched it, the flaming gems of light seemed to infuse his spirit. He thought: You, river, have seen it all, haven't you? But be patient, Moskva. Soon, very soon, you will witness the greatest victory of all.

There was a soft knock on the door.

"Come in."

One of his young assistants entered, braced. "Sergeant Baklanov has arrived, sir."

"Send him in."

A moment later, a young, husky man strode through the door and stood at ramrod attention. "Sir," he barked.

Zgursky smiled warmly. "At ease, Sergeant. Sit, sit."

Stiffly Baklanov settled into a leather chair, his palms on his knees, eyes straight ahead.

"Would you like some vodka?" Zgursky asked gently.

"No, thank you, sir."

"Come, do," he said, pouring out a glass. "I would consider it a great honor to toast with you."

The sergeant took the proffered glass. Zgursky touched it with his own and both men drank. The general sat on the edge of his desk and studied the young man.

"Are you afraid, comrade?" he asked finally.

"No, sir."

"Even though you know you may die?"

"It does not matter, sir. The beloved Motherland will remember me."

"Indeed." He straightened. "There are not many hours left. Do you have any request? Special food, vodka? A woman?"

"Nothing, sir."

"Very well." Zgursky stood and Baklanov immediately sprang to his feet. The general moved forward and embraced him, kissing him lightly on both cheeks. There were sudden tears in the sergeant's eyes.

"Thank you, sir," he murmured emotionally.

Zgursky stepped back. "All right, prepare yourself and your weapon. And, Sergeant, do not miss."

"I will not, sir."

Then Baklanov, the man who had volunteered to be Viktor Seleznov's assassin, snapped his heels, spun around, and quick-stepped out.

From the helicopter the land was brown and barren, rolling, stony hills, absolutely treeless. Everywhere shallow waddies and pressure valleys cut the landscape where swatches of blackfruit wolfberry and tamarisk grew in the bottoms. They resembled smears of thinned paint.

Yet superimposed on the land were the marks of men: vehicle tracks, scattered tent bivouacs and stone buildings under construction, freshly dug missile pits and rows of parked trucks and light motorized infantry vehicles. Back toward the east, more vehicles were coming in, snaking in a single line, churning dust. Far to the right, another dust cloud marked where engineering units were cutting an airfield across the gypsum flats.

General Qin shifted in his seat and took a long pull of *unkape*. His buttocks hurt. He had been in the air for nearly six hours, traversing the nine-hundred-mile frontier with Kazakhstan. He was presently over the great detritus zone known as the Dzungarian Gate, a fan-shaped hilly plain formed by ancient rivers. On the western horizon, within Russian territory, he could see the thin line of dark water that was Ozero Balkhash.

He tapped the pilot on the shoulder and pointed toward the airfield. The chopper tilted sharply as they swung northeast. He took another drink.

Throughout the morning, Qin had received relayed messages from Urumchi, primarily from Marshal Peng, detailing the situation in Beijing. They made Qin fume. Holding to character, Premier Sichen was trying to generate solid backing in the State Council and Politboro so he could pressure the PLA to slow its rapid build-up of forces in the northwest. Such a move, he maintained, would be perceived as provocative throughout the world. Particularly in the U.S., with whom he was seeking closer treaty relations.

Still, Qin found an upside. The very fact that the premier was having to seek backing within the factions of the government meant that powerful forces were in agreement with the PLA position to strengthen the northwest frontier. Qin knew who those forces were. They included some of the most influential men in the State Council, Politburo, and even the Committee of Elders.

The helicopter reached the dust cloud over the field and swung around it. The general leaned out and studied the configuration of the twin runways, each nearly a mile long and capable of the largest cargo jets. He saw that several huge maintenance buildings and a control tower were already completed. Parked near one end of the first strip were over a dozen Tianjin-J-208 jumbo jets, part of the contingent that had ferried in the elements and equipment of the Sacred Lightning Division.

The general was pleased. His troops had proven to be quick and efficient in this harsh, remote land. They were tough and seasoned, and he knew they would be rapacious when it came time for them to cross the frontier.

If they ever got the chance.

That tag-end thought chilled his mood. He had another go at the bottle and sank into brooding. What was truly needed, he thought, was another incident similar to the attack in Tibet. Only here, across *this* frontier. Then not even Sichen could hold back the whirlwind.

Jackie came up out of a doze to find her body cramped and sweaty, one leg numb. In the humid air, perspiration clung to the secret parts of her body like glue. For a moment she kept her eyes closed, feeling the hot wind flow over the Rover's windshield.

At last she opened them and sat up. Bonner was driving. Across the rear seat, Hak was scrunched down with his head on a tool box, his Aussie jungle hat pulled over his eyes.

"Where are we?" she asked Cas.

"About ten miles from Dibrugarh." He glanced over. "Manage any sleep?"

"Not really. God, my mouth tastes like shit."

"There's some water in that bag."

She reached for it. It was made of goatskin with a

little spigot like a Spanish wine bag. She squirted some into her mouth. It tasted rancid.

They were on a narrow dirt road that paralleled the river on the left. The Brahmaputra was nearly a half mile across here, and white sandbars along the near side jutted way out into the water. Yellow hornbills stalked delicately in the little riverlets formed by the current.

She stretched and squeezed her leg. Needles of discomfort prickled her skin. "What time is it?"

"About four in the afternoon."

"What will we do when we reach Dibrugarh?"

"Get a radio and some weapons," Cas answered, his head tilted toward her. "Hak knows a gun dealer."

"Then?"

"We'll head for Lake Sonai, get some hard recon on those missiles."

"Is it far?"

"About fifty miles straight upriver. But Hak says we'll have to go through Dum Dum and then cut back. Maybe a hundred miles all told."

"That'll take us all night.

He glanced over and smiled. "Not us, honey, just McCarran and me. You're staying in Dibrugarh."

"Why?"

"Because from here on in it gets rough."

"And from here on back wasn't?"

"Child's play."

"Oh, crap! I'm going, too."

"No."

"Who the hell died and made you boss.?"

He merely chuckled.

Several hours later, they pulled into the grim town of Dibrugahr. It lay under an unmoving strata of oily smog from the drilling rigs on the opposite bank of the river. It felt thick in the throat and gave a faint, yellow gloominess to the ramshackle oil town.

Yet everything seemed normal as the Rover, now with McCarran at the wheel, swung onto Jewel Harbor Road, the main thoroughfare. It was a wide, gravel-topped street lined with vendor shops and open markets. Prostitutes lounged under purple and yellow doorways in shabby saris with brass jewelry in their noses, idly fondling their "mistresses," personal lovers who were mostly younger, less gaudy girls.

Hak was stiffly alert, head swiveling as if testing the air. They left the main street and passed through a congested *chawl*, a slum area of tin and cardboard shacks and makeshift tents formed from sheets of asbestos. Beyond the slum was a temple dedicated to the goddess Ma Kali. It was made of terra cotta with crenellated archways and corner beehive towers. In front of the temple a low-walled courtyard was filled with men and tethered goats. Several large bier fires burned near the temple's huge banyan tree.

McCarran pulled up beside the outer gate and put his hands wearily over the wheel. "See that?" he said, nodding toward the courtyard. "That's *becara ki puja karna*. Very heavy prayer ceremony. It's only performed in times of great stress to appease Ma Kali for sending her demons from the river."

Jackie glanced around at him. "The fungus?"

"I suspect so," McCarran said.

Gopalpur-on-River General Hospital was situated on two acres of unkempt lawn filled with walkways overgrown with weeds. The main building had been erected in colonial days: twin stories with dirty white walls and an upper balcony. Behind it was a convent house of drab gray stone, where the Sisters of Angelique who staffed the hospital lived.

The parking area was packed with people: village men still filthy from rice paddies, women with their saris wrapped around their legs to form *luggudes*, children, dogs, oxen carts, bicycles and rickshaws, over-flowing onto the outer grounds. Yet the crowd was utterly silent; even the children were motionless and waiting. The only sound was the distant, steady throb of the drilling platforms across the river.

Hak parked the Rover beside a deodar tree, and the three of them made their way through the throng to the hospital entrance. Inside, more people were pressed tightly in the corridors. Some were on make-shift stretchers, others lay on the floor. The rooms stank of saffron and sweat and excitement. Stony-faced nuns, in stained white uniforms with black wimples, moved like swift spectres through the assemblage.

They found the chief of hospital on the second floor in a room filled with prone bodies. Some were obvi-ously dead, others with bodies constricted in tetanus dorsalis, their torsos arched. The floor was soppy with runny excrement that slushed under the nuns' shoes. The smell was even worse than on the lower floor.

The chief was a young, thin Bengali doctor with skin the color of roasted chestnuts. He was dressed in a sweat-soaked safari suit. At first he refused to talk to them, mumbling to himself as he rushed from pa-tient to patient, desperately, helplessly administering hypos that he carried in a small green bag.

Bonner grabbed his arm and held him still. The man stared into Cas's face, his eyelids blinking rapidly. "Please, you must wait your turn," he cried franti-cally. "Please, you must wait." He tried to pull away.

Bonner held him. "Settle down. We're here to help."

"What? What?"

Jackie stepped forward. "I'm a doctor. And I know the cause of all this."

The Indian stared at her, then shook his head rap-idly. "No, you must wait your turn."

"Listen to me," Jackie said firmly. "I know why these people are sick. It's a fungus from the river, a mutated form of fungus."

"No, these people are with dysentery."

"It's *not* dysentery, dammit." She launched into a long burst of medical terminology. The man stared and stared, his long-lashed eyelids fluttering.

When she finished, he said, "You are indeed being a doctor?"

"Yes. How many physicians are here?"

"Only two, which is including myself. The other is *ayurvedic*."

"What anti-fungial serum do you have in your inventory?"

The Indian frowned. "I am not aware of what there is at this very moment. We have been treating with—"

"Do you have any amphotericin B? Hydroxystilbamidine isethionate?"

"Oh, yes, yes, Amp-B, we are having that. But very little amounts."

"Get more."

"I have already notified the Delhi Disease Center. But they will be most surprised if I ask for such medicines."

"I don't a give a shit if they are surprised. Just get it here. Along with—" Her words were cut off by a scream across the room. A man thrashed on the floor, his breathing coming in short, tight gasps through clenched teeth. Two nuns rushed over to him.

The Indian doctor's face contorted and he began to weep. "Oh, sweet, blessed Kali, I cannot bear this. What can I do?"

Jackie took hold of his shoulders and shook him, glaring into his moist eyes. "Do as I tell you. Now! We need huge amounts of Amp-B flown in. And all the defibrillation equipment Delhi D.C. can lay its hands on.'' She shook him again. ''Do you understand?''

The Indian's eyelids began fluttering again. He stared dumbly at her.

''We must have defibrillation capacity. That's how you destroy the pathogen.''

''But these peoples are not dying of heart seizure.''

''They must be shocked to kill the fungus. Then hit with massive doses of amp-B or HI to detoxify their bodies.''

''No, no!'' the Bengali cried. ''I cannot allow this thing.''

''But it's the only way. I've done it.''

''No, I cannot make such responsibilities.'' He pulled free. ''No, you are going away.''

''Look around you, you goddamned idiot,'' Jackie screamed at him. ''They're all dying. You don't have a choice.''

''No, it is terribly against regulations. Delhi would be most displeased.'' He turned and hurried away.

Jackie stood looking helplessly after him. ''Jesus Christ!'' she cried in frustration.

McCarran jerked his head to Bonner. ''Come on, lad. We're of no use here.''

Jackie whirled around. ''Where are you going?''

''To have a little chat with an old friend,'' Hak answered. ''We'll be back in an hour.'' He headed for the door.

Jackie grabbed Bonner's arm. Her eyes searched his face. ''You *are* coming back?''

He nodded. ''We're going for weapons.''

She relaxed. ''All right.'' She squeezed his bicep. ''Be careful.''

''You, too. And keep on that jerk, make him listen.''

Her eyes went as hard as gray agate. ''Oh, he'll

come around, regulations or no regulations. Or I'll
tear his goddamned nuts off.''

He grinned down at her, then reached up and lightly
ran his finger over the hair on her temple. She cupped
her hand over his. After a moment he turned and followed McCarran.

Sagub Gupchat owned a goldsmith shop located in
an alley filled with piles of refuse down near the river.
Bracketing it was a vegetable shop and a tailor's. At
the far end, the passageway devolved into an oily backwater where hulks of sunken boats protruded through
the surface.

Hak eased the Rover gently along the alley. The air
was stifling and ripe with the odor of slowly rotting
fruit, especially spoiled papayas. Rats nibbled at refuse. Against a wall squatted *harijan* beggars, the untouchables called by Gandhi the Children of Light.
Some had arms or legs missing, others eyes.

Gupchat's shop was filled with shadowy light from
several kerosene lanterns, which made the beaded curtain across the front shimmer. Hak parked directly in
front. Inside, they could see two young Indians sitting
cross-legged over stone anvils, hammering on bundles
made of sheep intestine called *cutchs* that were
wrapped around thin sheets of gold.

The shop itself was cluttered with statues, wooden
utensils, and leather books, all etched in gold Davan-
gari script filigree. Joss sticks, bamboo slivers impregnated with sandalwood and rose powder, hung on
threads, their thick perfume a barrier against the stench
from the alley.

The two young men glanced up sullenly as Mc-
Carran and Bonner came through the beads. There
were bells on the bottoms of the tassles that tinkled
softly. Hak spoke to one of them. The man shouted

something over his shoulder. A moment later, Gupchat emerged from an inner room.

He was a tall, very dark Tamil. His face was shaped like the figure eight, the lower half ponderously jowly. One eye was black as an agate, the other a milky orb from glaucoma. There was a horrible scar on his neck that looked waxy in the flickering light.

"*Acha!*" Gupchat cried and flashed a betel-stained smile at McCarran. He clasped his palms together, bowed in *namaste*. "Sahib McCarran, how good you come to my shop." His words came out softly but rapidly like the gentle rustle of water over rocks.

"Hello, Sagub," Hak said. He returned the *namaste*. "I need to talk"

"Ah?"

"In private."

Gupchat stepped back, indicating they proceed into the back room. Hack and Bonner entered. The room was small, its walls blackened from smoke residue. In one corner was a cement fireplace with two grilles over white-hot coals and a grimy chimney that went up through a hole in the ceiling. Beside it, a tiny alcove displayed a figure of Ganpati with a wreath of marigolds around its neck. The floor was covered with a red rug.

The proprietor had been eating. He offered them food, but Hak declined. Everyone sat down on the rug. Gupchat put his rice balls and bowls of sauce aside, tented his fingers, and looked at McCarran. There was a faint smile on his thick lips, but it did not go up into his good eye.

"So?" he said. "On what matter are you wishing to converse with me, my English friend?"

"I need automatic weapons," McCarran said evenly. "And some explosives, with fuses."

Gupchat blinked slowly. "But why do you come here?"

"I know you supply the BIM, Sagub. And you know I know. So let's dispense with the ruddy crap. I'll pay well."

The Tamil scratched delicately at his scar. His diseased eye seemed to shift slightly back and forth like an ivory bearing loose in its socket. "So you are intending to capture your crocodiles with explosives now?"

"No, I'm after bigger bloody game. Gulab Dau Singh."

Instantly Gupchat's brow lowered. He intently studied McCarran's face for a moment, then asked, "Why you do this?"

"Because the bastard's got Russian biological missiles up at Lake House."

"Ah, yes. I am knowing about the Russians. But there has been no talk of missiles."

"They're there." Hak waved his hand. "And all the bloody sickness here is the result of it. So far it's probably only from an accident. But we believe Singh intends to launch them against your people."

The Tamil sprang lightly to his feet and paced the small room in agitatation. Finally he paused. "How do you intend to proceed?"

"We'll make a run on the island to find out what missiles he's got and precisely where they are. Then we'll bring Delhi into it."

Gupchat looked surprised. "Only you and this one?"

"Yes."

"That would be most dangerous."

"Your ordnance would make it less so."

"Ah, well, perhaps I can render further aid. Two,

three days from this there will be . . . certain fighters in Dibrugarh.''

Hak shook his head. "Too late. We're going now."

"You are a fool, McCarran. Singh will kill you both." Then he snorted through the beak of his nose and jerked his head. "Come."

They walked down the alley to the oily backwater, Gupchat carrying a flashlight. Out on the river they saw tiny fires floating. Hak explained to Cas they were images of papier mâché and clay in small leaf boats that the people had set adrift for Ma Kali.

For a few moments they moved through the grass, unseen things rustling ahead of them. Several yards down, they reached the stern of a partially sunken tug with a ramp of two-by-fours. Bonner and McCarran followed the Tamil up onto the tug's stern deck.

All the up-machinery had been stripped, and the metal hull was heavily rusted with its entire foredeck under water. As they went down through the main-house companionway, Cas caught sight of a snake as it uncoiled and slithered off a forward hatch to go swimming across the water, its sinuous movement making a spreading ν of light.

The mainhouse deck was coated with bat guano, white as chalk. Gupchat opened a deck hatch and led them down a narrow ladder into the boat's engine room. The single engine mount was empty, and they saw that the bilges were filled with black water. In the flashlight beam, several rats, huge as cats, scurried away into the shadows.

The Tamil's stash of weapons was packed in three straw-wrapped boxes near the gutted transmission housing. Gupchat tore aside the straw, sending huge yellow spiders plopping onto the deck, and opened one of the boxes. It contained eight M1 Thompson

.45-caliber submachine guns with thirty-round stick magazines. Their blued barrels gleamed in the light.

The second box held two dozen handguns: Colt .45 Combat Commanders and Beretta 9mms, neatly packed in a wooden jaw frame. There were also fifteen glass acid bombs made from net floats and filled with hydrochloric acid. The third box had six satchels of C-4 plastic explosive, each satchel holding four two-and-a-half-pound blocks that looked like bricks of vanilla fudge. The satchels had the old X timer/fuse system, with a battery-operated timer clock in the center along with a packet of detonator wires which, when inserted through rings in the fabric to each C-4 block, formed an χ. There were also four boxes of detonators, each one in its own slot like drill bits.

Cas picked up one of the Thompsons, rapped back the cocking lever. The *chunk* of it was sharp in the closed space. It was a good sound to him, a familiar sound. He hefted the weapon and inhaled its clean, acetate scent of oil. He glanced over at McCarran, knocked his knuckles against the butt, and grinned at him.

McCarran smiled grimly back. "Aye, they're a bit out of date, lad, but first-class all the same."

They chose two Thompsons, a Colt, a Beretta, and four satchels of C-4 with fuses. Gupchat led them forward into a second compartment, where he had six boxes of ammunition. Squatting on the deck with the light, the Tamil watched as the two men loaded their weapons. Next they transferred some of the 9mm ammo into one of the .45 boxes and slung the satchels.

Cradling his Thompson, McCarran turned to Gupchat. "How much for the lot?"

The Tamil grinned, his teeth looking black in the half-light. "You do not have enough money."

"How bloody much?" Hak repeated.

"Nothing."

Hak grunted. "Most gracious of you. But there's still something else we need. A mobile transceiver."

"Ah, radios. Unfortunately, of these I am most barren."

"Who can I see, then?"

"Wait a moment, let me consider." The Indian's white eye quivered, a celestial sphere encased in his face. He nodded. "Yes, I believe there is a man. Come, you can wait for me at my shop."

Gupchat was gone for twenty minutes. Bonner and McCarran watched the two apprentices laboriously pound their gold ribbon. Neither man seemed startled to see their weapons. When the Tamil returned, he put a box in the Rover, then poked his head through the beaded curtain. He snapped an order to one of the men, who silently went out and down the alley.

The box was stamped with French stencils, indicating it contained a Belgium Brussel-Comm 310 HF/SSB Transceiver, a BRV 003 amplifier, and a collapsible whip antenna. Inside, the components were encased in fitted styrofoam squares.

Hak shot Gupchat a sly look. "She's a beauty, Sagub. How much?"

The Tamil flicked his hand. "This was stolen from one of the oil companies. I persuaded my Chinese friend it should be put to proper use as forgiveness for such terrible thievery."

"Bravo," McCarran cried, grinning.

A moment later, the apprentice came back up the alley struggling with another box. He slid it onto the hood of the Rover and silently went back into the shop. This one held a 24 VDC cadmium battery with a 110/220 automatic switcher. Bonner put it in the back of the Rover.

Gupchat held up a finger. "I am desiring but one item. Before Singh and his men kill you, you perhaps will send several of my bullets into his testicles. Thus, his next incarnation will be without sons."

"Agreed," Hak said.

The tiny blue flame of the acetylene cutting torch looked amber through the welder's mask, a sputtering blob of incandescence in an otherwise black field. Kurisovsky, stripped to the waist and drenched in sweat and groundwater, tried to keep the dot steadily moving in a straight line across the I-beam of the launcher's frame. In the darkness under the mask, he had to remember the chalk line by the impressions left on his retina.

Since late afternoon, he and his men had been frantically working to re-assemble the launcher and create a new platform for the BEARCAT-214s. Many of the parts had been warped and sheared by the crash of the C-47. The Russians had to cut and reweld whole sections before even starting on the revised firing sleeves.

Moreover, in order to fix a firm foundation for the launcher, they had had to dig up the floor of the courtyard down to seepage water and cable the different sections to posts driven deep into the sandy ground. Also, once the monsoon hit, the pit would fill with runoff, which would absorb much of the shock of the launch.

Earlier, around twilight, Kurisovsky, two of his troopers, and the handful of Singh's militiamen he'd left behind had gone down the hill to the drilling camp. A crew was still working the main drill derrick, but most of the off-duty men were at mess. Everybody looked up when the grimy, armed men came in. All conversation abruptly ceased.

Kurisovsky strode to the center of the room. "Who is leader here?" he shouted.

A huge, bearded man in white coveralls and a hard-hat stood up. "I'm toolpusher, mate. What d'ya want now? Another bloody barge?"

The colonel walked around the table and stood in front him. The toolpusher towered above him. "We need welding equipment and tools," he said.

"Do you now?" The man looked him up and down. "Where the bloody hell is Singh?"

"Across the lake."

"Well, you go get that bleedin' kafir. I ain't given' out tools without him telling me to."

Kurisovsky's eyes were steady, flat. "*I'm* telling you."

"Not good enough, mate." The beard parted into an insolent smile.

Kurisovsky's expression did not change. He dropped his hand. When it came back up, his Beretta was in it. He shoved it against the man's heart. Everybody jumped, and in a hushed voice someone said, "Ay, God!"

"You will do as I say," Kurisovsky snapped.

The big man's sneer disappeared for a fraction of a second, then came back. "Bullshit, mate," he growled.

The twin reports of the pistol were muffled against the toolpusher's body. A wild expression came into his eyes, the massiveness of his chest taking the impact. Then he let out a soft groan and slumped to the floor. All around the room, men were frozen in place, jolted into utter silence. In it, the two spent rounds rolled off a table and tinkled on the cement floor.

Holding the Beretta at port-arms, Kurisovsky said, "Now get me the tools."

A bald man at a nearby table hurriedly lifted his leg over the bench seat. "They're out here, mister." The colonel nodded to his two troopers, who instantly followed the man out the mess-hall door.

Kurisovsky turned back. "No one is to leave the island."

There was a general groan. Someone near the door called out. "But we're on rotation, man."

"No one is to leave the island," Kurisovsky repeated in the same icy voice. "Anyone who attempts to will be shot."

No one spoke.

The colonel ordered several men to cart the toolpusher's body down to the lake and throw it into the water. While they were about it, he placed a militiaman at each of the entrances. The remaining three he sent down to the main freight dock to guard the drilling company's two cargo gigs. Then, commandeering a jeep, he and his troopers hauled two acetyleyne tank rigs, work lights, and a huge box of tools back up the hill.

Someone tapped his shoulder. He sat back, snapping the welding mask up. It was Corporal Modin, who had been assigned to monitor the bungalow radio. "A signal from Mr. Andropov, sir. They request a specific launch time."

Kurisovsky cut the flame and climbed out of the launcher pit. Work lights had been strung from the main house, and their brightness glistened and danced on the ankle-deep water in the pit as he pulled his boots free. He whistled for one of his sergeants who was working on the firing panels. The man ran over.

"Status?" Kurisovsky barked.

"We've got the adapter rails mounted, but there's trouble with the recoil pads and fire doors, sir. All the bolt holes are way off alignment. We also have to recut the entire base plate and use shims to keep the rockets from creating warp vibration."

"How long?"

"Three, four hours at least, sir."

"What about the firing panels?"

"I've got the sections rewired, but I had to bypass

the warm-up connectors in the packet system. That'll throw off the firing sequence.''

Kurisovsky thought a moment. ''All right, set firing to auto with a ten-minute lag. We'll use the torches for warm-up once we've started launch sequence.''

This would make the firing touchier, he knew. But there was no choice. His initial intention had been to fire each missile individually, allowing repair time for any damage the blast created in the launcher before firing again. But in auto mode, the three mounted missiles would be fired in a ripple salvo with only fifteen seconds between each launch.

The sergeant frowned. ''How will we pre-check the system, sir? The BM-27 auto gear isn't functional with such a wide lag.''

''Then triple-check every component visually before switch-on.'' Kurisovsky gave the man a cold stare. ''Make certain, Sergeant.''

''Yes, sir.'' The man went back to his panels.

Kurisovsky turned to Modin. ''What's the forecast for the monsoon?''

''It has already struck Visakhaptnam and Cuttack on the Bay, sir. Latest estimate of arrival in Assam is dawn.''

Kurisovsky wiped mud off his watch and checked the time. It was 8:01. Dawn lay nine hours away. He figured a moment. They'd need at least an hour to allow the monsoon to come in fully so that its downpour and lightning would cover the launch. ''We'll launch at six A.M., Assam time.''

''Yes, sir.'' Corporal Modin hurried away.

Kurisovsky refired his cutting head, snapped down the mask, and returned to his amber flame.

The crowd at the hospital had increased, yet it was still enveloped in that eerie silence. Like stone statues in the darkness, they waited. Adding to the macabre mood were flecks of heat lightning far to the west that touched the high leaves of the deodars.

Bonner left McCarran to assemble the radio and went into the hospital. He found Jackie in a small operating room near the back. It was little more than a lab with a single table in the center under a reflecting shade of fluorescent lighting. Beside it was an oxygen tank and a mobile fibrillation machine, its twin paddles hooked to a wire under the shade.

A young woman lay on the table, her upper body naked. Her breasts were thick and heavy with large, dark nipples. A nun in a feces-stained operating gown was giving her oxygen.

Jackie, also in a gown, glanced around when Cas came in. Her eyes rested for a moment on the Colt .45 he had tucked into the band of his shorts. Then she turned away.

Bonner came over. "I see you convinced him."

Jackie grunted. She slipped a hypo into the girl's arm, snapped off the rubber hose, and felt the carotid vein with her other hand.

"How's it going?" he asked.

"We've saved three."

"All right!"

She ignored him, glancing over at the nun instead. "Get another one in." The woman adjusted the oxygen mask and hurried out.

"You're going," Jackie said. It wasn't a question.

"Yes."

"I'm not."

"I know." He looked at her back. It shifted under the gown, pulling tightly across her spine when she withdrew the hypo and tossed it into a corner.

"I came to say good-bye," he said.

"Good-bye." She didn't turn around.

Her abruptness shocked him. For a moment he stood

there feeling a little foolish. The nun returned with a young boy on a gurney. The cart knocked loudly on the swinging door of the O.R. The boy turned his head and looked at Cas, his eyes wide, showing yellow.

"Prep him," Jackie barked to the nun. "No, over there, over there."

Bonner shrugged, turned away, and started for the door. As he reached it, he heard Jackie call out: "Cas."

He glanced back. She was staring at him, a strange expression on her face, the tight, still, shocked look of a woman who has just been told she has cancer. Then she advanced quickly across the small space, her gown whispering softly. She reached out, put her hands against his face, and pulled his mouth to hers.

He felt the full length of her body come to him. He pulled her even closer, catching the faint redolence of jasmine in her hair. Her lips quivered on his, parted, bringing teeth on teeth, tongue tasting hungrily.

She broke the kiss. "Oh, dammit," she gasped, clinging to him.

Aroused, he bent and kissed her neck. They swayed against each other. Then someone out in the corridor let out a groan. It pierced their spell. Jackie gently pulled back, her eyes flitting across his face.

"Don't get killed," she whispered feverishly, her eyes filled with an aching tenderness. "Just don't die, okay?"

"I won't," he said.

She whirled and hurried back to the operating table, snapping out an order to the nun.

15

In Washington it was 12:11 P.M., yet Scott Clark had bypassed lunch. In truth, he'd had very little to eat since a jelly roll at six, along with tons of coffee. His stomach felt like a tin drum full of gas.

Nevertheless, he was exhilarated. Earlier that evening, British Intelligence had passed along its findings of the Russian commandos in Assam, and the Defense Secretary had ordered that Clark be directly linked into a CIA intelligence search. The amount of information he had been receiving because of Secretary Moffett's intervention was astounding. Ordinarily, trying to find solid ground in the data chase of the U.S. government was like climbing a stairway of wax while drowning in molasses. But tonight his requests for access were being handled with businesslike alacrity. Not only from the CIA, but also from such sensitive departments as the Office of Strategic Research and the Department of the Army's Intelligence Bureau.

Using specific information from these sources, reinforced by his own war game results, he had already formulated a cohesive Theater of Operations composed of a cast of "characters," each representing the various forces involved in the entire Sino-Chinese-Indian-Russian-Caspian Alliance situation.

An hour earlier, he had begun uploading the T.O. into the logic systems of the Cray 250 computers in the NDF at Fort McNair. Working from it, the big analog machines would run forecast scenarios in which the force-characters improvised their way through hypothetical events leading to theoretical outcomes.

On this he had worked completely alone, keeping his computer room above the Mock-up Center locked. This was primarily to minimize the interjection of subjective factors into his T.O. due to operator mind-set. Further, he assiduously sought to keep his own gut feelings of Russian involvement out of the mix as well. It proved difficult, particularly since the word of Soviet mercenaries in India had come in.

Still, in the broad picture that single item remained isolated, incidental within the confused melange of other forces. And it was a hellish melange, created from a plethora of reports on internal affairs within India, Moscow, and peripheral intelligence out of Beijing. Along with satellite reports of the Chinese build-up along NEFA and the old Russian republics, even meteorological updates of the monsoon could play a part in any Sino-Indian fighting. To expedite, he'd chosen only those highlights that would have significance to his projection goals. He hoped this admittedly subjective choice would wash out in the long run.

At 12:12 the forecasts began coming back from McNair. As expected, their main focus was on the possibility of an Indian-Chinese confrontation across both the Kashmiri and NEFA borders. Although there were other projections, it was the expansion of the first one that instantly caught Clark's attention. If the Chinese not only crossed into NEFA territories but also the Kashmiri frontier in the north, this could result in a massive spillover of Chinese invasion forces into the old Soviet republics of Tajikistan, Kyrgyzstan, and Kazakhstan.

Studying the printouts closely, Clark immediately

realized the great deal of "gray" in the projections. The Crays had encountered too many data tolerances in the T.O. framework, resulting in parameter assumptions within too wide a projection scale. This, in turn, created unacceptable variances in forecast accuracy. He had expected divergence, since he had "topped-off" the data input and done it with too much speed. But this was too broad. He'd have to fine-tune before submitting any coherent blue paper to Moffett.

Quickly he chose a single force-character scenario to begin tightening the system. This one concentrated on the Chinese invasion of Russian territory. Running a random search through his own data bank, he drew up deeper Beijing intelligence material, followed by all the information he had on the present situation in Moscow. It included the latest item concerning the meeting of the ICS Council of Ministers. Last, he infused the material on Kurisovsky.

For a moment he sat back and surveyed the workup. He knew he was deliberately guidelining this one. But what the hell, he thought, at least he'd get something with a narrower assumption base. He leaned forward and sent it to McNair.

Six minutes later, it came back. The Cray logic system had projected initial confusion within the Russian CIS at the onset of a Chinese invasion. This would be followed by pleas to the U.N. for condemnation of the Sino forces and immediate intervention.

But while the Chinese continued to sweep easily into the old republic territories, the U.N. and the world would hesitate. Within that momentary vacuum, McNair's computers predicted the possibility of a re-emergence of Soviet right-wing factions, reinforced by across-the-board outrage throughout the entire USSR. The result could be a swift coup in Moscow that would initiate the decisive return of centralized power into the hands of the Communist hard-liners.

Clark's pulse went up. He was looking at the first substantive statement of his green light. But, he quickly saw, there were contingencies tacked on. First, the Beijing government under Sichen had not yet exhibited enough of a swing to the right to justify the probability of preemptive invasion against Russia. Unless there was a change in present policy, or a military coup within Beijing that would oust Sichen, the Chinese government would never launch such an invasion.

Second, and more important, ever since the abortive coup against Seleznov, the Communist factions within the old USSR had been fragmented, without a powerful enough cadre to generate the decisive usurption of the CIS. The projection indicated that a dedicated force, even a small but highly skilled and efficient one, would be needed to accomplish it. Nothing in his T.O. data had given the Crays enough to form the assumption that such a force existed.

Clark was on his feet all the same, moving distractedly about his consoles. He paused at the window. From his room he looked out on the Pentagon concourse from ground level. Out there it was bright and sunny, but he didn't see any of it. His mind was humming, instincts fired. He knew he was on the right track.

Two items were still missing, pivot points. Their absence formed a big hole in the Cray run around which he sensed things swirling. He prowled back to his terminal, studied the display. It triggered the distinct feeling that he was looking at a box of dynamite, smoldering, ready to go.

But where were the fuses?

Tadhunter snored softly, sitting back in his chair. Weariness had finally caught up to him around nine o'clock. Affairs in Thailand had finally come under control as the Thai king rode herd on his subjects enough to cause even antagonistic factions to sit down and discuss possibilities. But Tadhunter had decided to remain at his office in the event of another flare-up. At seven he had dinner with the commissioner, Sir Frederick Hume, then returned to his station. His doze had started as a mere rest period but had soon escalated into this snooze.

Suddenly through it burst Booker, wide-eyed. "Sir! Sir!"

Tadhunter blinked and sat forward. His mouth tasted slightly sour. "Ah, Booker." He frowned as he read the shock on the man's face. "What's happened?"

"The bleeding Russians have biological missiles," Booker cried.

"What?"

"In Assam, sir. Those Russkie mercenaries with Singh have bio-missiles."

Tadhunter was jolted. "Good God!" His gaze wandered a moment, came back. "Has Jeffry verified the report?"

"It didn't come from Jeffry, sir. It was from Tiger Stripe. Hak McCarran!"

"McCarran? What is this?"

"I was down in Dispersal, sir. One of the operators showed me a low-priority info-chit signal that came in from the New Delhi embassy. He thought it was a bloody joke, didn't know what to make of it." Booker leaned over the desk and held out a yellow sheet.

Tadhunter took it and read:

To: Commissioner: Singapore
    RR ID Section
Time: 1531 NDST//6-8-92

Request clarification and verify on relay from con-
sulate:Calcutta CR (Log: 1324 NDST//6-8-92 . . .
Calcutta CR received open radio message using defunct code term: Sickle Round . . . Message claimed
Russian biological missiles in Assam state . . . Further
claimed unknown fungial infection has been discovered in upper Brahmaputra. Message source identified
as Tiger Stripe . . .

That was as far as he got. He looked up at Booker
in disbelief. For ten solid seconds they stared at each
other. Then Tadhunter gently lowered the signal to his
desk. "Booker," he said tightly, "we've got ourselves
a potential disaster."

"Maybe it's just some twisted joke of McCarran's,
sir?" the aide said hopefully. "Perhaps the booze has
finally sopped him."

Tadhunter shook his head. "No, not McCarran. This
is for real." He thrust himself to his feet. "Get in
direct link with Calcutta. Tell them we want everything they can find out about McCarran's whereabouts.
Everything on Red Clear-Through. And find out where
the bloody hell Jeffry is."

"Yes, sir." Booker darted out as Tadhunter lunged
to his feet, rounded his desk, and headed for the radio
room to call John Williamson in London.

The Indian night flew past the Rover in a sultry,
storm-laden stillness. Banks of trees flashed in the
headlights, their dark branches seeming to droop like
giant, exhausted runners in the humidity.

Cas was at the wheel, bombing along the jungle road
toward the tea town of Dum Dum. Since there was no
direct river road from Dibrugarh to Lake Sonai, it was
necessary for them to cut inland to Dum Dum, then

turn north and head for the shore *jheels* of Talab. Hak estimated they would reach Sonai around one in the morning.

Ever since leaving Dibrugarh, he had been trying to raise the British consulate in Calcutta on the Brussel-Comm. Hunched low behind the driver's back rest, the radio's antennae whipping in the breeze, he'd continuously probed for the consulate's C.R., now openly using his code identification of Tiger Stripe. It was no use. The radio's range was insufficient on battery power.

Finally, he gave up with a curse and lay back, his leg up on the passenger seat. He reached over, pulled a bottle of whiskey from the tool box over the wheel well, and drank.

Bonner glanced around. "Is there anyone between here and Calcutta you can raise?" he yelled.

Hak shook his head and handed up the bottle. "Nobody with any bleeding authority."

Up ahead, three deer suddenly exploded from the trees, and flashed across the road in a bounding blur. Cas hit the brakes and the Rover fishtailed violently. He finally got it straightened out again.

A moment later, he shouted over his shoulder, "What about your wife? Could she relay to Calcutta?"

Hak, about to take another drink, stopped, sat upright. "What a splendid idea, lad. Why in bloody hell didn't I think of that?" He twisted around and put his flash on the transceiver, began whirling the dial.

Malli McCarran came back with her soft Hindi voice clothed in a static warp that surged and crackled like sticks burning. Hak acknowledged and reached over to tap Bonner's shoulder, indicating he pull up. They slid to a stop in a cloud of talcum-like dust.

"Listen very carefully, *priyvar*," McCarran said

into the mike. "I am near Dum Dum. Bonner with me. Headed for Lake Sonai and Singh's stronghold at Lake House. Repeat, over."

Malli did so.

"There is outbreak of disease at Dibrugarh. Very bad. It is a fungus. Write that down." He spelled it for her, using the Hindi alphabet. "Cause is from Russian missiles at Lake House. Repeat, over."

Again his wife complied.

"Radio British consulate in Calcutta," Hak went on. "Use call name Tiger Stripe." He gave her the consulate's frequency, twice. "Tell them about the missiles and disease in Dibrugarh. Tell them I am going to Lake House. Have radio but they must relay through you. Do you understand fully? Over."

Malli came back: "Yes, *samajh me ana*." She repeated what he had told her, word for word. Then: "*Patidev*, there is one thing most important I must tell. A man has called to you on telephone. His name is Jeffry. He say you must know that he is of George Tadhunter. Over."

McCarran cried, "Bloody good." He keyed. "Where is Jeffry now? Over."

"In Gauhati. He is to come here in one hour. Over."

"Bravo, love. Give Jeffry this frequency." He read it twice off the radio display. "Tell him he must raise me as soon as he gets there. If I do not hear from him in one hour, I will call. Over."

"*Samajh me ana, Patidev*. Over."

Hak cleared after a few intimate words to his wife, then sat back with a grin on his long face. "British Intelligence is in it now, lad," he said. "Tadhunter is MI-5 head in Singapore. This Jeffry must be his A-agent in Assam." He lifted his bottle, took a long pull. When he lowered it, he raised it on high. "Go, lad, go! Now we've got some bloody backup in our kit.''

Bonner shifted into gear. But in that second before the Rover moved, he felt a breeze lift past his face, touch his arm lightly. It felt cool, the first faint disturbances from the massive front of the approaching monsoon.

''Impossible!'' Indian General Moraji Shastra shouted when informed by Secretary Amit Chedi that British Intelligence claimed there were Russian biological missiles in Assam state. ''I have had no such reports.''

''But MI-5 claims to have eyewitnesses,'' Chedi persisted. They were in the prime minister's quarters in the Rashrapati Bhavan. The room was done in rich red cedar, and through a massive bay window they could see the distant lights of Gandhi International Airport.

''Eyewitnesses? The goddamn English always have eyewitnesses. They only want to stir up trouble.'' The general waved his hand disdainfully and jammed an unlit cheroot into his mouth. He was an imposing man, tall and deep-chested. His bright red uniform, glittering with gold epaulettes and ribbons, added to the air of Raj indomitability.

Seated at an ornate desk of marble, Prime Minster Jurigan Anduri said, ''They have conceded it is as yet only an unverified rumor.''

''You see?'' the general said. ''Rumors! They make all mischief but cover their pricks with claims of rumors. It is outrageous.''

Chedi turned to the P.M. ''But what if it is true, Jurigan?'' As Secretary for State Affairs, Chedi was the closest cabinet member to Anduri and one of his major supporters in the Rajya Sabha, the upper house of the Indian Parliament. ''If Singh does indeed possess such missiles, there could be devastation anywhere in Bharat.'' Bharat was what Indians called India.

Anduri nodded solemnly. In contrast to the others, he was small, almost fragile. Once he had been a firebrand who twice was put into prison for sedition before finally winning the Congress Party's power seat. Since obtaining it, however, he had become equivocal, his decisions timid. The apology to China had already created a backlash within the powerful Council of Ministers, adding to the general feeling of discontent with him.

''We should have dealt with Singh earlier,'' he hissed petulantly.

General Shastra snorted, withdrew his cheroot. ''Singh is a pissant. One company of my Fourth could destroy him in a day.'' Before becoming chief of the General Staff, Shastra had been commander of the XXXIII Corps. The unit he referred to was the Fourth Grenadiers, paratroopers in summer quarters in Gorakhpur in Uttar Pradesh Sate, west of Assam.

''Do that and you would creat instant civil war all over the northeast,'' Chedi cried hotly.

''We'd crush that, too.''

''But what if Singh does have such missiles? Mm? What then, General?''

Shastra stared at the secretary, one cheek quivering slightly. Anduri held up his hands. ''Gentlemen, please.'' He put his head down, balanced on the tips of his forefingers. Finally he looked up at Chedi. ''What do our own intelligence people say?''

''They have no reports of missiles.'' He looked uncomfortable. ''But it is suspected that many of their agents in the northeast have been corrupted by Singh.''

Anduri's eyes flashed. "Why wasn't I told of this situation?"

"Look!" Shastra crowed, "Now the secretary even accuses our own I.B. of laxity and corruption."

Chedi ignored him. "There were other, more pressing matters."

Shastra swung to face the P.M. He put his huge hands on the marble desk. "Do you believe these bloody English?" he demanded.

"How can I know?" Anduri answered helplessly. "It is all insane."

"If you do believe, then let me strike Singh now, before the monsoon reaches the upper Brahmaputra. I can have paratroopers over Lake Sonai within two hours."

Anduri's face contorted as if in pain. "But we cannot act too rashly. These are only rumors."

"The rain has already entered Bangladesh," Shastra said. "If you decide to strike it must be done quickly."

"Be prudent, Jurigan," Chedi warned quietly. "If you send government troops into Assam, it could precipitate chaos."

"Goddammit," the general shouted at Chedi. "You are the one who believes these idiotic reports of missiles."

"I do not totally believe," Chedi shot back. "I think it could be a possibility. But one we must move very cautiously with."

Anduri nodded. "Yes, I agree. We will wait."

General Shastra growled, clamped his teeth onto his cheroot, and glared out the window.

At 12:45 A.M. the tiny chime of Dave Bass's clock made a delicate dollop of sound in the dark cabin. Instantly Bass was awake. He uncoiled his tall frame and sat up. For a moment his head ached slightly; he'd only been in the bunk for less than two hours. He flicked on the bunk light.

Below him, his cabin mate, Charley Mirisch, opened his eyes sleepily. "Oh, Jeez, don't tell me it's time already."

"Rise and shine, pal," Bass said. He dropped to the deck and began pulling on his coveralls. The cabin was small, and he had to bend when moving around.

Charley slid his legs over the side of the bunk and sat there, dark circles under his eyes. "I feel like I've been hit with a handful of shit," he said gloomily.

"I'll see you in the O.P. room," Bass said and left.

As he made his way along the narrow companionway, he could feel his energies beginning to hum. All through yesterday they'd been checked and frustrated. The *Yuma*'s estimate of down time had been off and was continually lengthened. Noon came and went. When they'd finally gotten a clearance signal from the sub, it was too late in the afternoon for a launch. Now the new time was set for 0500.

Ross had managed to hide his pique around Garretson behind a lopsided grin. But he knew the bastard was gloating over the new tracking protocol, his eyes glinting in spite. Since all the equipment and grid reassignments had been completed, it had been decided to hold to the multiple survey setup instead of again redoing the schedule. But Garretson's little victory left a sour taste.

Up on deck, the *Explorer* was full of lights as the deck watch and survey crews ran through last-minute checks of cable gear and the SAR units, three seven-foot tubes filled with sonar and environmental monitors. These would be deployed and towed as soon as the *Explorer*, sitting five miles from the Mascarene, entered the post-explosion zone.

The weather was perfect, night cool under a clear

sky lit by a misshapen moon. The ocean stretched away
in all directions, long, gentle swells out of the southwest that gave the ship an easy roll at her sea anchors.

Bass talked with the quartermaster for a moment,
then ducked below and went into the galley. The mess
tables were already full, everybody eating quietly but
with expectant eyes. He got himself a bowl of dry
cereal and a fresh bottle of orange juice and headed
for Operations.

The Operations Room was located just aft of the
bridge, a compact space filled with batteries of electronic equipment, computer terminals and screens,
timing systems, environmental monitor consoles, sample analysis machines, and radio and radar gear. A
chart table in the center was covered with tracking
grids. The overhead lights were faintly tinged blue,
which picked up little metal flecks in the deck lino-
leum.

Several console operators were already at their terminals, headphones and stick mikes clipped to their
heads. Bass paused behind Tom Lasco, his chief assistant of Operations. "Everything still on go, babe?"

Lasco nodded. "Clean and ready."

"Where's Garretson?" He gave a clown leer at Skip
Haley, who had taken over the videotaping of the pre-
launch activity for the Defense Department's research
archives until Mirisch came up.

"Chow, I think," Lasco said.

Bass wandered around, peering at things. At the radar tracking screens, he synchronized his wristwatch
to the digital readouts showing on the sides of the displays. These indicated the date and time-to-launch of
the XGB-3AS. They showed 3 hours, 59 minutes, 04
seconds.

16

The wind had picked up, slashing restively through the jungle and making the higher branches whip about. Now and then gusts would dip and swirl dust ahead of the Rover as it bore through the night. Hak had left the radio and was sitting in the passenger seat, one of the Thompsons across his legs, drinking stolidly from his whiskey bottle.

They had already crossed through Dum Dum, a dark town filled with tea *godowns,* shacks, and ancient, peaked Buddhist stupas below which were courtyards filled with silent monkeys.

It was a little after one when they reached the Lohit River. Coming down a slight hill, they saw Lake Sonai a mile to their left. Its surface was etched with windcaps, and out in the middle the lights of Lake House looked like a ship on a stormy sea.

At the bottom of the hill, Hak told Bonner to swing left so they could skirt the river and head toward the lake. It was heavy going, the ground mushy. On the right, the river was sluggish, almost still, and there were pan shoals covered in floating lily beds and freshwater mangrove forests where Hak said crocs hid.

The Garo village was perched on the lake shore where the jungle came right down to the water. The Garos were originally Nagaland Mountains tribesmen who had been driven out of their homeland several years before by Burmese bandits. Seeking to get protection from Singh, they fled into the Brahmaputra plain and became fishermen around Lake Sonai. But Singh had proven more ruthless than the bandits. Periodically he raided their villages for the prettiest virgins to service his militiamen. The Garo had come to hate him but were helpless against his weapons.

The village was made completely of bamboo, houses on stilts set in a semicircle facing the lake. Even the raised chicken coops and pigpens were of bamboo. In the center of the compound was an open pavilion called a *nokpanti*, where the bachelors of the village lived. Long, slender canoes were pulled up onto the shore, and there was a bamboo fence like a lattice across the open end of the compound as protection against night-marauding crocodiles.

Jungali and seven of his men were sitting cross-legged around a large fire beside the *nokpanti* when Bonner pulled the Rover into the compound. The wind made the flames roar, sending sparks up. From high in the night sky came the forlorn honks of river geese riding the monsoon winds to sanctuaries in the Bishemna foothills.

The Carib waved a strip of turtle belly meat as Cas and Hak came up. "HakMcCarran, you goddom Englishman," he called happily. "I'm tinkin' dat sombitch monsoon gonna cotch you." He spotted Hak's Thompson. "Hey, whot's dat you got dere, mon?"

Hak handed over the weapon. Jungali examined it, grinning, turtle fat glistening on his lips. He slipped out the stick clip and peered down at the cartridges, then replaced it and handed the gun back. "Das one scornful gun, I tell you dat, mon." His men giggled childishly. They looked drunk. From the shadows of the *nokpanti* came furtive whispers.

Hak squatted down. "Bonner and I are going to Lake House right now. You coming with us?"

"Goddom right," the poacher chief cried. "Best time, too. Dat bastard Singh an' his thieves is campin' back in de jungle." He sliced the air with an open palm. "Two, tree mile in."

"Good," Hak said.

Jungali gazed out at the dark lake a moment. "But we boys betta be gettin' on. De wind blowin' fifteen, twenny knots on dat lake. Gonna be a hard pull in dem skinnny Garo boats."

"Then let's move," Hak said.

They chose two of the larger canoes. Three village elders, short, gnarled men with dark skins and faces like pygmies, stood around silently while the men loaded the canoes. The vessels were twenty feet long, made from a single balsa log impregnated with jackfruit sap. In the water, they barely had a six-inch freeboard, but they were extremely light. Each canoe had several bailing buckets made from turtle shells that looked like World War II helmets.

Bonner and Hak put the radio and battery in the center of their boat and covered it with a tarp from one of Jungali's Rovers. Just before they pushed off, he raised Malli again. She informed him that Jeffry was there. Through the static wash, the MI-5 agent's voice sounded very young and very British, out of place amid the high, wild rush of the wind and the calls of the river geese.

"I say, Tiger Stripe, bloody glad I've finally tracked you," Jeffry said. "We've got ourselves a rather sticky situation here, haven't we? You say you're on the lake? Over."

"Affirmative. Heading for Lake House now. What is status with you people?"

"Tadhunter is on the way, old chap. Intends to set

up C.P. at Calcutta consulate. Needs absolute verify from you on missiles, over.''

''We'll get it. What does London intend to do about it when we do?''

''Not privy to that, I'm afraid. Sorry. Over.''

Hak shook his head disgustedly, and Jungali said. ''Dat mon sound like one goddom pussy.'' Bonner chuckled.

McCarran keyed. ''Are you aware of full extent of the epidemic in Dibrugarh?''

''Yes. Beastly affair, that. Understand that Delhi Disease control is mounting offensive now. Over.''

''Do they realize it is caused by a fungus?'' A particularly strong splay of static washed through the last part of his sentence.

''Say again, please.''

''Do they realize it is a fungus-caused disease?'' Hak repeated.

''I have notified Tadhunter of that item as per your instructions to your wife. It has created a decent amount of confusion, however. Over.''

''The disease is caused by a mutated form of river fungus. Undoubtedly due to contamination by the missile agent. The only thing that will kill it is electricity.''

''Electricity, you say?''

''Yes, directly into the patient.''

''I don't quite understand. Over.''

''You don't need to bloody understand. Just relay what I've told you.''

''Affirmative, old man. What is your estimate to verification? Over.''

''Two hours.''

''Right-o, then. I'll raise you first if there's urgent news. I have your frequency. Good hunting, old chap. Over and out.''

Hak mumbled something to himself and replaced the mike under the tarp. He straightened. "Everybody ready?"

"All set," Bonner answered.

They shoved the canoes out into knee-deep water and then slipped onto the seats, three of Jungali's men going with Cas and McCarran. Before they could get their paddles in, the wind side-slipped the prows and the chains of white caps slapped against the gunwales, casting water into the bottom.

Cas took his position as coxswain and finally got the canoe straightened out. Grunting as he stroked, he pointed the prow toward the lights of Lake House. With each sweep of the paddles, the balsa vessels leapt forward, cutting diagonally across the face of the wind.

Defense Secretary Moffett stood waiting under the White House portico. Down below, at the foot of the curving staircase, the President talked amicably with a cluster of Future Farmers of America delegates. He had just given them a short tour of the building.

When the farewells were completed, the President came back up the stairs. A tall, dark-haired man with a soft tan from daily jogs, he was smiling and joking with his security men. When he saw Moffett, he gave him a sidelong glance. "Problems?"

Moffett nodded. "I'm afraid so, sir."

They walked through the diplomatic reception room to the library. It was a long room filled with dark panels and leather-bound volumes. It had the feel of early America, hewn woods and pipe tobacco. The President closed the door and put his hands on his hips. "Well?"

"We just received another message from London. It seems those Russian mercenaries in northeastern India also have biological missiles."

The president's expression didn't change but his eyes narrowed. Then he lifted his head and murmured, "Jesus Christ."

"Nothing really definite has been established yet," Moffett said. "MI-5 says one of their retired agents in Assam, man named McCarran, is making the claim. But there's some doubt about his credibility."

"How much doubt?"

"We don't know yet."

"What does Delhi have to say about it?"

"I talked with Tachter before coming over." Frank Tachter was the ambassador to India. "He's heard nothing so far. Apparently Anduri's people are still occupied with damage control over the border incident with the Chinese." He frowned. "But there's something else. This McCarran also claimed that the bio agent has already created a deadly disease in the Brahmaputra River."

The president looked shocked. "What? You mean there's already been a launch?"

"No indication of that, sir. But there have been reports that an epidemic of some kind has just hit an upriver town called Dibrugarh."

The president strode away for a moment, then dropped into a leather chair. "My God, Jack, what are we looking at here? Biological missiles rammed into those packed Indian cities? The thought makes my heart freeze."

"It could get hairy, all right."

"Who, exactly, is supposed to have these missiles?"

"From what I can gather, the British believe that both the Russian mercenaries and the missiles belong to a local warlord. Some Punjabi who dominates the Assam plain east of Bangladesh. The whole area's a mishmash of warring religious and political factions."

"So where does that leave us?"

"On the outside looking in, I'm afraid. At least for the time being. This could turn out to be wholly an internal problem."

The President snorted. "Like hell! Some warlord nut starts throwing bio-missiles around, it's everybody's problem." He shoved himself to his feet. "Goddammit, I don't like the direction this whole Indian thing is taking. First a Chinese firefight, then Russian mercenaries, now this."

"I agree, sir. Something's in the wind here."

The President was silent for a moment. "What's our surveillance capability in this . . . Assam area?"

"We have no agents in the sector. We've depended on British Intelligence for the bulk of our data."

"What about satellites?"

"A KH-11 photo-recon unit transits the vicinity every twenty-four hours, but its sweep-track is along the NEFA frontier. Besides, I understand the annual monsoon is about ready to enter the area. I think cloud cover would prohibit any concise location shots of missile emplacements."

"Joint Chiefs aware of this development?"

"Yes, sir, I called Hoskins from here." Admiral Ted Hoskins was chairman of the JCS.

"What about your man in JAD?"

Moffett nodded. "Yes, I put him in the loop earlier. Open clearances all the way. I assume he's onto this missile thing already."

"Check it out. Now."

"Yes, sir."

It took Moffett a few moments to clear through to JAD on a secure line from the library phone. While he did, the President walked about the room, distractedly pulling books out, fanning pages a moment, then returning them to the shelf.

The S.D. spoke for several minutes. When he hung up, he said, "Clark's got the missile data and is infeeding it into McNair now."

"What's he come up with so far?"

"He says he's formulated some parameters but wanted to wait until he could utilize a wider data spectrum before submitting his blue paper. He was pretty excited about the missile item."

"Well, screw the blue-paper route. I want his results verbally. Directly to me as soon as he's got them."

"Yes, sir."

The President sighed. "All right, let's try to cover all the bases here. Notify Hoskins that I want some force assessments of what we've got in the Indian Ocean. Both strike as well as medical assistance capabilities. Also, some protocols from Justice on what we can legally do in case this thing blows."

"Right, sir."

'Get Brough in the loop, too." Bernadette Brough was the U.S. representative to the U.N. "Have her start setting groundwork for a special session. Probe London about what the British intend to do. I want definite coordination already in place. And get Tachter moving, right now. I want statements of intent from Anduri and his military people concerning these missiles.

"Yes, sir."

"Keep me on it, Jack."

"I will, sir." Moffett departed, leaving the President staring at the floor, his earlier good mood vanished.

Thirty-three minutes earlier, Premier Anduri had been shaken by a phone call from his Officer for Medical Affairs, retired General Ram Kalnari, notifying him of the outbreak in Dibrugarh.

"I am most sorry for disturbing you, sir," Kalnari apologized. "I had wanted to wait until morning. But it has become quite terrible in Dibrugarh. Already there are many dead, sir."

After the meeting with General Shastra and Chedi, Anduri had asked the secretary to remain. Since then the two of them had been sitting near the window, sipping heavily sugared tea and discussing the deteriorating political situation in Delhi. The premier was restless, charged with anxiety. Now he looked utterly stricken. He couldn't speak for moment.

"Sir?" Kalnari said. "Sir, are you there?"

"Yes, yes. Go on."

"I have never seen anything of this nature," Kalnari continued. "It is a most peculiar thing. Many aspects of the disease are of tuberculosis, some aspects are of tetanus and other muscular disorders. There are also cases of infectious pneumonia. I am most alarmed."

"Has there been further infection downriver?" Anduri asked softly. Chedi, aware that something of great import was being discussed, had quietly come to the desk and was watching, his teacup held in both hands.

"Yes, there are scattered reports of deaths in Majuli and Sibsagar."

"What is being done?"

"I have authorized that Disease Center send several teams into Dibrugarh before the monsoon." Kalnari hesitated a moment. "There is an American doctor there also. She has made a request for many fibrillation units. It is most peculiar. And she speaks of strange things, mutations of river fungus and biological missiles and such."

Anduri froze: *There it was, the link!* He glanced, terrified, at Chedi.

"I would humbly request, sir," Kalnari said, "that

you mobilize military units to aid us. The monsoon will create much chaos and spread of the infection.''

''Yes, of course. I will do this immediately.''

''Thank you, Prime Minister.''

''I want continual updates, Kalnari. Is that understood?''

''Oh, yes, sir. I will be most prompt.''

After Anduri hung up, he explained the news to Chedi. The secretary became pale. He gently lowered his teacup to the desk. ''So, it is true,'' he whispered.

The P.M. stood still for a moment, then paced to another position, remained only a few seconds before pacing again. ''What can I do now, Amit?'' he moaned.

Chedi's cold eyes followed his erratic passage. Finally he said, ''Strike at Singh. Now.''

Anduri turned and stared at him. ''Dare we do that?''

''There is no longer any choice. Singh is responsible for this. Now I am certain. He has already struck and will do it again. Perhaps the next time it will be Bangladesh. We must destroy his capability immediately. We can deal with the infections after that's done.''

''How do we go after him? Shastra's paratroopers? It is too late.''

''No, I would suggest an air strike.''

The P.M. sighed, put his head down. Without lifting it, he said, ''Yes, an air strike.''

He returned to the desk and picked up the phone.

The launcher was finished. Kurisovsky and his men gathered around it under the floodlights. The wind, thick with the smell of rain, lashed over the courtyard walls and moaned through the columned walkways.

The colonel checked his watch: 2:36. He shaded his

eyes and studied the sky beyond the glare of the lights. It was dark and the clouds moved like great slabs of black ice on a winter river.

Perhaps, he thought, they would be able to launch earlier than planned.

It was time to bring the missiles down from the bunker they had dug beside the bungalow. He barked out orders. Several of the troopers instantly double-timed it out the courtyard gate and headed up the hill.

Kurisovsky and the others climbed into the oil company jeep and drove slowly around the courtyard, studying the balcony floor. Finally, choosing a section of solid teak timbers, they ran chains up to the floor joists, hooked their ends to the vehicle's trailer hitch, and began pulling.

It took several lunges, the jeep's wheels screaming on the cobblestones, before first one timber jerked free, then another and another until the entire balcony came down in a shower of stone dust and splintered wood. The upper roof hung precariously against the adjoining supports.

Quickly they fashioned a skid for the missiles from the floor planks. Earlier when they'd taken them up to the bungalow, Singh's men had been there to help bodily carry the units. Now it would have been time-consuming to do it manually.

At last the skid was ready and hooked to the jeep. With two men standing on it to keep it from tipping over, they went slowly out the gate and started up the grassy slope, the runners gouging dirt.

Once more Kurisovsky glanced at his watch. It read: 3:06.

Clark had actually shouted when he first received the message from CIA headquarters about the presence of biological missiles in northeastern India. He was certain it was one of his missing links.

He was working up a new T.O. when Moffett called. From the secretary's terse remarks, he had the impression the president was also there. A momentary prickle of heat skittered up the back of his neck. The assumption was strengthened a few minutes later when Moffett called back and ordered him to contact the president directly when he had any results. To do it, he gave him the chief executive's instant-access code number.

To enhance the missile T.O. input, Clark had initiated a scan of CIA, NSC, and Pentagon data files on known Russian warhead and missile inventories. After years of hard intelligence following the Geneva Protocol on Chemical/Biological Weapons, coupled with the recent openness of the CIS in Soviet internal and military affairs, the stored data was surprisingly vast. Added to it were the trackings of Soviet rocket sales, both published and covert, to foreign countries, particularly those in the Middle East.

Out of the data overload he managed to isolate three specific types of delivery vehicles produced in Russia that had been designated to carry either chemical or biological warheads. These he ran through his own logic units to see which would be most viable within the framework of the Assam situation.

The first two were immediately discarded. Both, adaptations of the SS-22/SCALEBOARD high-acceleration missiles, were silo-based ballistic units. Such missiles were far too cumbersome and satellite-visible for operational efficiency using a small field crew within a guerilla-type situation.

But the last missile had workable possibilities. It was the BEARCAT SSR-214, a mobile-launched unit manufactured by the huge Soviet Kranoyarsk Munitions Works outside Leningrad. In addition, reports indicated several hundred such missiles had been sold to Iran, Iraq, Libya, Egypt, and even India.

Then he ran into a slight glitch. All warheads designed for the BEARCAT were chemical-oriented, not biological-capable. Momentarily stumped, he left his terminals and wandered around the room. He was sure those missiles in India were carrying biological agents: bacteria or virus. The tag on the MI-5 reports about infections in the Brahmaputra River seemed to nail that certainty down. Well, he thought, maybe the missiles were Russian, but the warheads something else.

He quickly ran a scan of CIA data on world production of biological agents. Again, the file was heavy. He focused on China and Germany. The material on China was shadowy, everything clothed in layers of sub-components and manufacturers. Germany was more accessible.

Astoundingly, the links from German chemical and pharmaceutical companies to Middle Eastern countries was absurdly blatant. He managed to glean an inventory of over two dozen biological agents, all scatter-virulent under varying environmental conditions. The data also included potential delivery vehicles for the specific bio canisters.

One was adaptable to the BEARCAT SSR-214.

He backtracked and isolated the German manufacturer. It was the I.T. Gramrauch Chemical Corporation of Dusseldorf. In 1989 the company had been suspected of shipping chemical agents to Libya and Iran. It, of course, had denied the charge, and evidence was insufficient to impose sanctions pursuant to the Geneva Protocol.

However, secret Interpol papers showed indications of a solid link between the company and Tehran. Also, an interview with a disgruntled ex-worker of Gram-

rauch gave investigators an alleged inventory of bio-
agents and warhead adapters the manufacturer had
secretly produced.

Only one had the specific weight, aerodynamic and
milling configurations adaptable to the BEARCAT. It
was designated the BISS-56 and designed to carry a
vacuum-burst canister containing a biological component in a pressurized alcohol suspension. The agent was
either anthrax bacillus or pneumococcal pneumonia,
strain three.

With this injected into his updated T.O., Clark shot
it to McNair. Forecast feedback returned within eighteen minutes. With the presence of bio missiles in Assam, assumption parameters had changed.

First of all, the assassination scenario had been
downgraded, the McNair computers considering a missile attack as an assassination weapon highly unlikely.
On the other hand, the threat of a vicious escalation in
the internecine conflict throughout the Indian northeast
had been driven way up, primarily one created by a
local guerilla force such as Singh's.

Also tremendously increased was the possibility of
renewed Sino-Indian tensions. China's reaction, once
Beijing discovered the presence of potentially dangerous missiles only a few hundred miles from her borders, could result in a direct face-off with India and the
resulting possibility of open war.

A Caspian scenario had also been expanded with
Muslim fanatics striking an Indian city with bio agents.
Still, the computers included a qualifying addendum to
this. From their data, such a mindless act of terrorism
would actually bear very little strategic result within the
framework of Caspian Alliance aims in the region. Nevertheless, consideration of it had to be studied, since
terrorism of any sort usually broached the parameters
of logic.

Clark returned to the Sino-Indian scenario, again riding out impulses. Although the injection of the missile data into the mix had not totally altered the earlier projections of possible Chinese invasion, he immediately saw one startlingly obvious fact. If fired into China, a missile attack would be an initiating factor, one that would instantly coalesce the entire Beijing government into violent retaliation.

In other words, it was one of the fuses that made his green light glow brightly.

"But where the hell is the other?" he demanded loudly to himself. In a moment he was back running data scans, this time focusing on everything he had concerning Communist hard-line activity within the CIS.

What he found was a patchwork of light and shadow. Most of the once powerful hard-line organizations within the Communist party were so destroyed or fragmented that their efforts were too feeble and disorganized to mount a major coup. As a result, dissident reactionary forces had gone underground, into a dark labyrinth where quickly appearing and disappearing factions shifted.

He managed to work up a list of possible faction leaders from CIA analysis reports. Then, starting from the point that these factions would need cash resources first and foremost, he went back into the agency files for specific international connections in which these men had been involved.

The network that began to evolve on his screens was astounding. Cash transactions of one sort or another appeared from sources as varied as the Iranian government to the French Communist party, Cuban military attachés, and Irish terrorist organizations. But the pastiche was made up of too many transient contacts for Clark to isolate individual leaders.

For a while that stumped him. But then he decided

simply to isolate those factions that appeared most frequently in the run. This was quickly done. He now had three factions along with their alleged hierarchy.

The first and seemingly most powerful was the Vladykin Group, made up of deposed members of the SIS, the old Soviet Secret Intelligence Service. The second was also intelligence-oriented, its members coming from the GRU's Special Committee of Information, initially started by Beria. The last faction, called Phoenix, seemed to be made up strictly of military men, the entire cadre either active or retired officers. Their leader was a deposed general named Valeri Zgursky.

Clark's eyes ran over the data, yet he kept coming back to Zgursky. Where had he seen that name earlier? he wondered. It was there, somewhere in his data runs. He shifted to a second terminal and requested a search-scan for the general.

It shot back:

Zgursky, Valeri Stanislav
Born: Gdansk, 1919
Military Career: Chebrikov Academy (1939)
                 Captain: 478th Armored Division
                    (highly decorated)
                 Colonel: 129th Infantry Regiment
                 General: 178th Armored Corps
                 CO: Spatnez team des. October
                    Force

Clark's mind went *click*! Instantly he scooted his chair to a third terminal and brought up the file on Colonel Kurisovsky. And there it was, twin links. General Zgursky had been Kurisovsky's commanding officer in both the 178th and again with October Force. He returned to the Zgursky file, quickly scanned down through the remaining data, which included his alleged affiliations with the Phoenix group. The final file notation was small, containing no hard evidence. It stated that Zgursky was suspected of negotiating the transferral of stolen Russian art in exchange for a substantial amount of cash and arms. The file did not indicate who the recipient of the art works was but assumed transfer point had been Budapest, Hungary. Active date was somewhere between June and September 1991.

Clark hurriedly extracted what he had on Zgursky, Kurisovsky, and the Pheonix group. With this he formed up another T.O. and shot it to McNair. Then, prowling around the room, cracking his knuckles, he waited. Five minutes later, his main terminal started coming up.

He stood, mesmerized as the projected scenario reeled off on the screen. It was all there, the entire plan, designated by the big 250s as the Phoenix Strike. His green light was blinding.

Clark took one deep breath, then whirled and headed for his phone, hauling the president's instant-access code number from his pocket.

17

It was frustrating toil crossing the lake. Frantically jamming his paddle from side to side between bailings, Bonner had managed to keep a fair hold on the canoe. The three poachers and McCarran were definitely not mariners. Their strokes were weak, their rhythm chaotic. The wind came at them from crazy directions, blowing mostly from the southwest, but then it would suddenly shift around, whipping the surface into foam flecks.

Fifty yards back, Jungali was also having difficulty holding course. Although an expert steersman, his crew was as bad as Bonner's. Occasionally his voice would drift faintly past on the wind as he scourged his paddlers.

Gradually the island drew closer, the drilling rig taking shape under the lights of the derrick and the bright playing-field wash of the main deck. Beyond, the red top lights of the storage tanks and the yellow windows of mess and barracks buildings looked cozy under the wind. To the right were floodlights in the courtyard of Lake House and, down near the shore, the blue glow of the pavilion.

Fighting the stern, Cas aimed toward the docking area on the south side of the island. He could see it was darkest there, with only small wharf lights and a long string marking a tanker-loading slip, which went out a hundred and fifty yards into the lake. But his men were rapidly becoming exhausted, hanging on their paddles as the wind steadily shoved them up toward the drilling platform.

While still beyond its reflected light, Cas paused long enough to give it a quick study. Years before, fresh out of high school with his father dead, he'd spent a season as a roughneck on two drilling rigs in the Gulf of Mexico to earn enough money to send himself through Stanford. Eyeing this one, he immediately realized something was wrong.

It took him a moment to understand what it was. The rig wasn't drilling, pumping, or pulling pipe. There was no hum of machinery, no flame on the gas burn-off tower. The pressure valve housing on the wellheads, blowout preventer, and Christmas tree valve stacks near the pumping motors were all under green lights, indicating a shut-down. A section of pipe was still hooked to the pedestal crane's messenger lines, but the bottom swing tongs were free, the kelly cock motionless. No one was in sight on the drilling deck.

Bonner leaned forward and slapped McCarran on the shoulder. "Something's wrong," he shouted over the wind. "That rig's shut down. Looks like it was done in a hurry."

"Maybe they're clearing for the monsoon," McCarran panted.

"No, those rigs can stand a hundred-fifty knots and all the rain you can give them. They'd never shut down unless there was a blowout."

Hak gave him a guarded look. "You saying that bloody thing is liable to explode?"

Bonner shook his head. "If there was a blowout, there'd be a fire crew on deck." He stood for a moment and waved to Jungali, pointing toward the platform. When he sat down, he told McCarran, "We'll go in under it."

It was like entering a cliff cave, albeit one that smelled of crude oil and new cement and the sharp magnesium stench of the betonite mud that was pumped down the drill holes to stabilize pressure. The wind, hot and heavy with moisture, created hollow *whomping* sounds as it swept past the foundation legs and vertical braces.

There was a small dock on the shore with matrices of electrical and pressure conduits snaking across the bottom of the platform. Cas guided the canoe to the dock and slipped up onto it, the Thompson slung over his shoulder. A moment later, Jungali's canoe slid up alongside, the Carib still cursing.

Bonner squatted beside Hak. "I'm going topside, have a look around."

Hak nodded, panting over his paddle.

Going cautiously, Cas mounted the stairs to the main deck. They were grimy with oil. As he reached the top, he realized Jungali was behind him, grumbling to himself: "Dem goddom boys pull poddle like old womans." He growled in disgust. "Dey ever see some real ocean in de windwards, dey be floatin' wid dere bellies down."

Cas hissed, raised his palm. The Carib fell silent.

The ladder came up beside a series of bulk storage tanks. He and Jungali squatted, surveying the open deck and draw-works sheds aft the derrick.

Cas looked up at the monkey board deck halfway up the derrick, where the derrick man usually operated the pipe lifters. It was empty. Telling Jungali to stay there, he dodged through the tanks, and climbed the outside derrick ladder swiftly, the Thompson banging against his spine.

The monkey board cables were humming softly in

the wind. He braced himself beside the operator's shed and slowly scanned the island, starting at Lake House. Despite the height, he couldn't see over the courtyard wall, although floodlights were visible, swaying on their lines. Up beyond the main house, thin stands of scrub oak thickened into deodars and lake pine. The lights of a bungalow shone through the swaying trees.

He swung his gaze back toward the drilling barracks and storage tanks. He focused on the largest building in the living quarters compound. It was near enough for him to see a figure move across a lighted window. Then one of the side doors opened and an Indian dressed in a white robe stepped onto the rampway. He lifted his robe, squatted, and urinated Indian-fashion over the edge of the ramp. An assault rifle hung over one shoulder, and bandoliers were slung across his chest.

At that moment the wind dropped slightly, and Cas heard the sound of a gunning jeep engine near Lake House. He swung around. Headlights snapped on up near the bungalow and began to move down the slope, proceeding jerkily, the engine roaring and ebbing. As it cleared the trees, he could see that it was towing something, a skid or trailer. On the trailer was a long white tube that caught the reflected lights of the vehicle.

A missile!

Bonner scooted back down the derrick ladder in a half fall, half lunge, and raced toward the bulk storage tanks. Jungali's head and weapon snapped up as he pounded around the corner. Cas slid to a half squat.

"Goddom, mon," Jungali croaked. "Don be comin' on me dat fast."

"Get back to McCarran," Cas snapped. "Tell him I think they're moving missiles now, up there in the woods. I'll be back."

Before the old poacher could say anything, Bonner was already descending the after ladder to the shore ramp. Dropping off the last few rungs, he landed first on wood and then rock, stumbling. Quickly he righted himself, moving up the beach at a dead run. Several yards beyond the ramp, he cut across a patch of lake grass to a road that curved off toward Lake House.

His legs setting a steady rhythm, he sprinted on, squinting ahead at the dim ground for the telltale dark line of a snake. Off to his left, the jeep's headlights continued making progress.

Five minutes later, he left the road a hundred yards from where it entered the courtyard gate and made for the thick shadows under the outer wall. For a moment he leaned over, palms on his knees, and gasped for air. He could faintly hear men shouting on the other side of the wall but couldn't make out words.

Lights flashed suddenly and swept toward him as the jeep reached the road and swung toward the gate. He dropped to the ground. It was rocky and jabbed into his ribs. The jeep straightened out and came on, the missile skid bouncing.

As the rear of the skid finally passed through the gate, Cas bounded to his feet. He made it to the edge of the gate and pressed against the huge hinges of the opened doors. They were made of thick iron slabs that smelled of rust and sandalwood. Lowering slightly, he peered around the gate frame.

His blood froze. Several men, their bare backs glistening with sweat, were bustling around the skid, unstrapping the missile. Beyond them were four more missiles lying on the ground. In the center of the courtyard, its frame and firing panel partially hidden in a huge pit, was a treadless mobile launcher lashed to cables. Thrusting upward were three firing tubes, obviously jury-rigged, their metal sheeting covered with black cutting-torch marks.

Cas stared at the tubes, for a moment confused. They were aimed due east, not downriver. Then the point of it hit him. He ducked back, pressing his spine against the wall. "Sweet Jesus," he murmured.

Ten seconds later, he was headed back down the road, going full out.

"Well, crap!" the President said. He'd just nicked his chin while shaving. Disgustedly he dabbed the tiny spot of blood with a washcloth and stared at his own eyes in the mirror. At the moment they were slightly glinted with impatience.

There was a soft knock on the door. The President leaned around the door frame. "Come in," he called.

Roy Swan, deputy chief of staff for White House Affairs, stepped in. "Sir, you have a call on your I.A. line. A Mr. Clark from JAD."

"All right." In his undershirt, and still holding the washcloth to his chin, the President headed down the hall to a small communications room beside the Lincoln Suite. Still in the corridor, he paused. "Get Moffett and Doole up here." Donald Doole was chief adviser of the National Security Council.

"Yes, sir." Swan hurried off.

There was an operator sitting before a compact but sophisticated radio-telephone panel with side computers. He was a tall black FBI agent. He stood immediately when the President walked in.

"Hello, Frank," the President said.

"Good evening, sir." Frank immediately withdrew to the outer hall.

The President picked up a red phone. "What have you got?" he said.

For the next two minutes, he listened while Scott

Clark laid out the parameters of the Phoenix Strike. As he did, his face went through a plethora of emotions from stunned shock to revulsion. Once he inhaled deeply and leaned against the radio panel.

When Clark finished, the President didn't say anything for a long moment. Then: "Could you be wrong?"

"I don't think so, Mr. President. I've assiduously checked the entire T.O. in-feed."

"I don't accept that answer," he snapped. "I want one with no think in it. Run the works again."

"Yes, sir."

"How long?"

"Ten, twelve minutes, sir."

"Make it ten."

"Yes, sir."

The President hung up and leaned around the door frame. "Frank, on the double."

The agent came running.

"Get McNeely at CIA here. Now! And Admiral Hoskins. If they can't make it in ten minutes, get them on a secure conference line."

"Yes, sir." Frank slipped into the operator chair and began bringing up a scan of security access numbers on one of the computer terminals.

The President returned to his bedroom to finish dressing. Secretary Moffett showed up five minutes later. He had been in a meeting at the Senate Office building. Flushed and slightly sweaty, he found the President pacing in the front room of the Lincoln Suite.

The President glared at him as he came in. "It's bad," he said simply.

"What happened?"

"I'll let Clark tell you. He'll be on the line in three minutes."

The President continued pacing, his brow deeply furrowed. The room seemed energized with his agitation. Soon Don Doole appeared. The NSC chief, in a tuxedo, was a burly-faced man with a discordant, high-pitched voice.

"What the hell is up, sir?" he blurted.

The President nodded to a chair. "Wait and listen."

The FBI agent came to the door of the suite to notify the President that Hoskins was on the conference line. McNeely, he said, had been contacted and would be on line in two minutes.

"Patch everything in here."

"Yes, sir."

Clark called back precisely eleven minutes, four seconds after his earlier call. He said, "There's no error, Mr. President."

The President quickly brought everybody up to speed, explaining that Scott Clark of JAD had been running projection scenarios on the Chinese-Indian situation in NEFA. He paused. "All right, gentlemen, listen up. You're about to hear something that'll shrivel your nuts. Go ahead, Clark."

There was a moment of silence, as if Clark were arranging his thoughts. When he did speak, his words were rapid and to the point. "There is to be a biological missile strike across the Sino-Indian frontier, either into northern Yunnan or eastern Sichuan provinces of China. The missile warheads will contain either or both the biological agents for anthrax or a highly virulent strain of pneumococcal pneumonia."

"Jesus Christ!" Doole whispered.

"Missile launch," continued Clark, "will be conducted by a small force of Russian mercenaries now in Assam state of northeastern India. The purpose of the strike is to initiate an immediate Chinese retaliatory attack and invasion across the NEFA and Kashmir frontiers. It will also include a concentrated Chinese attack against the old Soviet republics of Tajikistan, Kyrgyzstan and Kazakhstan.

"The mercenary force in Assam is led by a colonel of the Russian Army named Andrei Kurisovsky. He's Spetsnaz and was a commander of the KGB assassination team called October Force. He is now aligned with a secret Communist organization in Moscow named Phoenix, composed of anti-CIS military officers. Its leader is deposed General Valeri Zgursky.

"Projections indicate that once China invades old Soviet territory, the Phoenix group will initiate a coup against the Seleznov government, with a high rate of probability that Seleznov himself will be assassinated. The Phoenix group is also counting on a general uprising of the Russian people at the Chinese invasion to solidify their coup and subsequent return to centralized Communist power."

The men in the room shifted slightly, uncomfortably, and their eyes met each other's. Everybody looked stark.

Clark went on: "These projections also note the strong connection between the present convening of the Russian Parliament in Moscow and the commencement of the monsoon in northeastern India. From these key facts, forecast indicates that the missile attack will take place on or soon after the monsoon strikes Assam. Present weather data shows that monsoon conditions will begin in the area within two hours.

Clark stopped, leaving the room in a vacuum of utter silence. Everybody waited expectantly for the President to speak. When he did, he began snapping orders to Moffett.

"I want to speak directly with Sichen, Seleznov, and Anduri." As Moffett lunged to his feet, he added: "First Sichen. Everything keys on China's reactions."

Moffett hurried away.

"Admiral Hoskins," the President went on. "I want JCS contingency options in thirty minutes or sooner."

"Yes, sir," Hoskins said.

"The same with you, Don," he said to Doole. "Get your staff cracking."

The NSC chief departed on the run.

"McNeely, raise Whitehall and apprise them of what we've come up with. I want their reaction in fifteen minutes."

"Yes, sir," McNeely answered.

The President took a deep breath and eased himself back into his plush green Victorian chair. For a moment his eyes sought the last gleam of sunlight over Washington.

The two Sikhs were large men. They walked with a cautious, lumbering gait, their rifles gripped low. They patrolled along the beach from the direction of the docks, exchanging guttural comments.

On the south side of the derrick, McCarran and Jungali were pressed into the cone of shadow formed by the shore side hull column of the derrick platform. There were rocks at their feet, slimy with algae and shallowly washed by the lake. The wind whipped across the lake, propelling insects which slapped and thumped against the great cement column.

As the Sikhs approached the rig, they separated, one moving close along the shore, the other veering off toward the main ramp. This one passed within three feet of McCarran, so close that he could smell the rancid odor of clarified butter in his beard and hair.

Perfectly motionless, his right hand pulsing, Hak glared as the Sikh passed. He inhaled open-mouthed and then leapt forward, his left hand grasping the trailing tail of the Sikh's turban. He jerked it back, bringing the man's head up sharply, flung his arm around the Sikh's neck, and sliced back and away. The blade made a soft rasp like the fanning of the pages of a book. Continuing in an arc, he twisted the knife and then drove it deeply into the man's kidney.

The Sikh dropped without a sound as McCarran melted back into the shadows.

Beside him, Jungali snickered with savage relish. He held up a finger and then soundlessly slipped around the other side of the column. Hak tensed, head cocked, trying to catch any sound in the wind. In less than a minute, the Carib was back, leering devilishly and wiping his long knife across his shoulder. "Dat make two monkeys for de butcher sack," he said.

A sudden blur of movement up along the road made both men whirl, crouching. On it came, into the penumbrial half shadows of the derrick lights. It was Bonner. McCarran stood up and whistled. Cas's head cocked up and then he raced toward them, his chest heaving with exertion. He drew up, leaned against the column to catch his breath.

"They're readying for launch," he panted. "Five missiles already in the courtyard."

"Bloody hell!" Hak cried.

"There's a mobile launcher in the ground, three fixed sleeves. Looks like they had to make modifications."

"How many men?"

"I counted eight. All Russian and well armed." As McCarran started forward, Bonner grabbed his arm. "There's something else. Those missiles aren't going downriver." He pointed with his hand, palm vertical. "The launcher sleeves are pointed east."

Hak paused. "East? That makes no bloody sense. Nothing up there but isolated mountain tribes that

Singh's already—'' He stopped abruptly, his eyes wide. ''Good Christ, man. China?''

''China.''

Hak lowered his head and stared at Bonner from under his eyebrows. Finally he said, ''First we'll get word out, then go after that launcher. How much time do you figure we have before they launch?''

''I don't know. They're goddamned close.''

Hak swung around to Jungali. ''Get your men up here fast.'' The Carib nodded and disappeared around the column.

He slapped Cas on the shoulder. ''Let's go.''

''Wait a minute, there are Sikh guards carrying assault rifles at one of the buildings in the drilling compound. I saw 'em from the derrick. I think they've got the oil crews in there. We'll have to take them out. If we attack the launcher first, they'll have us in a cross fire. Besides, we could use those automatic weapons when we take on the Russians.''

''All right, lad. While I radio Jeffry, you set up the attack. Make it silent.''

''Right.'' Bonner went up onto the main ramp and waited for the men to assemble.

Below, a glitch developed. The radio wouldn't work. Somehow the battery unit had taken water and shorted plates during the trip across the lake. After a moment Cas came halfway down the ladder. ''What's the matter?'' he called over the rising roar of the wind.

''The bloody battery's gone west.''

''Shit!'' Cas thought a moment. ''Bring the radio up. Maybe we can run off the power panel on the monkey board.''

While Jungali and his men headed down into the compound to take up attack positions around the mess hall, Cas and McCarran scrambled up the side of the derrick, with Bonner carrying the sixty-pound radio under his arm, the whip antenna trailing.

The derrick man's station was the size of a large closet with a wind wall and steel deck. It was packed with hydraulic and pressure lines, banks of metering gauges, and switches for the blowout valve stacks. A central computer screen and terminal for calculating pressure and mud injects into the bore hole sat in the center.

Using a valve wrench, Bonner tore off a panel face and traced the conduits. He decided to hook into the computer terminal line. While Hak disconnected the whip antenna socket head and ran the wire to the steel wind wall, Cas used a knife to scrape the radio leads, screwed them into the computer line, and flicked the terminal On switch.

Instantly the small red signal light on the radio receiver popped on. Hak scooped up the mike and keyed: "Tiger Stripe here, over."

"Ah, yes, old boy," Jeffry's Oxford tones came back in a high whistle. "Where the bloody hell have you been? I have astounding news. The—" The radio went dead.

"Bugger!" Hak barked. He frantically clicked the mike button.

"Hold it," Cas said. "One of the leads came loose." He put his knife to it and pressed it to the terminal post. A snapping blue spark sizzled across the post, and he felt an electric sting in his fingertips. He'd forgotten to flip the terminal's off-switch. Cursing at his stupidity, he did so and soon had the lead on again.

"—any verification? Over," Jeffry's voice whistled back.

Hak keyed: "Momentary power loss. Say again."

"Repeating, have just received red signal, Whitehall. Relay designate Washington. The Yanks've discovered that your bloody Russian mercenaries intend to mount a missile attack against China. Repeat, attack on China provinces, assumed Sichuan or Yunnan. Estimate indicates attack will commence on or soon after onset of monsoon in area. Do you have any verification? Over.''

Bonner and McCarran exchanged hot glances. Hak keyed: ''Plot true. Mobile launcher presently in Lake House. Russians now in process of mounting missiles. Pointed east. Repeat: pointed east. We intend to attack them.''

''God's sake, man, this is turning into a bloody cock-up, this is. Have you capability to intervene? Over.''

''We'll give it a decent go. Advise London.''

''Will do, old chap. Suggest you maintain constant radio contact if possible. Take care and good lu—''

Cas and McCarran had already pulled the wires and were headed back down the derrick.

18

The President's data sources expanded rapidly. To expedite operations, he had withdrawn to the small War
Room in the basement of the White House. From it
his probes were reaching all over the world. One of
the first was to the highly secret Homestead Biological
Research Depot near Price, Utah. Another went out
to the Center for Disease Control in Atlanta.

From both came consensus on two particular points.
The first was that the deadliest of the two possible
biological agents was the pneumococcus. Once introduced in a free state into a region, the contagion's
spread would be swift, infecting entire infrastructures
through water and sewer systems. Under monsoon
conditions, diffusion would increase tremendously.

The second was just as ominous. In order for the
missile warheads to be rendered inert, they would have
to be completely dismantled, using decontaminating
procedures and equipment. If the pathogen units were
breached in any way, the spread of the agent would be
as if the warhead had exploded on impact.

The high-priority calls, of course, were those to the
three leaders of the nations involved. Reaching Sichen
proved extremely difficult. No immediate access to the
Chinese premier was possible, since no network like
the red phone between Washington and Moscow had

ever been set up. The U.S. calls to Beijing were being filtered through layers of bureaucratic sub-officials.

The CIA's Office of Electronics and Satellite Intelligence came up with an idea. They suggested that the probe, instead of going through Beijing's official network, go via the Chinese Air Traffic Control system. Since Sichen was titular head of the Air Ministry, he had to be informed immediately of any Chinese air disaster. Therefore, the CATC always had instant access to him. Perhaps that access could be used, thereby circumventing Beijing completely.

The President authorized an attempt.

The call to Russia also ran into problems. Ever since the decentralization of the Soviet command in Moscow, normal diplomatic and military networks had become disorganized, some lapsing into a chaotic tangle. Even the red-phone link had been affected. On two earlier calls between the President and the leader of the CIS, the system's decay had forced them to actually speak over regular phone circuits.

Compounding this was the hesitancy of Washington to impart secret information to subordinate officials. There was no way of knowing who might be involved in the plot. Individual calls were being made all over Moscow in the hope of finding Seleznov.

The Anduri call, however, got through fairly quickly. The President was going over strategic field maps with Doole, McNeely, and newly arrived Admiral Hoskins when Roy Swan called out, "We have the Indian prime minister on the line, sir."

Anduri's voice was subdued with tension. "Yes, Mr. President," he said, "I am aware of terrible missiles in my country. It is a most agonizing knowledge."

"I am told you are considering an air strike on the missile site. Is that correct?"

"Indeed, it has already been authorized."

The President stiffened. "Have you already sortied your aircraft?"

"They will be taking flight at any moment. It is most essential they hurry to their target before monsoon."

"You must stop them, Anduri," the President barked. "Those missiles cannot be bombed!"

"I do not understand, Mr. President. These terrible things must be destroyed."

"If the warheads are blown open, the biological agents will be scattered. It could be just as dangerous as if they had exploded."

"Ah, dear Vishnu," Anduri whispered.

The President paused a moment for his voice to settle. "Premier, we have strong reason to believe that these missiles are to be launched into China, not into your country."

"China? What is such madness? Singh does not care about China."

"This Singh is merely a ploy," he said. "The whole plot has been engineered by a Russian reactionary group." Quickly he summarized the scenario and the means by which it had become known. At the other end of the phone, the Indian gasped and murmured Hindi invocations. When the President finished, he waited while Anduri absorbed the full implications.

At last the premier said, "I am stunned."

"Will you recall your air-strike order?"

"But how can we stop these fiendish things?"

"At this moment, I don't know. I'm trying to contact Sichen and Seleznov now. But we must not let this incident escalate into full-out war. Even if these missiles are launched and many people die, we must not let it trigger a worldwide catastrophe. Do you fully understand that?"

"Yes."

"Will you recall your aircraft?" he repeated.

"Yes."

"We'll talk again very soon."

"Thank you Mr. President."

"Thank *you*, sir."

McNeely approached and quietly laid a sheet of fax paper before the President. It said:

To: CIA Station: Langley//Base Fax no. 11354//
From: London: MI-5 CH via London Station: 2-C
Time: GMT: 1801 Langley EST

British agent (des. TIGER STRIPE) has made visual confirmation of bio-missiles and fixed launcher ///Location: Namak Island (des. Anath-Sonai): 5:31 E/28:56 N///Launcher azimuth fix: due east/// Launch imminent.

End of message

The President stiffened, his mouth set in a grim line. "McNeely, contact London. Instruct this Tiger Stripe to delay the launch for as long as he can. But caution them that the missile warheads must not be breached under any circumstances."

The CIA director hurried off to one of the main radio panels.

The President swung his chair around. "Hoskins, what do your people have?"

The admiral had just finished speaking with his JCS analysis chief at the Pentagon. His bulldog face looked anxious. "They've come up with an option," he answered slowly. "But it's extremely risky and may not work."

"What is it?"

"Within the given time frame and biological prohibitions, the only chance of interdiction is our own preemptive strike.''

''You already know that's impossible.''

''Not quite, sir.'' Hoskins paused a tiny second. ''We could use the XGB-3AS missile. Its heat blowout could conceivably destroy the warheads without breaching them.''

When Cas and McCarran came down from the derrick, Jungali and his men awaited them in the shadows near one of the storage tanks. They were sharpening their *ags,* fourteen-inch knives with slightly curved blades that legend held were always tempered in horse shit and the testicle blood of a muscular man. The edges gleamed evilly.

Jungali immediately demanded the right of first blood on the Sikhs in the mess hall. ''I be wantin' to send dem Punjabi bastards to damnation, mon.''

Hak nodded. ''All right, but keep it silent.''

''Oh, we be silent, mon. You can know dat.''

The Carib had already worked out his assault plan. It depended on swiftness and the poachers' ingrained ability to see in the dark. The Sikh guards, he said, were separated, one at each doorway. In order to attack all at once, the lights would first have to be turned off. Then he and his men could slip into the huge room unseen, and in the ensuing confusion, with their eyes already accustomed to the darkness, they'd easily pick out the white-clad Sikhs and slit their throats.

Bonner volunteered to take care of the lights.

Going like shadows, Jungali and his men took up their assault positions. Two beside each door, their heads down, eyes closed. Meanwhile, Cas skirted a huge mud pool and went around the back of the hall to search for the main light box.

A *godown* stood beside the hall, grass poking up

through its foundation planks. The wind moaned through the narrow space, and far off to the west he saw lightning flash.

He followed the overhead electrical wires to the junction box. It was painted orange with glass-headed fuses in a double line. A main on-off lever was on the side of the box. He gripped the lever and turned his head against the wind, listening.

Two minutes later, Hak's "Go" signal drifted with the wind, the melancholy hoot of a river loon. Cas pulled the lever down, its rusty shaft scraping metal.

Instantly all the lights in the mess hall went out. Still holding the lever, he listened for the sound of gunfire. Long seconds went by, full of the howling wind.

Then, distinctly, he heard an Aussie voice yell, "Bloody hell! They're killin' each other." This was followed by boots hitting the floor in a general rush. On the side of the building, one of the windows was smashed out, and men began crawling through the shattered frames.

Cas counted to ten, then hit the lever. The lights went back on. Two oil workers came running up the alley between the buildings. One spotted Bonner's shadow and stopped dead. "Oh, Jesus!" he cried, turned, and ran the other way. The second man simply swung around and followed.

Cas dashed around the corner of the building and up onto the porch. He saw Hak go through the nearest door carrying the radio. Inside, the oil workers who hadn't yet managed to get out the windows were pressed up against the opposite wall, milling anxiously about. A Sikh lay with his boots through the doorway, one foot trembling slightly.

Cas stepped over the body. Its head was nearly severed. The eyes stared glassily at the ceiling, and a pool of blood, thick and red as a rose petal, spread across the floor. At each of the doorways lay the other Sikhs, their white robes covered with blood.

Unsure of what was going to happen next, the workers edged back toward the tables, keeping them between themselves and the two white men and bloodstained poachers. Their eyes darted back and forth expectantly.

One, with a pushed-in face like a boxer's, approached Hak. "Aye, mate," he said quietly. "What's up here? You ain't wi' them bleeding Ruskies, are ya?"

"No," Hak answered. "Are you?"

"Not bloody likely. They're the dingos what put them raghead guards on us. An' flat karked off our boss neat as you please and throwed him in the bloody lake."

"Where's a 220 outlet?"

The man nodded toward the kitchen. "Back there. What you intend doin' with us?"

"I suggest you get your arses downriver." He eyed the Aussie. "Unless you want to join us to fight Russians."

The man stared back at him as Bonner came up. The Aussie looked him up and down, then spoke to McCarran. "No, thanks, mate. Them dingos are armed to the fuckin' teeth. Soljers, they are." He nodded toward the dead Sikhs. "Not like these bloody swaggies."

"Then get out," Hak barked. "But make it quick and be quiet."

"We're gone, mate." He turned and jerked his head. All the workers made a rush for the doors, stopping long enough to step gingerly over the Sikh corpses, their eyes squinting with revulsion. Jungali's men had already stripped the bodies of bandoliers, knives, and Kalashnikovs. They squatted nearby, fooling with the breeches of the unfamiliar weapons.

Cas and McCarran took the radio into the kitchen. It was a large room filled with dirty stainless steel tables and two big commercial grills. The floor was greasy, littered with bits of vegetable and fruit. It smelled powerfully of garlic and beer.

They found a 220 outlet for a steam washer and laid the radio on top of the broad surface of the washer. It took Cas a moment to wire the plug while Hak mounted the whip antenna. The instant power entered the unit, Jeffry's voice snapped and crackled into the air: "—Stripe, Tiger Stripe, where the bloody hell are you?"

Hak keyed. "Tiger Stripe here. Go ahead."

"Thank God," Jeffry said. His Oxford smoothness had disappeared. "Don't break off transmission. Have you managed to intercept launch? Over."

"Negative."

"Then London instructs that you stand by. Repeat, you are to stand by. Over."

"What's happening?"

"The Americans are considering sending a cruise missile into Namak. You are ordered to stand by for further instructions. Over."

Cas looked up and locked into McCarran's gaze. "What was that?" he said. "They're gonna put a Big-C in here?"

Hak keyed: "Repeat last transmission."

Jeffry did.

McCarran inhaled and let the air out slowly before speaking again. "When is this bloody missile due to arrive?"

"No time frame yet. But for God's sake, don't break contact. Over."

Hak said, "Understood. Standing by." He lowered the mike and gave Bonner a mirthless grin. "I think this one's going to be a bit antsy, lad."

"More than antsy," Cas said. "That damned thing's probably coming off a warship in the Bay of Bengal." He shook his head. "One helluva long shot over heavily populated areas."

"Indeed," McCarran said.

Precisely six minutes after Hoskins's announcement, Captain Towne of the *Explorer* poked his head around the bridge bulkhead and pointed a finger at Dave Bass. His face was stark. "Up here. Now!"

Bass had been in the final stages of his pre-launch checks. He shot a "What now?" look at Tom Lasco and went forward to the bridge.

The captain thrust a radio phone at him. "It's the president."

For one tiny moment of complete confusion, Bass thought, What president? He put the receiver to his ear. "Yes, sir?"

The President said, "One question, Bass. Is it possible to put that XGB of yours onto a burning oil rig in northeastern India?"

Bass glanced at Towne. What is this, a fucking joke? he thought. "I don't understand, sir."

"You don't need to for now. Just answer the question. Is it possible?"

"Well, ah, theoretically, yes, I suppose. But a tremendous amount of readjusting would be necessary."

"Could it be done within a time frame of, say, forty-five minutes?"

Forty-five minutes? His mind was beginning to race. This was no joke. Acceptance of that fact made a hard knot in his stomach. "I can't answer that immediately, sir. I'd need some time to work up all the mechanics."

"You've got ten minutes to give me a possible or not possible," the President said. "Move it." He was gone.

Bass stood there with the receiver still to his ear. As his mind came around, he realized he was staring into Towne's eyes. "He wants us to fire that missile into India," he said with awe.

Towne's eyes widened. "What!"

Rousing himself at last, Bass lunged back into the O.P. room. "Everybody, cut everything!" he bellowed. "We just got a whole new ball game." Heads swiveled, chairs spun around.

"I just got a presidential order," Bass said grimly. "He wants us to put the XGB into northeastern India."

Everybody jerked up. Mirisch said, "You're fucking kidding."

"No, I'm not," Bass barked. "We've got ten minutes to come up with whether we can do it or not." He leaned on the chart table and glared around the room. "All right, gentlemen, input."

There was a moment of coiled silence through which whispered the soft paraphernalia of ship sounds. Then, in a rush, everybody leaned in like boxing spectators at the bell, shooting questions, formulating problems, countering with solutions. Bass and his missile men led the charge. Someone produced a map of India and the southern ocean and unrolled it onto the chart table.

For the next five minutes, it was like one of those midnight blast sessions in grad school, everybody jamming input. Voices shouted, cursed, everyone's mind zinging.

Some solutions proved simpler than others. Fuel, for instance. Since the XGB for this test flight was rigged for only a thousand-mile range, spare fuel cells would have to be added. Solution: the sub crew could reload. That meant the *Yuma* would have to surface so the men could get top access to the unit. That could also help: firing from a surface platform would allow just that much more thrust to the flight.

But *that* created the necessity of entering the missile's guidance pod for resetting of altimeter and inertial systems from the baseline of a ninety-foot depth of underwater launch to that of sea level. No problem, everybody decided, the crew could do that, too. Also, the sub's firing system could pre-launch infeed the new target program by running directly off the *Explorer*'s own mainframe.

The real problem was guidance control. Since the XGB test had been set up so that the missile's guidance system was homed directly to the command impulses of the *Explorer*'s transmitters, the sub's firing system was not programmed to monitor the missile to its target. It was merely the launch platform. There was no time to completely transfer guidance command. So, in-flight adjustment commands to the XGB would have to come solely from the *Explorer*'s tracking system.

That's where they hit a stone wall. The research ship could not maintain control throughout the complete flight. Its transmission range would be overextended and compromised once the missile reached a point approximately two thousand miles from the ship. Guidance data to the XGB as well as its return sensor reads and response acknowledgments would be jumbled, possibly enough to create chaotic drift and send the missile wildly down into the sea.

The obvious answer was a command relay source.

Lasco suggested the *Yuma*'s fire control. Bass shook his head. "Too dangerous. By the time she got to the edge of the sub's signals, she'd be over land. If we lost control then—" He didn't have to finish the thought. "No, we need a sky platform that can carry full relay all the way to the target."

"What about one of our NAVSTAR positioning satellites?" video-processing officer Bruce Morrel put in.

Bass's eyes brightened. "What's their frequency capability?"

"Shit, that's right," Morrel answered. "They're assigned-locked on a spectrum of between 3700 to 6400 MHz." The XGB was design-set for in- and out-links using an 11–14 GHz frequency spectrum.

Bass thought a moment, then swung around to Garretson. "What weather satellites cover the Indonesian Quadrant?"

"The Australian GeoStar-5 is the only one with clean focus on both us and northeastern India. It's assigned the same band as the NAVSTAR, but I think it's capable of station change."

"As high as 11 to 14 GHz on isolate mode?"

"I'm not sure."

"Where's its control station?"

"Jambi, Sumatra."

"Check it out."

Captain Towne, who had remained silent during the high-tech chatter, said, "I'll do it." He disappeared back onto the bridge.

Bass glanced at his watch. There were four minutes left before the president's call. "All right, let's assume we can use the GeoStar-5. Thoughts?"

"First off, will the XGB accept transmissions from the satellite?" Mirisch asked.

Bass nodded. "We can reposition antennae and give her new AV alignment to the sat just before we cut her loose."

"But will she hold it?" Garretson put in. "Remember, there's monsoon conditions over the Bay of Bengal and southern India. Signals could go all to hell."

"Dammit," Bass cried. "I forgot about that fucking monsoon.'' He leaned forward over the map. ''Show me exactly where it is.''

''Latest reports put the entire front right about here,'' Garretson said, drawing an invisible line with his thumbnail. It ran diagonally across northern Bangladesh into Burma.

Bass studied the line, realizing that the missile, with a design altitude maximum of 12,000 feet, would have to pass directly through the heart of the monsoon. Still, he knew, one of the elements that had been built into the XGB was its frequency tolerance in chaotic ambient conditions. As long as the incoming signals were strong and the receiving platform had the capacity to isolate the weakened return from the missile.

Tracking supervisor Darryl Bheme apparently was thinking the same thought. ''With the GeoStar in the loop,'' he said, ''I'm certain we could handle input. But I'm not so sure about the return. There might be heavy scatter.''

Morrel said, ''Those weather sats have a dense Pseudo Random Noise signal capability. If we concentrated the span cone tight enough, I think we could isolate the missile's return and obliterate scatter.''

Garretson, still brooding over the map, spoke up. ''There's something you've forgotten. That storm front'll be packed with heat cells.''

''Jesus, she could home to them,'' Bass hissed.

''Exactly.''

At that moment the captain returned. ''The GeoStar station says it can handle gigahertz frequencies up to nineteen. But the operators flatly refuse to issue a command unless directly ordered to do so by Canberra.''

Bass waved that off. With the president of the United States riding this one, that little jog could easily be handled. He turned instead and studied Lasco's goateed face. "If a cell took her, we could override homing before she went out of control. What do you think?"

Lasco looked skeptical. "Would we have enough time to react? I mean, what sort of lag time in the data loop are we talking about?"

"I figure maybe five, six seconds before she drifted too far to recover. One in, one out, two for the mainframe correction."

Lasco grunted. "That's cutting it close."

"But possible."

After a moment, both Lasco and flight coordinator Terry Freiden nodded.

Again Bass checked his watch. Two minutes to the president's call. For the remainder of the time, they cleaned up some of the minor details. By now, word had spread throughout the ship. Crew members crowded in the corridor beside the O.P. room, everybody silent and watchful as Towne signaled to Bass that Washington was on the line.

The President said, "Mr. Bass, I have several colleagues of yours in the hook-up. Reynolds, Handover, and Gilstrap. So far, I'm getting positive feedback for an XGB attempt. I want consensus. What's your opinion?"

Bass shifted the receiver slightly and felt a furtive drop of sweat slip down his spine. Although he knew the three men named—Roy Reynolds of NASA, Jock Handover and Ned Gilstrap of the Ballistics Research Center at Table Island, Tennessee—he felt suddenly naked among strangers.

"A successful launch of the XGB missile into India is possible, Mr. President," he said slowly. "If certain pre-flight functions can be performed adequately."

"How much time?"

"We could be on Go in thirty minutes, barring unexpected glitches, once procedures are started."

"Fair enough. You and these gentlemen work out priorities. You'll have my final decision when you're ready." There was a pause, then, "Good luck."

"Thank you, sir," Bass said. He turned slightly. In the O.P. room, strained white faces stared back at him, seemed to float in the blue-tinted air.

He nodded solemnly. The faces whirled away.

This time Jeffry's voice came to them through a long, modulated tunnel of static: "Tiger Stripe, hold on, over." Several seconds of sputtery, perforated air followed. Then: "Missile launch is on tentative go. Do you copy, over?"

"Reading fine," Hak answered. He lowered his head and placed the mike against it, listening. Bonner moved closer.

"You are instructed to detonate drilling platform and all adjacent fuel-storage tanks. Repeat, you must detonate all fuel facilities on Lake House. Missile must have massive heat source for homing target. Do you understand? Over."

Hak cupped the mike. "Understood. Will comply."

"Further, you are to prevent Russian launch as long as possible and then vacate target area," Jeffry continued. "One major caution. Bio missiles and warheads must not be breached under any circumstances. Repeat, missiles and warheads can not be breached. Do you understand? Over."

"Understood."

Cas turned and glanced out through the kitchen door to the mess area. His mind was already positioning the charges out on the platform, around the casings of the storage tanks, running the fuse wires, coordinating the blast chains. Behind him, Jeffry was still talking.

Out in the hall, Jungali sat cross-legged on one of the tables, playing with a Kalashnikov. Holding the butt in the crook of his arm and grinning fiercely, he brought it down in a make-believe burst at his men. "Goddom," he cackled gleefully, "dis beautiful sombitch can tear up the whole dom world."

At that moment a tremendous crack of lightning blew out of the sky. Its pure white shaft, jagged as the edge of broken glass, struck the drilling derrick. For a flashing moment, almost too rapid to form an image on the eye, the struts and girders and cables of the derrick glowed like the lines on a negative as the charge went down into the grounding posts. A second later, the cold, sharp odor of ozone swept into the building.

There followed a drawn-out moment of elemental stillness, utter, absolute. Then, very faintly at first, came the rain. It pattered lightly on the roof, pecked uncertainly at the windows. Gradually the sound increased, the impacts heavier. Solid sprays of drops lashed against the building. Within seconds, cascades formed, pouring off the eaves. A warm rush of air washed through the doors and open spaces. Bonner turned his face to it, caught the sweet, heady smell of open ocean.

The monsoon had arrived.

19

Kurisovsky didn't see the great electrical discharge that heralded the start of the monsoon. He was still hunched over his welding torch, putting a final bead along the launcher's main trunnion. Only a dim flash registered through the mask, but he heard and felt the thunder a fraction of a second later as it rumbled through the courtyard.

Little more than a feathery mist at first, floating in on the wind, the rain came. He flipped up his mask. In the floodlights the rain looked like snowflakes.

Then the drops became larger, slashing in at an angle until they were pounding on the cobblestones. The troopers laughed and called happily to one another, letting the downpour wash over them like schoolboys.

Kurisovsky checked his watch: 4:09. He was pleased. The timing of everything was merging neatly together. In a few minutes they would run a final check of all systems and then warm up the missile packets and begin the pre-launch sequence.

He set actual salvo for 4:49 A.M. He began to hum, little snippets from a Vologdan drinking song.

As the third missile was being eased down into its firing sleeve, using the launcher's small cherry-picker winch, he and the firing sergeant went over the electrical systems, connected ignition circuits and inserted blast cartridges into their slots forward of the engine impellers. When detonated, these cartridges would create a blast of hot air to set the missile's small TK-44 turbofans spinning into full ignition.

Abruptly a problem developed. The floodlights began to short out. One by one, the bulbs exploded with little blue discharges as the rain crept down into their sockets. Hurriedly the men attempted to make protective shields for the remaining lights with strips of fiberglass packing from the missile fin assemblies. But before they could do it, the rest of the string went out. The courtyard was plunged into a rain-roaring blackness lit only by bursts of lightning.

Kurisovsky dispatched a man to the bungalow for flashlights. As he squatted on the firing platform waiting, a sharp series of lightning bolts crackled in the sky, the thunder right behind them. For a full five seconds, the entire landscape was lit in blue-white. Then up on Lake House, a bolt, looking like a ragged, white-hot slash cut across the darkness, struck one of the brass spires. For a moment the spire glowed, the metal ringing as the charge was carried off through the grounding wires.

Suddenly alert, Kurisovsky shot a glance up at the missiles, protruding fifteen feet above the courtyard. Although the entire launcher system was thoroughly grounded, he knew, a powerful enough lightning bolt striking one of the missiles might create enough static electricity to set off the igniter cartridges prematurely.

Bellowing, he lunged to his feet. "Pull the cartridges!" Then, fumbling around in the dark, he and the firing sergeant extracted each cartridge until all of them were back in their rubber storage casings.

When the trooper returned with the flashlights, they discovered another problem. The launch pit was filling with water too rapidly. Soon the level would reach the launcher's power boxes located on the bottom side of the platform and short them out.

Everybody began wildly bailing, using anything that would hold water. But it was useless. The rain came down faster than they could get it out. Cursing at his stupidity for not foreseeing this, Kurisovsky plowed around in the pit and frantically tried to figure out what to do.

Playing his flashlight beam across the courtyard, he quickly saw that the water was draining away from the center of the enclosure toward the main gate. He had an idea. If they could cut a narrow ditch from the edge of the pit to the gate, they could drain out enough water to keep the power boxes safe.

But there wasn't enough time to dig it; they'd have to blast it out. Working furiously, they laid out a line of de-pinned grenades from the pit to the gate, spaced six feet apart. A single trip wire was connected to each detonator lever, then the grenades were packed in sand to keep the levers compressed and to direct the blasts downward. Finally, heavy Kashmiri rugs dragged from Lake House were spread over the entire grenade chain to act as blast mats.

Everybody took cover. Crouched behind the corner of the gate, Kurisovsky yanked the trip wire. The explosions made muffled, ragged blasts under the rugs and blew tendrils of smoke through the weave. Instantly the water in the pit began to funnel out along the created ditch. Within minutes, the level had dropped a full two feet below the power boxes.

Kurisovsky again consulted his watch. Damnably, they'd lost eighteen minutes. But no matter. He quickly recalculated and set the new launch time to 5:11 A.M.

Forty-two minutes earlier, Commander Rockliffe had begun readying the *Yuma* for launch of the XGB to its target on the Mascarene. Ever since 0300, the sub had been executing slow, wide circles at her launch coordinates, running at a two-hundred-foot depth.

The firing of a missile from any American submarine always involves a complicated set of rules, even when the launch is categorized as a non-combat firing. Usually a sub begins this formal step-to-launch immediately after receiving an Emergency Action Message from its home base. But since the XGB test was already part of his cruise orders, Rockliffe had decided to complete some of the procedures well before placing his ship into Man Battle Stations, Missile status.

The first was the validation of the launch order. It was necessary that the captain and his three senior officers fully concur that the order was legitimate. Momentarily relinquishing the conn to Lieutenant Duquette, he returned to his cabin to get the written order from his safe. A second, similar order was already in the C.C. safe and would be taken out by the officer of the deck upon presentation of the captain's copy.

Once more in the Control Center, he took the conn again and ordered the O.D. to retrieve the second copy. Visually he compared both copies and nodded.

"Very well," he said. "I have a properly formulated order."

"Permission to authenticate, sir?" the O.D. asked.

Rockliffe turned to his XO. "Mister Duquette, do you concur?"

"I concur, Captain."

"Mister Misner, do you concur?" he asked his navigation officer.

"I concur, sir."

He repeated the question to the O.D., who answered in the affirmative.

"You have permission to authenticate."

The O.D. immediately ran both copies through a

machine that resembled a fax unit. It contained a secret code that had to match the code series on the order.

In a moment the O.D. said, "Captain, the order is authenticated."

"Very well, we have validation of order." As he turned to the chief of the watch to order him to Sound General Alarm, the loudspeaker crackled.

"Conn, Radio, we have ELF requesting we attain radio-depth to receive Emergency Action Message, sir."

Rockliffe nodded, feeling a bite of irritation. He suspected there had been a glitch aboard the *Explorer*. They might have to do more three-sixties until it got straightened out.

"Helm, bring her to eight-zero feet. All ahead two-thirds."

"Eight-zero feet, aye. All ahead two-thirds."

The *Yuma*'s deck tilted slightly as she ascended. The C.C. came alive as officers and seamen gave status relays. As the sub reached the eighty-foot depth and leveled out, Rockliffe ordered deployment of the radio antenna and instructed the helm to decrease their speed to four knots during the radio run.

Thirty seconds later, the receiving light on the C.C.'s FSK unit came on as the incoming radio message was automatically transcribed into written symbols on the machine's video screen. Rockliffe crossed the deck and read it as it printed out:

EAM12//0312z//WR1539967
ULTRA SECRET
FM: COMSUBPAC//1194
TO: USS YUMA
AUTHORITY ASSIGN: PRESIDENT//WR-BRAVO BRAVO
KILO 0045
/////////////

1. YOU ARE TO EXECUTE IMMEDIATE SURFACE
2. MAINTAIN CONTACT SHIP DES: EXPLORER TO COORDINATE LAUNCH OF MISSILE: XGB-3AS
3. DES EXPLORER GIVEN FULL AUTHORITY BY PRESIDENT
4. STAND BY FOR LAUNCH ASSIG ALERT-ONE COMBAT
5. ASSIGN TARGET: 05:31E/28:56N
//////////////

code reference: bravo: 25364KKT
BRAVO: 68746ITY
KILO: 84756HIY

//////////////
endendend

Rickliffe thought, What the fuck is this? He whirled about. "Radio, Conn, request verification." His eyes met Duquette's. They were shocked. "Navigation, bring up those coordinates."

A few seconds later: "Captain, I have coordinate fix."

Rockliffe darted to the bank of consoles near the chart table. One of the screens held a map magnification of northeastern India. A tiny fix light sat squarely in the middle of a lake designated Sonai.

The FSK unit light came on again. Once more the message was printed out. It was identical to the first.

Rockliffe conferred with his senior officers. Everyone was astounded. The whole thing made no sense. First, an order to surface was counter to the entire purpose of the cruise, something never done unless the submarine was experiencing catastrophic malfunction.

Second, they were being ordered to fire a missile

from the surface. Another abrogation of mission purpose. Technically it could be done, but the entire concept of submarine ballistics was based on underwater firing.

Third, the content of the EAM implied that the *Yuma* was literally to come under the direct command of the *Explorer*. Rockliffe's military instincts rebelled violently at that scenario.

And, finally, they were to send a missile into a sovereign nation, India. What in holy Christ is there? Rockliffe thought wildly.

Still, the message was apparently a presidential directive.

"Gentlemen," he said grimly, "I question the validity of this directive." He polled his officers. They all agreed with his assessment. He turned slightly. "Quartermaster, specify the plot log that all senior officers bear question of this order."

"It is so specified, sir."

The O.D. said, "Permission to authenticate, Captain?"

Rockliffe again polled his officers for concurrence, received it, and issued permission to the O.D. The message printout was run through the code unit.

"Captain, the message is authenticated."

"Very well," Rockliffe snapped. "Place the ship in condition 1-SQ."

"Condition 1-SQ, aye," Duquette repeated. The command was echoed in the C.C. In a moment the X.O. said, "We have 1-SQ status, Captain."

"Chief of the watch," Rockliffe called. "Sound General Alarm."

"General Alarm, aye." Immediately the Klaxon blared throughout the ship, a surging and fading horn similar to a London police van's.

"Man Battle Stations; Missile."

The order was quickly relayed.

"Helm, give me ten degrees up and proceed to surface."

"Ten degrees and proceed to surface, aye."

"Surface, surface, surface," the chief of the watch intoned.

"Blow the main valve stages and maintain high-pressure air."

"Main valve stages are being blown. High pressure in green."

"All ahead one-third."

"All ahead one-third, aye."

"Depth six-zero feet," the dive officer called out.

As the commands and acknowledgments flew through the hushed, tense C.C., Rockliffe stood motionless, his eyes cold and hard as the *Yuma* rose through the increasingly sun-pierced depths.

Holding to a geostationary orbit twenty-two thousand miles over the island of Borneo, the Australian-owned GeoStar-5 satellite soared through space, monitoring its plethora of meteorological activity, which included weather front movements, ocean circulation, eddy patterns, and data for ozone mapping. This information, stored and transcribed into six thousand code signals, was then transmitted to weather stations throughout the Indonesian Quadrant over a twenty-four-hour cycle.

Eighteen feet long and six wide with an earth weight of thirty-three hundred pounds, the satellite was shaped like a silver beer can sitting on an overturned cup. Deployed at one end were reflectors and vertical polarizers shaped like butterfly wings; at the other end was the cone-shaped assembly that contained the apogee-motor booster. Within the main cylindrical body were fourteen thousand solar cells that provided over eight hundred watts of power to the internal systems, with backup power provided by a bank of nickel-cadmium batteries.

At 4:01 A.M., Assam time, the satellite received a command alert signal from its control station at Jambi. First it was ordered to activate its redundant receiver subsystem. When this was done, it was told to boost its primary transmitter band to 14 GHz frequency and adjust the redundant receiver to 11 GHz.

After Jambi received compliance status, it issued a series of further commands. Instantly the satellite's secondary transmitting antenna swung slowly until it achieved a center-of-dish position homed to ground coordinates 86:31 E/8:11 S, the present position of the surfaced *Yuma*. Once the home was fixed, the antenna's automatic-repositioning sequence was activated. This would allow it to continually shift position to maintain a center-of-dish fix to the XGB as it moved along its flight path to northeastern India.

Finally, in order to prevent chance intrusion from any transmitters also operating on the 11 or 14 GHz frequencies, both receivers were issued an accept/no-accept code.

Seventy-four seconds later, the satellite acknowledged full completion of its setup. Jambi turned over total control of the vehicle to the radio operators aboard the *Explorer*.

The guidance loop was now complete. As soon as the missile was airborne, direct guidance signals from the *Explorer* would travel to the satellite's primary radio unit. There the signals would be multiplex-processed and down-frequencied. They would then be transmitted by the secondary unit to the main computer aboard the XGB to effect necessary adjustments for flight-track stability.

The return loop simply reversed the process. As the

missile's sensor and inertial systems fed constant position and attitude data to its own computer, this information would be transmitted back to the GeoStar's 11 MHz receiver, converted to the primary transmitter's higher frequency, and sent on to the *Explorer*.

Bass's first transmission was a code check. Two seconds later, *Yuma*'s Fire Control, which would monitor the missile's signals until actual launch, came back. Quickly the *Explorer*'s operators check-listed the system. The loop was clean.

At 4:16, the ship ordered the satellite into holding mode to await the launch of the XGB-3AS.

Bonner, his tennis shoes slipping on the sleek metal surface of the drilling platform, headed for the main derrick. The entire platform was flooded with water. It swirled around stanchions and storage tanks, and poured off all four sides of the rig in a steady waterfall. But above the rush he could faintly hear the revving of boat engines on the wind as the oil workers left the island.

For an aching moment he felt a sense of desertion. He glanced southward and saw the bobbing lights of the boats headed out into the lake. And safety. Cursing, he shook off the feeling and started up the derrick ladder.

Below him, McCarran was hunkered down beside the Christmas tree valve nest with two C-4 satchels and fuses. Earlier, Hak had dispatched Jungali and his men in the two canoes. They were to return to the shore at the pavilion, disperse up through the main buildings and gardens of Lake House, and set up field-of-fire positions above the courtyard. The moment the charges on the drilling rig went off, they would begin harassing fire against the Russians.

"But you must not strike the missiles," Hak cautioned. "When you shoot, make bloody certain you hit what you're aiming at and nothing else."

The Carib caressed his Kalashnikov and grinned impishly. The killing of the Sikhs had made his old bones feel young again. "Oh, I tell dem dat for sure, HakMcCarran. But dey good boys, dey no miss."

With the rain pounding at him like mercury pellets, Cas scampered up to the monkey board and slipped into the derrick man's shed. Inside, the rain rumbled wildly on the overhead. He studied the control panel until he found the line of emergency switches for the eight Christmas tree valves.

Each of the switches had a toggle shield. He flipped up the shields and, using the edge of his hand, activated the switches to On position. Instantly, down on the drilling deck the lights of the Christmas tree shifted from green to red, indicating the flow valves were open.

When he returned to the main deck, he could see McCarran had already tied the two satchels to the Christmas tree stanchion. As he passed the doghouse shed, he ducked into it for a moment. There were spools of wire stacked by the door, and coveralls hung from name-plated pegs in the wall. A storage bin was set at one end, filled with assorted gear. He dug through it until he found two waterproof box-battery flashlights.

He and Hak set to work charging the explosives. First, they inserted the detonaters into their lock rings and connected the four timer wires, crimping the insertion sleeves with their teeth. Next, they precisely set the satchels to the main valve casing so that each was offset slightly from the other. In this way the combined explosive charges would sheer the casing completely. The pressure-vaporized crude oil in the valve recesses would then ignite and chain-explode the oil both in the bore-hole pipes and in the lines that led down to the storage nest.

Finally, they set the timer clocks to an eighteen-minute delay before detonation. Hopefully, this would allow them enough time to get down into the compound, place the remaining satchel charges on at least two of the storage tanks, radio a message to Jeffry, and then head for Lake House.

Cas glanced over at McCarran. "Set?"

Hak nodded.

"Let her go."

Both men released their timer dials simultaneously. As the tiny clickers started, they lunged away and headed for the ramp ladder. At the bottom, they retrieved the other satchels and sprinted across the small stretch of beach to the shore berm surrounding the utility compound. A moment later, they disappeared down among the buildings.

Anduri was shocked into silence when the President informed him that he was considering the option of sending a missile into Assam.

"I am fully aware of the tremendous risks involved here, Prime Minister," the President quickly added, his words carrying a tiny modulation echo. "It is a great agony to me. But at this juncture, my advisers say there is no other option but to intervene in this situation."

At last the Indian P.M. found his voice. "This is monstrous, Mr. American President. How can you think of it? This is—is an act of transgression to my country's territories."

"That is precisely what it is," the President shot back. "And that's why I need your cooperation. These Russian missiles must be stopped!"

"But how can I assent to this? If your terrible missile is incorrect, there will be thousands of dead in my country.''

"The alternative is a hundred Chinese missiles in your country.''

"No, you must not ask me to do this thing.''

The President studied his hands. They were steady. He found a gold pen on the desk. He picked it up assured by its solidity. He tried to think of something more to say.

Before he could, Anduri's voice came back. "I will discuss this with my minsters. It is they who must make this terrible decision.''

"There isn't time for that.''

"I must have time.''

The President gritted his teeth. "Anduri, please understand that these missiles could be launched at any moment. You must decide. Alone. It is your duty as leader of your country.''

"No, I cannot do it.'' The line went dead.

"Dammit!'' the President hissed violently.

The wind swept out of the southwest and gave projectile speed to the rain as it howled among the buildings. From the overcast, lightning bolts hurled sharp blue pyrotechnics, and their thunder rumbled across the island.

Down in the compound, Bonner and McCarran found an old American military half-ton ammo carrier that had been adapted into a service truck. Its bed was filled with tools and pipes and two canisters of gasoline. A foot of water was trapped on the floor of the driver's compartment.

Bonner checked for the ignition key. It was there. He tossed his satchel onto the seat and slid behind the wheel. The engine snapped to life with the first flick of the key. He turned on the lights, waited for Hak to

climb in, then gunned off through a crazy quilt of
feeder pipes that ran toward the south loading dock.

McCarran tapped his shoulder, pointed to his wristwatch, and held up the fingers of both hands: ten minutes before the timers on the rig went off.

They reached the main storage nest. Cas chose the
largest of the storage tanks and skidded to a stop. Four
smaller ones formed a circle around it. He grabbed a
satchel and flashlight and leapt out. Hak immediately
took the wheel and tore off toward one of the smaller
tanks.

The wind nearly pulled Bonner off the tank's ladder
as he scurried to the top. The structure was painted
yellow, and there were dark streaks of rust along the
seams. He reached the top and crawled along the ladder to the main valve upright. There was a red light
on it alongside a large metal wheel. Straddling the
stanchion, he cradled the satchel and began inserting
the detonators. He could hear the buzz from the light
filament near his head. The glow made the silver
detonator tubes look like thin rods of ruby.

When the charge was set, he jammed it between the
valve wheel and the stanchion casing and checked his
watch. It was 4:44:45. Six minutes, fifteen seconds
left to the rig detonation. He set the timer dial to co-
incide, then crawled back to the edge and started
down, literally dropping, his tennies gripping the out-
sides of the handrail. Across the tank nest he caught
sight of Hak's flashlight up on the tank to his left.

He hit the ground running.

The War Room in the White House crackled with
incoming and outgoing calls. The small group of men
who had been there at the start had grown as more and
more of the president's staffers and military men came

in. Everybody moved around with the hushed expectancy of people about to witness an execution.

The President, his restless tension forcing constant movement, prowled between the radio-telephone panels and wall maps. He was still enraged over Anduri's refusal to cooperate in the XGB strike. The man was a damned weakling. Yet at the same time he understood his dilemma. To acquiesce to a foreign government sending a missile into his country would be devastating. Even if it was successful, it would be the end of his power.

He had finally reached Premier Sichen as well. But the Chinese leader had refused to promise he would not retaliate, even after the situation was fully explained to him. He simply wasn't sure he could control his hard-liners if disaster struck.

McNeely said, "We've just received word from the *Explorer,* sir. The XGB is ready to fire."

The President nodded solemnly.

McNeely's voice was barely a whisper. "What is your decision, sir?"

For a moment the President experienced an almost overwhelming desire to jump to his feet and run from this place. But he didn't. Instead he rolled the gold pen back and forth with his fingers. Its substance helped draw his mind into a tight focus. He thought of all the consequences, all the moral issues. They paraded by like marching soldiers, full of ominous pageantry. And death.

Would he be savior or slaughterer?

He lifted his eyes. "Launch it," he said.

20

Sergeant Georgi Baklanov hung his handkerchief on the branches of a mulberry bush. On it he had scribbled a single word: Motherland. It was a Leningrad ritual usually reserved for weddings when a bride and groom hung a handkerchief to something green and leafy for luck. But here the union was between Baklanov and death.

Since midnight he had been hiding in a small stand of linden trees and mulberry brush on the western edge of the Krasnokazarmen Cultural Park. At first the night sky had been filled with cold stars. But now fog hung over the mile-long stretch of rolling grassland of the park. Once the czar's Imperial Army cannoneers had exhibited their killing power here for the amusement of silver-helmeted Hassars and their bejeweled ladies.

To his left stood the gate to Seleznov's dacha. Built in 1832, it had been a convent for the Sisters of St. Catherine. It was stark white with arched walls and tiled onion domes topped with golden crosses. A high wall surrounded the grounds. But from Baklanov's position, he had a clear, one-hundred-fifty-yard fire line to the brightly lit front entrance of the dacha, where several black Zil limos were parked and a handful of security men idly roamed between the courtyard and gate.

The sergeant shifted his legs. They were stiff, the

thick, powerful muscles bunched. Baklanov was a *kul'*
turizin, a body builder. He lifted his head and sniffed
at the air. The fog held a chilly sourness.

For a moment his thoughts drifted back to boyhood
when he used to fish with his father from the banks of
the Neva River in Leningrad while the city was still
and bathed in twilight at 2:00 A.M. during the long
white nights of June. With a snort of impatience at
himself, he forced the thoughts away.

In an attempt to refocus his mind, he lifted his rifle.
It was a Volga 300, a sniper's weapon. Sleek and
deadly with a black barrel and receiver and camou-
flaged stock. He brought the rifle to his shoulder and
looked through the mounted Red Star sight. Instantly
the hands of a security guard came into view. The man
was scratching his testicles.

Baklanov scanned away, fixed on the front door of
the dacha. It was made of dark wood with tarnished
brass rivets. For a long moment he held the cross hairs
on the precise center of the door, his muscles gone to
stone. The tiny lines of the cross hairs were absolutely
motionless.

After a full minute, he lowered the weapon and laid
it across his knees. From somewhere a dog began to
bark, the sound of it drowsy and melancholy in the
stillness. He would sit there until Seleznov finally
emerged.

Jungali's men didn't like the idea of going up against
Russian mercenaries. Cutting Sikh throats had been
acceptable, even fun. But Russian combat troops were
another matter. They had been grumbling sullenly
among themselves ever since getting into the canoe
under the oil derrick. Still, fearful of Jungali's wrath,
they dutifully paddled toward the pavilion.

Once they were out from under the drilling plat-

form, the wind hit them hard off the starboard quarter
and kept pushing them toward the rock-strewn shore.
In the dim light, their poacher's eyes picked out the
dark shapes of crocodiles in the small patches of
beach. The rain came down so hard, they had to yell
at one another to be heard.

At last they reached the pavilion. Its blue lights illuminated the rain, turning it to shimmering sheets of
azulene. Jungali swung the stern of his canoe against
the pavilion wall and leapt out. The three men with
him followed. They hauled the canoe up onto the par-
apet.

The other canoe banged into the wall right behind
them. But the men refused to disembark. Jungali raged
at them, but they remained seated, their rain-soaked
faces looking dumbly back at him.

The Carib paced back and forth, his face contorted
with fury. "I don' believe dis goddom shit," he
roared. "You little stinkin' chilrun frightened of dem
goddom Russians." He spat on them in utter contempt.

The men looked uncertainly at one another.

"Den tink about dis." He pointed toward Lake
House. "Dat ting got plenty booty, I tell you dat.
Fuckin' Singh booty." He reached down and gripped
his genitals. "You goddom fools got enough of dis to
go an' take it? Have you?"

To Jungali, this whole affair had become more than
the mere payback of his debt to Jackie Dunbar. His
blood was in it now, drawing up the memories of days
gone by when he was young and wild and had fought
for hunting grounds against the Burmese *macchars* in
the Patkai Hills and the Log tribesmen on the Dabang
River.

Gradually his contempt and the talk of riches coaxed
the men. They climbed slowly out of the canoe and

hauled it up beside the other. Down in the water, crocs slid along the edge of the pavilion, their knobby snouts probing the rain.

Going in single file, Jungali led them up toward the main house. The pathway wound among wildernesses of creepers, unkempt patches of rose and jasmine and alongside pools thick with canna and frangipani brush. A cobra, long as a bullwhip, slithered through the slosh of water on the ground and disappeared into one of the pools.

To the left was a stand of palms and jacaranda, to the right a grassy field fronting the fence line of a corral. Now and then in rain pauses they caught the sharp whinnying of horses as the animals plunged against the fence, smelling the strangers on the wind.

They entered the main house through the *khansama,* or cooking area. It reeked of charcoal and horse manure. All the cabinets had been torn out, and there were ashes of cooking fires on the tile floor. A corridor ran past the room and into a large, open veranda. Beyond was what had once been a ballroom. The men went about in the darkness stealing things.

Rugs were hung on the walls. As the men came close, cockroaches scurried away, making tiny clacking sounds under the steady drone of the rain. There were hunting and polo trophies mounted between the rugs. All the heads were filled with bullet holes, their skulls shattered, and the walls were pockmarked. The men's sandals crunched in mounds of bat guano.

Jungali paused beside a huge window covered with *tatties,* bamboo and straw strips to keep out the dust. He peered through. Directly in front was a colonnaded walkway with curving steps that led into the courtyard. Dimly he could see flashlights moving out there. Suddenly the entire western sky lit up with a flash of sheet lightning. For an instant he saw the three mis-

sile shafts stark white in the flash and below them the
Russians, their glistening naked backs caught in a
stopped moment of blue light.

Quickly hissing, he directed his men into position.
He sent two to each of the gardens that bracketed the
house. The remaining three were ordered upstairs to
take up firing posts on the balcony. He commanded
everyone to kill swiftly and accurately the moment explosions from the oil compound started.

The men melted off into the darkness. Jungali turned
back to the window. He poked the muzzle of his Kalashnikov through the bamboo, bracing it with his
palm, and sighted down at the moving flashlights. His
finger toyed with the trigger.

A tiny shaft of blue light snapped out like a candle
flame. A welding torch. Grinning devilishly, he homed
to the dark shadow that held it.

The mess hall was filled with the pounding rush of
the rain, the howl of the wind. The Sikh corpses were
still sprawled on the floor, but each had been turned
so the heads pointed south. A Jungali insult. The moist
air held the sickly sweet stench of coagulated blood.

Dripping wet, Bonner and McCarran knelt beside
the radio in the kitchen. Hak clicked the key several
times to let Jeffry know he was there.

Jeffry came right back: "Tiger Stripe, have just received Washington signal." His transmission was full
of lightning static. "Missile on go. Repeat, missile on
go. But it is contingent on your affirmative on oil fire.
Over."

Hak keyed: "She'll be blowing in two minutes."

"Tiger Stripe, must have absolute affirmative."

"I'll tape the key so you can hear the bloody thing."

"I roger that. Missile launch set for four fifty-five,

your time. Repeat, four fifty-five, your time. Do you understand? Over.''

"Understood. What is impact time?''

"Flight set for forty-one minutes. Impact your time is five thirty-six. Repeat, impact is five thirty-six.'' Jeffry's voice wavered through the static.

Bonner searched the slicing table, found a filthy apron. He ripped a tie off, handed it to McCarran. Hak keyed: "Impact five thirty-six. Understand. Out.''

"Tiger Stripe . . . Tiger Stripe.''

Hak keyed. "Shut the hell up and listen for the explosion.'' Then, holding the key down, he wrapped the strip of cloth around the mike and locked it open. Gently he laid it on the washer, turned, and sprinted through the door with Bonner right behind him.

Going with lights out and engine whining, Cas drove the ammo carrier between the buildings of the compound. A mud pool loomed directly ahead. He swung the wheel and they skidded sideways for a moment before the rear wheels grabbed and they careened around the rim of the pool. They sped on, the rain lashing them.

Driving on instinct, Cas squinted out at the dark objects hurtling past, trying to remember the way he'd come off the road to Lake House. The rain whipped his face, made bee stings on his lids.

He spotted a small intersection, reached it, and swung right. The road ahead was awash in water, and the ammo carrier bounced and lunged over runoff ditches that had already formed. Underneath, the water slammed into the chassis and sprayed off the wheels.

Hak hunched forward, his body riding the lunges. He pointed the flashlight at his wristwatch. Up the hill they went. Hak put out his hand with fingers extended.

He began retracting them, one at a time. Three seconds—two—one—

He snapped around and pointed back at the compound.

Dave Bass was running on adrenaline and orange juice power. One sped his blood, the other filled his stomach with citric acid needles. Aboard the *Explorer,* everybody was into the act, the tension heavy, like humidity in the air. Even petty differences were forgotten. When the president's decision came through for them to initiate the launch, stomach muscles clenched several more notches.

Yet despite the frenetic pace, preparations had gone without a hitch. The necessary reprogramming was completed expeditiously and all the trivial glitches anybody could think of planned for. The *Explorer's* mainframes were linked to the fire-control panels of the *Yuma,* which would continue to handle the launch until the moment the missile cleared her tube.

In the *Explorer's* O.P. room its men sat poised in tense silence, broken only by the pop of transmission keys and the hushed voices of the radiomen as they talked to the sub's operators directly through cleared UHF bands. Only Bass, wrapped in a controlled frenzy, darted from the consoles to the tracking boards, making last-minute checks.

Since the *Explorer* was positioned at the very edge of the same time zone as Assam, her clocks held the identical launch set as those given to McCarran. That was two minutes away. If, however, verification of the fire on the drilling platform at Lake Sonai failed to come in before launch, Bass would abort for a ten-minute wait. And keep aborting until it did come through or until Washington called for step-down.

Still, each stoppage would necessitate another frantic revamping of the preset flight track within the research vessel's mainframes as well as those of the F.C. computers aboard the submarine. Although everybody dreaded going through with this insane thing, they hoped that at least they wouldn't have to sweat out delays.

Bass paused near the bridge. His forehead was awash with perspiration. He glanced at the digital time read-out on the track panel: 004:54:49. He drew spittle through his teeth. "Come on, fuckhead. Have you lit that fire or not?"

As if in answer, the loudspeaker from radio 3, linked directly by communications satellite to the War Room in Washington on the marine emergency frequency of 2182 kHz, flashed a blow of static. Then: "CQ Whiskey Oscar Kilo two Mike three three, this is Whiskey Charlie one. Do you copy? Over."

The *Explorer* radio operator rogered receipt of the War Room's signal.

"We have affirmative on Fire in the Hole," Whiskey Charlie one continued, referring to the assigned code for the fire on the oil drilling platform at Lake House. "Repeat, we have affirmative on Fire in the Hole." Someone in the O.P. room gave a small cheer, which died off as Whiskey Charlie one came on again: "You are authorized under presidential code Bravo-Bravo-Kilo zero-zero-four-five to execute assigned launch when ready. Repeat, execute assigned launch when ready. Acknowledge and verify on TAC-COS designate COMMPAC Pearl Harbor on frequency two-zero-eight-two-point-five. Over."

While Captain Towne went about verifying the order through Pearl, Bass and his men were already moving. Click-ons were tapped into computers. The *Yuma* C.C. link was coordinated to the tenth of a second, and all tracking circuits via the GeoStar-5 were checked and cleared. Every screen in the room came alive with number sequences, reeling backward to track baseline.

A moment later, they heard Towne's return message to the War Room. "Whiskey Charlie one, we have verification from COMMPAC. Countdown now in effect. Stand by."

He paused and glanced at Bass. Bass yelled, "Coming up on two minutes . . . now!"

Into the mike Towne said, "Time to launch designated at two minutes and counting. Over."

On the main tracking screen, arc parameters shifted, converged. There was a slight deviance that was automatically corrected. Soft hums and clicks issued from the data-processing consoles as the machines came up to function status.

Whiskey Charlie one said, "You are instructed to hold open channel until TTL and ignition complete. Over."

"Roger on open channel. TTL is at one minute, fifty-three seconds and counting."

Bass's eyes bored into the flitting numbers on the side of the track panel. The acid in his stomach was forgotten. Remaining was only adrenaline and the quick, sharp thud of blood in his head.

A tiny *ping* sounded as each second clicked off: 1:50—1:49—1:48—

During the preceding twenty-two minutes, the *Yuma* had maintained a general fix at her assigned firing position on the surface by holding just enough power to offset a four-knot current from the northeast. She lay on a tranquil gray-black sea. In the west a few stars still lingered. But across the sky the eastern horizon showed a widening wash of dawn light.

Aboard the sub was a frenzy of activity. Following

the commands issued from Bass aboard the *Explorer*—which felt like rusty nails in Captain Rockliffe's teeth—the crew had initiated an entire set of adjustments to the XGB and its launch tube.

They replaced the fuel canisters with larger ones and added spare units. The booster charge was changed along with an increased number of igniters. Flood-valve lines were linked to the adjacent launch tubes so a higher pressure feed could be used when water was pumped into number nine to offset vibration damage during the "dry" launch. Meanwhile, Fire Control relayed the updated flight program coming directly off the research ship's mainframes into the missile's computer.

All of it was completed by 0450 hours. One minute later, Lieutenant Duquette hurried in from the Radio Room with a printout of the president's order to launch the XGB in precisely four minutes.

Rockliffe thought, *Here we go!* He felt a dryness in his throat. Quickly he ran through the formal concurrence procedure for the message, and then it was run through the code machine.

"Sir, message is authenticated," the O.D. said. The other two officers again concurred.

Rockliffe nodded. "Very well, we have a properly formulated order." Since the ship was already in 1-SQ state, he began the actual firing sequence: "Officer of the deck, achieve and maintain launch position designated delta-one-three."

"Maintain delta-one-three, aye, Captain."

Orders and acknowledgments echoed back and forth in the C.C. as final engine settings were issued to bring the *Yuma* to its precise firing position as dictated by the inertial navigation gear.

"Weapons, Conn, you have permission to activate circuits," Rockliffe said.

Fire Control repeated the order. In the Weapons bay the main launch panels came alive. On the firing grid were two sets of lights for each of the twelve launch tubes. The left bank was green, the right white. Only the whites came on during this initial phase.

The captain turned to Duquette. "Executive officer, break out the CIP key."

"Break out the CIP, aye."

The CIP key was kept in one of the C.C. safes. Retrieved by Duquette, it was inserted into a box beside the navigational panels. When properly aligned, it completed full activation of the sub's firing circuits. Instantly in the Weapons bay, the green bank of lights in the grid came on.

Rockliffe glanced at the chronometer over the chart table. Designated time to launch was two minutes, fifteen seconds away. He reached up for the loudspeaker mike. "This is the captain. We are in condition 1-SQ. This is a Missile, Combat launch."

He then handed the mike to Duquette. The ship's crew had to recognize both the senior officers' voices. Duquette identified himself and repeated the command.

"Officer of the deck, recommend position for hover."

"Captain, recommend hover commence in one minute."

"Do so."

"Aye, sir. Helm, achieve hover in fifty-seven seconds."

"Fifty-seven seconds, aye."

"Stand by Fire Order," Rockliffe called out. His heart was beginning to thud against his chest wall. He touched a finger to his right temple. It was a little trick he used to maintain calm.

"Stand by Fire Order, aye, sir," repeated the chief of the watch.

"The Fire Order will be nine."

The command was relayed and acknowledged by the Fire Control officer. In the Weapons bay all the firing grid lights went off except the number nine green and white.

"Weapons, Conn, open outer door."

"Open outer door, aye." A moment later: "Outer door open and locked."

"Conn, Helm, permission to initiate hover."

"All right. Dive master, all stop and commence hovering."

"All stop. Hover has been initiated."

Rockliffe paused for a moment before issuing the next order. "Officer of the deck, retrieve the firing keys."

"Firing keys, aye."

The three firing keys, tiny metal fans resembling spark-plug spacers, were the last security step in a launch. Kept in seperate safes, they were retrieved by two officers. The third was constantly worn around Rockliffe's neck.

"We have the keys, sir," Duquette said.

Quickly the three officers exchanged their individual sets. These were then inserted into a code machine called the Doom Box. Within seconds a printout clicked from the machine. It was handed to the captain.

He studied it a moment, then called, "Weapons, Conn, the printout has been validated."

The Fire Control officer acknowledged.

Rockliffe checked the chronometer. Twenty-four seconds to launch.

"Pressurize tube nine."

"Tube nine pressurize, aye." There was a soft hiss

as several atmospheres of air were pumped into the XGB's launch tube. "Nine on full pressure."

Eleven seconds . . .

"Conn, Helm, we have full hover on delta-one-three."

"Very well." Rockliffe did not look at his officers, or at any of the enlisted men in the C.C. Yet he could feel their eyes on him. Felt it right down in the skin of his neck.

Five seconds . . .

The sweep of the chronometer second hand was like a fall in slow motion.

Two seconds . . .

One . . .

"Weapons, Conn, you have permission to fire," he said sharply.

"Initiating fire," came the call.

In the Weapons bay, the firing officer punched a large red button. Instantly the single green light on the number nine slot replaced the white one. There was a powerful jolt as the missile's booster packet went off. This was followed by a high-pitched sound indicating the sudden release of air pressure. The deck and bulkheads trembled.

A few seconds later, the loudspeaker blared: "Nine away."

Rockliffe leaned against the chart table. His body was taut. It's done, he thought. Jesus, it's done. He and the *Yuma* had just entered history as the first American submarine to launch a nuclear missile against human beings. It made his heart ache, as if someone had actually reached in and gripped it.

"Dear God!" he whispered and closed his eyes.

Under normal firing conditions, the pressure-sensitive booster rocket igniters would have activated as soon as the missile cleared its sixty feet of water. Since there was no water, the igniters held ignition until the blow of the pack had carried the XGB to a height of 470 feet. Then the igniters, responding to the slightly thinner pressure differential of the upper air, lit the booster rocket into full thrust.

Velocity was sixty miles per hour and accelerating.

Jet tabs in the thrust flow vectored the missile to a fifty-five-degree angle of ascent off the horizon. Forward of the booster canister, the set of three tail fins deployed, rolling the missile to a stabilized 0 base position. Gyros automatically spun up, and the LOS inertial navigation system in the auto-pilot fixed on the preset heading of 31 degrees, 12 minutes True relative to the bow of the *Yuma*.

Eight seconds into the flight, the booster burned out and was jettisoned. The short, stubby forward hull wings swung out and locked into position while the main air scoop was deployed from its position forward of the turbofan engine impellers.

A half second later, the engine's ring of AG starter cartridges blew, jamming a blast of superheated air sternward, spinning up the turbofan engine to 30,000 rpm and into ignition.

Velocity climbed to 600 miles per hour, increasing rapidly. Thrust vectors in the jet barrel adjusted the missile nose to a twenty-degree angle off the horizon. Down-track position was 5.6 miles from the *Yuma*, altitude two thousand feet.

As the speed reached Mach 1.5, the auto-pilot clicked on the missile's environmental sensor system. Immediately it began absorbing data on attitude, outside air pressure, propulsion temperature, fuel status, and inertial navigation readings of position. Five seconds later, it commenced transmitting its status reports via the GeoStar on 11 mHz.

Velocity: Mach 2.5 and still accelerating. Altitude: 4,000 feet. Down-track position: 9 miles.

The stern thrust vectors brought the angle of the nose to seven degrees of the horizon. The turbofan jet was nearing the end of its first-phase thrust. Speed had reached Mach 4.2 and altitude was now 6,000 feet.

As the missile approached its cruise level of 6,500 feet, the thrust vectors brought it to a horizontal position. The moment it achieved a 0 angle to the horizon, the engine shut down. The XGB, carrying full momentum holding to Mach 4.9 velocity, continued through the air, the sudden silence broken only by the whir of its impellers and the electronic pings of the sensor circuits.

Four seconds later, as momentum began to dissipate, the engine reignited, blowing out a second blast of superheated air astern. Once more the missile was driven forward, everything holding to a track that would take it to a marble house on a lake in northeastern India in precisely 39 minutes, 51 seconds.

21

The C-4 charges on the drilling rig went off several seconds before those in the tank nest. On the derrick floor, the Christmas tree stanchion was completely sheared, blowing a two-foot-wide, high-pressure geyser of raw oil a hundred feet into the air. Ignited by the heated metal, it erupted into flame with a whooshing roar. This was instantly followed by a jolting explosion as the derrick's upworks, storage tanks, and crane disappeared in a searing, boiling burst of fire.

It was then the nest charges went. Like fuses, they fired the trapped oil fumes in the tops of the two tanks. Both exploded with a gigantic, metal-rending blast. Fiery chunks of metal arced into the sky, their flight silhouetted against a great mushroom of black smoke laced with sheets of coiling fire. Twin concussion waves hurtled outward.

Up in the Lake House courtyard, Kurisovsky and his men jerked upright in shock at the detonations, then instinctively dropped to the ground. Above them the rain-filled sky lit with red and orange as the rolling thunder of the explosions *whomped* and surged off, riding the wind. A second later, the concussion waves hit and seemed to suck the air upward.

With his face pressed into the flooded cobblestones, Kurisovsky's mind raced wildly for an explanation. What was this? From the gigantic sound of the explosions, he surmised they had either been from storage tanks or the derrick itself. But why? Was it an accident? Or, worse, some gigantic diversionary tactic before an attack?

Preparation for the launch of the first three rockets had been nearly completed. The men were merely running one final check on the circuit systems. Even the welding torches had been relit to begin the igniter warm-up and ten-minute firing sequence.

Still caught in the tendrils of the pressure wave, Kurisovsky shoved himself to his feet, turned to shout an order. Before the words came out, a barrage of automatic fire interspersed with the throatier booms of big-bore Mauser rifles erupted from the main house. The air was filled with a deadly rain of bullets that screamed off the cobblestones.

Five of his men were instantly hit. The rest, frantically grabbing their weapons, raced for cover. Kurisovsky dashed to the left and hurled himself behind a huge marble statue of Ganesh. It had a thick layer of moss on its base that smelled like vomit. Twisting, he cautiously peered around it, trying to pinpoint the muzzle flashes.

A new barrage of bullets opened up. As they did, he managed to spot a series of flashes up on the first balcony of Lake House. Propping his 9mm on the palm of his left hand, he emptied the clip at the spot where the flashes had been. Behind him, the others opened up, too. Out in the courtyard, one of the wounded men dragged himself to the edge of the launch pit and disappeared into it.

A corporal named Papalorev crawled up beside the colonel. "Five down, sir," he said quietly. He had their only machine gun, a light Heckler & Koch HK11A1 clip-fed 7.62mm, cradled in his arms.

Quickly the firing from the house diminished until

there were only sporadic Mauser rounds. Kurisovsky studied the field a moment, then turned to the corporal. "Set up in the launcher pit and lay covering fire for us. We'll flank them through the gardens."

"Yes, sir."

As the man started to turn away, Kurisovsky grabbed his shoulder. "If we're not back in fifteen minutes, launch the rockets immediately."

The corporal nodded, paused a moment, then zigzagged back across the courtyard, and dropped over the lip of the launch pit. In a moment he had the machine gun set up on other side closest to the house and began pouring bullets into it in five-round bursts. The tracers made white-hot lines over the courtyard. Up on the balconies, the Gunjarati filigree and arabesque *pietra dura* blew into showers of marble.

The colonel took a quick position fix of his men. One was under the opposite gallery, three on his side. He raised his arm in the "Converge on me" sign. Immediately the three came up and knelt around him. Overhead, a fresh deluge of rain started, the water sizzling off the upper gallery floor.

He tapped one of the troopers on the shoulder. The man's short beard sparkled with raindrops. "Cross to the other gallery and wait until you see us move. We'll go in through the gardens."

The trooper sprang to his feet and sprinted straight across the courtyard. He drew a single shot from the garden. Kurisovsky and the other two troopers opened up on it.

For the assault he placed one man on point, the other on his left flank. The point man carried a Spagin 1200, a 12-gauge pump shotgun firing Double 0 buckshot loads; the other had an AKMS paratrooper Kalashnikov. Each had managed to don his battle harness, which contained two grenades apiece.

Kurisovsky paused long enough to insert a new clip into his pistol. Then, moving silently, the three men skirted the gallery wall and melted into the underbrush of the first garden.

Before the explosions, Bonner's mind had been racing ahead, up the slope toward Lake House and into the courtyard. He pictured those Russian missiles pointing toward the eastern sky and experienced a momentary, crazy compression of time. Were they too late? Had the missile igniters already been circuited and were now nearing launch? He squinted through the driving rain, expecting to hear the sudden rumble of engines.

Then Hak was grinning at him, counting down and pointing. As the derrick charge went, the column of oil ignited from the bottom like a gasoline-soaked rag. When the main explosion came, it sounded like a five-thousand-pound bomb and lit the rain-dark landscape with a bright white-orange glow that illuminated the flooded road ahead and the high walls of Lake House, only two hundred yards away.

The tank explosions were even louder. Cas felt the ammo carrier shake violently, and then the concussion waves passed over them. That nearly tore the steering wheel out of his hands, and the vehicle surged to the left. Fighting to regain control, Cas felt a rolling wall of heat sweep over them. He jammed on the brake and finally got the ammo carrier stopped.

The fires began creating a steady roar that sounded like an approaching tornado. Yet under it he caught the pounding chatter of automatic weapons from Lake House. He glanced at McCarran and grinned. "Jungali and his boys have started."

"Aye, lad," Hak snapped. "We'd best be quick in support."

A heavy squall swept in off the lake. Through it Cas studied the courtyard wall. He could barely see it save for the dancing black and orange shadows on the outer stones. He released the clutch and they moved ahead slowly.

As they neared, he noticed a grove of palms and jacaranda to the right, nearly hiding that portion of the outer wall. Instantly he swung toward them, and a moment later they went in under the trees. Overhead, the branches whipped violently in the wind.

On the far side of the grove was a walkway amid overgrown patches of brush. He eased the ammo carrier to a stop and killed the engine. The firing from Lake House had stopped, but now and then came the short, powerful bursts of a machine gun. Between the bursts he thought he detected horses screaming from somewhere down near the lake.

Hak handed him one of the Thompsons. Cas jacked a round up into the chamber, then did the same with the Colt. He tucked the pistol into the band of his shorts above his buttocks. It felt icy cold and heavy against his skin. Last, he clamped a spare clip between his teeth.

Both men dismounted and scurried between the trees until they reached the walkway, then went more cautiously toward the house. All around them the brush crackled under the impacts of the rain. The air was thick with the stench of crude oil. They could feel cinders and droplets of unburned oil slanting in on the wind.

Beside a pool filled with wild roses, Cas halted. Through the rain the marble facades of Lake House glowed with firelight, their glistening brass domes just barely visible. Nothing moved save the whipping branches of the garden trees and the hissing flood of water across the ground.

He glanced back. Hak was on the other side of the pool. Returning his attention to the house, he saw that a corner column of the walkway rose to his left. The balcony it supported extended over the garden and then curved to form the courtyard gallery on his side.

He felt nervous bursts of energy tingling through his body, became aware of his muscles tensing. Soon, he knew, he'd be in personal combat again, that groin-aching, heart-pounding insanity he had experienced so many times before. Yet each time it was new, always filled with that wild, almost painful thudding in his head as instinctive fear boiled through his blood to make his ears whistle.

He let the tensions concentrate until his fingers tingled, focused on the metallic, oily taste of the clip in his mouth. Then he shifted around and motioned for McCarran to hold his position. He rose and, hunched over with the Thompson at high port, he started forward.

He had gone about twenty feet when from the corner of his eye, he saw a man rise beyond the upper balcony railing. There was a powerful crack and a quick tongue of fire blew out. He heard projectiles slashing through the trees and underbrush around him.

Moving faster than his own thoughts, he swung the Thompson around and blew a burst at the balcony, the weapon's recoil pulling upward. His bullets slammed into the man and he dropped out of sight.

Instantly Cas threw himself to the ground and rolled to the left. As he did, a returning burst from another part of the balcony sprayed across the spot where he'd been. He fired again, fanning the weapon across the muzzle flash, which he could still see on his retinas.

Silence.

He heard a grunt, then another. It had the odd,

straining murmur of a man trying to lift a great weight.
The hair rose on his neck.

Hak!

He remained absolutely motionless for several seconds, his eyes sweeping the flickering shadows up on
the balcony. Nothing moved. Finally, inching forward
from elbow to elbow, he slithered backward and
crossed the walkway to McCarran.

Hak was leaning crookedly against a jacaranda
trunk. He had taken the full blast of a shotgun in the
groin, a plate pattern, the buckshot blowing his lower
body into a mass of torn flesh and intestines.

"Oh, Jesus!" Cas whispered around the edge of the
spare clip. He leaned forward, his nostrils catching the
raw smell of the wound. Clenching and unclenching
his hands, he reached out and touched Hak's carotid.
He could feel a heavy thump of blood under his finger.

McCarran grunted again. Cas looked into his eyes.
In the flickering light they blazed with rage. Bonner
put his arm under McCarran's legs, the other around
his back. He started to lift. Hak grunted again. This
time it made a little sinking arc of sound that slowly,
delicately faded away. His eyes still held the hot fury,
but now they were glazed. He was dead.

The blast of a grenade erupted from somewhere on
the other side of the house. Cas released McCarran
and rolled away as a handgun opened up, followed by
two quick bursts of automatic fire. A high-pitched wail
was cut off abruptly, as if operated by a switch. A few
seconds later, there was more gunfire.

Silence again, overlaid with the distant roar of the
fires, the sough of the wind, and a scream of a horse.
Cas lay with his face to the ground, felt the steady
collisions of the rain on his back. The earth fumed
with jungle wetness, the fecund chlorophyll tang of

vegetal growth. His heart felt large in his chest, and anger welled up against the insides of his temples.

After a moment he rose slowly to his feet. He leaned over McCarran's body and picked up the other Thompson. Hak looked like a tired hobo sleeping in the rain. The brim of his Aussie hat trembled in the wind. Cas ejected his empty clip and replaced it with the one from McCarran's weapon. One final glance, and then he moved away.

"E Acquisition Gate coming up," Bass called out loudly. A second later, he added, "Achieved." The XGB, seven hundred and thirty miles down-track from the *Yuma*, had just crossed the line of the equator.

Bass was seated at the Central Command Unit, the semicircle of display screens and computer boards situated on the starboard side of the O.P. room. Lined on either side of him were secondary consoles and radio panels. In the gear bank was the complete Closed Loop Computer System that controlled the XGB's flight.

A TADL-(Link 11) communications system received constant position/status data from the missile's auto-pilot. This was instantaneously filtered through transducers and logged into an interface of parallel analog and series digital memory/data processors called the CMP unit, which logic-scanned for any divergence error off the preset track.

Within milliseconds, the CMP's Automatic Direction System calculated response factors that created a Zero-Base Error alignment to the present trajectory. Correction commands were issued, sent through the transducers, where they were changed to frequency pulses and transmitted back to the missile's auto-pilot through the TADL return-loop circuit.

In addition, all this electronic processing was in-

stantly projected onto status screens, which include
Cathode Readout and Fixed Action panels, an Interjec
Action Entry unit, and the primary Trackball Assem
bly screen, which carried the actual red position trac
superimposed on a geodetic map.

Without taking his eyes from the displays, Bas
yelled, "Somebody get me another goddamned bottl
of juice." One of the mess boys obeyed, dodgin
through the crowd in the corridor.

A bell rang on the bridge. When it stopped, the cap
tain said something over the loudspeaker to the dec
crew. His voice echoed back through the portholes
which were showing an orange fusion of light on th
eastern horizon.

Before his juice arrived, Bass ran a quick opera
tional check on the other panel men. He started wit
the Comm panel. "How's R and A feedback holding
up?"

"Response functions all clean," Lasco shoutec
back. "No interference and holding point-zero-zero
one percent modulation."

One of his displays suddenly turned a bit fuzzy.
"Hold it! Bruce, I'm getting slight distortion on the
TA visual."

"I've got it," Morrel answered. A moment later,
the display screen shimmered, then cleared.

"That's it." Bass turned to Bheme, seated beside
him at the Fixed Action readout. "Darryl?"

"I picked up a tiny oscillation moment during en
gine restart. But it's gone now."

"Dammit! How near breakout divergence did i
get?"

"No problem, less than one-fiftieth of CTD." CTD
stood for Chaotic Trajectory Divergence.

Bass snorted. "Well, she's still riding soft air right

ow. But wait till she sticks her nose into that mon-
oon.''

''Right,'' Bheme answered tightly.

Bass returned to his main console. Numbers along
he sides indicating track components flashed and
lanced. He focused on the Time-to-Impact set. It read
0 minutes, 12 seconds.

Two minutes earlier, Kurisovsky had heard firing
rom the other side of the house. Shotgun blasts and
he heavy chatter of an American automatic weapon.
He paused to listen, then crawled onward. A second
ater he bumped into the point man's boot. It smeared
mud over his nose. It was so close, he could see the
pattern of hobnails. They pointed upward.

He froze, listening intently for sounds. All around
him, the undergrowth whipped and thrashed. Gently
he ran his hand up the soldier's right leg to his thigh
and felt for a pulse through the fatigue trousers. He
could feel the heavy testicles but no pulse.

He inched forward on his belly until he reached the
man's throat. It was slit wide open, from earlobe to
earlobe. His fingers went into spongy, warm flesh.
Withdrawing, he wiped his hand on the man's chest
and felt around for the grenades on his battle harness.
He unhooked them and then felt around the ground for
the shotgun. It was gone.

Directly ahead was a pool about thirty feet wide. It
was choked with water lilies, creepers, and rotting
leaves. Where the surface showed, it was corrugated
by the rain and faintly reflected the flickering light
from the oil fires. His skin tightened with repugnance.
He'd seen cobras in these pools.

Twisting his head slowly back and forth, he finally
picked up the soft sheen of the other trooper's back,
another corporal named Fjodorov. He was ten feet to

his left, lying flat on the ground. On the right, a ston
path skirted the pool. Beyond it was the side verand
of the main house.

At that instant he saw a solid, dark shadow mov
against the inner wall. He pulled the pin on one of th
grenades and heaved it, hearing the fuse click as i
sailed through the rain. Body tensed against the water
soaked ground, he waited.

The explosion made a hollow, echoing *wha-whomp*
and rock slivers wet slicing overhead. Instantly he wa
up, running forward, firing the 9mm. From behin
him came two three-round bursts from Fjodorov. A
man screamed, then the sound was cut off.

Suddenly two Indians rose out of the shadows in th
garden and ran off toward the back of the house. Bot
Russians cut them down, the rounds hurling one for
ward into the pool. When he stopped firing, Kurisov
sky remained motionless, waiting for the ringing i
his ears to dissipate.

Finally he raised his hand and motioned to Fjodoro
to advance to the veranda. The corporal came up of
the ground and scurried past him, his boots slapping
in the water. He reached the veranda and dropped flat.

Kurisovsky waited a moment, then moved up beside
him. A dead Indian lay crumpled near the wall, the
corpse looking like a pile of dirty clothes. A large
door with blown glass panels stood ten feet beyond.

Moving with silent, coordinated precision, they took
the room beyond the door. First grenading it, then
rushing in, Fjodorov lay a fan barrage and then Kurisovsky lunged forward and darted from wall to wall,
scanning. It was the billiard room. There were saffron-
colored rugs full of crouching tigers and peacocks
hanging on the walls lit by a shimmering orange twilight that sliced the gently swirling grenade and gun
smoke into glowing layers.

Satisfied the area was clear, the two men crossed to a wide archway that Kurisovsky knew led into the main ballroom. Poised, one on each side of the door, they listened. Finally, Kurisovsky tossed in a grenade, waited for the explosion, and then followed the corporal into the room, blowing rounds.

For the next few minutes they went from room to room, clearing them: dining area, den, mistress's parlor, *khansama*. Each one was broached with solid, methodical assault technique. During it all, Kurisovsky kept his ears tuned for other firing. The machine gun in the courtyard had stopped to allow the assaulting troopers time to clear the mansion. The colonel nodded, pleased. Continued silence from it meant the launcher was not under attack.

He glanced at his watch: thirteen minutes since they'd left the courtyard. He turned and looked down the long corridor that led directly to the front veranda and then the courtyard. Out there, Papalorev would soon be starting the ten-minute countdown on the rockets. And apparently he would be unmolested.

Kurisovsky felt a wash of pleasure warm his neck. The mission was almost complete. He signaled to Fjodorov, and they turned toward the ornate curved stairway that led to the second floor. Pausing a moment to listen, they finally started up, going in slow motion, muscles straining to hold silence, three steps at a time with muzzles probing forward.

In the flickering gloom, the colonel found himself humming silently deep in his throat.

Bonner's instincts were focused on the dark, wind-tossed underbrush ahead of him. His mind ached with concentration: *Put a foot down slowly, ball to heel, brush leaves aside.* Now and then the muffled blasts of grenades came from the main house, followed by quick bursts from a single Kalashnikov. He knew the Russians were going after Jungali's men.

His body jarred at each explosive outburst. Memories flashed into his mind, encapsulated images of 'Nam. The scene was rife with similarities. When he turned his head, he could see the firelight-etched spires of Lake House, which resembled the domes of pagodas along the Mekong, shimmering from the light of artillery salvos.

He reached the archway under the balcony where it crossed to the courtyard gallery. Water rushed across the pathway beneath it with the swiftness of a turbulent stream. Beyond it, he saw the entire courtyard and the launcher with the three missiles dramatically thrusting upward, their slanting white shafts high enough to catch the full glare of the oil fires.

Two Russians worked on the firing panels at the stern of the launcher. One man moved awkwardly, his arm in a makeshift sling. Mounted on the house side of the launch pit was a machine gun.

Crouched, Cas studied his field of fire. From where he was, he saw that to get to the soldiers he'd have to fire through the missiles. He couldn't risk that. He'd have to attack from a different position.

He slipped his arm out enough to pick up light and squinted down at his watch. Eighteen minutes, fifteen seconds before impact of the American missile.

He pressed his back into the shadows, cursing bitterly. *Move*, his mind shouted. *Get out there, disable that godforsaken launcher, and then get the hell off this doomed island.*

Desperately he studied the underpinnings of the balcony, searching for a way to get to a higher firing position. Finally he spotted two ornately carved columns that supported the fore wall of the gallery. Slinging his Thompson, he scurried to the columns and began o climb, bracing his feet against each column and working himself up over the complicated bas-reliefs of aging elephants and gods.

The balcony was strewn with straw sleeping pallets, bits of rotting food, and the remains of cooking fires. Inexplicably a woman's sari was draped over the railing. It fluttered soggily in the wind.

He made his way along the balcony and slipped into the courtyard gallery. There were small rooms along it, each with a cupola-shaped door fashioned out of tiles. At the end, the curving gallery butted against the courtyard wall. The wall was about three feet wide, its top hidden under vines and the overhanging branches of the palms and jacaranda trees.

He chose a position in the far corner. Squatting, he gingerly unstrapped his Thompson. He took the spare clip from his mouth and laid it on the railing. As he did, he noticed a new light coming from the courtyard: sharp, flickering flashes of blue and white.

He peered through the arabesque carvings. The Russian troopers were using acetylene torches on the after portion of one of the missiles. Cinders and unburned oil had invested the rain, turned it black. Yet he clearly saw the hoses for the torches, draped over the firing panel and then running to the twin tanks braced against one of the anchoring cables.

Oh, yeah, Bonner thought.

Quickly he rose to one knee. Wrapping the weapon's strap around his palm for steadiness, he lifted his body and rested the back of his hand holding the forward grip of the Thompson on the railing. Then, settling the butt solidly against his shoulder, he scanned until his front sight picked up the blue flame of the first torch. Slowly he followed the acetylene-oxygen line across the panel to the tanks. He inhaled, let a little air out, and held.

His finger began tightening on the trigger. His heart pounded, thumping against the stock. Killing from ambush was not the same as a firefight. Instinct, buried moral interdictions, created a moment of abhorrence at such furtive murder.

He hesitated, but only a moment. Bonner's blood was too hot. Death hovered in the air, and he knew that more of it was already soaring toward him on the monsoon wind.

He fired, a single ten-round burst. The weapon jumped, its stick clip knocking against the railing as he strained to hold the weapon down against the muzzle's tendency to climb.

Before the burst was complete, there was an explosion in the courtyard. It had a peculiar, tinny resonance to it. Cas released the trigger and peered through the railing. Blue flames surrounded the stern of the missile launcher. One trooper had been blown completely off the firing platform and was rolling on the ground beyond it, covered with fire.

Cas lunged to a crouching position and threw a second burst at him. The rounds lifted the Russian off the cobblestones. He searched for the second man. Something moved down in the pit. Squinting and cursing, he tried to fix a clean line of fire to it.

Suddenly the machine gun opened on the gallery. With tremendous rapidity the slugs crashed into the marble balustrade and overhang. Stone chips and chunks of wood sizzled through the air as Cas hit the deck.

All of Jungali's Carib-Indian blood was aflame with rage and shame as he squatted against the teak-scented bed frame in an upper room of Lake House. The last of his men had just deserted him, fleeing out windows n the rear of the house. He'd watched them go in silent ury.

For the last few minutes they'd listened to the Rusians blowing and gunning their way through the first tory. Each thundering explosion had drawn the eyes f the poachers wider and wider until they could no onger withstand the mounting terror.

He alone remained, armed only with an empty Kaashnikov and a short boot knife. Above the drumming f the rain he heard the horses scream. He listened a noment, discovered a new timber of terror to it, then he thrashing of animals in water. Obviously the horses ad broken through their fencing and were now on the lownside of the bluff in the lake. Then, like a great :ounterpoint bass note, rose the charging roar of a :rocodile.

He returned his attention to the house. The air eeked of burnt explosives and cordite. The room he vas in was large, filled with wickerwork furnishings nd a nineteenth-century piano. To the right a door ed to a small purdah terrace that overlooked the garlens.

The squeak of a floorboard on the terrace cut through he thrumming rain. Jungali felt his bowels grip up vith fear. Then he sniggered disgustedly at himself. 'Goddom ole duppy woman,'' he murmured. ''You in't gon' die, nigger. Jus' get up on yo' feet and fights lem, mon. *Fights* dem!''

He searched the room once more, finally paused at he bed. It was covered with a straw pallet, but beieath it was a thick mattress. Laying down the assault ifle, he quickly, silently withdrew the mattress. With t wrapped around his body, the knife in his right hand, e crept to the terrace door and crouched beside the ill.

He knew the Russians would first toss in a grenade

and then come blasting. If the mattress protected him
enough from the explosion, he was sure he could kill
the first man through the door. Then, using the man's
body as a shield, he'd go after the next one. It was all
he had left.

He waited.

Surprisingly, Jungali found his fear dissolving. Instead his mind found silly thoughts. He pictured the
calm blue ocean off Gun Bay, Trinidad, where turtles
ran in the green shallows and the sun shone like a pure
flare of light. "Dat mean dry weather, mon," he murmured over the image to himself. "Oh, yeah, dem
catboats be ridin' low with catch."

He smelled the Russian: diesel oil and acetelyne and
white-skin, flat-head sweat. Close, very close. He
braced his legs, tensed his body for the explosion. He
heard the click as the Russian pulled the pin on his
grenade.

From outside the house there was a sustained burst
of gunfire and a muffled explosion. A quick flash like
lightning, only lingering, throwing the shadow of the
Russian across the door frame. For a stultifying moment of indecision, Jungali stalled. Then, almost
without conscious volition, he lunged forward.

The Russian soldier was silhouetted against the blue
glow, his head turned to look at it. Beyond him was a
second soldier. Jungali's boot knife came around in a
sweeping arc and plunged into the first Russian's left
eye, going in deep, straight into the brain. Instantly
all structure went out of the man, and he started to
slump toward the floor.

His momentum carrying him, Jungali grabbed the
flesh around the Russian's chest and shoved him forward, holding tightly. He heard the other man grunt
with surprise. Three quick shots rang out, the bullets
thudding into the dead soldier's back. As the echoes

faded, there was a tiny fizzing sound and then the grenade went off.

The powerful blow hurled the corpse against Jungali, lifting him off his feet. He tried to turn in the air, but before he could, he slammed into the door frame. The shock knocked him out.

Kurisovsky had been startled by the sudden gunfire and subsequent explosion in the courtyard. From his vantage point, he could see only the sheet of blue flame that swept beyond the edge of the house. When he turned back, there was Fjodorov's back coming toward him, propelled by a shadowy figure. Instinctively he fired, heard the spent rounds tinkle onto the floor.

But he heard another sound, the lethal fizz of an armed grenade.

He twisted away, diving to the floor. The grenade went off. He felt the concussion and tiny metal fragments blow across his back. He was bodily heaved against the railing and, somersaulting, went out into midair.

He hit the garden pool facedown, sank through prickly brush and slime soft as shit. Thrashing to find air, he surfaced entangled in creepers. The pond stank of rotted vegetation, the water thick and oily. His back burned as if hundreds of tiny fires were being pressed against his skin.

Head whirling and vibrating with the captured sound of the grenade, he stood up and began wading toward the edge of the pool. Ahead was a thick growth of roses, the leaves shiny with unburned oil. He reached out to brush it aside, felt the thorns tear into his palms.

A slender, dark shadow lifted suddenly out of the bush. It came up in a sinuous thrust. Cobra! For a fleeting moment the snake flared its hood. Kurisovsky gagged, tried to throw himself backward. The snake struck, coming straight in at his face.

Kurisovsky threw up his hands, his eyes clamped shut. He felt the snake's forebody collide against his wrist and then came the powerful needle thrusts of its fangs into his forehead. *They bracketed the precise spot where the little virgin goddess had touched him.*

He heard the snake expel air in a soft grunt, and then it withdrew, recoiling, the scales like ice across his arm. There was a moment of wild entanglement, creepers and snake all around him and himself panting with terror, his feet sliding in the slime before he once again went down into dark water and vaguely saw the blue shimmer of the courtyard flames dance on the shattered surface.

22

Time to impact: 16 minutes, 12 seconds.

For the past quarter hour, all data streaming through the CCLC of the *Explorer*'s O.P. room had remained within green parameters as the XGB motored itself through a beautiful dawn sky. At 0515 hours it had passed due west of the Nicobar Islands. Three hundred eighty miles to the northeast lay the Andamans, the gateway to Burma and the Bay of Bengal.

Then, thirty seconds before the missile reached 89'21″E/14'01″N position designate, west of the Andamans, Bheme's Fixed Action board started flashing numbers as a rush of new data zinged in from the XGB's auto-pilot. External temperature had increased while barometric pressure had dropped. This instantly resulted in a climb of the drag component with an accompanying steepening of the fuel-consumption curve.

The missile had just reached the outer perimeter of the monsoon, and the moisture-saturated atmosphere was causing a heat-friction rise on its flight surfaces. Moreover, since moist air affords less lift than dry air, the vehicle was experiencing an increased drag and thereby an automatic power compensation and heavier fuel usage.

Bass caught the data on Bheme's board. "God damn it!" he yelled, "She's entered the storm a minute too soon.'' According to the latest meteorological updates, the trailing edge of the monsoon had been fixed eighty miles to the north. ''Well, gentlemen, here comes tight-asshole time.''

As everyone watched, the FA board again clicked off number chains as the ADS's automatic processing system analyzed the situation and issued adjustment commands.

Within seconds, the data showed a return to normal parameters as the XGB's auto-pilot complied. Fuel mixture was leaned, the rpms of the air-duct fans were speeded up to compensate for atmospheric saturation. Only a slight differential remained, a small increase in velocity due to tail winds.

Suddenly things began to change. Lasco was the first to indicate problems. ''Heavy electrical disturbance on my circuits,'' he called out. ''Modulation waver in orange and increasing.''

''Can you wash?'' Bass called back.

There was a pause. ''Yeah, I'm getting override—there! How's the board?''

''Slight lag showing,'' Bass answered. ''But acceptable.''

Bheme said, ''I don't like the PE read, Dave.'' He referred to the Parasite Error, a divergence from normal track caused by factors in addition to heat build-up that created unstable aerodynamic forces on the missile. These included gravity changes, wind shear, even the Coriolis effect, which became distorted in turbulent air.

''I see it,'' Bass snapped. A drop of sweat fell from his chin onto the χ key of his board. Oh, shit, he thought irrationally. The χ was the Cancel key! An omen? He forced the thought away, refocused on his huge display.

Immediately he saw that the situation was worsening, even while the ADS computers fed data to offset. Missile velocity had already reached a loss rate of three seconds per quarter minute, and flight angle was showing a 15 MIL drop off the nose. The fuel curve also steepened again as the XGB auto-pilot commanded its SM systems to compensate.

Bass entered an override command for a two-second, full-open fuel-injector position of the missile's engine, well beyond the preset ADS maximum. Although this action would eat fuel, he knew, it would also give the rocket a sudden burst of speed. Hopefully, that would carry it beyond this particular swirl of heavy turbulence.

He leaned in anxiously, eyes riveted to the return data series. As expected, the initial reaction was a strong steepening of the fuel curve. It actually touched into the orange zone for a second, hovered there. "Come on," Bass groaned. "Clear, clear."

The fuel curve suddenly slipped back into outer green as the two-second max burn completed out. Then, gradually, the other parameters began shifting back to normal. Bass heard Bheme let out a sigh. The XGB had re-entered comparatively mild air again. Only one number showed a set change. Time to Impact had been updated to a new fix due to the loss of a full 12 seconds. It was now set at 14 minutes, 6 seconds. . . .

The firing from the launch pit stopped, yet the rain patter echoed with a high, sharp ringing that Bonner realized was in his head. He leaped to his feet and swung the Thompson up over the railing, jerked the trigger. A single round went out and the ejector slammed back into open-lock position. The clip was empty.

Jacking it out, he felt for the other clip he'd placed

on the railing. It was gone, probably knocked off by a flying piece of concrete. Still crouching, he pulled his Colt from his waistband, released the safety, and fired three rounds down into the pit.

Instantly a new barrage fired back at him, this one coming high, exploding against the overhang and then cutting across to the outer wall. The air was filled with projectiles, whipping, zinging all around him. He could feel the heated pressure waves from the incoming rounds.

He lunged away, his body curled, and struck the edge of the railing. Momentum rolled him right over it and down onto the top of the outer wall. The firing continued, bullets chewing up the front side of the wall.

Cas was aware that he was yelling, incoherent phrases he couldn't hear. Desperately trying to escape the line of fire, he clawed through the vines and overhanging branches. There was a moment of sponginess and then he plummeted through.

He landed on his right hip, a jolting impact. The ground oozed up around him like warm pudding as he fell over onto his back, momentarily dazed. Vaguely he felt a throbbing in his leg and the rain on his face.

Through the whirl in his head rose a command: Get up! Run before they come and shoot you like a goddamned dog lying flat on your back. The firing stopped. He forced himself to his knees, then stood up. Unsteadily he moved down through the trees toward where he had left the ammo carrier, his leg and hip throbbing dully.

The vehicle's tool boxes drummed hollowly in the rain. But Cas's head had cleared. He leaned against the fender and flexed his leg. His muscles felt bruised and hot. He looked back toward the courtyard. Everything danced with fire shadows. He glanced at his watch. It was covered with mud. He rubbed it away and peered at the tiny hands.

It read 5:26. *Ten minutes before impact of the American missile.*

For one overwhelming moment, Bonner wanted to run wildly for the sanctuary of the lake. In ten short minutes everything would be disintegrated. And him with it! He actually pushed himself from the fender, started off.

But then he stopped. Another force swelled in him, overcoming the fear. It was rage, pure as the tip of a laser. At the whole stupid thing, all of it, even himself for getting into this mess.

He turned and looked down through the trees at the shadows where McCarran lay. A good man gone, he thought bitterly. And why? For killer missiles full of poisonous fungus and a handful of stinking Russians who wanted to play at war again. And what if that savior of a missile never came? What if it got lost somewhere up there in the heavens?

Then the bastards would have won.

He walked slowly around the ammo carrier, feeling the rage boiling. A grayish light, faint as a smear across the darkness, was beginning to seep through the rain. Dawn.

He spotted the two gas cans. He paused, then climbed onto the tailgate and hauled them back against the right wheel well. Moving methodically, he lashed them to tie-down eyes with a length of electrical cord, both of them turned broadside to the rear of the vehicle.

The seats and floorboards were slimy with oily water when he got behind the wheel. He tucked the Colt, its hammer still in full cock position, into his waistband and started the engine. It caught immediately. He swung the vehicle around and went back through the trees toward the entry road, driving slowly at first while he fumbled with the throttle lock on the accelerator pedal.

As it clicked in, the engine roared, and the ammo carrier lunged ahead. He reached the road going hard, the steering wheel yawing wildly back and forth through his fingers. He hauled it to the right. The vehicle's lunge smoothed out as it went up onto the road. He held it straight ahead, going for the courtyard gate.

As the truck passed through it, its wheels suddenly hummed on the cobblestones. Almost instantly the machine gun from the launch pit opened up with twin short bursts that slammed into the front of the vehicle. The engine went dead.

Bonner shoved his feet against the floorboards and threw his body off the seat. Curling, he hit the courtyard like a paratrooper coming down with a collapsing chute, rolled to the right, and stopped, up on one knee. He whipped out the Colt, double-gripping it.

The ammo carrier's momentum still carried it toward the launch pit, but it was starting to curve to the right. In the pit the acetylene flames were gone, but Cas could see the muzzle flashes of the machine gun on the missile tubes, could hear the bullets sizzling overhead.

He took aim at the two gas cans and fired twice. He saw one can jerk against the electrical cord. He held steady on it, knowing he had to put a second round into it in order to detonate the released fumes. He fired.

There was a quick white flash and then a whooshing, muted explosion. The vehicle was engulfed in an orange cloud of fire. The tail lifted, twisting with the force of the explosion, and crashed onto its back, throwing tongues of burning fuel like molten rivulets down into the launch pit.

* * *

As the updated Time-to-Impact readout clicked through 13 minutes, 31 seconds, the XGB picked up the first heat cell.

Within all sea-generated storms, great air masses shift and spiral up off the ocean. Created by areas of extreme low pressure, they roar up through the main storm like miniature typhoons, drawing massive amounts of moisture with them. As the moisture reaches higher elevations and cools, tremendous heat is given off and formed into large pockets with temperature gradients higher than ambient level by as much as 20 degrees C.

The first indication to the CCLC was a sharp linear divergence of the XGB from its track line. Readouts quickly escalated into a rapid shift toward a chaotic state. Right behind it came verification that the missile's infrared-homing packet had just locked onto a heat cell and was relaying distance and trajectory data: 100 miles NNE on bearing 031 degrees.

Bass felt his belly go hollow. With his gaze jumping all over the main display, he watched as the ADS countered with the contingency adjustment commands he had input before launch. But the auto-pilot seemed unable to comprehend or accept them. Activation of the IF packet had thrust the on-board computers into their Final Flight Phase mode.

In a moment of panicked indecision, Bass stared at the furiously moving numbers showing the worsening condition. Although he had planned what to do if this happened—force a complete quarter-second shutdown of the entire auto-pilot system—now that it was here, he froze. The disastrous possibilities rose like a tidal wave. If the XGB's auto-pilot refused click-on, or, worse, if it returned with the same commands intact, he'd have a completely out-of-control missile. In either case, the XGB would continue on its set heading until fuel ran out, and then it would plunge to earth somewhere in northern Thailand or Vietnam.

At last his cognitive mind reasserted itself. There was no choice: he *had* to momentarily shut down the missile system. Even if the click-on failed, he knew, the missile would impact, but it would contain no detonation of the warhead, since the final arming command would not have activated.

His hands shot over the input board as he furiously interjected the kill sequence. He didn't even have to look up to know compliance had been performed as Bheme yelled, "All screens dead."

A heartbeat later, Bheme said, "We have click-on."

Bass lifted his eyes. All the board men were yelling frantically. His own display was a mass of flicking numbers like tiny insects under the glass. The kill sequence had indeed obviated the IF block, but now the missile was nearing full Chaotic Track Divergence. The display numbers shifted from deep orange to red.

Bass's fingers jammed down on the keyboard, inputing the code sequence for Full Reprogram. Seconds whipped past like bullets in the compacted air of the O.P. Room as the ADS sent out a completely new set of program commands.

There was a moment of blur on the screen, and then the color overlay shifted back into orange, lightening steadily like a sunrise as the data sets began fluttering again.

"Sweet Mother Mary," someone whispered behind Bass.

With agonizing slowness the XGB returned to its preset track alignment, and the data back-feed showed normal stability parameters. Still, the missile was now fifty-three miles east of its original line. If not corrected, the preset guidance bearing would carry it off target. Automatically the ADS did just that, recalculating for the slight angular offset.

Bass surveyed the damage. The divergence had eaten over two percent of fuel. Also, the Time-to-Impact fix had changed, now showing 12 minutes, 17 seconds, a full thirty-two seconds behind the original TTI. Although the actual impact time was negligible within the overall framework of the flight, the increased air time pushed the envelope on fuel reserves.

Another question skewered him. Was the warhead IF packet now totally inert, unable to form up a homing fix to the actual target of the oil refinery? When the earlier contingency procedures had been worked out, refunction of the infrared homing system had shown an eighty percent positive span. But now that twenty percent negative span looked ominous.

The answer came three seconds later when the IF packet locked onto a second heat cell. Bearing: 351 degrees, NNW. This time the linear divergence was not as great as the first. Bass, his brain still at warp speed, immediately ordered the auto-pilot shut down.

Once more the screens experienced blackout for a fraction of a second before the automatic ADS restart and reprogram. Everything slid back to the normal track with an updated bearing. But another nine seconds had been used. New TTI: 12 minutes, 14 seconds.

Hissing with tension, Bass nevertheless allowed himself a moment of triumph. His counter procedures had overcome the pull of the second heat cell so expeditiously that, along with the fact that the shutdown mode hadn't thrown the IF system into malfunction, he felt a tenuous confidence the ADS could handle more cells. Undoubtedly, it would have to. Already the XGB was nearing the inner periphery of the monsoon's main vortex, where more powerful cells lurked.

Still, precious fuel was being eaten during each recovery. If too many cells appeared, the missile would never reach the target and would burn out somewhere over India. As his eyes followed the screens, Bass's mind began probing for solutions.

The XGB found a third heat cell, heading 083 degrees, range 78 miles. This time the vehicle responded to the IF home as if struck by a blast of wind. Track divergence registered instantly and began a rapid deterioration.

"I'm getting forty percent CTD," Morrel shouted. "Fifty! Sixty! We're fucking losing her!"

Bass's fingers rammed down on keys.

"Oh, Jesus," Bheme groaned over his Fixed Action console. "The IF's gone into full-arm phase."

An instant later, Bass saw his own display indication. The XGB, less than seventy miles from the cell, had just armed the warhead for impact detonation. That sent everything out the door. If not recaptured, the missile, hunting for a solid physical target, would pass through the heat cell and home to whatever other heat source drew it. With a jolt of ice down his spine, Bass saw the present bearing line displayed. It crossed directly over the mass of heat of Rangoon, Burma.

"CDT on eighty percent," Morrel called wildly.

Bheme: "All screens dead."

One second flashed past. Another.

"No click-on."

Another second.

Bass felt a moment of utter helplessness. Had the missile gone into total track divergence and was completely beyond their control? Yet even while he roiled in his dark impotence, his fingers punched in a second override Kill command. His screens flared, then faded to black again.

"No click-on."

Bass was aware of every sound in the O.P. room. It was as if his blood had stopped flowing, his heart beating, and in the vacuum his hearing, like an orgasm, had blotted out all the other senses.

The screens came on.

For the next few seconds, panel men shouted back and forth, and the screens laid out a fluttering pandemonium of numbers as the ADS automatically sorted out the in-feeding impulses, fixed new parameters, and made adjustment commands.

Gradually, like a puppet master, the main command system regained control of the XGB's flight. Normal set runs began appearing. TTI readout indicated twenty-one more seconds had been logged off the preceding fix. New fix stood at 11 minutes, 59 seconds.

But Bass's agonized gaze sought two other readouts. The first was the fuel curve. While all other warning overlay lights had changed tone, the fuel color remained in orange. With the oil rig target still over eight hundred miles away, the missile's fuel supply had just become marginal.

But it was the second readout that really wrenched his guts. It indicated that although they had again regained missile control, the click-on had not wiped off the IF's arming command. At this moment the XGB, plowing through the monsoon, was carrying a fully primed warhead.

It took a tremendous concentration of his rage for Bonner to force himself to his feet and move toward the launch pit. He knew he had only three rounds left in his Colt, a few in his pocket, and he was going up against an automatic weapon. Even though the firing had stopped the instant of the explosion, he couldn't be sure the Russian wasn't down there, hidden by the flames and waiting for him to come in.

But he had learned the value of head-on assault in 'Nam. Carrying shock power, it could give an edge. Besides, he had neither time nor ammunition to flank and set up a perimeter firefight. So he committed himself full-out, running straight at the fire and through it, his shoes splashing in flaming water with the fire burning fiercely all across the stern of the launcher and down in the pit.

The Russian trooper was dead, his machine gun torn from his hands and rammed barrel first into the water. A piece of metal from the ammo carrier had ripped into his throat, and flaming gasoline was burning and sizzling on his back, the skin curling away and turning black.

Cas's charge took him right down into the pit. For a few seconds he floundered in fire, but then managed to grab hold of one of the wheel drums of the launcher and pull himself up onto the stern platform. The metal scorched his hand.

Squatting in a corner of the platform that was free of fire, he studied the launcher and tubes, their fixed missiles protruding up into the rain. The casings were nicked and fire-scarred, but all three were intact. Heat from the platform deck plates came up through his shoes as he lowered his eyes to the firing panels.

They were formed into a confused series of metal boxes that he immediately saw had been jury-rigged with extension plates. Down along the trunnions of the launcher frames were welded recoil pads and make-shift deflection tubes to funnel back blast.

Over the steady pounding of the rain he heard one of the panels clicking. Quickly he moved closer, holding his arms tightly against his sides to keep from touching hot metal. One panel box was covered with dials and a bank of switches with brightly colored tips: yellow, green, and red. Below the dials was Thai writing. None of the gauges seemed activated. But the next box, which had been welded over a second panel board, had eight red lights in a vertical line.

Three were lit.

Cas shifted around to the third panel board. It was about four feet high, a buffed black box with more stenciled Thai words on it. It was so large it nearly filled the right side of the control platform. It had two narrow inspection doors on each side and another switch panel beneath a dozen gauges and electrical power jacks. This was the one that was clicking, the tiny metallic ticks coming in one-second intervals.

He bent down and peered at the dials. Heat fumed off the face of the box. The glass faces of the gauges were scorched, one shattered. He could sense electrical power moving inside the unit, could see the faint tremor it made in the dial faces.

His eyes fixed on the bottom left-hand gauge. It held four digital readouts, each one only a half inch high. The top three were dead. The bottom, its numbers glowing green, read: 00707. As he watched, the 7 clicked to 6, then 5 . . . 4 . . . 3 . . .

The launcher was in automatic countdown.

Bonner jerked away from the panel as if he had just heard the fuse of a grenade. For a confused moment he glanced up at the missiles, jolted with the knowledge that in six minutes they would be propelled skyward.

Then he went into action, twisting this way and that, trying to find the main power cable from the panel box. A heavy deluge of rain swept across the courtyard. It made the burning water in the pit sputter and crackle, and the heavy drops formed little impact craters on the fiery surface.

He found the main cable. It coiled out the back of the big panel box and went down between two recoil pads. It was wrapped in metal webbing. He tried to reach it, to pull it from its recessed insert jack, but the surrounding metal was too hot. His shoulder touched the corner of the box, sending a searing pain down his arm.

He pulled back, frantically searching for a better access to the cable. It was no use, he couldn't reach it without burning himself. Gritting his teeth, he jammed his arm in between the box and closest recoil pad. The pain was excruciating, momentarily numbed his tissues.

Closing his mind against it, he fumbled for the cable, touched it with his fingers, missed, touched again. He clamped down but instantly let go as the hot metal webbing scorched his palms. He jerked free, panting from the pain that still echoed through his body. His eyes darted to the countdown gauge. The rain ran over the glass face, blurred the tiny green numbers.

They read: 00538 . . .

He was so frustrated he began loudly cursing the cable. Finally he dropped into a squat and brought up the Colt. Hesitating for a second to steel himself against a new rush of pain, he jammed his back against the edge of the panel box, picked up the cable over the sight, and fired until the receiver slide locked back on empty.

The bullets tore through the cable and *whanged* into the recoil plate. Instantly he lunged away from the panel box. Needles of pain flashed across his back, seemed to collect along his spine as if a knife blade were slicing into vertebrae. He whirled around and glared down at the countdown guage.

00454 . . . 00453 . . . 00452 . . .

"Goddammit!" he bellowed. He popped the empty clip from the weapon, held both in one hand, and jammed the other into his pocket. He pulled up four rounds. They tinged softly like marbles in his palm. He began loading the clip. The first bullet slipped off the spring lip and fell to the floor. Cursing, he rolled another between thumb and forefinger.

A deep, throaty growl came through the sound of the rain. It had the timbre of an animal's charge, guttural and inhuman. Bonner's head jerked up. There, six feet away, a Russian, his half-naked body covered with rain-streaked mud and entwined in vines, came at him, one arm low, coming up with a long-bladed knife.

For a fleeting moment Cas froze, staring into the man's face. It was misshapen, so swollen the eye sockets were mere slits, the cheeks puffed outward as if air had been forced into the bloated tissues under great pressure. Right in the center of his forehead, seen clearly for a second as his lunge carried him across a bright band of firelight, were twin circles of black flesh, as if a cobra had bit him.

A decision loomed over Bass. It was a decision in a nightmare where he had to choose between two different kinds of terror, both stark and deadly. The prospect was so harrowing that he closed his eyes and sought a moment's respite.

Over the past several minutes the XGB had run into two more heat cells. Each had been successfully countered. But the fuel curve light was showing a faint scarlet through the orange. If another cell were struck, the missile would be unable to reach its target.

There was Bass's dilemma. If allowed to continue on its present track, when the last ounce of fuel blew through the igniter jets, the missile would plunge to earth somewhere in the densely populated Brahmaputra plain.

On the other hand, he could initiate an alternate

command system, gain altitude, and play for distance. But if that failed, the missile would impact somewhere east of Lake Sonai, in the less populated Lokit Mountains. Either way, people would die. It had become his choice as to which people it would be.

A God-like decision.

He turned slightly and looked into Bheme's face. The man's eyes held a painful ambivalence: horror mingled with relief that the decision wasn't on his shoulders. But the look also told Bass something else. Bheme, and probably the others, no longer believed they could strike the oil rig. With a pang, he realized he didn't believe it, either.

He refused to accept that. No, you son of a bitch, he thought fiercely, I'll ram your nose into that island if I have to fucking *will* it there.

With lightning rapidity he began mentally running through procedures and potential obstacles. First, he had to interject a change in course status, go for altitude and distance. All his instincts told him that was the only way. To preserve concentration, he forced out the other factor, the human one.

Under normal circumstances, stretching a missile's range involves certain designed operations. Unfortunately, the designers hadn't done their calculations on a vehicle in the middle of a violent storm that created chaotic variables and unknowns. For the moment Bass focused on the basics.

Altitude was the key. The higher he could take the missile, the longer its glide range would be once power cutoff came. But that presented a delicate exchange. For each incremental increase in altitude, he'd have to use more fuel with a corresponding decrease in linear range. Would the end result give the edge to the altitude choice?

Next, once in glide configuration, there would be a

rapid deceleration of the missile, all the way down into subsonic speeds. In that state the force and direction of the monsoon winds would became critical. The vehicle could literally be shoved beyond the homing system's capability to control airfoil guidance.

Finally, the heavy turbulence within the storm could accelerate the normal vibrational component as the missile passed through the sonic barrier and bring on harmonic overload and subsequent air-frame disintegration.

Steeling himself, Bass thought: Well, let's find out.

"Garretson," he shouted. "I want an update of weather conditions within a fifty-mile radius of Lake Sonai. Focus on wind direction and speed. Get it as precise as possible."

"I'm on it," the meteorologist called back and disappeared onto the bridge.

Bass turned and pointed at Morrel. "Work up a fuel-weight ratio for maximum glide and set up the climb chart. Also, factor for wind and earth-spin component on a north-northeast span of twenty-five degrees off present heading." In order to compensate for wind force and Coriolis effect, the missile's track heading had to be altered, offset into the wind so that the vehicle's homing system could drift it into the target. "What was your last wind vector?"

"Two hundred sixty-three degrees at thirty-four knots."

"Go with that until Garretson verifies. I want an ERC in one minute." The ERC referred to estimated range capability.

"Right."

He whirled around to Bheme, who had anticipated him and was already furiously working his keyboard. "Input deceleration parameters and give me a time set."

Bheme nodded, their eyes meeting for a charged second.

"Work out the automatic air-foil deflection sequence," Bass continued. "And set up for barrier pass-through. Use the high side of the OP graph. She's gonna be a bitch."

"We're liable to cross margin. Do we cage?"

Bass considered the pros and cons of that. Like everything else, it was a balancing act. Caging meant locking down all systems into the inert state they had been in during the launch phase. This would prevent drift damage during the shock of crossing back through the sonic barrier. But one of the systems included the main stability gyros. If the subsequent click-on failed to spin them up again, the missile would have no baseline reference for guidance. As a result, the auto-pilot computer would become "frustrated" at being unable to orient itself and automatically shut down.

Bass's instincts again pushed forward. "We cage," he snapped.

"I've got ERC," Morrel yelled. "Zero position plus point-zero-one-eight percent CPT at twelve thousand feet." This indicated the XGB would travel eight-tenths of a mile beyond the target from the point of CPT, or complete propulsion termination, at an altitude of twelve thousand feet.

"Yeah!" Bass shouted. Eight-tenths of a mile leeway, a goddamned gift wrapped in a red ribbon. *If* the missile didn't hit another heat cell. "What's CPT fix?" he snapped.

"Sixty-eight-point-three miles."

Garretson returned. Morrel waved him over. They talked a moment and then Morrel called to Bass, "Wind vector holding two hundred sixty-five degrees at thirty-six to thirty-eight knots."

"Run it through," Bass commanded. He glanced at

his displays, instantly read the XGB's present position. It was passing over the eastern Meghalaya Hills, two hundred thirty miles SSW of Lake Sonai. He began imputing interject commands to the ADS.

For the next minute the panel men called to each other, checking off as their computers fed them data. Readouts shifted on the display screens, showing projected parameters, time plots, and new engine power-setting sequences during climb. Lasco was back in the loop, too, giving ADS status updates as the mainframe ingested the imput flood and formed up electronic commands.

At last everything was ready. Bass watched as the power burn came up, the digital readout clicking off in tenths of a second. 3.1 . . . 3.0 . . . 2.9 . . .

The air-foil deflection command went out.

2.8 . . . 2.7 . . .

Compliance. A slight velocity drop registered. The ADS automatically compensated.

1.9 . . . 1.8 . . .

Power burn.

One-point-four seconds later, Bass's displays jumped as numbers and graphs everywhere registered the altered state of the XGB: engine temperature and propulsion arcs, drag coefficient lines, thrust-time curves, wave propagation buffet indicators. His eyes, unblinking, scanned back and forth as the voices in his head moaned like a recalcitrant wind.

Altitude: 8,000 feet. Velocity holding on Mach 4.4.

The red glow of the fuel curve deepened. Bass blinked.

Altitude: 9,500 feet, velocity steady. Down-range distance to target: 186 miles.

"Come on, baby," Bass hissed.

Altitude reached 10,600 feet, velocity on Mach 4.2. There was utter silence in the O.P. room save for the soft blips and ticking hums of the machinery. A brilliant morning sun sent a beam of pure light through the starboard porthole that touched the edge of Bass's panel with gold.

As the missile neared 11,300 feet, the burn sequence command shut down the engine. The XGB hurtled on thrust momentum, the velocity dropping rapidly as it achieved the set cruise altitude of 12,000 feet.

Once more the engine kicked in. Velocity climbed, passed through Mach 4.7, and held. The fuel-curve light blinked slowly, methodically like a neon sign at a cheap motel.

Bheme whispered, "Damn, we're gonna do it."

"Not yet," Bass croaked. "Not yet."

Down-range distance to target: 105 miles. The XGB had just crossed over Dibrugarh.

Bass's gaze shot to the CPT fix, watching the numbers reel down. His heart hung isolated somewhere in his chest. Target distance: 97 miles. Again the engine shut down. Glide. Restart for final burn.

Target distance: 76 miles . . . 71 . . . 69 . . .

Complete propulsion termination. The fuel-curve light went steady.

Morrel whooped. "She's done it! Right on the fucking button."

Once again the screens became furiously active as the XGB's computer scanned its sensor system and rebounded stabilization commands, keying on Bheme's air-foil deflection sequence. Velocity held for a few seconds of glide, then began to drop. Mach 4.4 . . . 4.1 . . . 3.7 . . .

It contined to plummet, all the way through Mach 1.4 as the missile steadily arced into the thickening air over the Brahmaputra plain. As it neared the peed of sound, buffet readings began to cross into range.

Bass leaned forward, shouted, "Go for full lock and age."

"L and C command on," Bheme came back.

An instant later, the screens went black. Bass lowered his head. Microseconds of time seemed to hurtle past his head like bullets. Later, he would swear he felt their passage in the air.

"No click-on," Bheme yelled wildly.

Oh, Jesus, Bass thought. Not after all this way!

"Overload it," he yelled. To overload a signal meant to break it into minutely spaced impulse segments, each creating a burst of accumulated power. Sometimes a receiving unit would respond to the bursts much as the nerves of a human eye react more to a powerfully flashing light than to a steady one. But there was a danger the receiver would jump sequence gaps, creating a garbled command chain and possible shutdown.

One blink later, Bass's screens came on again.

"We've got her!" Bheme cried.

Bass frantically searched his number sets to see if guidance stability had also been achieved. Had the gyros spun up? Yes!

All four panel men cheered. The others looked at one another, not totally aware of what had just occurred. Their mouths showed tentative smiles.

Bheme's shout drew their attention and the smiles faded. "I've got IF fix."

"Bearing?" Bass yelled.

"Zero-one-five degrees off the nose."

"That's it!" Bass bellowed. "She just locked onto that beautiful fucking oil fire."

Now everybody cheered.

Through the noise Bass called to Bheme: "Is she

taking override?'' When the IF locked onto a target
the main guidance system instantly turned the vehicl
directly to it. Since the ADS had placed an overrid
command into the guidance track to account for the
wind's force, the question now was whether or not the
on-board unit would accept it and thus allow the mis
sile to drift in along a curving approach to the target
If it didn't, impact would occur east of the oil rig.

Bheme was silent.

Bass whirled around. "Is she, goddammit?''

Bheme's head began nodding, slowly, then faster and
faster. He glanced up, grinning. "She's holding to the
approach curve.''

Bass sat back. Everything in him seemed to drair
down. He felt his groin muscles go soft, thought for
an exposed moment he was going to urinate.

His eyes sought out the Distance-to-Target set. I
read: 59 miles. His gaze swung to the Time-to-Impac
set. It had just completed a rapid re-adjustment due to
the constantly changing velocity data during climb and
burn-out.

The numbers glowed: 7 minutes, 58 seconds.

The Russian's charge carried Cas directly onto the
command platform of the launcher. Bonner, bracketec
by the main power box and the recoil plates, had no
space in which to move. In the Russian came, knife
low, his other arm up in the parry position.

Moving on instinct, Cas countercharged. His legs
coiled and boosted him directly at the man, his left
arm slanted across his groin to intercept the upward
thrust of the knife. With his other hand he swung the
empty Colt down, slamming it into the Russian's fore
arm.

He felt the barrel smash bone and then the knife
come up, the man's face so close, his lips drawn back

nd then the full impact of bodies colliding. His elbow
inioned the Russian's thrusting arm, but the hand
olding the knife curled over it. He felt the blade go
nto the fleshy tissue under his shoulder, an instant of
ot pain, and then a duller, sickening nerve blow as it
liced upward and cut through, cleared skin.

Both men disengaged and fell back. For a fraction
f a second they glared at each other, each panting
vith combat blood high in their veins. The fires made
ne Russian's bloated face resemble a gargoyle. His
novements, Bonner noted, were sluggish, automaton-
ke, the arms coming up again into a fighting stance
efore another charge.

But Cas moved first. Once more he lunged forward,
urling inward to lessen the outline of his body, ig-
oring the throbbing of his wound. When they col-
ded, the Russian's voice blew out of him. Bonner
eard himself bellowing, a primal, incoherent, animal
xpulsion of sound.

They grappled for holds. The Russian's strength was
nhuman, his fingers grabbing chest skin, climbing up-
vard like a steel tarantula to Bonner's throat. They
)cked on. But the collision's momentum carried them
) the platform edge and over it, down into flame and
vater, the light snapping off for an instant as they went
nder. Bonner felt the fingers still on his throat. It
nade the blood in his head begin to roar. A hint of
ausea crossed through his consciousness.

His foot touched something solid. Metal. It moved.
rantically he twisted to reach it with his right hand.
'he Russian was enfolding him in a powerful em-
race, the knife arm trying to slice along Cas's spine.
he fingers on his throat tightened, a band of steel.
le couldn't loosen them.

Then his own fingers gripped the metal object. It
vas the barrel of the HK-11A1 machine gun. They

rolled in the darkness in soft sand. With one last surg
of strength, Cas shoved his body against it, liftin
himself and the Russian toward the surface.

They broke through, still entwined. The Russian'
face was against his cheek. He could smell his breath
oddly tainted with ammonia. He drove his free han
into the face, felt the spongy texture of it as his finger
sought the eye sockets and gouged them. The Rus
sian's head reared back and he gagged.

In that moment of slight release, Bonner swung u
and across with the machine gun. The forked tripo
struck his adversary in the throat and ruptured th
swollen skin, ripped it open to expose the man's jaw
bone. The Russian screamed. Cas hit him again, th
machine gun coming around in a full swing, this tim
across the cheek, which also blew open, spewing blac
blood into Bonner's face.

The Russian went completely limp and sank unde
the water. Gasping, Cas fell back against the edg
of the launcher. His body was so full of adrenaline
he didn't even feel the heated metal. But then it seare
him, and with it came the throb and flush of othe
pain—his side, his throat, the hot ache of muscle.

He stood up.

The clicking came through the rain.

With it were other sounds from the sterns of th
three rockets: little hums and electronic pings. H
whirled, his eyes seeking the tiny lighted countdow
gauge on the power box.

It read: 0032.

He spun the machine gun in his hand and pulled th
trigger. Nothing.

0025 . . .

Cursing insanely, Bonner searched the rim of th
pit, spotted the other dead Russian. His waist la
stretched across an anchor wire, exposing his battl

arness. A clip packet was attached to it. Cas surged
cross the pit, ejecting the empty clip, and ripped the
acket flap open.

0016 . . .

His hand shook, trying to insert the new clip. It was
eavy with new rounds but kept misaligning with the
eed slot because of a slghtly bent lip. At last he got
t in, rapped back the cocking handle to chamber a
ullet.

009 . . .

A sharp whir came from the missiles. It sounded
ike the blades of a large food processor, starting
lowly, then rising, faster and faster. The engine im-
ellers were spinning up. Lights began flashing on the
nain control board.

Cas braced the butt of the weapon against his thigh
nd fired. The air was shattered by explosions, all of
hem coming together so rapidly they molded into a
ingle sound. The butt plate rammed against his leg,
nd empty casings flicked from the breach as the bar-
el lifted in his hand, the metal instantly hot.

The first rounds slammed into the main control box,
he spaced tracers impacting with showers of phospho-
ous. Electrical shorts blew, sizzling with acelytene-
olored flames. As the recoil pulled the muzzle farther
pward, the bullets went across the courtyard, the
racers leaving brilliant white streaks through the rain.

Bonner stopped firing for a second, lowered the
nuzzle, and cut loose again. His palm against the bar-
el was stinging from the heat. He could smell the
umes off the metal. Forcing the muscles in his shoul-
ers and arms into immobility, he held the weapon
teady and poured rounds into the control box. The
ain turned to steam on the barrel, and slivers of metal
lew through the air.

He stopped again, ears ringing. He moved up close

to the edge of the platform, trying to hear through th
roar. Faintly he caught the sonance of the impelle
still whirring.

But then the sound began to wind down. Softer an
softer it became, and then there was silence, a grea
vacuum of it into which other sounds crept like furtiv
mice: the wind, the steady patter of drops on th
launcher and in the pit, the faraway scream of a horse

Cas put back his head and inhaled deeply. Again
The rain peppered his face.

The Russian exploded out of the the water to hi
right. He came up as if shot from a catapult, a demo
with face torn open to bone, springing at him, arm
reaching, reaching.

Bonner spun to meet him. The knife flashed in a
arc right past his face. He felt the Russian come u
against the muzzle of the machine gun, the impac
jarring back through the breach. The knife came back
this time in closer, the man leaning in, swinging back
handed.

Cas pulled the trigger. Buried in the man's stomach
the muzzle reports were muffled under the hard rap c
the ejector slide slamming back. The Russian wa
lifted up and away, literally flying, his ripped fac
jerking back for an instant and the slitted eyes rolle
back, showing pure white through the mud smear. An
then he was gone, beneath the rain-ruptured surfac
of the water.

Bonner fell back against the edge of the pit. Hi
breath felt like knives in his chest. He let the machin
gun slip from his fingers and half squatted in the wa
ter, feeling his muscles locked tautly, his nerve
thrumming inside his skin.

Once more he slowly lifted his head and inhaled th
night air, smelling of burning oil and cordite and th
raw fume of torn flesh and blood. His mind raced t

ultuously, images tumbling over each other, but
owing like the missile impellers, slowing.

It's over, he thought.

No, it isn't!

Realization cracked through his brain circuits like a
ullwhip. *The incoming missile!* "Oh, Jesus!" he
urted. His head jerked upward. It was descending
rough the air, its nose pointed right at him. He
oked at his watch. It had a sheen of oily water.

Four seconds to impact.

Blind terror exploded through him. Releasing an in-
oherent whimper, he hurled himself onto the side of
e pit, drove his face, chest, arms, legs into the sandy
ud so powerfully that it seemed to meld into him,
ecome himself. All sounds evaporated. He lay, feel-
ng the tissues of his back recoiling from the coming
xplosion like wisps of tinder held against a white-hot
eel bar.

Seconds fragmented into a thousand chips of time.
e closed his eyes so hard it made tiny lights and curls
icker in the darkness. I'm going to die, his mind
creamed.

Nothing happened.

He waited, burrowing even deeper.

Still nothing.

Cas opened his eyes. The oily mud stung his lids.
is mind registered the sensation like the clear, icy
rick of a needle through the vacuum of his terror.
hen all the sounds came back.

He lifted his head. Rain drummed on his skull. He
oked upward. It's not coming, he thought deler-
usly. It was all a lie. He rose slowly and stood in
e water. He wanted to laugh crazily with relief. The
in poured off his face. He opened his mouth, let it
n in. It tasted oily and thick.

A flash of lightning rippled above the rain. For a

fraction of a second, it illuminated the underside the clouds, a great, shifting mass of moving blue-gra ghosts. And in that instant, felt down to his very cor Bonner knew it *was* coming.

Once more terror reared up like a dragon, but th time it was laced with defiance. He wasn't going to l down and just wait for death, not again. "No, you so of a bitch!" he screamed at the sky. "You want me Then catch me."

He clawed at the pit rim and hauled himself out the water. As soon as his feet hit the cobblestones, l was running full-out, bounding toward the gardens Lake House and the blue pavilion.

23

He fled through a dawn-graying landscape alive with flickering shafts of orange and black. An El Greco painting with the trees and walls all deformed and fire hanging in the sky. His feet splashed over the ground, muscles pulling smoothly, drawing him forward through the dancing shadows. He crossed under the walkway, where the discarded sari still fluttered on the railing, raced on into the gardens. The rain made the shrubs whisper like old men telling secrets. Then from the lake came the low, primordial roar of a crocodile. Another. The wild screams of horses and thrashing water.

Hak's corpse still reposed against its tree, the water funneling off the brim of the hat. Cas didn't slow as he passed; only his eyes darted for one last look.

He ran down the slope of the garden. Branches whipped at him. The ground was a torrent filled with tiny eddies and curling gravity currents. Ahead he could see the vague outline of the pavilion, its blue lights glowing, an island in the mist.

He drove for it, the word "Go!" repeating itself in his mind. A mantra linked to the slam of each foot as when he had run the four-hundred meters in college with the tape so faraway and his muscles screaming to stop but his mind winging up there, exhilarated and the tape coming closer and closer. Only now the tape

was a shadowy blue pavilion signifying not a meda
but his own life.

A man lunged up out of gray darkness directl
ahead.

Cas, startled out of his concentration, hauled back
stopped. The man was crouched low in a wrestler'
stance, all shadow, a long, curved knife in his hand
Bonner's lips drew back and he lowered, too, leg
gathering to spring.

The man suddenly grinned at him and straightened
Bonner could actually see the flicker of firelight on hi
teeth. "Som'bitch, mon," the man said cheerily. "
be tinkin' you was dem goddom Russians." It wa
Jungali.

Bonner released a lungful of air, then started wildl
waving his arm toward the pavilion. "Run, Jungali!"
he yelled. "The missile, it's coming!"

"Ah," Jungali said, half whisper, half groan.

Side by side, they started off. Nearing the pavilion
they saw the horses out in the water close by, blacl
heads and necks bobbing in the reflections of blu
light. Back on the shoreline, others raced back an
forth.

Suddenly one horse was lifted partly out of the wate
as a huge crocodile struck its flank. The croc's tai
whipped the water furiously as it got a deeper pur
chase. The horse lifted its head and screamed. Its eyes
wide with fear, glistened for a second, and then it wa
pulled under.

They reached the pavilion. The marble floor wa
slippery with oil and shone like glass. Only one cano
was still on the wall, the other having been taken b
Jungali's fleeing men. Below the wall, crocodile
lunged agitatedly through the water, excited into
feeding frenzy. Jungali slashed at them and muttere

Trinidad obscenities as he and Bonner slid the canoe off the wall and climbed aboard.

The Carib took the prow, Bonner the stern. Digging their paddles deep, they spurted away from the pavilion wall, the canoe's curved bow hissing, the hull rocking with their shifting weight. They went a few yards out and then Cas braced his paddle against the gunwale and swung the prow with the wind. Cleared of obstruction, it lashed their backs with rain. Beneath the hull they could feel crocs nudging against the wood.

Cas leaned into the paddle with all his might, fear and rage mingled together like a glowing furnace in his belly. Time whipped past in the wind. He squinted through the rain. The surface was full of white caps. Beyond, the lake stretched off like etched pewter to the distant shoreline, where the jungle formed a black line above the beach.

Lunging and pulling, he drove the canoe ahead with powerful sweeps of the paddle, his eyes fixed on that distant shore, mind creating the image of himself and Bungali reaching it, running up into the sanctuary of its trees.

Time to impact: 2 minutes, 37 seconds . . .

The XGB, soaring through the air at just under six hundred miles an hour, was approaching its target still slightly off the wind. Altitude was twenty-two hundred feet with distance to the impact zone twenty-three miles.

In the warhead packet, a click-on command was received from the auto-pilot. The unit, no larger than a basketball and encased within a titanium nose, contained a compact firing assembly of electronic and gravitational-monitoring gear. Independent of all flight and homing functions, its only command link was with

the main computer of the auto-pilot. Although the A
already contained the activated arming sequence, th
warhead itself had until this moment been inert.

Within its miniaturized circuits, impulses raced
drawing it to setup phase. Around the inside rim c
the nose cone a grid of steel filaments was embedded
Called the GTN, or Gravitational Trigger Net, each c
its strands was one-thousandths the width of a huma
hair. Suspended across minute pegs, these filament
were subjected to displacement from their linear aligr
ment by the gravitational field directly ahead of th
missile, the rate of distortion being monitored by th
warhead's computer. So delicate was the GTN that
was able to detect the sudden, looming gravitationa
mass of the target within 1.2 seconds of impact.

At this point the computer would issue the firin
command to the detonation assembly. The resultin
thermal out-throw would thus occur when the missil
was still two hundred feet above its target, creating a
in-air spread of heat energy that would cover a cor
centration zone approximately a half mile in width.

Nuclear reactions creating such powerful heat ger
eration were based on the so-called carbon cycle, th
fission loop that makes stars glow. However, in th
XGB carbon was not used as the initiating nuclea
source because of its higher fission state and its heav
gamma radiation contamination. Instead, thalliur
bromoiodide crystals made up the bomb's heart.

The detonation unit was a small hemisphere compose
of graphite magnetically suspended in an atmosphere c
low-pressure helium. Inside the hemisphere was a "fis
sion capsule" containing the thallium bromoiodide cry
tals. Into this capsule a beam of photons would be sho
causing immediate fission and the creation of the isotop
Th-203.

A fume of infrared, alpha, and gamma radiatio

would erupt from the isotope field. Since Th-203 has
a half-life of only 0.0000002 second, the shorter alpha and gamma waves would dissipate almost instantaneously, while the longer infrared radiation would
remain long enough to be captured by the free helium.
Enclosed within the graphite, which has the property
of blocking neutrons, the heat would be concentrated
to levels in excess of thirty thousand degrees Celsius.

Like the filament in a heat lamp, the graphite shell
would become incandescent, flashing a burst of heat
and green light that would instantly vaporize the entire
nose cone assembly, allowing the full energy of the
blast to be directed downward. At actual missile impact, the full isotope loop would be completed, and
the Th-203, like the carbon isotopes in its cycle returning to carbon, would have become inert, non-
radioactive thallium. Contamination within the target
zone would be less than 50 rem, below acceptable levels for immediate human habitation.

Time to impact: 1 minute, 41 seconds . . .

Within the detonation system, power circuits now
became charged. The core of the system, called the
photon cannon, was attached to the flat after surface
of the graphite hemisphere. It resembled the bell housing of a tiny automobile's transmission. Within the
housing was an electromagnetic field "plate" that
contained a film of photons in zero-momentum state.

As power increased through an intricate series of
no-stop switches around the electromagnetic field, the
"plate" began to spin counterclockwise. As its velocity gradually increased, the photons were excited into
parallel momentum flow. Faster and faster it went
until momentum flow reached a state just under the
so-called CP Conjunction in which anti-photons are
created.

Time to impact: 1 minute, 3 seconds.

At this point the computer held the power stage in equilibrium, awaiting the GTN to indicate imminent impact. Upon receipt of it, the computer would send a full power surge to the spinning field "plate," turning it into full CP Conjunction. Anti-photons would instantly materialize out of the electronic soup and merge with photons to create a single-wave accumulation beam of highly charged quantum particles. Funneled by a cladding tube, the beam, like a bolt of invisible lightning, would strike the core of the fission capsule.

Yet despite all these intricate electronic impulses and subatomic mechanisms, no sounds issued from the warhead's basketball. If any had, they would have been lost in the hissing, moaning rush of the wind across the air foils and metal skin of the missile as it hurtled into its final plunge through the stormy Indian night.

Time to impact: 21 seconds . . .

A big croc had trailed them, lying a few yards off the stern of the canoe. Normally crocodiles are cautious, wily animals, preferring to wait in ambush for their victims. But the tumultuous flight of the horse into the lake, the stench of their fear mingled with blood, had driven the animals into a killing frenzy.

Bonner, lost in concentration, was completely unaware of the croc's presence. The canoe was about four hundred yards from the shoreline and going well, driven by the heaving strokes of the paddlers and the force of the wind. Jungali's instincts, however, were deeper rooted than Bonner's. In the increasing light Cas saw the Carib turn and look back. He straightened, took another stroke, then turned around again staring hard. For a moment Bonner saw, felt, something in that look. The thought shot through his mind: *He sees the missile!* A frozen hand gripped his heart.

Jungali shouted, "Look out, Bonner. *Magalmach!*"
What? What?

Something struck the right side of the canoe so powerfully it was lifted two feet out of the water and slammed sideways. Bonner was thrown toward the impact. As he fumbled for the seat ahead of him to keep from falling out, the canoe came down hard.

From the corner of his eye, he saw a huge black head explode out of the water less than four feet away. The skin was gnarled and scaly, its eyes yellow. Instantly it sank out of sight.

"Oh, Christ," he yelped as a new kind of fear knifed through the other, this one from the dark recesses of his primitive instincts. Momentarily frozen, he sat there, gripping his paddle like a baseball bat and furiously searching the surface.

In the bow, Jungali had stood up and was doing a crazy little dance, trying to keep his balance in the rolling canoe, at the same time smacking the surface with the flat of his paddle. He screamed, "Stand up, mon. Stand up, make big body." A croc, even attacking, could sometimes be bluffed away by the sudden appearance of a victim's full size. In the lowered, almost hunched position of paddling, Cas had shown a low silhouette to the animal, thus drawing the charge.

He heard what the Carib was saying, but at the moment it seemed totally insane. Stand up? In a wildly rocking log of a canoe with a man-eater under you? He remained riveted to his seat.

There was a hushed moment, like a warm breath in the air. Even the rain and wind seemed to pause. Then the bull croc struck the canoe again, coming in hard and lightning fast. Bonner saw its open mouth, a great vertical V of yellow-white filled with teeth. The croc took hold of the gunwale of the canoe, crushing it. A gurgling growl came from the throat.

The stern of the canoe went under water. Blindly Cas swung his paddle, felt it crack across the animal' head. It made a thick, padded sound as if striking heavy leather chair. He back swung, aiming for the eyes. Vaguely he was aware of Jungali coming toward him, scrambling over the center seats. Just as the paddle hit, the croc's tail flailed out of the water, again so quickly it was only a sensation of blurred movement water exploding.

Cas felt a shock of pain explode on the right side of his back as the after part of the tail caught him. I lifted him upward. But his legs, curled under the seat sprang him back down again. The croc, half of it body lying diagonally across the sinking canoe, rolled furiously, its tremendous weight splintering the already sundered gunwale. The huge jaws snapped at Jungali, who frantically scrambled forward again, up the now steeply slanted hull.

The fear in Bonner was horrific. He kept swinging his paddle again and again, feeling the jarring impacts come up through the haft. Imprinted in his mind was the image of those gigantic jaws taking him, the thumb-sized teeth making holes in his flesh through his bones. Yet a totally incongruous thought also formed. How ironically unfair it all seemed suddenly. He was a seaman, and a seaman's grave should be the sea, not a godforsaken lake, devoured by a beast from a million B.C.

The thought fled as the canoe went under completely, and he felt the violent vibrations of the croc's tail thrashing through the water. It whacked his belly and his chest, and then he went under totally, down into black water filled with the croc's thrashings and savage growls and beyond, as if in another world, the faint drum of the rain.

Then his underwater instincts took over. In turbulent, dangerous water, a diver always heads for the bottom to escape the tumult. Slanting downward on his back, arms gyrating, legs driving with the frenzied impulses from his heart, Bonner bore deeper as the tiny dancing flecks of firelight on the roiled surface above him grew fainter and fainter.

Detonation.

For a millisecond a blinding green flash a thousand times brighter than a sheet of lightning illuminated Namak Island, the lake, and surrounding shoreline. The undersides of the storm clouds glowed aquamarine; the rain, sweeping in slanting lines, glistened like strings of emerald chips.

Immediately behind it came a gargantuan thunderclap as the air molecules within the impact zone instantly vaporized. Under the thunder, smaller explosions sounded, the sharp cracks of rocks blowing apart, high-pitched metallic whistles from steel foundations instantly superheated as the tremendous burst of thermal energy from the still airborne warhead spread over the island.

A second later, at precisely 5:42 A.M., the smoking remnants of the missile struck the ground at a point two hundred feet north of the oil rig, its homing sensors drawing it to the greater heat of the burning tank nest.

Immediately the oil fires were extinguished in the suddenly oxygenless atmosphere. Down in the main compound, every wooden structure, dock, walkway, instantly vaporized. The charred, skeletal shaft of the drilling rig melted, its beams and struts and Christmas tree valve columns collapsing into boiling pools. In the storage nest the exploded tanks also melted down. Their molten liquid, pitch black, spread over the ground with the consistency of water, splashing into the remnants of the barracks and repair shops.

Then great waves of surrounding air slammed back into the vacuum over the island. Instantly the lava of steel, drawing oxygen, turned blinding white. The oil vents, ignited by the melted rig, blew columns of fire into the air. Massive heat tornadoes were created, roaring and whipping across the island, out into the lake. Fresh deluges of rain set off violent, riffling explosions above the tank nest, billowing clouds of steam.

Up the slope from the compound, the forest of pine and deodar and eucalyptus simply disappeared in flashing bursts of white smoke, leaving only delicate skeletons of sap. Each trunk aorta, every tiny branch vein, was intact but turned to glass. Underbrush, tiny forest animals, snakes, mosquitoes, flies, everything, went in the blink of an eye. Rushing sheets of rain-water evaporated, exposing carbonized ground.

Lake House itself was turned into a blackened, glazed ruin, its sandstone facings metamorphosed to glassy kaolin, the marble walls and columns sundered by exploding fracture seams. Wooden window sills, doors, internal walls, and furniture vaporized. Above the balconies of melted wrought iron, the tall brass spires were crystallized into a thousand pieces like shattered vases. Under a flash of lightning, the sap sculptures in the garden glistened as if made of blue ice.

In the courtyard, the mobile launcher and mounted missiles melted into a single fiery liquid mass that dropped into the launch pit, engulfing the remains of Kurisovsky and the trooper. It boiled and crackled as the rain struck its surface and hurled streaks of rainbow colors. The cobblestones were carbonized; the ammo carrier had become merely ribbons of white fire seeping among the seams. Beyond, the body of the other Russian trooper was no more than a carbonized skeleton, all its flesh and viscera boiled away.

In the first massive blast of heat, the water around the entire shoreline of the island for a hundred yards out had been instantly turned to invisible superheated steam. Completely exposed, the entire bottom was sucked dry, the mud turned to solid carbon. Huge shrink fissures cracked open, releasing geysers of natural gas that immediately exploded with rending detonations.

Farther out, where the heat was less, billows of visible steam poured into the air. There was an instantaneous drop of thirty feet in the level of the lake as the water beyond the steam eruptions flooded into the exposed zone. At first this, too, instantly became steam. But as more water came in, cooling the heated bottom, it formed a tidal surge that rushed up onto the shore and higher ground.

More violent steam explosions followed until the remaining water lost its momentum and began to recede, pouring back down the slopes. At the beach, now a ribbon of pure glass, it collided with new waves of incoming water. A turbulent jam of water was created until there was more over the once exposed zone than beyond in the lake itself. Now a counter wave formed, a twenty-foot-high tsunami. Hissing loudly, it raced away from the shoreline at sixty miles an hour.

Bonner had continued his flight toward the bottom, his rationality overtaken by a wild rush for survival. He was down about twenty-five feet and could feel pressure building on his eardrums. But frantically he kept pulling through the darkness, all the time his body feeling the water for the first coils of a pressure wave that would come off the gigantic crocodile's snout before it lashed into him.

A flash of light came, one brilliant burst like a single pulse from an enormous strobe light. It lit the water all around Bonner into a virescent gloom. In that instant he saw Jungali on the surface and the crocodile several feet below the Carib, both silhouetted against the light. As if he were looking at an X-ray plate, he saw the bones in the croc's clawed legs, the tiny chain of vertebrae in the end of its tail. Jungali's body burst into flame.

Gagging with horror, Bonner was plunged into darkness again. Only a shimmering spot of flame hovered above him, which was Jungali's corpse, crackling and sizzling in the water. Suddenly the water turned scorching hot. It numbed his exposed body tissue and drew forth a million needles that seemed to puncture his veins. He coiled into a ball and felt a powerful pressure wave wash over him as something huge rocketed past. He caught a rumbling grunt riffle off it. It was the croc. Frightened by the light and perhaps burned by the burst of heat, it was plunging for the safety of the lake bed.

Massive, sizzling eruptions from the surface mingled with sharp explosions farther off that riffled through the water with cruel, slamming vibrations. Uncoiling, Bonner lengthened out in the darkness and began swimming furiously away from where he thought the island was.

Abruptly he was wrenched backward by a tremendous force in the water. Straining against it, he kept swimming. But it was too strong. It pulled him upright and then over and over in a series of somersaults. A moment later, he was bodily flung through the surface into air as blistering as that from the open door of a steel furnace.

Once more he crashed back into the water. Helplessly floundering, he was swept toward the island. But then the force stopped pulling. He sculled, looking frantically around. The surface of the lake around him fumed with smoke that he immediately realized was steam. It whirled and eddied, scalding his throat when he breathed. Through it he saw several fountains of fire shooting into the sky from the oil compound, their plumes as tall as twenty-story buildings. To the east, the island was covered with steam clouds painted by the firelight. They boiled and churned up into the rain.

Taking as much air as he could stand, he went under again and swam away. A wild mingling of separate terrors gave power to his arms and legs, his body rolling smoothly with each pulling stroke. His eyelids stung from the heat, and his entire body felt as if he had a horrible sunburn.

Sixty yards on, he heard it coming. The sound of it was a massive hissing that blew through the water. Angling up, he broke the surface and swung around. There, like a moving hill, a huge wave roared toward him. The front boiled and rolled, the crests etched by the light from the fires.

Facing directly into it, Bonner dived, driving with all the power in his legs to get below the surge. The welling of displaced water before the wave front caught him, threw him back. He flailed, spinning crazily. He lost all sense of direction as surges pulled him this way and that. He curled over again and let the force of the wave tumble him. Then he was on the surface again, the great looming wave directly over him, his body sliding and skidding across the top of the water like a beachball bouncing off the slanted front of the wave.

The wild tobogganing seemed to go on and on. But gradually the wave lost its momentum as the bulk of the lake absorbed its surge. At last it swept on past him, declining to merely a large swell that left whirlpools which bounced Bonner up and down. He lay on

the surface like an exhausted whale, pulling in lung
fuls of rain-cooled air and feeling the tumultuous
pounding thrum of his body slowing.

Finally, aching down in his bones, he rolled and
began swimming to the far shore. Images of long, ser
pentine bodies lunging up out of the depths to devou
him haunted each stroke. He held them off and kep
going, trying to hold his concentration fixed onto
tiny glowing triangle in the center of his head.

At last he reached a series of serrated sandbars tha
spread out into the lake. They were covered with
charred lumps like black, misshapen stones. He pulle
himself up onto the sand and flopped down. The sand
was hot as if sun-washed, and the air stank of burning
flesh. He lifted his head and looked at one of the lump
near his arm. He could see that it was the remains o
a lake bird, probably an egret. It had been turned into
a pile of charcoal, its beak merely a white smear o
the burnt flesh.

He turned and looked back at Namak. In the gray
dawn, seen through the rain, it looked like a black
volcanic island lying in some arctic sea. Steam cloud
still rose from it in swirling, pure white columns.

He was able to walk all the way to the shore on the
sandbars. They were part of a river delta. Beyond
heavy gallery trees came down close to the water. The
were scorched, all the leaves turned golden, and in
places fires had been started by the blast but were
quickly extinguished by the rain. Rushing streams o
runoff water folded around the trunks and made a grea
dark stain in the lake. Farther up the river, he hear
the roar of crocs.

He went up onto high ground and headed inland
The ground was mushy, covered with grass that had
been pounded down by the force of the rain. In low
places the water formed pools, and green snakes were

ying in the rain. As he walked, his body felt hot, stiff
nd unnatural, as if his skin were too tight for his skeleton.
There were large, painful blisters at his joints.

He reached a road that ran into the jungle. It was
overed with water, gray-brown in the strong light of
lawn. The jungle rose on both sides of the road in
heer walls, looking dark and menacing. It seeped mist
n the thick humidity.

Suddenly something darted through the shadows,
nd Cas stopped. To his right stretched a small glade.
ts grass was thick and green, about waist-high, and
here were orchids and crystal fern right at the edge of
he trees. Among the ferns he caught another move-
nent: a small, gnarled man paused for a second in the
hadows and then disappeared.

Garos.

Cas put his hands over his head to show he was not
rmed. For a long time he stood there, the rain coming
n squalls that pounded the road and made the jungle
oar. But the Garos remained hidden. Finally he sat
lown and crossed his legs.

At last they came, slowly, cautiously. First faces
eering out, then whispers. Then a man stepped from
he underbrush about sixty yards away. He stood look-
ng at Bonner. His thick bush of black hair was dotted
vith raindrops, and his face was wide and deeply
vrinkled, giving the impression it had been squeezed
ogether from chin to crown.

"Santi," Bonner called. The word meant peace in
Iindi.

The little man studied him. He carried a bow and
everal arrows, both gripped in one hand, and was
ompletely naked.

Cas tried to remember the word for friend but
ouldn't. *"Santi,"* he said again.

The Garo eventually approached and squatted in

front of him. He wore a brass ring in his chin. Slowly
like ghosts emerging in the rain, others slipped out o
the trees and came to squat beside their leader. They
too, were naked. They looked at Bonner and mur
mured excitedly among themselves.

Furtively the leader reached out and touched Cas's skin
He ran his fingers over his chest, paused at the blisters o
his elbow. The Garo's fingertips felt like sandpaper. H
said something and pointed toward the lake.

Cas pointed in the same direction and then at himself

All the men made a startled, whispering sound with
their lips. It resembled the fluttering rush of quail from
brush. Finally the leader rose and indicated that Bon
ner follow him. They went off through the jungle in
single file, Cas in the middle.

Twenty minutes later, they reached a village like the
one from which Jungali had obtained the canoes. The
central compound was covered with water and the hut
surrounding it were sodden and stank like a sewer
Cas was ushered into a *nokpati*. It was low and ha
grass matting on the hewn-wood floor. The men le
him, and several old women came in.

With gestures they told Bonner to disrobe, and the
they rubbed a thick salve all over his body, puttin
large mounds of it on the blisters and into the woun
Kurisovsky's knife had made. The salve was the colo
of tapioca and smelled like rotted flowers. The wome
cooed and giggled at the size of his shoulders and bi
ceps and penis.

Afterward, they went away and he lay back on th
grass and listened to the rain pouring off the eaves an
the tiny chirp of mice that had been driven to shelter
He fell asleep.

At 8:53 A.M. that morning, helicopter assault team
from General Shastra's Fourth Grenadier paratroope

division attacked Singh's encampment southeast of Lake Sonai. Following word of the XGB's successful destruction of Namak Island, Anduri's timidity had finally turned to anger and he had authorized Shastra to strike. Helicopter recon flights over the area pinpointed Singh's camp before the main force came in.

The Sikhs fought bravely during the vicious firefight that followed in the dense, monsoon-lashed jungle. But they were out-powered and out-gunned. Singh was killed in a tiny glen, roaring like a wounded lion as he was cut down. His head was brought back to the the divisional command base on a bayonet. Broken, the remainder of his militia scattered into the underbrush, where they were hunted down and massacred.

In Delhi and Calcutta, politicians and administrators suspected of aiding Singh were arrested, as were local state and province chiefs throughout Assam, Nagaland, Meghalaya, and West Bengal. Local bands of Singh's militia were wiped out. Anduri's swift, brutal action destroyed the core of Sikh power throughout all of northeastern India within hours.

Still, the future would not be bright for the prime minister. As news of the American strike seeped out, a momentum of outrage in the Congress developed over his "acquiescence" in letting the president of the United States fire a missile across Indian territory. It quickly reached fever pitch. Some opponents even demanded a declaration of war be made on America. Fortunately, as the full parameters of the situation emerged, Anduri was able to quell that outcry. But within a year, his government would be deposed.

Meanwhile, the President was riding the coattails of the XGB's success. Reports from Shastra's helicopter crews had verified the missile's accuracy and destructive power. But even before that, satellite thermal monitors had precisely pinpointed the massive heat out-throw even through the thick overcasts of the monsoon.

Within minutes of the detonation, the President was on the phone with Sichen. It turned out to be a short, rather grim conversation. The Chinese premier's attitude was stiff-backed, almost belligerent; he seemed insulted by the entire situation. He finally assured the President that he would attempt to defuse the aggressive forces calling for retaliation within his country. But it would be nearly two months before recon satellites and in-country reports showed a gradual pullback of Chinese forces along the old Soviet frontier and a stabilization of tension on NEFA.

Making contact with Seleznov proved much more difficult. Moscow had suddenly become shrouded in a deathly, foreboding quiet. Diplomatic circuits were tangled as low-echelon officers continually shunted incoming and outgoing calls through complex nets of other excited-sounding menials. Even the direct line from Washington to Seleznov's offices within the Kremlin was not answered.

Within the city, the tension was like that before a major hurricane among higher-grade government officials and the gathered ministers. Word had filtered out well before dawn in Moscow that an assassination attempt had been or was about to be made on President Seleznov. Rumors claimed people had already been killed.

In truth, Seleznov was still alive. The American ambassador Massie had reached the president's dacha two hours before the XGB struck Namak Island. His news had jolted everybody. Although Seleznov's security police had been monitoring the Phoenix group and General Zgursky for some time, until this moment they had considered it a minor opposition group.

Immediately, the security men at the dacha scoured the entire building and surrounding grounds for assassins or explosive devices. Further, it was decided to move the president to the better-fortified Yoshkar-One. This was the old Soviet underground ABM deployment center located a few hundred yards south of the Kremlin that had been built to protect the military command authorities during a nuclear crisis. It still contained its complex command network.

In thickening fog the move was carried out, first the security men lunging out to form a protective gauntlet from the house to the limos, and then Seleznov and his aides coming, Ambassador Massie among them. The night was sour and cold, and moisture dripped from the trees. The president reached his automobile, lowered to enter. His coat caught on the door. A security man leaned forward to free it.

Baklanov opened fire. The crack of his Volga 300 was like a cannon in the white darkness. The security man's head blew apart. Instantly everyone dropped to the ground, two security men throwing their bodies on top of Seleznov.

The assassin, as if infuriated by his initial miss, began shooting wildly. Another man was hit in the chest, the power of the round skittering him along the gravel. By now the main contingent of security people was up and charging out the gate toward the muzzle bursts. A fourth man was hit. There was a furious chorus of automatic weapons and then utter silence.

Less than an hour later, Seleznov struck back. At 6:27 A.M., Moscow time, a powerful explosion crashed through the suburb of Katsova, and General Zgursky's old house overlooking the Moscow River blew into a flaming inferno. When fire crews finally got the conflagration under control, the charred remnants of fifteen men were found. Eventually some of the bodies were identified, including those of the generals Zgursky and Ostalsky and ex-KGB First Chief Granov.

Cas Bonner awoke with a gun muzzle in his face. Squatted around him were four Indian soldiers in muddy battle dress. It was late afternoon and the rain made rustling sounds on the roof of the *nokpati*.

One of the soldiers said something to him in Hindi.

"I don't understand," Bonner answered.

The soldier said, "English?"

"American."

The soldier snorted. "Bu'sheet! You Russian."

Cas tried to sit up, but the soldier pressed the gun muzzle into his chin. "Goddammit," he cried. "I'm an American, I tell you."

The soldiers talked among themselves. They looked as if they wanted to kill him. Finally they told him to get dressed. He stood up. His whole body ached, but the blisters on his joints were gone and his skin felt cool.

The soldiers took him to a military radio van parked off the road near a grassy field a half mile from the Garo village. A huge Indian officer in a red turban was seated in the van smoking a Marlboro. The front of his tunic was covered with blood. The soldiers explained to him where they had found Bonner.

"What's your name?" the officer asked him. He spoke very good English and had beautiful white teeth and an ugly scar over one eye.

"Cas Bonner. I'm an American."

"Why are you here?"

"I was on the oil rig in Lake Sonai."

The officer's ugly scar lifted slightly. "Ah," he said. "You're very lucky."

"You believe me?"

"Of course. You don't smell like a Russian." He flashed his beautiful teeth. "Actually, you smell like puke."

"Can I get transportation to Dibrugarh?"

"Perhaps." The officer chain-lit another Marlboro. He started to put the pack back into his tunic pocket.

"Mind if I have one of those?" Cas asked.

"Ah, of course." He lit it for him and leaned back. "Tell me of the inferno."

For the next thirty minutes, he interrogated Bonner. Now and then the radio crackled with Hindi calls and an occasional burst of gunfire chattered way off somewhere.

Night came. The officer, who said his name was Captain Din, offered Bonner food, British field rations. Cas ate it all and asked for more. Din laughed at his appetite.

Two hours later, an American-built HH-53 helicopter landed in the field. It was painted in jungle camouflage. The huge rotors whipped up a whirlwind of water, and its lights flashed red and white. Din tapped Bonner on the shoulder and pointed to it. "Dibrugarh," he shouted.

There were eight wounded paratroopers in the chopper, lying on the corrugated floor with their field gear and weapons beside them. The inside of the aircraft smelled of blood and iodine. The men watched him in silence as he climbed aboard. In the light from the control deck, their eyes look yellow in their mud- and blood-smeared faces.

Forty minutes later, the aircraft landed on a little hillock in the grounds of the Gopalpur-on-River Hospital, the craft settling heavily and the blades idling. One by one the wounded soldiers got out and walked in single file across the lawn, which was under six inches of water. Bonner followed.

The parking area before the hospital was still crowded with people waiting silently. They held broad banana leaves over their heads and squatted sullenly in the water. Several ambulances were pulled up near

the emergency entrance. They were painted yellow
with the International Red Cross emblem stenciled on
the rear door.

Bonner made his way through the main entrance.
People lay everywhere and the air was hot and wet and
stank of medicine and shit. He continued on into a
corridor equally crowded, then up a stairwell. It came
out on a veranda. Wind gusts whipped rain across the
floor, and there were clusters of men and women huddled against the inner wall.

He walked along the veranda. Out on the grounds,
he could see the helicopter. One of the yellow trucks
had pulled up beside it, and men were transferring
cartons to the aircraft. He rounded the corner of the
veranda and found a large room with shuttered windows. The double door was open. Inside were people
on dozens of military cots with others stretched out on
the floor between.

He saw Jackie with a nun on the opposite side of the
room. She wore a filthy green operating gown and was
administering to a soldier on a cot. The man was naked save for his battle tunic. Both legs were swathed
in bandages. He gritted his teeth each time he breathed
while the nun hung an intravenous bottle on the wall.

Jackie straightened, smiling down at him. She lightly
touched his forehead, then turned. When she saw Bonner,
she stopped. For a long moment she just looked at him.
Then she wound her way through the bunks and reclining
patients and silently put her arms around him.

"I thought you were dead," she whispered.

As they clung to each other, Cas felt her tremble.
At last she released him, took his hand, and led him
back out onto the veranda. They found a spot where
the rain didn't sweep in. Tiny sparrows were crammed
up under the roof beams. They made little chittering
sounds like mice.

With her head leaning on his shoulder, Jackie sighed and gazed out at the night. "Was it very bad?" She shook her head. "No, I don't want to know yet. Someday when we're faraway from this place you can tell me." She looked up at him. "Where's McCarran?"

"He's dead."

She sucked air in sharply, held it a moment, then released. She put her head down. When she lifted it again, she said, "Jungali?"

"Yes."

"Insanity."

"You look like you're ready to drop. Have you had any sleep at all?"

"I don't even allow myself to sit down. If I did, I'd never get back up again."

"You've done enough, Jackie. Let someone else step in now. It's time to leave."

"No, I can't. Not yet, but soon." She straightened and turned her face to the wind. Her features were drawn and pale, and there were dark circles under the gray eyes. "I've watched over seven hundred people die here in the last forty hours, Cas," she said quietly. "From fungial infection and pneumonia. Seven hundred helpless, frightened people. And still more are coming. I try to—God!" She closed her eyes and seemed to weep.

He touched her hair. It was moist with perspiration. "Were you able to save any?"

She nodded. "Yes. I think we've stopped the worst of it. And the rest of the world's finally gotten into it. Supplies and doctors are being flown in all along the river."

He hissed bitterly and looked out at the town of Dibrugarh and across it to the river. "That thing's still full of more poison and flooding."

"No, we may at least have that part of it controlled. Would you believe sugar?"

"What?"

"That's what kills it, the fungus. Common, ordinary glucose dissolved in chloroform. We discovered it by accident. Nobody's certain of the exact process yet, but we think it penetrates the epidermal wall of the organism's nuclei and combines with its alpha naphtol component to produce pure sulfuric acid. Dissolves the whole goddamned thing."

He shook his head, amazed.

"Delhi just notified us that Indian, British, and American air tankers will start spraying the river and flood areas at first light."

"Then it's almost over."

"No. It'll never be over for some of these people." She leaned back and looked up into his face, studied it a long time. "You're beautiful," she said.

"So are you."

"And you smell terrible."

He grinned at her. "So do you."

Slowly Jackie's expression changed, the eyes darting, the face slack with a sudden sweep of emotion. She lunged back into his arms, drawing him desperately to her as if he might fly away into the night.

"Will you come with me afterward, Casimir Bonner?" she finally murmured.

He rubbed his forehead across her moist hair. "Of course. Where shall we go?"

"Any place far from here. Maybe to where it's snowing and the air's so cold and dry it'll hurt when we breathe." She laughed and tilted her head back. "We could run naked and get roaring, crazy drunk and make love all night."

"You're on," he said and pulled her lips to his.